W9-CMN-335

A Breath of Hope

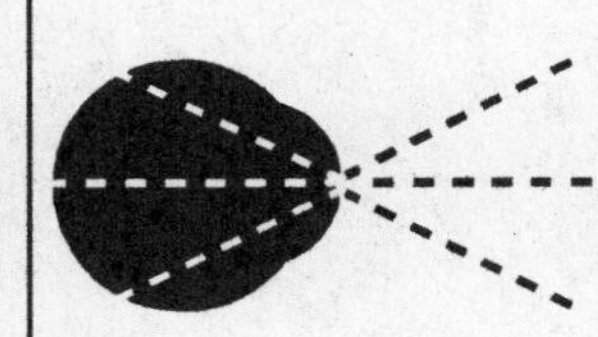

This Large Print Book carries the Seal of Approval of N.A.V.H.

UNDER NORTHERN SKIES

A Breath of Hope

Lauraine Snelling

THORNDIKE PRESS
A part of Gale, a Cengage Company

Farmington Hills, Mich • San Francisco • New York • Waterville, Maine
Meriden, Conn • Mason, Ohio • Chicago

Scripture quotations are from the King James Version of the Bible.
Thorndike Press, a part of Gale, a Cengage Company.

This is a work of fiction. Names, characters, places, incidents, and dialogues are products of the author's imagination and are not to be construed as real. Any resemblance to actual events or persons, living or dead, is entirely coincidental.
Thorndike Press® Large Print Christian Fiction.
The text of this Large Print edition is unabridged.
Other aspects of the book may vary from the original edition.
Set in 16 pt. Plantin.

LIBRARY OF CONGRESS CIP DATA ON FILE.
CATALOGUING IN PUBLICATION FOR THIS BOOK
IS AVAILABLE FROM THE LIBRARY OF CONGRESS.

ISBN-13: 978-1-4328-4836-1 (hardcover)

Published in 2018 by arrangement with Bethany House Publishers, a division of Baker Publishing Group

Printed in Mexico
1 2 3 4 5 6 7 22 21 20 19 18

A Breath of Hope

CHAPTER 1

Nilda Carlson stared at the money in her hand. This was a week's pay. Her last week's pay. "I will never, ever be able to save enough money to buy a ticket to Amerika."

"Ah, Nilda," her mor, Gunlaug, said softly. "Never is a long time. Somehow we will find a way."

Nilda stared out the window at the snow drifting down, the flakes float-dancing, since the wind had given up. Would spring ever come? Each year, winter seemed to take up residence for longer spells. She knew she was being unreasonable. She'd been admonished for that before.

"Spring always comes. Our Lord ordained it so. And He has heard your cries. He promised He would always listen and answer."

How many times had she heard that? But hearing and deep-down believing were two entirely different things. As were hearing and answering. Did she believe God heard?

Ja, she had to answer ja. But she had already learned that sometimes the answer was *yes,* sometimes *no,* and sometimes the hardest to deal with, *wait.*

"I know how hard you worked."

"But, Mor," Nilda insisted, "the shop is closed. True, Mrs. Rott is too sick and feeble now to keep the store open, and that is a shame, but still, I have no more work." She thought a moment. "Perhaps the Nygaards are hiring. I'm sure I would dislike working for them. No one likes working for them. But the money . . ." Two of her older brothers had stuck it out until something better came along, and now it seemed to be her turn.

"Ja, I know." Gunlaug threw the shuttle on the loom, where she was weaving another rug. When finished with one, she always restrung for the next. Slamming the batten vigorously, she forced each strand tightly into place to make the rugs last longer. "This one is for you, you know."

"You will have that done long before I can buy a ticket, that is for certain."

"Then you will have the first layer in the bottom of the trunk Far and Johann are making for you."

Nilda tightened her fists in the folds of her wool skirt, fabric her mor had woven in years past.

Mor eyed her. "I have learned that weaving is a good way to work off despair. Throwing the shuttle and slamming the batten in place are good for one's soul — and letting loose your feelings."

"As is kneading bread. It is nearly time for that." A smile tickled the corners of Nilda's lips, but she clamped her teeth against it. "Mor, you make it hard to stay angry."

"Takk, I guess." Eyebrows arched, she looked at her daughter with a nod. "And the bread is much lighter for the extra kneading, like a rug is tighter for the extra slamming."

"My one day at home, and I'm wasting it fussing like this."

"Why don't you write Onkel Einar a letter and see if he is interested in bringing over another family member to help him?"

"That is a good idea. I will do that as soon as I knead the bread back down. When you are a shopkeeper, your work just disappears out the door. At least with baking bread, you have something to show for it when you are finished."

For a while, at least. She shook her head at the thought and returned to the kitchen, the slam of the shuttle accompanying her.

The fragrance of yeast raising the bread dough permeated the room. Both of these everyday tasks would be needed in Amerika too. After setting the bowl of dough on the stove's warming shelf, she added more wood and fetched paper and pencil. They were out of ink, and she did not want to spend time making more.

By the time she finished the letter, the dough was crowning the bowl again, ready to form into loaves. "Shall we have some of this fried for dinner?" she asked her mor.

"Ja, that will be a nice treat. Make enough for Ivar for when he comes home from school. He can mail the letter for you in the morning."

"I will take it in myself after the bread is finished. Do you need anything from the store?"

"Need or want?"

Nilda nodded. How true. Every winter they ran up a bill at the store and paid it off as soon as spring work brought in more cash. Winters were always sparse.

A couple days later, Ivar burst through the kitchen door just as dusk was bluing the snowbanks. "Mor, letters from Amerika!"

"In here," Gunlaug called from her loom. "Sweep off your boots."

"I did. Is Nilda home yet?"

"Nei, but soon." She smiled at her youngest as he, minus his coat, stopped beside her at the loom. "You'll want some wood in that stove. It's cold in here." She took the letters. "Takk. One is from Onkel Einar."

Ivar grinned. "I saw that. Wouldn't it be funny if he is asking for more helpers and Nilda just mailed him a letter? If Nilda goes to Amerika, I will really miss her."

"Ja, I will too." Gunlaug blew out a deep sigh.

"I will take you there someday, Mor. I will. At least for a visit."

"Takk, my son, but . . ."

"I will take Far too, if he will go."

She patted his hand. "You keep dreaming that." Nodding and almost smiling, she threw the shuttle again and slammed the batten with extra force. "I better hurry and finish this so I can make one for Rune's new house."

"If Nilda goes, it would be good to send another loom along with her. And a feather bed for Rune and Signe. At least they are no longer sleeping on pallets on the floor." He paused and turned his head slightly to the side so he was not looking directly at his mor. "Onkel Einar is not a very nice man, is he." He was not asking a question.

"I'm afraid not, but he has not struck anyone — at least as far as we know." Gunlaug stared out the frost-painted window. The frond patterns near the top were winter's curtains. The intricate design feathered on the glass always made her wish she could weave such a pattern into her rugs.

Ivar asked, "Did Nilda get the job at the Nygaards'?"

"Ja, I think so. She went there this morning and promised to return if she did not get work. We were thinking to clean the kitchen."

Darkness fell, bringing all the family home but for Nilda. Gunlaug set the table and stirred the beans and smoked mutton she'd baked all day. Guilt at wasting wood moved her to use the oven when the cookstove was helping to heat the house. The round stove in the other room was only lit on the coldest days or when she was at the loom, which was most of the time. Even so, she wore gloves with no fingers, a sweater, and a shawl.

The letters in the center of the table were pleading to be read, propped up against the sugar bowl.

"You could go ahead and read to us," Thor said with a slight raising of his eyebrows. "She might have had to spend the night for some reason."

"Nilda would find a way to let us know." Ivar propped his elbows on the table. "Wouldn't she, Mor?"

The knock of skis sliding into the rack outside made him jump to his feet and run to throw open the door.

"Hurry up, we have letters from Amerika, and Mor won't read them until you are here."

Coming through the door, Nilda scowled at no one in particular and everything in general. She unwrapped her scarf.

"Your supper is in the warming oven." Gunlaug could tell something was bothering Nilda, but she wisely kept her own counsel. "As soon as you are seated and eating, I will read." Nilda had been known to eat standing up by the fire when in a hurry.

Gunlaug began:

"Dear Thor and Gunlaug,

"I hope all is well with you in Norway. As we get busier here, Gerd and I agree that we need more help, especially since Rune and Signe will be moving into their own house this summer. They told me that your daughter Nilda would like to emigrate to Amerika, so if she still desires to come . . ."

Nilda screeched so loudly they must have heard her clear to Valders and threw her hands in the air. "I get to go to Amerika! I really do!"

Gunlaug rolled her eyes at her husband and returned to the letter. "If we could have a chance to hear, I will continue." She paused, looking over the top of the paper at Nilda, who bounced once more in her chair and nodded. "Now where was I? Oh, here. 'I will purchase a ticket for her with the agreement that she will help us here on the farm to reimburse me for the ticket. If you have any other family members who would appreciate starting a new life in Amerika, have them write to me, and we will see what we can work out.' "

"What about Ivar? You said you wanted to go." Nilda flashed her younger brother a face-splitting grin.

He nodded solemnly. "But I do not want to be beholden to Einar. From what Rune and Signe have said, he is a tyrant. I want to be able to leave him and go work for a real logging company. Not that I would, but still. . . ."

"Surely he can't be that bad," Nilda said, staring at her brother, who had always been the careful one.

"Well, we really do not want Nilda traveling alone. So many horror stories I have heard." Thor stared at his daughter. "Something to think about."

Nilda huffed out a sigh, her head slightly wagging.

"May I continue?" Gunlaug glanced from her daughter to her husband. The last thing she wanted was anger at the dinner table.

"Ja, go ahead." Thor still looked upset.

" 'The winter has been especially hard this year, but we continue to fell trees as much as the weather allows.' "

"You think Rune exaggerated the size of the trees?" Ivar asked.

"Rune is not one to exaggerate." Never had Gunlaug had so many interruptions reading a letter. "I think they have not been telling us how bad it has been for them there." She found her place again. " 'Spring will be here one of these days, and travel by ship will be much easier then. If you can plan to leave in mid-May, that would work well. I look forward to hearing from you. Einar and Gerd Strand.' " Gunlaug laid the letter down to be reread later.

"I could use another cup of coffee." Thor raised his cup.

Nilda leaped to her feet. After pouring coffee for all who wanted some, she paused. "Do we have anything to celebrate with?"

"Fresh bread with butter and jam. I thought about making a custard but was too busy weaving." Gunlaug looked around at her nodding family. "Perhaps tomorrow we can make snow candy. We have syrup."

Nilda fixed everyone a slice of bread and jam. "Are the hens still laying?"

"Not much. Another reason not to make custard."

"Mid-May." Nilda set the half slices of bread on a plate to serve. "We need to start lists of what can go with us." She paused and stared at Ivar. "I have some money saved that we could put toward a ticket for you. Do you have anything saved?"

"I do," Johann volunteered. "You can have that. Mor, can you ask Tante Gretta?"

Gunlaug nodded. "I will write a letter to them tomorrow. Somehow we will collect enough for Ivar's ticket. I know we will."

"But what if we can't in time?" Nilda sighed again. "I have a dream. Onkel Einar offers to pay for my dream. Now I must wait until Ivar can come too. Wait. Wait. Wait. I will never be able to get to Amerika."

CHAPTER 2

Keeping the house warm was near to impossible, cold as it was outside.

"You boys make sure you wrap that horse blanket around you while you are riding and then blanket the horse." Signe watched her two younger sons, Knute and Leif, nod like they had heard her say those words every day for years. She handed them a gunnysack with their dinner pails in it. Good thing Mr. Millhause, the school custodian, always had the school rooms warm before the children arrived. Of course, with school only half days on Saturdays, it hardly seemed worth the effort.

They waved as they went out the door. Three-month-old Kirstin shifted in the sling around Signe's shoulder, in which she had spent most of her life. While Signe and Gerd had always taken turns wearing the sling, Kirstin was getting too big for the older and much weaker woman to carry, especially while making breakfast.

"You sit in that chair and nurse her, and I will fix us something to eat." Tante Gerd brought the chair closer to the stove. "You would think she already knows when any mealtime for us comes."

Signe patted the baby through the sling. "I think she forgets she has already been fed once." While the baby slept through the night now, she was ready to eat long before dawn cracked the horizon. Signe pulled the coffeepot to the hot part of the stove again and settled into the chair. The gray-furred Gra wrapped herself around Signe's legs.

"Sorry, cat, you will have to wait until the baby is done."

"Anytime there is a lap, she thinks she should curl up in it." Gerd paused to take a deep breath. And then another.

Setting the baby to nursing, Signe threw the shawl over her shoulder and the baby. "My goodness, but you are a noisy one this morning." She watched Gerd for any other signs of recurring weakness. "Did you not sleep well last night?"

Gerd stirred the oatmeal before slicing some bread to toast on the stove top. "No worse than usual. Einar's snoring must keep all of you awake."

"Nei. We don't hear him upstairs."

Signe refused to refer to the second story as the attic. After all, her whole family slept up there. At least now they all had beds, a very real improvement over sleeping on pallets on the floor. If she allowed herself to dream, she pictured the house they would build on their own land come summer. She and Rune had to fight with Onkel Einar to force him to follow up on his agreement with them, but it would be worth it. If she furthered the dream, someone from home in Norway would come to live with them or with Tante Gerd and Onkel Einar. She knew for a fact that Einar had written to Rune's mother about bringing Nilda over; he had asked Rune about Nilda's work habits. There was certainly enough work around here for another person. Of course, Einar would be overjoyed to have another logger helping him fell the big trees. Not that one would ever be able to tell if Einar was pleased with anything.

Glancing down, Signe realized her daughter had already slipped back to sleep. While she was awake more now, as she should be, she found comfort with a full tummy, snuggled against her mor or Tante Gerd. When she was sitting down, Gerd could still wear the sling.

"You ready?" At Signe's nod, Gerd

spooned oatmeal into their bowls and pulled a plate of the toast she'd been making from the warming oven. Hands on her hips, she studied the table. "Anything else?"

"Sometimes I feel guilty seeing you work while I am sitting here."

Gerd looked at her like she was losing her mind. "After all you did for me?" She heaved a sigh. "I would not be standing here, working in my kitchen, enjoying that baby, if it weren't for all your persistent hard work. I will never be able to thank you enough."

Signe stared at Gerd, making sure her chin was not touching her chest. Could this be the same woman who had screamed at her every moment she needed something? Who refused to even try to do things on her own? Who slept all the time? She sniffed back tears of relief — or was it joy? Or gratitude? After all, only God could work miracles like this. Last night she had read in the Bible about being thankful — the hard part — for everything. She would never have said thank you for *that* Gerd, and now she couldn't say it often enough. More than one miracle had occurred here, that was certain.

She sniffed again. "Takk, tusen takk many times over." Signe resettled the baby and turned to her bowl. Nothing tasted as good on a cold morning as steaming oatmeal. "Today is Saturday."

Gerd turned to look at the calendar on the wall. "Ja, why?"

"That means tomorrow is Sunday, and I really want to go to church. The weather is not so bad."

"Will you take the baby?"

"I planned to." She paused. Might it be better to leave Kirstin here? Gerd could feed her with a bottle. "I have a better idea. Why don't you come with us?" She was as surprised as Gerd at the spoken thought. This would be their first Sunday at the church, but . . . why did there always have to be a *but*? She ate a couple bites of toast and took a sip of coffee. Still no answer from the woman across the table, who was staring down at her bowl. "We would really be grateful if you came too."

Was that pain in Gerd's eyes?

Gerd shook her head. "I think not. There is too much bitterness for me to go." As she spoke, her head kept moving from side to side.

"But this is church."

"A church made up of people who have come to despise us. You go and see what it is like, and we shall see."

"You know Mrs. Benson and Mrs. Solum.

They were friendly and helpful." Signe returned to her oatmeal. "When we have Kirstin baptized, I really want you there. I know Einar won't come, but I have learned that Einar will do what Einar will do. You have been so good to this baby — you saved her life and mine. I will be in your debt forever." *And one day, we will really be a family, even when we live in the new house.*

Gerd shook her head and brushed Signe off with a flutter of her hand. "We will just say we are even, then, and go on from here. Remember, if you decide to leave her with me, mostly because it is so dreadfully cold outside, I will be grateful."

Grateful. Such a marvelous word.

"And now, you need your coffee heated. Can I get you anything else?"

Signe raised her eyebrows. She dropped her voice and leaned forward. "Are there any cookies left?"

Gerd almost smiled — at least that was what Signe thought the fleeting commas that edged her mouth were. Gerd pushed back her chair and fetched the cookie tin. "I will have to bake again this afternoon. Perhaps Leif will help me. He likes to."

"As soon as they return from school, they're going down to the barn. He said he was going to let the cows out for a while and sweep up hayseed for the chickens. But maybe afterward he will help." Signe lifted her newly warmed coffee cup. "Takk." She dunked her cookie in the coffee. "Cookies are such a treat. When I was little, my far let me dunk cookies in his coffee like this," she said with a drawn-out sigh. "Which reminds me, I need to write a letter to Rune's family. Good thing they pass the letters around." She paused and gestured with what was left of her cookie. "These are so good. Sugar was often at a premium in Norway."

"Ja, life is better here in Amerika." Gerd carried their dishes to the pan on the stove. "I'll start churning next."

"Why don't I do the churning, and you start the cookie dough? I will put her in the cradle first." The baby cradle they kept near the stove was one of the first things Rune had made after the beds for the boys. Signe and Gerd were both adept at keeping the cradle moving with one foot while their hands were busy with something else.

Late in the afternoon, Leif came slamming in with a grin that delighted his mor. The cookie dough was ready to roll out, and the butter was set in their winter food keeper, a niche installed in the pantry window. That room was so cold, even the cats ate fast and ran to curl up by the stove to wash.

"The chickens really liked the hayseed! You should have seen them scratching and clucking." While he talked, he hung up his outer things and made sure there was no snow on his boots. "Cookies. Can I help roll them?"

"Ja, I waited for you." Gerd pushed more wood into the firebox. She glanced at the clock. "You hungry?"

He grinned at her. "I am always hungry. Can we cut the cookies first?"

Gerd almost smiled again. Signe couldn't stop smiling. She patted the baby nestled on her shoulder and swayed her instinctively from side to side. *Thank you, Lord. I cannot say thank you enough.* Signe tucked Kirstin into the cradle so her hands would be freer to help with the cookies and dinner. *Thank you, Lord, for such a contented baby.* What if she was a fusser? Another gift to be grateful for.

"Can I go out to the woods to drag branches after we eat? I'll come back early for chores."

"I don't see why not. Fill the woodbox first and take some cookies with you for the men."

That night, after all the others had gone to bed, Signe sat down in the kitchen, where it was the warmest, to read her Bible, hopefully without falling asleep with her cheek on the table like she had the night before. Rune had found her that way when he came down to see why she had not come to bed. Perhaps she should get up earlier and read in the morning. In her last letter, Mor had asked if she was reading her Bible. Signe knew she felt better when she did. But like last night, her body overruled her mind. Uff da.

This time Kirstin woke her, probably when Signe's foot stopped rocking the cradle. She nursed the baby, changed her, and dragged herself and the baby upstairs to bed. Rune drew her close to warm her up.

What would church be like in the morning?

"We're on our way." Signe felt like singing the words. It had been a rush, getting the children ready and the baby tended to, but they made it. Now that they were out on the snowy track, Rosie pulling the sledge, she felt almost like a new woman. They were going to church like regular people, like they had in Norway. *Thank you, Lord, for this breath of normality.*

Rune patted her knee through the robe

that covered her and baby Kirstin. "I'm sorry it has taken so long. We could ski faster than the horse and sledge."

"Hmm." She looked at Rune. "Have you thought of making skis?"

He shook his head. "Nei. I'm surprised Bjorn hasn't suggested it."

Bjorn, their oldest son, popped his head up from the mound of quilts and horse blankets in the wagon bed. "Hasn't suggested what?"

"Us making skis."

Knute joined him. "For all of us?"

"Kirstin is a bit small to learn to ski," Leif added.

"Mor could put her in a backpack." Knute had either thought of this before or was thinking fast now. "What kind of wood do we need?"

Signe nearly laughed out loud. "Have you ever made skis?"

Rune smiled at her. "Nei, but then, I've learned to do any number of new things since we came to Amerika."

The jingling of the horse harness rang out across the glitter-frosted snow. Laughter, delighted laughter came from their boys — how long since she had heard that? Back home there used to be laughter. Had they lost it on their journey, left laughter behind in the horrible hold of that ship? Signe held her baby closer. *Lord, is it that house? Or is it Onkel Einar and Tante Gerd? There will be laughter in our house,* she promised herself. *From the time we lay the foundation.* She let the thought keep going. Anger and meanness could permeate a house like it did a human soul. What would it take to open the door and let laughter clean out Einar's house? Gerd had almost smiled a couple times yesterday.

"You are being mighty quiet," Rune said.

"Just thinking. I guess the icy air is clearing my brain. I need to be outside more. Can you make skis out of pine, or do you need a hardwood?"

"We could use deer hide for boot straps." Bjorn was obviously already planning on making skis.

Rune nodded. "Ash would be best, but I haven't seen any ash around here. I'll ask Einar."

A horse and sleigh caught up with them, and the occupants waved as they passed. Just that bit of kindness made Signe feel calmer. How would they be received at church? No, Mrs. Benson would make them welcome, and the boys already knew other children because of school. The breath she huffed out bloomed in front of her. Rosie probably already had ice crystals about her nose.

When they turned right onto the road to Blackduck, they passed the school, and Rune turned the horse onto the church's property. Several houses fronted the road beyond that. Signe realized that on her trips to Benson's General Store, she'd never taken the time to look at the rest of Benson's Corner — not that there was much to it. The railroad ran along the east side of the town, if one could call it that. Rune pointed ahead to the tracks and a station of sorts.

"That's where we'll bring the logs to ship. Einar said we would load them on the sledge before the snow and ground thaw out." He stopped the horse next to another team tied to the railing. "Bjorn, Knute, blanket the horse and tie on the feed bag." Behind the school was the shed where the horses spent the school days sheltered from the weather.

Rune came around the sledge to help Signe down, the baby in her sling. "Careful now."

Another team joined the lineup, the couple nodding and smiling a welcome. Rune shepherded his family to the front of the church, where three steps led up to the carved double doors. He held the door for Signe, then followed her in.

"Mrs. Carlson, you came! Welcome to Our Savior's Lutheran Church." With hands outstretched and a smile that warmed Signe from the inside out, Mrs. Benson shook hands with both of them. "And your boys?"

"Taking care of the horse." Rune pulled off his ear-flapped hat and clutched it to his chest. "I hope we are not late."

"Right on time. Come inside where it is warmer." Mrs. Benson beamed. "I am so happy to see you here." She leaned closer and peeked inside the sling. "Oh my, she is growing so fast. Look at her, still sound asleep. What a beautiful little daughter you have. I know some of the others are anxious to meet you."

Mrs. Benson led the way through the swinging doors to the sanctuary, where the sun shone through the stained-glass window to jewel the white-painted altar. A man at the organ filled the room with music, calling people to worship. Those already seated in the pews kept their eyes forward, as was proper.

"I think we should sit in the back in case Kirstin gets fussy," Signe whispered.

"Of course." Mrs. Benson ushered them into a pew and smiled at the boys, who joined them. "Now, as soon as the service is over, I will introduce you to our pastor, his wife, and some of the others."

Signe inhaled the fragrance of worship and exhaled the fear of meeting the church people — who might hold a grudge against her family because of Onkel Einar. The organ music swept over her and carried her home to their church in Norway. *Thank you, Lord God,* she breathed. She could feel Rune studying her, so she nodded, a simple message he would understand. He took the hymnal from the rack on the back of the pew in front of them and found the right place.

When the pastor stood before them and opened the service in Norwegian before switching to English, she felt the tears burn her throat. Had she always been this way back in Norway, or was it because it was so long since they had been to church? With a whole lifetime lived in between?

When the pastor read the gospel passage for the day from Matthew, the words of *blessed are they who* poured over her. When he reached, "blessed are the peacemakers," she felt herself flinch inside. Wasn't that the way she'd been feeling? Living in a house with so much anger? But how to be a peacemaker when others did not want peace?

Kirstin stirred in her arms, so Signe swayed gently, hoping the movement would calm her infant daughter, but at the same time, knowing that if this baby was hungry, she would want to be fed — *now.* But the motion settled her down again, and Signe glanced down at Leif by her side. He and Knute were quietly entertaining themselves. Bjorn leaned against the corner of the pew, looking like he was about to fall asleep — or was he daydreaming? How long since he had been forced to sit this still and be silent? She knew he would rather be out in the woods, but Sundays in church were more important for the rest of his life than felling one more tree.

The singing just before the sermon woke Kirstin again, and this time swaying did not help. Before Signe could gather herself to rise and leave the sanctuary, the woman in front of them turned enough to give her a nasty look. She nudged the man beside her, and he glanced back too with a slight shake of his head.

"Sorry," Signe murmured as she pushed her way past Rune and Bjorn.

"You need help?" Rune whispered.

Signe shook her head. Surely there was a

room where she could sit to nurse her baby.

As the congregation sat back down, Kirstin moved from fussy to wailing. In the momentary quiet as the reverend waited for calm, everyone knew there was a baby in the back.

Signe slipped through the door to the vestibule, where one of the ushers rose from his chair.

"Ja, can I help you?"

"Is there some place I can feed and change her?" Signe motioned to the squirming bundle in her sling.

"Ja, this way." He led her to some narrow stairs to the basement. "There are chairs down there."

"Takk." She clutched the rail attached to the wall with one hand and the sling tighter with the other. She knew everyone could still hear them and felt her face blazing hot as she took the final steps. She thought of home and how her mor or one of the other ladies would have leaped to come help her. Tears burned her throat and made her sniff. Babies did not seem to be overly welcome here.

Pushing her way through a set of swinging doors, she breathed a sigh. At least the room was warm. She lifted the shawl from around her neck and laid her squirming bundle on a table while she unbuttoned her dress. A bottle might be easier, but then she would need to heat it up. Finally the squalling stopped when Kirstin latched on. The front of Signe's camisole was soaked with milk that had begun leaking when her baby started fussing. With the shawl tossed over her shoulder to shield any other eyes, she breathed a sigh of relief. Nursing a baby would be far easier in warmer weather.

She put herself back together, changed Kirstin's diaper, and started toward the stairs, but her sweet baby decided to talk. Shushing an infant did not work, and baby chatter would surely offend those folks sitting in front of them. So she spent the remainder of the service in the basement.

When Mrs. Benson and another woman came down to set out the coffee Signe had been smelling and wishing for in her banishment, gratitude made her own smile wider.

"You remember Mrs. Olavson?" Mrs. Benson leaned over to hold out her finger for the baby.

Signe remembered all right. This was the woman who had been rude in the Bensons' store. She made sure she smiled and nodded. Mrs. Olavson did not.

"May I hold her?" Mrs. Benson asked.

"Of course." Signe tucked the blanket

around the baby's kicking legs and handed her off.

Mrs. Benson rocked Kirstin in her arms, talking sweet nothings and grinning from ear to ear. "Oh, she is so precious. I must come out and visit one day soon. I'm so glad you were finally able to come to church today. I've been hoping —"

"I will start setting things out." Mrs. Olavson turned away without another word.

Signe watched her go. A sigh escaped before she could trap it.

Mrs. Benson leaned closer and dropped her voice. "Don't pay any attention to her. She'll come around in time."

"But what did I do?"

"It wasn't you. It was Einar. It had nothing to do with you, but some people do manage to carry a grudge." She tickled Kirstin's cheek and received a wide smile for her effort. "She is so happy."

"She wasn't, there for a bit. When she is hungry, she lets the whole world know."

"But look at her now."

"I know. Leif thinks she is the best thing that ever happened. His brothers tease him about not being the baby anymore."

"How is Mrs. Strand? Gerd?"

"She is getting stronger all the time but still tires easily. She plans to get more yarn to knit sweaters for the boys." The chords of a new hymn drifted downstairs.

"Oh, I better go help. That is the final hymn. Will you be able to stay for coffee?"

"As far as I know. Who were the people right in front of us?"

"Ah, Mr. and Mrs. Eriksen. I'll introduce you when they come down for coffee."

Signe had a feeling those people were among the families Onkel Einar had caused to dislike him so intensely. Why did people have to take sides, even in church?

But she just nodded and thanked Mrs. Benson.

Knute came down the stairs. "Mor, Far wants you to come back up so we can all meet Reverend Skarstead at the door." Signe nodded and bundled Kirstin back in her shawl. "Hurry."

Other folks were standing at the top of the stairs, waiting to come down. Signe nodded when she reached them and followed Knute. Rune still stood in their pew, talking with a man. Signe waited, swaying slightly to keep her baby content.

Rune smiled at her and motioned to the man. "My wife, Mrs. Carlson, this is Mr. Garborg. He has a farm west of ours. They passed us on the way to church."

Mr. Garborg nodded to her. "I am glad to

meet you. Welcome to Our Savior's Lutheran Church."

"Takk — er, thank you."

"Many of us speak Norwegian here, so *takk* is good." He had switched to Norwegian too.

Signe knew her smile was wider now. Trying to keep up with the English, her baby, and checking on her boys made her weary. "Did you emigrate too?"

"Nei, my parents did. They live in Blackduck. I took over the family farm." He beckoned to a woman talking with a couple of others. "This is my wife. Come meet Mrs. Carlson. We are near neighbors."

"Do you live near that lake Onkel — er, I heard about?" Rune asked, nodding toward Knute. "My son wants to go fishing."

Knute nodded.

"We are ice fishing now. If you come over, I will take you out to our camp."

"Really?" Knute's eyes widened and a grin took over his face.

"Ja. Of course."

"Mr. Garborg loves to fish nearly as much as he loves to farm." His wife smiled at Knute too. "Perhaps you have met our sons, Thomas and Soren, at school?"

"They are older, like my brother Bjorn."

"Today is a good day if you want to come

over after church and go fishing," Mr. Garborg said.

Knute looked to Rune. "Could I?" But his grin disappeared. "I don't have hooks or anything."

"Oh, we have plenty." Mr. Garborg turned as the robed pastor approached them. "Reverend, have you met these people yet?"

"Nei. But I am glad to see you here." He held out his hand to Rune. "Reverend Nels Skarstead."

Mr. Garborg completed the introduction, and Rune included his three boys, laying a hand on each shoulder as he said, "Leif, our youngest; Knute, middle; and Bjorn is our oldest." He nodded to Signe. "And this is my wife, Signe, with our baby, Kirstin."

"Welcome to you all. I hope you will join us in the basement for coffee before you bundle up to head home. I believe Mrs. Benson said you came to Minnesota to help your relatives."

"Ja, in June."

"I have heard glowing reports on how much help you have been for both of them. Now, can you come to the basement for coffee so you can meet more of our people?"

Rune looked to Signe and then shook his head. "I think we must decline this time, but we will plan on that next week, if all is well at — at home."

Signe made sure the surprise of him saying "home" did not show on her face. Had they really come to think of that house and farm as home? Had she ever used that term? Home meant so much more to her than the house they were living in. She nodded and half smiled. What more would she need to do to make that house feel like a real home?

Once they were all bundled up and heading back to the farm, she thought on her question. They had good food to eat, the house was clean again, the boys were in school, the men had plenty of work in the woods, while the two younger boys pretty much handled the farm chores. Gerd had gotten much stronger and was able to help with the cooking and keeping the diapers washed and folded. Signe needed to remember to thank Gerd more often for taking charge of the diapers and baby things. First she had sewed the diapers and knitted soakers, and since Kirstin was growing fast and the box of baby things Mrs. Benson had brought was dwindling, Gerd had sewed more gowns and blankets too.

So what was missing? What made a home?

Chapter 3

Although there were no mountains at all in this area, or even any sharp rises or vales, the countryside was very pretty. Especially in morning sun like this. The shadows and light beams set the snow to sparkling.

Rune grabbed the seat as their sledge bumped across a rut. "Onkel Einar, you ever made skis?"

"Waste of time."

"Did you learn to ski at home?"

"Ja, didn't we all?" He stared over the top of the scarf he wore around his lower face.

"If you were to make skis here, what wood would you use?"

"Waste of time."

"But think about it." Rune realized he'd not pushed an idea like this before. He usually just agreed and let it go. "If I make skis for the boys, they won't have to ride Rosie. I know there is a shed at the school, but the barn here is much warmer." *Besides, then*

Signe can use the horse if she wants. He shook his head. With no sleigh . . . He started to ask another question but let it drop. "Birch should do well."

"Too hard and brittle." Einar shook his head. "Makes good firewood."

Would the lumberyard in Blackduck carry seasoned birch? Perhaps they could recommend something better. Maybe they even carried ash.

Einar drew the horses to a halt and climbed down onto the crusted snow. "Time to move the logs to the railroad at Benson's Corner."

"How?"

"Thinking Bjorn could skid them with the team. Never had so many to move before."

"Not on the sledge?"

Einar shook his head. "Can't load 'em. If Knute didn't go to school, he could skid them or keep limbing. Going to slow me down."

Rune didn't even bother to shake his head. They were not about to change their minds on the boys going to school.

Bjorn took care of the horses as usual, though he could not take them to drink at the creek, since it was frozen solid. Near dinnertime, he started a fire so they could have hot coffee.

"After we eat, you go chop a hole in the ice so the horses can drink," Einar said.

"What about bringing out the washtub and setting it beside the fire, melting them water?" Bjorn asked.

"Won't work," Einar snapped.

Rune nodded to his son, but trust Onkel Einar to throw ice water on any idea he did not come up with.

Today Signe had sent soup in a kettle, which they set into the coals to heat. Hot food and drink, even though they ate standing, was a welcome respite. Rune reminded himself to thank her.

Bjorn wolfed his soup hungrily. "Far, you really think we can make skis?"

"I don't see why not, if we can find some suitable wood. We could try pine, but it's pretty soft and would warp easily."

"Waste of time," Einar said more forcefully this time, including his traditional glare. He tossed his coffee dregs in the direction of the fire. "Bjorn, start a new pile closer to where we are. We sure could use another hand."

Rune ignored him and headed back to the last tree they had felled to start cutting off the branches. He started working from the bottom, and Bjorn started halfway up. Einar returned to the tree he'd started. If they hurried, they'd get another tree down today. The next time they went to Blackduck, he would check with the lumber company. Perhaps Sunday he could ask Mr. Benson if he had wax or could order some.

A blizzard day would give him more time in the woodshop. Much as he liked farming, he liked building things in the woodshop far more. Felling trees would never be a pleasure. So far he had built a table and benches for their new house and was working on a chest, a surprise for Signe.

Rune focused on his work, and the rest of the day passed quickly.

"A letter from Norway," Leif announced before supper. "Onkel Einar got one too."

Tante Gerd turned from the stove. "Bring the cream up when you come so we can churn tomorrow." She set the lid back on the pan and reached toward the line they had strung across the kitchen to unpin diapers. Some were still hanging, frozen stiff, out on the porch.

"I will bring in the others," Signe said when she had laid her fussing daughter back in the cradle. "Shhh, shhh, you sleep, and then we will all have supper."

Gerd snorted. "Funny how quickly babies learn to demand what they want."

"And with no patience to wait." Signe shrugged into her coat, even though she would only be outside for a few minutes. At almost four months old, Kirstin had been fussy lately. It had been so long since Signe had a baby that she often wished she could ask her mor or Aunt Gretta what they thought might be wrong.

She was shivering by the time she brought the stiff squares back in the house to re-hang. With most of the moisture frozen out of them, drying would be quick. She pegged them up in the kitchen and sat down to fold those already dry. The sourdough starter filled the room with thoughts of bread baking tomorrow. She would use the last loaf they had for breakfast and dinner.

While Einar never mentioned his letter, she read the one addressed to Rune out loud, since it was from Nilda.

" 'Dear Minnesota family: Ivar and I are so excited to be coming to Amerika to join you.' " Signe stopped. "Ivar is coming too?" She looked to Einar, who was going out the door. Was that news to him too? Why did he have to be so — so . . . ? She shook her head.

"Keep reading, Mor." Leif propped his elbows on the table and leaned forward.

She nodded. " 'We are grateful that Onkel

Einar will pay for one ticket, but since Far does not want me traveling alone, we are all trying to get the rest of the money to pay for the other.' "

Gerd nodded. "I will see about that."

Things had really changed around here, now that Gerd felt so much stronger.

Signe continued reading.

"If there is something you would like us to bring, please write back with your list.

"We so look forward to letters from Amerika. I tried to convince Mor to come with us, but she is not willing to leave Far. He has fallen a couple of times, and while he says they are all accidents, we are beginning to wonder if something is wrong to cause these.

"Mor's big news? She finally received a letter from Tante Ingeborg. I had no idea you live so far apart. Amerika is such a big country compared to Norway. We sent her your address, so perhaps you will receive a letter too. Please write soon so we can be prepared. Onkel Einar said the ticket will be in the mail soon. Where do you buy tickets back there?"

Signe looked to Gerd.

"Never fear, buying tickets just means Einar will have to make a trip to Blackduck."

Signe nodded. " 'We pray you are all healthy. I know that baby Kirstin must be growing like dandelions in the spring. Just the thought makes me yearn for spring greens. With love from all of us. Your sister, Nilda. P.S. Have you met any handsome loggers yet who might want a wife?' "

Signe folded the letter carefully and looked at Rune, who nodded and smiled.

Rune stood up. "We better get to the woodshop before the night is over. Such good news. Thank you for supper, Tante Gerd. What a pleasure to see you up and about."

Gerd looked up from playing with Kirstin, surprise widening her eyes. "Why, you are welcome. Signe and I . . . we did it together."

Signe grinned at her husband. "I will make pudding so it is warm when you all return. Knute, Leif, do you have homework?"

Both boys nodded. "I could do it after we come back," Leif offered.

"No, first."

Bjorn pushed his chair back and followed his far to the coatrack. He winked at his brothers and wiggled his eyebrows. Leif grinned back, but Knute glared at his older brother. Signe knew that if they offered Knute a choice between school and work, he would definitely choose the woods and the farm over book learning. He was counting the months until he was sixteen and could make the choice.

While she set the milk to heat for pudding, Gerd took out her knitting, making room on her lap for an orange body to curl up, purring. Gra of the gray stripes lay sleeping on the oval braided rug by the stove.

"Did you ski in Norway, Gerd?"

"Ja, of course." She leaned over, to the disgruntlement of Gul, to pick up her ball of yarn. "But there has never been time or a need for skiing here. I think skis for the boys to get to school would be a good idea. Leif, come here so I make sure the sleeves are long enough."

Leif stroked the wool as she measured out the sweater. "This will be so warm. Takk."

"Should have it done in the next week or so. I'm making it plenty big so you don't grow out of it too fast."

"Far says I am growing like a weed. I think corn would be better than a weed."

"You have to admit that weeds grow awfully fast." Signe dipped some of the milk into her mixing bowl with the eggs, which were beaten with sugar and flour, so they wouldn't cook too fast in the hot milk. Then she slowly stirred that mixture into the rest of the heated milk, which she'd pulled to the cooler side of the stove. She enjoyed making pudding on a winter's night. The warm kitchen, the boys studying at the table in the lamplight, the baby gurgling and kicking in her makeshift bed, the click of knitting needles — what more could one ask for?

The pleasure shattered when Einar kicked the snow off his boots and came in to hang up his coat. How could it be that his growling seemed to precede him and taint the whole house?

He rubbed his hands over the heat rising from the stove in shimmery waves. "You need to use so much wood?"

Signe rolled her eyes. Would kindness ever get through to this man? "I thought pudding might taste good when you all came in." She poured the rich mixture into the bowls she had lined up on the table. "Are the others right behind you?"

He glared at her. "How should I know?"

She heard Gerd sigh. Kirstin's gurgles and happy noises turned to a whimper. Even she could tell the difference.

Signe shoved two more chunks of wood into the stove and pulled the nearly hot coffeepot to the hottest place. After spooning a dab of jam into the center of each bowl, if for no other reason than to irritate Einar, she picked up the baby and rocked her in her arms. The sounds of Bjorn and Rune on the porch gave her a sense of comfort in spite of Einar. They both entered carrying an armload of wood and dumped them in the box. *Interesting,* she noticed. *Einar never brings in a load of wood when he comes.*

"Takk." She settled Kirstin on her shoulder and patted her back.

"Smells good in here." Rune eyed the pudding dishes. "What a fine thing for a night like this."

Einar grunted as he lowered himself into his chair. While he no longer favored the hand he had cut so severely, she saw him limping sometimes by the end of the day. She was not surprised, considering how hard he worked throughout the day. Rune had said more than once that keeping up with Einar took every ounce of willpower he could dig up.

"Would you like your coffee now?" Signe asked, looking right at Einar. He nodded without ever meeting her eyes. She poured a cupful, set it on a saucer, and the others passed it around the table to him. Rune raised one eyebrow at his wife.

While the others waited for everyone to be served, Einar was scraping the sides of his pudding bowl before the others had tasted their first spoonful. He drained his coffee, shoved back his chair, and headed for his bedroom. "I'm going to Blackduck day after tomorrow. Have the lists ready."

"Takk. I will go with you then," Rune said.

"You and Bjorn could fell another tree."

"I need to go to the lumberyard."

"Suit yourself." As always, the door shut more firmly than it needed to.

Leif let out a whoosh of air, as if he'd been holding his breath. Knute snorted a laugh, then both looked at their mor.

Gerd shook her head. "Well, good riddance."

Signe tried to keep a straight face, but when Rune and Bjorn both wiggled their eyebrows, she gave up. She nearly choked on the laugh she tried to swallow so Einar wouldn't hear. The boys stared from Gerd to their mor to Rune. They too tried to laugh without making noise, which only made them stutter.

"Tante Gerd, is there anything special you would like from Blackduck?" Rune asked.

"Just more yarn. Signe and I will make a

list of things we cannot get at Benson's."

"Do you ever go along to Blackduck?"

She shook her head. "I used to, but for the last year I never left the place, got too weak."

"Have you ever seen the doctor?"

"Einar got him when he found me on the floor. He said it sounded like my heart. But thanks to you, I am so much stronger now. He gave me some pills. I took them till they ran out."

Signe stared at the woman whom she thought so much older than she really was. It still amazed her, the differences between the old Gerd and the new. Such changes, and they'd not even been here a year yet.

Chapter 4

Nilda blew a strand of hair from her face and leaned back to stretch a kink from her spine. Being hired by Mrs. Nygaard to cook and clean seemed a blessing, if you only considered the money. Scrubbing floors was never fun, but the work was no harder than at home, and every day was one closer to earning Ivar's ticket to Amerika.

And that still irked her. Here she finally had a sure way to Amerika with Onkel Einar paying for the ticket, and now she had to pay for Ivar first. *Shame on you, Nilda! You would begrudge your little brother his big chance?* He had the same dream as Nilda.

With a happy sigh, she returned to the floor as she imagined her new life. According to her letters, Signe seemed to spend most of her time on the farm, but Nilda knew there must be a handsome lumberjack or two just looking for a wife in the nearby town — Blackduck, she thought it was called.

Without knowing why, Nilda was drawn out of her daydream and looked up. There, standing in the door, was Dreng Nygaard.

"Very nice," he said, raking his gaze along her kneeling form.

"Pardon?" Nilda didn't know Dreng well. He had gone to school with her older brothers but rarely interacted with them. Something about the way he was looking at her made the hair stand up on her arms.

Suddenly, Nilda remembered her friend Addy warning her not to take the position with the Nygaards. Addy had worked for Mrs. Nygaard for a short time and had pulled Nilda aside as soon as she learned of Nilda's new job.

"It's not a good place, Nilda," Addy had warned at the time, but Nilda hadn't wanted to hear her vague warnings. Now she wondered if she should have asked more questions.

"I said it looks very nice down there," Dreng commented.

Fairly certain he didn't mean the floor, Nilda sat up and dropped her brush in the bucket. Rising to her feet, she ignored his comment and asked, "Is there anything I can get you?"

She realized her mistake immediately as he took three steps toward her. "Oh yes, there is something you can get me."

Nilda backed up until she felt the doorframe hit her shoulder, and still he was only a step away. He wouldn't really touch her, would he? Surely that was not what Addy had warned her about. Frantically, Nilda searched the room for help. Should she call out?

"Dreng!" Mrs. Nygaard's voice rang through the house.

Nilda's sigh of relief turned to alarm when she recognized what it would look like if Mrs. Nygaard entered the room and found them in such a compromising position. There was no question whom she would believe. Realizing she still held the scrub bucket between them, Nilda gave it a quick flip and allowed the water to slosh out and over his pants and boots. Getting her own skirt wet was worth the look of shock in his eyes and the way he scrambled back from her.

"Dreng," Mrs. Nygaard called again as she entered the kitchen. She stopped as she noted the soapy puddle spreading on the floor. "Whatever happened?"

Nilda held her breath, waiting to see what Dreng would say.

"The girl is clumsy."

"Nilda, dear," Mrs Nygaard chided, "you must be more careful."

"Yes, ma'am," Nilda agreed.

"Now go change your boots, Dreng. You agreed to take your dear mor to the store."

Nilda watched them leave the kitchen. Surely it hadn't been as bad as it had seemed at the time. It couldn't have been, could it?

When Nilda arrived for work a few days later, Mrs. Nygaard waved a finger airily. "Clean that cupboard at the end of the upstairs hall. There are several bottles of Mrs. Sluy's Spring Tonic that I fear have spoilt. Throw them all away, and I will purchase new ones. Also, throw away the jar of face cream. There is mold on it. Of course," she added with a smirk, "if you cannot afford fine face cream, you may take it home with you and skim off the rot."

"Thank you, ma'am. You are very generous." Nilda tried to make it sound sincere. It was not.

"I will be gone for the morning at the mission society meeting. They need me there. Make certain you do a decent job."

Nilda fetched her bucket and rags, filled the bucket halfway with soapy water, and trudged up the stairs. She opened the closet door, and her heart sank. This closet must surely not have been cleaned out for years. On the bottom shelf were folded bed linens. That shelf would be easy. The next shelf up was filled with towels, more towels than Nilda had ever seen in one place before.

It was the middle shelf that was the problem. Bottles and jars and more bottles and jars. Boxes and packets, all stacked willy-nilly. There were the bottles of Mrs. Sluy's Spring Tonic, at least half a dozen of them. What was the elixir like? Nilda could not help wondering. Cautiously she twisted the cap off one of the bottles and sniffed.

What a wretched stink! How could anyone get past the odor to actually take the tonic? She would rather stay sluggish all spring than have to deal with this putrid stuff.

"Well! Look what we have here."

Nilda wheeled. Dreng stood in his bedroom doorway, leering. He came right up to her.

"Good morning, Mr. Nygaard." She felt a sudden wave of terror, but she tried not to let it show on her face.

"Yes. It is going to be a very good morning." He took her arm. "Come with me to my room."

She stiffened. "I think not."

"I wouldn't hurt you," he purred. "Come."

She started to turn. Suddenly she grabbed his arm and swung sideways with all her might. It caught him off balance, and he slammed into the open closet. Mrs. Sluy's Spring Tonic came crashing to the floor, along with other bottles and jars. Some bounced and rolled around; most broke, and the elixir's stench penetrated everything instantly.

He was surely faster than she was; would she be able to get away? She broke free of his grasp and ran down the hall toward the stairs.

Mrs. Nygaard! She stood at the head of the stairs with her hat and gloves in her hand and stared, openmouthed. "The mess! Just look at that mess! And what is that horrid smell?"

Dreng called, "Don't listen to her, Mor! She lies!"

She turned her steely gaze on Nilda. "I've a mind to fire you, you clumsy girl!"

"Oh, please do so!" Nilda bolted past her and jogged down the stairs. She grabbed her coat off the rack by the door and ran outside. She threw her skis into the snow, but the binding on one ski was twisted, so she slipped her left foot into the other ski, snatched up her poles, and pushed away.

She stood on the right ski and skated with the left, pushing furiously with her poles. Not until she got to the bottom of the village did she pause long enough to get her right ski bound on correctly.

Her skirt and shoes stank of Mrs. Sluy's terrible tonic, and she had left behind her scarf and mittens. She could always knit more scarves and mittens. At least she was safe; well, at least a little safer.

Would Dreng pursue her? Probably not, but she was not going to take the chance. Sweating even though her coat was not fastened, she skied home as fast as she could.

Her lungs burned from the cold as she kicked out of her skis and clambered onto the front porch. Why were her eyes so hot and wet? The danger was past. She was fine now. She tossed her skis toward the rack and hurried into the house she knew best.

"Mor . . ."

Her mother looked up from her loom and instantly leaped to her feet. "Nilda! What . . . ?" She opened her arms, her wonderful, strong arms.

Nilda collapsed into them and clung to her mor, sobbing. Her crying embarrassed her. Surely it was not that big a thing, was it? Finally she felt better, enough that she could stanch the sobbing and leave her mor's hug.

Mor led her to the kitchen and sat her at the table. She said simply, "Talk."

"It wasn't my fault." Nilda chewed on the end of one finger. "Dreng — you know Dreng Nygaard, he went to school with the boys. He made, uh, advances. Mor, I didn't encourage him. When he tried . . . I mean, I was upstairs in their house, cleaning out a neglected closet, as Mrs. Nygaard told me to. He came out of his room and tried to drag me back inside. I only got away because Mrs. Nygaard came upstairs for something."

"Oh, oh nei! He didn't —"

"Nei, but not for not trying. He cornered me a few days ago as well. I could not say anything for fear of losing my job. It was the only way to make some money for Ivar's ticket. I didn't even like the job, and Mrs. Nygaard's haughty ways. I hated it!"

"Hate is a strong word."

"Ja, but it fits. And you know if his mor found out, she would have blamed me."

"Of course she would." Mor's face looked so sad and pained.

Nilda shuddered a sigh. "When the boys worked for them, they didn't have to put up with him. Or at least they never mentioned it."

"Nilda. I did not know. You think he has bothered other girls?"

"I know he has."

"Addy?"

Nilda nodded. "She said she didn't want me to work there, but she didn't say exactly why. And I didn't understand what she meant."

"This has to stop."

"It has stopped. I won't go there again. And they didn't even pay me all the wages they owe me."

"Nei, I mean he cannot be allowed to — to . . ."

"Flirt with, attack, abuse girls who work there or anywhere else?" Nilda's weepy sorrow was turning rapidly into fury.

"Ja, all those things. You think his mor knows what is going on under her very pointed nose?"

"He is her darling baby boy who can do no wrong." Even being sarcastic felt good sometimes. "I keep thinking there must be a way to get even."

"Revenge is the Lord's job," Mor reminded her.

"Surely teaching someone a lesson to make them stop what they are doing is not a bad thing. You always said we should learn from our mistakes. I'd just like to help him learn."

Gunlaug shook her head, a smile tugging at her mouth. "Takk, I never have liked having my words of wisdom given back to me." She patted Nilda's shoulder. "I am so very grateful you have told me." She heaved herself to her feet and headed for the kitchen but paused at the doorway. "Promise me, Nilda."

"Mor. Oh, all right, I promise to behave myself." *But he will be taught a lesson, I can promise you that.*

Her mor stood there another moment, frowning. "And Nilda, what is that terrible smell?"

"Solveig, this chintz is absolutely beautiful!" Nilda stroked the sleek, folded fabric. The print was of cheerful summer flowers on a pale blue background.

"It's for kitchen curtains." Solveig paused as she mopped the corners of the kitchen floor. "The curtains in the rest of the house will be muslin. We cannot afford chintz for all the curtains, but I want the kitchen to be cheerful."

"Of course!"

Nilda rolled up her sleeves and carried a basin of vinegar to the window over the dry sink. Her task was to wash windows, which gave her plenty of time to think. Johann and Solveig, just married, were going to move into this little cottage half a mile from home. It was perfect for newlyweds, but filthy. Every inch had to be cleaned. No one had lived in it for over a year, ever since its former owner, Tante Slegg, had died. She was nobody's actual aunt that anyone could remember, but everyone in the whole area around Valders loved her and called her Tante. And she had loved everyone.

Would Nilda ever have a sweet little home like this was going to be? Oh, how she wished. Her husband would be an esteemed craftsman, and she would be mistress of the house. Dreams. How could she help them come true?

She heard skis clicking together out on the front porch.

"Oh, good! Johann is back." Solveig propped her mop against the wall and cleared the table. "We can rest a moment."

Johann came in with a big wicker basket. "Dinner!"

They unpacked the basket, which contained a bucket of rich soup and a braided loaf of bread. With a smile for her husband, Solveig brought the coffee to the table. There were only two chairs, so Johann plopped down on an overturned keg.

They joined hands and he prayed, *"I Jesu navn gär vi til bords . . ."* The familiar table prayer washed across Nilda's dreams. Her husband too would provide the mealtime prayers.

Obviously, Mor had packed this basket. Nilda would recognize her mor's delicious braided bread anywhere. Someday Nilda would bake bread this fine.

They ate in silence. Then, once their stomachs were full and their coffee cups refilled, Nilda asked, "Solveig, how long did you work for the Nygaards?"

Solveig cocked her head. "Somewhere between two and three months, I guess. Why?"

"Why did you quit?"

"Ah, well, Johann and I were talking about getting married and . . ." She shrugged and shot her husband a strange look.

I thought so. Nilda added another name to the tally she was keeping in her mind. That was three for sure. Keeping secrets that allowed a worthless young man to continue his bad habits.

"Why are you asking these questions?" Johann leaned forward, staring hard at his sister.

Nilda sorted through the thoughts that at

times kept her awake at night. Somewhere she remembered overhearing her brothers and a couple of their friends discussing young Dreng. He was never included in their circle.

"Johann, how come none of you ever were friends with Dreng?"

"Why do you ask?"

"Just curious."

"Nei, I know you, and you are up to something. What has that good-for-nothing done now?"

Nilda felt her eyes widen. She sucked in a breath of courage. "He's . . . well, have you ever noticed that several of us young women or older girls work there for a while and then get fired? One I know of had to leave home." She could feel Solveig's glare clear to the bottom of her stomach. "All I can really tell you for sure is my experience, but it is not something I want to talk about either." She shifted in her chair. "I'm sorry, Solveig, but this has to be stopped. Help me, please."

Johann stared from her to his wife, who was fighting tears. "Tell me." His voice was soft but undergirded with iron.

"Promise not to blame Solveig or me or any of us. I mean it, Johann. Promise." Nilda met him stare for stare. "We need help, so keep that in mind."

"Tell me!"

"You remember that Addy tried to talk me out of going to work for the Nygaards, but she would not tell me why. When I insisted it was the only way I would be able to pay for Ivar's ticket to Amerika, she made me promise to be careful." Nilda took a sip of her cooled coffee and shuddered.

Solveig pushed back her chair. "I'll get more coffee." She was up and at the stove before Nilda thought to stop her.

Nilda blew out a breath and rocked in her chair. *Come on, get this over with. I wish I'd never started this. Just get it over with.* Her mind seemed to argue with itself.

"Dreng starts by flirting with the help and persists until it is more than flirting. And goes to more than kissing, unless the girl or young woman flees, or fights back, or refuses to return to the house. I did not get all my pay." She nodded to Solveig. "Did you get yours?"

"Did he — ?" Johann stared at his wife, who shook her head.

"Nei, but I was so frightened, I got sick and threw up."

"On him?" Nilda choked out.

"The front of him. And his shoes."

"Did you really?" Nilda burst out laughing. She could no more contain it than she could stop the spring breakup on the river.

Solveig stuttered, then giggled behind her hand, then she too was laughing. "He — he was screaming at me, and his mor came running from the kitchen, and she was horrified and then angry and said I had to clean it up and go home so they did not get sick from my sickness. I did not go back because I was 'too sick.' " She looked at Johann. "It was not my fault," she whispered. "I did nothing to encourage him. He was, and is, vile."

"Why has this been allowed to go on so long?"

"Because I was afraid you would not want to marry me if you thought I was — well, you know."

"And the others? Besides Addy, who are they?"

"Does it matter? He is the problem." Nilda leaned forward. "I believe he should be taught a lesson, made to see the error of his ways. Don't you, Solveig?"

"Ja, but the women must not be made to suffer."

"True. Sadly this must be done in secret."

"Shame we don't pillory people here." Johann sighed and took his wife's hand. "You could have told me."

"No, she couldn't have," Nilda argued. "You are a lot wiser now than you were then. So what are we going to do?"

"*We* are going to do nothing. You started the snowball rolling down the hill, and now it will be encouraged along by someone else." He leaned over and stared Nilda back into her chair. "You know nothing about this, you will not talk it over with anyone else, and you will thus be safe from any danger from that family, either physical or hearsay. Do you understand?"

Nilda waited before nodding. It would be better this way. Hopefully Mor would not be able to blame her either. She surged to her feet. "Takk for the coffee, Solveig, and I better get home before dark and Mor starts to worry. I will do the windows tomorrow. After all, I am unemployed now."

Her brother walked her to the door. "Be careful, and I'm not talking about skiing home in the dusk either." He patted her arm. "Takk."

CHAPTER 5

"I do not want you out in the woods by yourself." Rune made sure his son was looking at him.

"But Onkel Einar said —"

"Be that as it may, your far says *nei.* I will deal with Einar."

"But I can work in the shop?" Bjorn made a face. "I thought I could catch up on the limb stacking."

"I figured that, but then you would decide you could finish limbing that tree." Rune knew he had hit home when the mask fell over his son's face.

Bjorn slumped slightly and heaved a sigh. "All right." He dropped his voice. "Will you get the ash for the skis?"

"If I can. I plan to talk with the men at the lumber store. Surely they know someone who makes skis around here who might be willing to share some information with me."

"Did you make the ones we had at home

in Norway?"

"Nei, my far did, years ago. Like everything else, if you take care of what you have, it will last longer." Not like Einar. He did take good care of his tools for lumbering, but the junk pile in the corner of the shop gave the boys plenty of things to sand and refinish to make them functional again, like the plane they used to smooth boards. The shavings made a great fire starter up at the house.

"I should spend some of the time splitting wood," Bjorn said.

Rune nodded. "I'll help you put that log up on the sawbucks so you can saw more spools for firewood, too." He heard the harness jingling. Einar was ready to leave, and patience was not part of his makeup. "Come on."

Signe met them at the door and handed Rune the page she and Gerd had put together. "Here are our lists. Takk."

"Make sure you get the coffee. Although Einar usually sees that we have that." Gerd swayed with Kirstin on her shoulder.

Outside, Rune and Bjorn dragged the dried tree to the sawbucks, but when they tried to lift it, they had to let it down with a thunk. It was just too big.

"All right, drive a wedge under the trunk

where you want to cut so the saw doesn't bind up. You wouldn't be able to drag it up by yourself anyway."

Bjorn nodded. "You better get going, or he'll leave you behind."

Rune laid a hand on his son's shoulder. "You better work on this first."

"I figured."

Rune swung himself up onto the sledge seat, once again aware of how hard Bjorn tried not to set Einar into a rage, or even a simmer.

Einar set the team to a trot, getting them to the turn at Benson's Corner in record time. All that time he never said a word.

Rune ignored him and enjoyed studying the other farms, dreaming of his own one day. They had the land, so step one was building their house. It would have been good to dig the cellar before the ground froze, but looking back never worked. He was saving every dollar of their wages to buy lumber for their house. But buying wood for skis was important too.

Finally, Rune broke the silence. "You ever thought of hiring one of those traveling sawmills to saw our logs here?"

"Ja, but the lumber will be too green to build with this summer."

Rune nodded. That made good sense.

"You ever thought about adding on to the shop?"

Einar glared at him. "What we got works fine."

"We could close in the remainder of the machine shed and add on a shed for the machinery."

"Ja, we could." Einar's forehead furrowed deeper as he glared at Rune over his shoulder. "You sure are good at spending my money." His bark bit. "We do not need more space in the shop. You want to build something bigger, you just go build your own shop."

Rune debated arguing but deliberately chose to let it drop. In these last months, he had learned that the best way to deal with Einar Strand was to drop an idea into his head, then let him work it around until it became his idea. "Just a thought. I figured that when you run out of pine logs to sell, you could use some other ideas for bringing cash in."

"I am going to farm. I told you that." The growl deepened with each word spaced to cut.

"I know, but from what I see, that soil isn't real good for growing things. Going to take a lot of building up. Lots of rocks to pick out too."

"That's what those boys are good for."

My boys will be working on our own home, at least part of the time. Not yours. "I've been wondering how to get those stumps out. A lot of stumps out there."

"Dynamite works."

"Dangerous."

"Not if you know how." At least Einar's voice was back to his normal growl. "I was hoping to get another couple of acres ready for spring planting. Going to need more hay if we get more cows. That wife of yours going to make cheese?"

Rune shook his head. "Her name is Signe. And now that Gerd is stronger, once the cows are out on pasture again, she is hoping to."

The snow cover gave Blackduck a crisp, clean appearance. Still, even if you flattened out Norway's hills and mountains into a level plain, this town looked totally different. In Norway, you were either in the town or not. Here, you passed a few farms, then more farms, and then a feedlot, and then the stores, which were, Rune assumed, the town proper. It was so spread out. Scattered. Norway's towns were compact, the buildings all huddled together.

Rune suddenly realized why. In Norway, land was precious and you used every inch.

Here, there was plenty of land for everyone. Einar's generous offer of acreage was not nearly as generous as it had sounded when Rune was still in Norway. Land in Minnesota was cheap and plentiful.

He pointed toward what appeared to be a mill. "How about leaving me off at the lumberyard, then I will meet you at Bergen's General Store?"

Einar nodded. "Going to the feedstore too. If you buy any wood, we need to load that before the feed."

Rune nodded. It would be easiest if Einar just waited for him at the lumberyard, but the thought of Einar getting impatient while Rune talked with someone there did not seem like a good thing.

Einar lined the team over in front of the lumberyard office. Rune barely had his boots on the ground before Einar clucked the team forward.

"Takk." Rune didn't expect an answer, and he didn't get one. He strode up to the building marked *Office* and opened the door. Overhead, a bell jangled. Monroe's Lumber was one of the largest businesses in town, and praise to God, the storekeeper spoke both English and Norwegian.

"Ah, Mr. Carlson, I haven't seen you for a long time. How can I help you?" The clerk greeted him with a smile.

"Good day, Mr. Hechstrom." Rune nodded. "I need both wood and information."

"Well, hopefully I have what you need on both counts. Let's start with the information." Mr. Hechstrom leaned on the counter. "What are you thinking to build now?"

"Skis for my boys to get to school easier."

"They know how to ski?"

"That they do. Don't all Norwegians know how to ski?"

"Depends on when and where they came from. You made skis before?"

Rune shook his head. "We used the ones my far made but could not bring them along. I know he used hickory, but I was thinking perhaps birch would be easier to find here. Or ash?"

"Most folks use black ash. Hickory is so heavy, and birch warps more easily. But if you soak black ash and bend up the front, when it dries, it stays that way. Keep 'em well waxed and stored straight, and you got skis for a lifetime. You heard about the ski clubs popping up? Big group down in Red Wing."

Rune shook his head. As if he went anywhere to hear any news. "So who is making skis? I just thought to make 'em for us. Skiing makes good sense here. Faster than horse travel and easier on the horse."

"The Halversons over in Bemidji are shipping skis back to Norway."

"Really?" Rune nodded slowly. "You have any black ash here?"

"I do, have to keep it in stock. Have birch too. How much you want?"

Rune reined his mind back to dealing with the here and now. "Ash, please. Enough for two pairs. Start there."

"I heard you got some land from old Strand. When you planning to build?"

"How did — ?" Rune cut off the question. Probably from the sheriff. Folks said women did the gossiping, but men told stories. Getting the best of Einar Strand seemed to be worth a tale or two. "Hope to start digging the cellar soon as the ground thaws."

"So we're probably looking at late June to build, then?"

"Depends on how fast my boys and I can dig it out."

Hechstrom snorted. "I'm sure old Einar's not going to help you any."

"Probably not. All he thinks about is cutting trees."

"You thinking a log cabin?"

"The trees are too big for that. I'll be ordering milled lumber when we get closer.

I thought about using some of our trees for the lumber, but that will be too green, right?"

Hechstrom nodded. "So for now, you just need ski planks?"

Rune held out his hand, measuring from the floor. "Knute is about this tall and Leif about here. But they sure are growing fast, so I suppose I should make all the skis six foot and let Leif grow into them. That way we could all use them easy enough." He shook his head. "I know my wife would love to ski again. You ever seen anyone carry a baby in a sling or backpack while on skis?"

"Might make her the talk of Benson's Corner, but . . ." He shrugged. "You do what needs doing." He grinned.

Rune smiled and nodded. "So where can I get good ski wax?"

"Over at Bergen's. They carry about everything. You going to build your house out of white pine?"

"Dry as it can be."

"We got some of last year's under a roof. Should be good by then. Still a lot of building going on around here. Makes you wonder, if you think about the diminishing acres of white pine left. Those big companies, they just clean out an area and move on. Watched 'em do that all across the northern part of this country." He leaned his elbows on the counter.

Rune nodded. "Farming will keep expanding."

"Yeah, but so much of that soil is only good for growing trees. Fella I met talked about planting hardwoods. That's what nature does, replants. Pine trees take a lot of years to grow back, but they will eventually."

"Planting hardwoods, eh?" Rune thought of all the birch already growing where the pines had either fallen or been cut down. "Black ash grows here?"

"Yup, and maple. Some make orchards of sugar maple too. Then cut the wood when it is big enough."

So how did you feed your family while the trees were growing? Rune couldn't see Einar being that patient, but . . . on his own five acres . . . he could plant trees on part of it. Half pasture, half trees. His head teemed with questions and ideas. He nodded. "Takk. You give me a lot to think about."

Mr. Hechstrom slapped his hand on the counter. "So, I got some real straight black ash, one by four by eight foot. You might want to get an extra board or two, just in case something goes wrong."

Rune counted out his carefully hoarded cash and paid, and together they walked out into the back of the long tall building where they kept the finer woods. He picked out six lengths. "We'll be back for them."

"I'll keep them right here for you."

Rune looked longingly at the different kinds and cuts of wood. He had always known he liked working with wood, a desire that came down from his far and his far's far. He inhaled the deep, rich fragrance of the gathered woods. Some, like cedar, smelled stronger, even drove the bugs away. He hated to be in a hurry to leave, but he had no desire to get left behind. "Takk. Tusen takk. I will see you later."

He walked out to the main street and turned toward Bergen's General Store.

Einar was inside, waiting at the counter. He had already amassed a pile of purchases. "You got the list?"

Rune pulled it out of his pocket and handed it to Einar. He smiled at the woman behind the counter. She smiled in return.

Einar frowned. "This all?"

Rune nodded. "Gerd and Signe both went over the list."

Still scowling, Einar slapped the list down on the counter.

To the clerk, Rune said, "Mr. Hechstrom

at the lumberyard said you carry ski wax."

"Ja, we do. Comes in a block." She reached behind her to some wrapped cakes that looked rather like soap packages.

He thought a moment and nodded. "I would like two, please."

Einar gave a snort of disgust.

Rune ignored him, something he was getting better at doing. "How long until the order will be ready?"

"Give me half an hour."

"Good, we need to pick up some other things." He turned. Einar was already halfway to the door. Rune turned back to the woman and smiled. "Takk."

She smiled and nodded, then sent a glare in Einar's direction. Seemed like he had a bad reputation in Blackduck too.

Outside, Einar untied the team. "How much wood you got?"

Rune told him. "Thought it would fit straight along the side of the bed."

"We'll get feed after that. You talk to that Hechstrom fellow about that addition to the shop?"

Rune stared at him. "But you said —" He cut off the rest of his surprise. "We haven't measured yet to see what we need. Besides, we can't add on until the snow is gone."

Einar grunted. "We can put the floor

down and continue that front wall. Build a door like the barn."

"You want to talk to him?"

Einar shook his head. "Tell him to put it on my tab, and we'll pick it up next Saturday if it ain't storming."

As if they had time right now to build that in. "When you thinking to move the logs?"

"Better do it soon, before the frost goes out. Tell him we need a pulley and tackle too. Need that today, and hawser rope, couple hundred feet. Tell him what we're doing. He'll know how much."

"We could use a pulley in the haymow, too. Especially since you're expanding your hayfields this spring."

Einar shook his head. "Just get one."

Rune returned to the lumberyard feeling a bit smug and with a lighter heart. He was finally becoming able to direct Einar's thoughts toward the future, away from negative things and toward positive things. And that was something he had not thought could happen.

But then, coming to this lumberyard always lightened his heart. Besides the wood aromas and stacks of milled lumber, there was Mr. Hechstrom. Together, by guess and by golly, they figured out approximately what would be needed for the extension on

Einar's shed in only ten minutes.

Once the ash planks, pulley, and rope were loaded, they drove to the feedstore, then returned to Bergen's.

"You remember this here dynamite needs to be kept dry," the man loading the wagon cautioned.

The look Einar sent him made him shrug and shake his head. But he carefully set the wooden box at the front of the bed on the floor. They tied down the load and climbed back up on the seat.

"Takk." Rune smiled at the store employee who had helped them load. "Appreciate the help."

Einar slapped the reins, and the team settled into their collars, somehow knowing that pulling the loaded wagon would take more effort on their part.

Rune's happy thoughts dissolved under Einar's black cloud. He gritted his teeth. Couldn't Einar Strand at least be a little polite?

CHAPTER 6

"So how did the trip go?"

Signe could feel Rune shaking his head. They had not had time to talk since the two men returned from Blackduck. She had been shocked to see such a huge load come jingling down the lane. They had yet to put away all the new supplies. Rune had promised to be careful with the box of dynamite. The box made her heart drop to somewhere around her ankles. The thought of having dynamite anywhere on the farm made her skin crawl. Accidents could happen so easily.

"I feel sorry for him."

She jerked herself back to the man beside her. "For Einar?"

"Ja. He . . ."

Signe waited, thinking perhaps Rune had fallen asleep. A thought tripped through her sleepy mind. What had Einar done to make Rune feel that way? Another followed. What would it take to make *that man,* as she'd come to call him, even look at her, let alone speak to her? How could he hang on to a grudge for so long? She could feel sleep creeping over her.

"He is never nice to anyone," Rune said.

Signe swallowed her snort. "I wonder if he was always like this." And why did Gerd ever marry him? That question had come to her before. What were they both like when they were younger? She trapped a yawn, her eyes closing in spite of her. Rune's breathing told her he had fallen asleep even if he desired to tell her more. She breathed her thanks.

Kirstin's squirming and hungry cries brought her mor out of a dream that left her wondering. Something bad had happened, but waking to her baby made her smile both inside and out. Kirstin was better than a rooster for an alarm clock.

Rune groaned and managed to pull his pants over his long johns and shove his feet into his boots. They were both adept at dressing in the dark. He moved to the wooden box where the kerosene lamp and matches waited. "Mornings like this remind me that spring can't come too soon."

Dressed in a robe and slippers, Signe picked up the baby and blinked against the lamplight. Rune carried the lamp down the stairs and held it up so she could see to follow him. In the kitchen, he started the stove while she changed the baby and sat down in the rocking chair to nurse her. The snapping of wood catching fire and the gurgles and throaty murmurs of the nursing baby made a fine good morning song.

"I'll call the boys."

"I heard someone moving around up there."

By the time Bjorn staggered into the kitchen, scrubbing his hair back with his fingers, she was adjusting the baby in the sling around her shoulder. No longer could she carry the baby in front. She and Gerd had devised a way to carry her on their backs, still leaving their hands free to cook or do whatever needed doing.

As long as her mor was moving around, Kirstin gurgled and made baby conversation until she drifted off to sleep again.

"What do you need from the well house?" Bjorn asked.

"Milk, cream, and the full churn." She smiled at her eldest son. "Takk."

He shrugged into his winter things, and as he went out the door to the porch, the other two boys blinked their way into the kitchen.

"What's for breakfast?" Leif asked.

"Bacon, eggs, fried cornmeal, and syrup."

"Can I cut a piece of bread to eat on the way to the barn?" Knute could eat a full meal and want more an hour later.

Signe nodded to the breadbox in the pantry. "Help yourself. Cut three."

Some time later, when all the menfolk were off to their labors, and Kirstin was demanding to eat again, Gerd fixed plates for both of them and set them on the table. She and Signe sat down at their places and heaved sighs of relief. The two cats sat side by side on the braided rag rug in front of the stove, tails curled around their front feet, eyes slitted. Signe happened to be looking at them when Gra's eyes flew open, and in one motion, they both leaped to their feet and tore into the pantry.

"Good hearing," Gerd said.

"Hope they catch it." One more thing to be thankful for — the mouse population had nearly abandoned the house. And now that they had inside stairs down to the cellar, the cats had taken care of that part of the house too.

"Do most babies start on real food at this age?" Gerd asked.

"My mor told me to, and it worked with the boys. But she also said that all babies do not do well with it." She looked down at her daughter's smiling face, milk drool leaking from one side of her mouth. "You don't want to waste any of that precious stuff, little one."

Kirstin waved her fist and gurgled an answer.

"I always dreamed of nursing a baby." Gerd swirled her cornmeal slab to mop up the last of the syrup on her plate. She nodded while putting it in her mouth. "Never did get pregnant."

"I am sorry."

"Perhaps it was better this way."

"I couldn't for a long time after Leif. Pretty much gave up hope." Signe stroked her daughter's cheek. "And then she came along. I think she is God's gift to us, being born in this country and all. We waited so long. Since I had lost several, we almost decided not to come when we learned I was pregnant. But we all got here just fine, and she is growing like those weeds that try to take over the garden. I thought about naming her Joy, but the boys liked the name Kirstin."

"So she is Kirstin Joy Carlson." Gerd nodded and held up her cup. "More?" She motioned for Signe to stay seated. "I'll get it." As she refilled their cups, she nodded to the churn by the stove. "I will do that while you get the bread going. Let's get that venison haunch started in the big kettle for soup."

Signe nodded and set her baby on her knees, propping her up with both hands on her sides. Jiggling her knees made Kirstin giggle, then laugh out loud. Joy was such a good name for her. There had been more laughter in this house with this happy baby than there had probably ever been before.

"Let's tie her in the rocker, and I can keep that going with my foot while I churn," Gerd suggested.

"Ja, fine idea." Signe drained her coffee cup and, baby on hip, set their dishes in the steaming soapy water in the pan on the stove. She paused and smiled at Gerd. "I am so grateful since you got better." She waved a hand around the kitchen. "I never dreamed this could happen."

"I didn't either. Bringing you and Rune and your family over here was the best thing Einar has ever done for me. And he thought it was all for felling more trees." She set to washing the dishes. "I even appreciate doing the dishes now."

Signe nodded and sniffed. She blew her nose on the bit of flannel she kept in her apron pocket. Thankfulness made even the cats and the kitchen smile. A streak of sun gilding a window design on the floor invited both cats to curl up there.

"Has Onkel Einar used dynamite to blow out stumps before?" Signe asked.

Gerd nodded. "He learned to leave a longer fuse and not stand too close. House shook every time. That was before I was too weak to get out of bed, but I didn't go out there." She shook her head while taking the dishes out of the rinse pan and drying them before putting them back in the cupboard. "I think my eyes see differently now."

Signe propped the baby against a pillow in the rocker and used a dish towel to tie her in place. Kirstin chortled and waved both arms while Signe carried the rocker over by the churn. "Here you go, little one. Have a good time."

Gerd dragged a chair over by the churn and sat down to begin, using one foot to set the rocker in motion. Kirstin stared at the *thunk* of the churn, her mouth matching the rounds of her eyes. Gerd nodded, so close to a smile that Signe held her breath. When the baby waved her arm again and garbled out some sounds, the corners of Gerd's mouth twitched, then spread. She leaned closer to the laughing baby. Kirstin stared at her, as if she too were waiting for a real smile. When it came, she stared right into

Gerd's eyes, gurgled, and reached for her face with one tiny finger. Gerd kissed the end of her finger, sending Kirstin into another round of chuckles.

Signe watched their game, ignoring the tears running down her face. All she could think was *Thank you, Lord God, thank you, Jesus, Holy Spirit, for being in this room with us. Surely this is one of your miracles.* She sniffed and beat more flour into the rising sourdough. Once it was thick enough, she dumped it out on a floured board and set to kneading. What a glorious day this was turning into.

The churn song deepened, the baby slumped into slumber, and Signe rolled her dough into a ball and laid it back in the crockery bowl. Now it would rise again, covered with a clean dish towel on the warming shelf above the stove.

"Why don't you go take a nap while I put her in her cradle?" Signe whispered, as always noticing as soon as Gerd started to fade.

"I was going to wash the butter."

"I know, but churning takes a lot out of you. Now is a good time to rest."

Gerd nodded and pushed herself to her feet. "Takk."

How that word made Signe's heart bloom.

It had been so long, but now it was worth all the times she had ignored the screaming and meanness. Illness truly did strange things to some people. Her mor had told her that years earlier. Never had she seen it so true as here in the Northwoods of Minnesota.

As Gerd made her way to bed, Signe carefully tucked her baby into the cradle and rocked it tenderly until Kirstin settled back into her morning nap.

Later, Gerd was back in the kitchen and the sun was already on the downward plunge when the boys burst through the door, laughing and waving a letter.

"From Bestemor," Knute announced.

"And Mrs. Benson said to tell you that if the weather holds, she plans to come visit tomorrow. She said she had to see that baby again and to have coffee with you and Tante Gerd." Leif grinned at his mor. "Good, huh?"

"Ja, indeed, very good."

"Oh, and Tante Gerd, she sent you more yarn. She just got more in. We are to tell her in the morning if you want her to bring more when she comes."

Gerd fingered the skein of yarn, nodding all the while. "I can always use more. It will be good to see her again."

Signe swallowed her shock and smiled both inside and out. How wonderful to have good memories in this house to blot out the earlier ones.

"I'm hungry." Leif sniffed the yeasty smell of rising bread. "Fresh bread would be good."

"We will have that for supper. There are some pancakes left you can butter and sprinkle with sugar. How was school?"

"I got a hundred on my spelling test." Leif brought the pancakes from the pantry to butter at the table. "Do we have buttermilk?"

"Since Gerd churned the butter today, we do. Look in the pantry."

"I have to write an essay." Knute shook his head as if this were a punishment rather than a simple assignment.

"About?"

No answer.

Signe rolled her eyes and lifted the lid to feed the fire. "You both better bring in wood before you start the chores."

"Joseph from two farms north of here said the wolves tried to get in their sheep pen. The ewes are having their lambs. I sure wish we had some sheep." Leif rolled another pancake and ate half of it in one bite.

"Maybe we could buy some sheep from them."

"We don't have enough animals to take care of now?" Knute shook his head at his younger brother. "Those two gilts mean we will have lots of baby pigs this year. And I want to work in the woods. Just think, Onkel Ivar will be here too. Means there are going to be plenty of branches to cut and haul to the piles."

"And we get to build our own house." Leif stuffed the last pancake in his mouth and drained his glass. "You get to milk Belle tonight. She tried to kick the bucket over last night. Wonder how come?"

"Maybe you pinched her teat."

"I didn't pinch her." Leif took a playful swing at his brother, who sidestepped him with a grin.

"Isn't the heifer due soon?" Signe asked.

Knute nodded. "She's pretty big."

"Have you put her in the box stall yet?" Gerd asked.

"No, should I?"

She nodded. "If she decides to have her calf during the day when they are outside, she might try to go hide somewhere."

"I won't let her out tomorrow. Far will know if she is getting close." Both boys headed out the door and returned with a load of wood.

"Takk."

"We'll bring in more later, after we put Jenna in the box stall." They laughed as they ran out the door, bounded off the porch, and chased each other to the barn.

Signe watched them go with a smile.

CHAPTER 7

Another job! Nilda was happy that she had been able to find a place with the storekeeper, Mrs. Sieverson, so quickly. It was only temporary, but it was money in her pocket. She entered the store, and the bell over the door tinkled.

"I am so glad you'll be filling in for Matilde until she is well enough to come back to the store." Mrs. Sieverson took Nilda's coat and showed her where to hang it up. "I have gotten behind on unpacking and putting out the last shipment of supplies, so that is where we will start." She led the way to the back room, where crates covered half the floor. "Some of this will go up on these shelves, then the rest out on the shelves in the store." She handed Nilda a crowbar to pry off the tops of the crates and left.

Nilda opened the first crate and lifted out paper-wrapped bolts of fabric and packets of notions, including thread. Yarn came in another wrapped parcel, and the bottom half of the crate was canned goods. She set the fabric and yarn on a shelf and lined the cans up on a table. Setting notions in a basket, she carried them out to place on the shelves that still held enough to guide her.

Dry goods! Nilda loved just being around beautiful dry goods. She smiled. This was going to be so much nicer than that Nygaard job!

Over the next few days, as she unpacked crate after crate, Nilda struggled to fight off the curiosity bug that kept attacking her. What did Johann mean when he told her to stay out of it, whatever *it* was?

One morning, she pried the lid off yet another crate. The last of Mrs. Sieverson's dry goods order. Excellent. She filled her basket with boxes of thread and took it out front to shelve the spools.

"You!" The customer at the counter pointed a long finger at Nilda. Mrs. Nygaard!

Nilda froze. Of all the people in the world — well, except Dreng — Nilda wanted to avoid this woman the most.

Mrs. Nygaard turned to Mrs. Sieverson. "You are employing a vixen. A hussy! A tramp! I insist you fire her immediately!"

"Why, Mrs. Nygaard —"

"She tried to seduce my poor Dreng. The boy knows nothing about the ways of the world, and she tried to pervert him. I insist! Out!"

Fury grabbed Nilda's heart and mind. And then that fury came flying out of her mouth. "Mrs. Nygaard, haven't you ever wondered why you cannot keep household help for more than a month or so? Your son makes unwelcome advances! Persistent advances! Not just to me; all of us! That is why."

"And you are a liar as well!"

"Miss Carlson is a splendid worker," Mrs. Sieverson barked, and she never raised her voice. "Industrious, fast to catch on, scrupulously honest, and pleasant to the customers. No, I will not fire her."

"Then I will not come here again."

"That is your choice, Mrs. Nygaard. Takk for coming in."

Red-faced with anger, Mrs. Nygaard marched out.

"I am so sorry." Nilda stepped toward Mrs. Sieverson. "You lost a customer, and it was all my fault. My terrible temper. I'm so sorry!"

Mrs. Sieverson studied her, and she did not even look upset. "I've heard rumors about Dreng. That woman called you a strumpet, it is no wonder you got angry. I would have as well." She smiled. "In fact, I did. Please resume your duties and think nothing more of it. I will see you first thing in the morning, right?"

"Ja, I will be here." Nilda's heart sang. Mrs. Sieverson believed her! She believed her!

That boy knows nothing about the ways of the world? Hah!

It was not as dark as usual when she left work that evening. The sky was still a bit light. Could spring be near? Nilda buckled into her skis and, digging her poles in, headed for home. Being outside with the cold biting her cheeks always made her want to shout for joy. Nothing felt more like freedom and flying than slipping over a hillock and up another. Except spring flowers. That was even better.

At the farmhouse, she loosed the bindings on her skis and studied them a moment. Would she be able to take them to Amerika? Rune had written that he was learning to make skis and how he wished he had spent more time with Bestefar in his woodshop. She needed to write to him and ask if he would have extra skis made by next winter.

Unwinding her scarf as she entered the

house, she could hear Mor in the kitchen talking with someone.

"That you, Nilda?"

"Ja." She hung up her things and followed her nose to the coffeepot on the stove. Once her cup was full, she joined her mor and Ivar at the table. "Something sure smells good."

"A leg of mutton, Ivar's pay for helping cut up the fir tree that blew down at the Stettlers'."

"Good pay."

"Ja. Ivar didn't plan on getting paid. So how was work?"

Even as she told Mor and Ivar about the confrontation with Mrs. Nygaard, she wondered — would this help or hinder whatever it was that Johann had in mind? She wished he had told her more.

She ended, "And Mrs. Sieverson wants me tomorrow too. Every day puts more in the ticket fund for Ivar." She sipped her coffee. "I don't think Far would have allowed me to go without Ivar. In a way, Dreng illustrates why."

Mor nodded. "I am going to miss you dreadfully. And two of you leaving at once."

Ivar laid a hand on hers. "You will get to come to Amerika, Mor. We will all see to that, and somehow you will see Ingeborg again."

"We were so close, Ingeborg and I, until that big feud that my far enforced. All those years we couldn't even talk to each other. Mor never got over it."

"I don't think you did either, not really," Nilda said.

Mor heaved a sigh and stood up. "That rug will never get done at this rate. How long until you are supposed to leave?"

"May twentieth. Right after Syttende Mai. I would like to take my skis along."

"You already have two trunks going and the loom, besides your clothes. I want to send Signe a yellow rosebush start too, and some more seeds. She has always loved our yellow roses. They will climb up anything. Perhaps she will have a porch on her new house that needs a yellow rosebush blooming in front of it."

Every time Nilda saw Johann, she wanted to ask him if anything was happening to teach Dreng a lesson, but some kind of wisdom helped her keep her questions to herself. One afternoon, she nearly pointed her skis to his house rather than straight home. Disgust dug into her skin like a sliver. She should have come up with an idea by herself. At least something might have happened that way.

Sometime later, Nilda was at work, setting the storeroom in order, when she heard the tinkling bell announcing a customer. When she didn't hear Mrs. Sieverson welcoming the person, she started for the front of the store.

"You won't believe this, Mrs. Sieverson." Mrs. Grosbach, one of the gossipers from church, had a voice that could carry across the valley.

Nilda told herself to go back to work but instead waited.

"Whatever has you in such a state?"

"Well, I can hardly believe this myself, but . . ." She dropped her voice.

Go back to work, Nilda instructed herself. *Now!* Still she waited. *Nilda Carlson, you do not like that woman anyway, what do you care about her tittle-tattle ways?*

Something kept her stuck to her spot. When she heard the name Dreng Nygaard, she leaned closer to the curtain-shrouded doorway. Hearing voices was different from understanding what they were saying.

"He was beaten up pretty badly, and when his far found out . . ."

Nilda fought to think of an excuse to go closer to them, but nothing came to mind. At least the men had inflicted some kind of punishment.

"And . . ."

And what? Never had Nilda's ears worked harder to decipher muttered words.

"What's the word? Oh I remember, *banished.* Mr. Nygaard is sending his son to Amerika to work for his uncle."

"When?"

"Immediately. His mor is going to be heartbroken."

"She's the one who spoiled him. You say no one knows who the girls were?"

"Pretty hush-hush altogether. The Nygaards would not want this kind of information out."

"How did you come by it?"

"I will never tell. Do you have any envelopes and writing paper?"

"I do, back here. Do you need ink for your pen too?"

"Why yes, I believe I do. And do you have any fresh eggs? Our hens are not laying yet."

Nilda shook her head and returned to her cleaning. So Dreng was receiving recompense for his vile actions after all. Banished. God help the young women in Amerika.

A couple of days later, she picked up the mail at the post office. A letter for Mor and one for . . . her? No one ever wrote to her.

She slid a fingernail under the flap and

pulled out a single sheet of paper.

On it in block letters, she read, *I will get you for this! DN*

Chapter 8

"Be sure to tell Mrs. Benson that I need more yarn," Gerd said as the boys headed out the door for school the next morning.

"I will!" Leif called over his shoulder.

As soon as they'd had breakfast, Signe set to sweeping the kitchen while Gerd washed the dishes. When things were put to rights, Kirstin nursed, and the coffeepot on, Signe sat down to finish a letter home for Mrs. Benson to take back with her.

We are so looking forward to Nilda and Ivar coming. Today is a beautiful day, but Einar said this morning that he thinks we are in for another blizzard soon. Gerd says he is right about the weather more often than not. Here it is, March, and I am already longing for spring. Kirstin is gumming everything, so I think she may be teething soon. I gave her a piece of bacon rind to chew on before she gnawed my knuckle off. That keeps her happy for quite a while.

Tante Gerd still needs occasional rests, but she is so much better, it is hard to believe. We all have scarves, hats, and mittens thanks to her knitting. We have rabbit skins to make outer mittens, so we are learning to do that. Bjorn is a good hole puncher with an awl they finally found in Einar's shop.

Rune bought wood to make skis, and they will plane those in the evening. They all like working down in the shop. Knute and Leif would be there more, but they have homework for school almost every night. Their English is getting very good, and they are teaching their mor. Gerd helps me too. Tell Nilda and Ivar the most important thing they can do is learn to speak and read English before they come. Their lives here will be much easier that way.

I hear a harness jingling. Mrs. Benson is coming, so I will say good-bye for now. We treasure your letters.

Your daughter,
Signe

She quickly folded the pages and slid them into an envelope. How she desired to see her family again. Writing should make the sadness go away, but it did not, not really. She grabbed her coat and headed for the back door to greet their visitor. The front door was all snowed in.

"Come in, come in. I will take your horse to the barn."

"No, no. With no wind, we'll blanket him and leave him here. I need to get back to the store soon, since Mr. Benson has to deliver orders later." Mrs. Benson smiled at Signe. "You see, that is what I am doing too, delivering yarn, and I am sure there are some other things in the sleigh. Isn't this a beautiful day? I think the icicles are even dripping on the south sides of roofs."

Together they settled the heavy horse blanket over the horse and retrieved a basket and packages from the back.

As they mounted the porch steps, Mrs. Benson said, "You have the nicest boys. You should be very proud of them."

Signe stared at her visitor while she opened the door. "I — ah — takk." She wondered what they had done to have earned such a compliment. "Let me take your coat."

"Good morning, Mrs. Strand," Mrs. Benson said as she walked into the kitchen. "How are you this fine morning?"

"Better. Sit down, sit down." Gerd pulled out a chair. "The coffee is nearly ready."

Setting her basket on the table, Mrs. Benson looked around. "Where is that baby girl of yours? You know that's who I really came to see."

"She is sleeping, but knowing her, she will be awake soon. She already doesn't like to miss anything." Signe glanced over to the cradle Rune had made for the downstairs. He had built another for upstairs, where the whole family slept. Wrapped in her blanket, Kirstin lay on her belly, one fist against her mouth.

Mrs. Benson handed Gerd a brown paper package of yarn the size of a soup kettle. Maybe even bigger. "This should last you awhile. For a change, I was able to buy two-ply in a soft yellow. I thought you might like to knit a dress for the little miss and perhaps a bonnet. But if you don't want it, I am sure I can sell it to someone else."

Gerd opened the package carefully, to save the paper, and fingered the soft fine yarn. "Oh, how lovely." She lifted a skein. "Won't this be perfect?" She held it out for Signe to see. "I have never knit anything so fine. Good thing I have my bestemor's wide collection of knitting needles. The ones I use for socks might work for this."

Signe gazed at Gerd's face in wonder. Soft to match the way she sometimes looked at Kirstin. She swallowed and took a deep breath. For this, God had brought her to this house and these people. She caught the look of delight Mrs. Benson sent her way and smiled back with a slight nod.

"I brought this for you." Mrs. Benson handed Signe a jar of honey.

"Tusen takk, we just used up the last. We can have that on the biscuits with our coffee." Signe made a face. "I almost forgot them."

The biscuits were a bit more brown than usual, but when she set the pan on the table, the fragrance invited them to pour the coffee. Signe glanced over when she heard her baby squirming and starting to wake.

"She likes the smell of coffee, I think." Gerd picked up the baby, who snuggled into her shoulder.

Mrs. Benson and Signe exchanged a smile. Gerd might not have been a mother, but she sure knew how to cuddle a baby.

"True Norwegian, the smell of coffee wakes her up." Mrs. Benson raised her cup as Signe reached her to pour coffee. "And no, nothing in it, black is best." She spread honey on her biscuit and passed back the jar. Signe sat down with her daughter on her lap, handed her the bacon rind, and ate with her free hand. "Your bees certainly produce good honey," she said.

"Mr. Benson considered no longer keeping the hives going, and there was such an outcry from our customers that he changed his mind and built two more hives, so when the queens decide to go looking for new quarters, they can move right in." Mrs. Benson dabbed at the honey that dripped on her plate. "That other package is baby clothes Mrs. Engelbrett sent for Kirstin, so she has some to grow into. She has been keeping these clothes in case she had another girl, but she thought you could use them in the meantime. She said she hoped you would come join our sewing circle when the weather lets up."

"I hope we both can come when spring breaks through." Signe bounced her knees gently as Kirstin fussed a bit. "I need to feed this one, so excuse me."

"Can you not nurse her where you are?"

"Ja, but . . ."

"Oh, for goodness' sake. As far as I can see, we are all women here. Go ahead."

With Kirstin content again, Signe finished her coffee. "We are about out of jam, I'm sorry to say. Do you know anyone who has strawberry or raspberry bushes we can buy?"

"Not for sale, but we share such things, all us women. If you don't mind, I'll ask when we have our next meeting." She looked to Gerd. "I hope you will come too, Mrs. Strand."

"We'll see."

Signe knew a smile did not stay down where she was trying to stuff it. *We'll see* was a far cry from an adamant *no.* "I have a question, Mrs. Benson. We want to have Kirstin baptized. Is there a process we need to know?"

"Just talk to Reverend Skarstead. I know he has been wanting to come out here."

Signe glanced at Gerd, whose shoulders hinted at a shrug. "It might be best if we talk with him after church on Sunday."

"Did you know that he preaches at All Saints in Blackduck every Sunday afternoon?'

"No, I didn't. His Sundays are really full then, aren't they?"

"Ja, but he says some pastors have three-point parishes. Two is hard, so three would be really difficult. Of course, he says at least he doesn't have to write two sermons for every Sunday." She glanced up at the clock. "Oh my, how the time flies. I need to get back to the store. Thank you so much for the visit. Can I hold that baby for just a minute?"

"Of course." Signe brought Kirstin around the table and handed her to their guest.

"Oh, you are just the dearest thing, such a sweet baby."

Kirstin stared at Mrs. Benson, wrinkled her forehead, and whimpered before shifting into full-blown crying.

"I'm afraid she is not used to very many people." Signe took her baby back and, swaying, shushed her with a gentle voice.

Mrs. Benson pushed back her chair. "I'll have to make sure she does not think me a stranger." She dropped a kiss on the baby's forehead as she made her way around the table. "Thank you, and I hope to see you again on Sunday. We are having a get-together meal after church, and I hope you can stay for that. You would be our guests, so please do not bring anything but your appetites."

"We'll see." Signe tried to smile.

"It would be a great way to meet more of our members." Mrs. Benson reached for her coat.

After she left, Signe refilled the firebox and put the remaining biscuits in a tin to keep them fresh. "Are you hungry?"

Gerd picked up her knitting, shaking her head. "Not really. Can we wait a bit?"

"Of course. I thought we might have fried cheese sandwiches." The last of the leftovers from the night before had gone to the woods with the men.

Snow had started to fall by the time the boys rode into the lane.

"Your turn to put the horse away," Knute told his brother from the porch stairs.

"I know."

Knute scraped off his boots and pushed open the door. "Getting colder."

Gerd looked up from her knitting. "The wind does that."

"Can we have something to eat before we start chores?"

"Ja, there are biscuits in the tin, or you could have bread and butter."

"With sugar?"

"Fix some for Leif too." Signe took the last of the diapers from the line and finished folding them. "Skim the milk pans so you have milk for the pigs and chickens."

"There is soured milk in the cans and plenty of cream to churn."

"Good. We sent the last of the butter with Mrs. Benson."

"I'm going to check my snares too." Knute sat down at the table with his bread and a glass of milk from the pantry. "I think we need a dog."

"Whatever brought that up?"

"We had to write a paper today about dogs, and we don't have one. So I wrote about our one in Norway, but it made me realize how much I want to have a dog again."

"We have two cats."

"They can't go along to check the snares or fishing or hunting or anything."

"Where would you get a dog?" Gerd asked. "We used to have one."

Leif blew in, stomping his feet on the rug. "We better get on those chores fast. Good thing we didn't let the cows out this morning. Onkel Einar was right. A blizzard is coming." He grabbed his bread and ate it standing in front of the stove.

"I'll go skim the milk pans so you can get to the animals." Signe reached for her coat and wrapped a scarf around her neck. "You want anything from the well house?" she asked Gerd.

"Just the cream for the churn. Let it warm, and I can churn in the morning."

The wind fought to tear off Signe's hat and drive the cold into her bones. Closing the door of the well house behind her, she paused to catch her breath before lighting the lantern on a hook on the wall. After skimming the cream into a crock, she poured the milk into one of the milk cans, filling a jug for the house. Knute had taken the full one down to the barn. They really needed more milk cans, especially now that the heifer had freshened. With a bucket of cream in one hand and the milk jug in the other, she stepped back outside and made sure the latch fell into place on the door. She looked toward the barn, hoping the men were already back, but she couldn't see through the blowing snow.

By the time she made it to the house, she had to stagger up the steps and stand there a moment, trying to catch her breath. Dark hovered overhead, making her glad to see the lamps lit and set in the windows, promising warmth within.

Concern had begun to gnaw on her insides before she finally heard the stamping of boots on the porch and the men filed in, brushing snow off their hats and coats as they came.

"Good thing we started back when we did," Rune said by way of greeting. "Almost hated to leave the quiet of the barn and fight the wind up to the house." He rubbed his hands over the heat of the stove.

"No frostbite?" Gerd stared at Einar, who

huddled over the stove with the others.

"Nei, but this might turn into a bad one," he grunted.

Rune inhaled. "Sure smells good in here. If it keeps on, there won't be any school for you boys, so we can work in the shop all day." He shot Einar a questioning look.

"Supper is ready," Signe said. "Wash, and we can eat."

Every time the howling wind woke him during the night, Rune gave thanks for the sturdy house and his family sleeping around him. He went downstairs and stoked the stove several times, and each time the storm seemed to have gathered new energy for another onslaught.

It was hard to tell when morning came with the storm still raging. The parlor windows were blocked by snow drifts, and all the windowpanes in the house wore delicate designs of frost. Only the kitchen had clear glass at the top.

"We will get the animals taken care of, then breakfast before we head to the wood shop," Rune instructed. "Einar?"

"Harness needs some repairs. That mower's not done yet." He glared at Leif, whom he blamed for the cut on his hand he had received from the mower, which had laid him low for a time.

Rune shook his head. Accidents happened, and most were not intentional. As if Leif would want to hurt anyone. "Bjorn, you can help by sharpening the blades, if you like."

Einar muttered something and raised his cup for Gerd to refill.

"Hang on to the rope," Rune ordered as they stepped off the porch and into the icy teeth of the storm. Earlier that winter, they had strung a rope from the house to the barn to keep anyone from getting lost in this kind of weather.

It took Einar and Rune together to pull the barn door open as the boys kicked the snow away. Inside, the barn seemed a haven of peace and quiet. One of the horses nickered, and the rooster crowed from the chicken house.

Rune made his way to the shop, lit a lamp, and started a fire in the stove. He set a bucket of snow on top to melt. The water barrel in the barn had frozen over. He set two more snow-filled buckets by the fire. The animals all needed water. The only pump not frozen was the one in the house.

"Wish you all could stay in the house," Signe said as the men and boys bundled up to head back out after breakfast.

"Me too, but don't worry about us. The shop will not be warm, but it will be tolerable, since we'll all be working. What's for dinner?"

"I brought up that ham hock and set beans to soaking last night. I thought ham and beans would be warming."

"And fried bread?" Leif grinned at his mor before he pulled his scarf up over his lower face.

"Ja. It should be ready for that. We'll have fried rabbit for supper, thanks to Knute."

"You two fill that woodbox before you come down," Rune told the younger boys. "I've got buckets of snow melting in the shop. Can you melt some here too?" he asked Signe.

"Of course. Bring me in a washtub of snow."

By noon, all the animals and chickens had been watered, and more buckets of snow were melting for later. Between Bjorn at the grinding wheel and the wind trying to collapse the building, sitting down for dinner felt like a reprieve for their ears.

Corn bread, ham, and beans with fried bread and bowls of syrup had everyone in a good mood.

Except for the baby, who woke from her

nap crying and hot enough to melt a bucket of snow.

CHAPTER 9

The wind no longer rattled the windows. It couldn't; the windows were covered by the snow banked on the windward side of the house. Rune and the boys were kept busy just keeping a path cleared to the barn. The snow drifted in almost faster than they could shovel.

There were chores to be done and dinner to be made, but Signe had a sick baby to rock. This fever worried her; there was no way anyone could reach a doctor, or even a neighboring farm, with this blizzard raging. She could not even tell the cause.

"Try this." Gerd handed her a baby bottle of vile-looking fluid.

"What is it?"

"A palm of vinegar and a palm of sugar in a cup of water."

"A palm?"

"You know, a palm." Gerd held out her cupped hand, palm up.

Uncertain, Signe offered the bottle to Kirstin. Kirstin took one suck and jerked her head aside, her arms waving. She fussed louder.

Boots thudded on the porch, and Leif burst into the room. "Mor, the calf is coming! You can see the front feet."

"Now?" The worst blizzard of the year, and the heifer was going to calve. "Is your far there?"

"Nei. Knute said to come get you."

"I have the baby." Gerd reached down.

Signe handed Kirstin off to Gerd, headed for the coat rack, and rammed her arms into her wool coat sleeves. This weather was far too cold for a mere shawl. The wind made her shiver the moment she stepped out the door. She tucked her scarf ends in her coat, grateful for the warm mittens, scarf, and hat Gerd had knitted for her.

Leif ran ahead to open the barn door for her. They both had to push and yank to knock aside the drift that already settled against it. The glow of the lantern hooked on a post by the heifer's stall drew her. From her stanchion, Belle was reminding the boys she had not been fed yet, while Rosie chomped hay in her stall. The team had hay as well. Had Einar fed the horses but not the cow? Where was Rune?

Signe leaned on the stall's half door to make sure all was well with the heifer. First-timers sometimes had more problems than an experienced cow. Knute sat in the corner beside her head, stroking her face and murmuring encouragement. "Is she progressing?" she asked.

"I think so. When she pushes, the front legs come out farther."

"And then they go back a bit," Leif added. "Baby pigs just pop out."

Belle lowed again.

"Leif, you better give her some grain so she doesn't disturb the heifer."

Leif did as he was told, then went ahead and set the stool down so he could get to milking. "You be good, now, Belle, you hear?" He brushed off her udder, and in moments, the ping of milk in a bucket added to the evening barn sounds.

Listening and watching the heifer reminded Signe of the years she had milked cows and taken care of the livestock in Norway along with her younger brother. In the winter in the barn under the house, and in the summer up at the *seter* where the older girls and younger children took the cows, sheep, and goats for pasture.

Knute came around to look. "Is the calf stuck, do you think?"

"It could be. Sometimes the head gets twisted out of line." Signe stepped into the stall and knelt by Jenna's tail. Jenna pushed again. The tiny hooves did not move.

"Knute, your hands are smaller than mine. Reach up into her and feel if the head is between the calf's front legs."

"She'll let me do that?"

"Try."

Knute took off half of his coat and rolled his sleeve up high. Warily, he worked his hand past the tiny hooves. He pushed farther, to the elbow. Farther. "I feel the head, and it's turned, kind of."

"Can you twist it back in place between the calf's legs?"

"I don't know." Knute forced his arm in farther; the whole arm was swallowed up now; maybe it would not be long enough. He grunted and squirmed. "Maybe . . . I think maybe . . . there." He pulled his arm out. It was slimy with placental fluid. "Yuck. But worth it if we save the calf, right?"

"Right! And save the heifer as well. She could die if the calf can't get out. Leif, bring a towel!" Signe called. The heifer pushed again, and this time the progress was clear.

"I'll get some sacks." Knute hustled away and returned quickly, drying off his arm. He beamed. "That was kind of fun. There's the nose! A couple more pushes . . ."

The miracle of birth, be it animal or human, never failed to bring tears to Signe's eyes. She glanced over to see Leif beside her. "You sure milked her fast."

"She's not giving so much anymore." He glanced over his shoulder. "I hung up the bucket." He grinned at his mor. "Pretty special, huh?"

"Ja, that it is."

The heifer groaned, lifted her head, and with a heave, the calf slid out onto the straw.

Leif grabbed the gunnysacks and handed one to Knute, who was lifting the calf's head already. He scrubbed the mucus out of the nose and mouth. The calf jerked and sucked in a breath of air.

Knute rubbed the rest of the baby's head to clean off the sac while Leif did the same, starting with the back.

"How come it didn't breathe right away?" Leif asked.

"Just needed a bit of help. Do we have a heifer or bull here?" Signe asked.

"Heifer." Knute blew out another breath. The cord lay flaccid, now that it was no longer needed. "Do we need to cut that?"

"You have a knife?"

"I do." Leif dug in his pocket for the knife he had been given on his birthday. He cut the cord about a foot away from the calf's belly, started to wipe the knife blade on his pant leg, then used the gunnysack instead.

"Good thinking." Signe left the gentle scene and went to open the barn door. She stepped outside at the same moment Rune came down from the house.

"Einar insisted we cut a path to the shed to fix the plow. I suggested waiting. He kept insisting, so we did. He's still in the shed. Something wrong?" He looked worried.

"Nei. We just had a calf."

Rune nodded and smiled. "The boys did all right, then?"

"You can be proud of your boys. They worked like they do this every day." She couldn't stop smiling. But suddenly she spun and headed to the house. "Kirstin! She is still fussy and fevered. I have to —"

"Isn't Gerd there?"

Signe heaved a breath and shook her head. "Of course." How silly. Months ago, Gerd couldn't have taken care of Kirstin but now she could. Miracles without end.

"Much as I hate to do this, I will have to miss church. Einar says we are hauling logs this week, and I — we have not felled enough to pay for the lumber for our house yet. Time is running out."

Signe nodded slowly, but hurt leaked out onto her face. "But when will we have Kirstin baptized?" Thanks to Gerd's ministrations, Kirstin's fever had quickly faded. With her daughter back to her usual happy self, Signe felt it was time to plan Kirstin's baptism.

"I thought we could wait until Nilda gets here, and she and Ivar can be there as godparents."

Signe nodded slowly. "I do like that idea."

"Good. Bjorn and I will fell the trees, and Knute and Leif can do the limbing. As the days get longer, I hope I can work on our property sometimes in the evening. We will have to pull some stumps to clear land to build the house." He scrubbed his scalp with the ends of his fingers. "I know Einar plans on Ivar working with him on Sundays, but I need him more. Besides, he will not be indentured to Einar."

The next morning, when he had finished eating his breakfast without waiting for the others, as usual, Einar announced, "We start hauling today. We will load the sledge, and then you and I will haul the load to the train at Benson's Corner." He nodded to Bjorn. "You will haul after that."

"Really?" Bjorn looked at his far, who nodded. Bjorn shoveled in the last of his pancakes and drained his coffee cup. "I'll go hitch up the team."

Rune half smiled at Signe. His boys were men. All they lacked were years.

Out in the woods, where they had built and erected a fifteen-foot-tall pulley frame to lift the logs onto the sledge, the men wrapped a chain around the end of the logs they had cut into twenty-foot lengths and dragged three of them over to the pulley, one at a time. Rune drove the sledge into place beside the logs and unhitched the team so he could hitch them at the end of the pulley rope. The men wrapped the sling and chains into place, hooked them to the pulley, and the team slowly raised one of the logs to be swung above the sledge and then lowered into place.

"We did it!" Bjorn whooped.

Rune and Einar exchanged a look along with a nod. "Let's do it again."

Dinnertime had rolled around by the time they'd loaded all three logs and hitched the team back to the sledge.

"Need that other horse out here," Einar muttered as he shoveled in his dinner. "Bjorn, you drive this trip."

Rune watched his son encourage the horses to dig in and get the sledge moving, and then he and Einar drove out to the lane and past the barn and house. *Lord, keep them safe. Keep my son thinking ahead and following Einar's orders.*

He repacked the basket, hung it up on a branch to keep it free of critters, and hefting an ax, headed for the tree they had felled yesterday to start the limbing. To think of all the trees Einar had felled by himself, it seemed impossible. Shame he hadn't learned to be grateful for the help Rune and Bjorn brought to him.

When the sledge returned, they loaded it up again, and while Bjorn hauled the load to the shipping station, Einar and Rune felled another tree. By the time they walked up to the barn, Bjorn had not returned.

"Shouldn't Bjorn be back by now?" Rune asked.

"He might have had to wait in line."

They left the saws and axes in the machine shed, and Rune returned to the barn to check on his boys. Knute was forking hay from the haymow, and Leif was milking.

Knute peered down from the top of the ladder. "Where's the team? And Bjorn?"

"He hauled another load of logs to the yard. Leif, run up to the house and ask Mor what she needs."

"She already said to bring the buckets and strainer up for scrubbing and bring the butter and buttermilk for breakfast. Oh, and eggs. Our hens sure aren't laying much."

"They will when it stays light longer. At least we can still have eggs once in a while."

The three of them headed to the house with all their buckets.

"I think Mor is getting worried about Bjorn," Leif said.

Rune nodded. So was he. Surely if something had happened, someone would come tell them. If only he had the skis finished, he could go look for him. Of course, he could ride the other horse. He set his load on the porch. "I'm going back to talk to Einar."

He pushed open the door to the shop and stepped in out of the icy wind. "Supper is nearly ready."

"Ja. Be there in a few minutes."

"Should I take the horse and go look for him?"

"He'll be here soon. They unload right up to dark."

Somewhat mollified, Rune checked on the press he had built to turn up the tips of the skis after he had soaked the planed and smoothed black ash. How would he know when it was dry? If only there were someone he could ask for advice. His far had not made skis, although he made anything else that was needed out of wood. So many generations of wood carving, for houses and other buildings, besides household bowls, looms, spinning wheels, furniture, wagons, even musical instruments. Perhaps there was someone at church who made skis. He would send a note to Mrs. Benson. She would know, she knew everybody.

Content with that decision, he looked at Einar. "Ready?"

"Ja." He passed Rune at the door, ready to blow out the lantern.

They were just sitting down to supper when Knute jumped up. "He's home." He grabbed his coat and headed out the door.

Rune nodded to Signe. If he looked as fearful as she did, they had both worried for naught.

When the boys stomped the snow off their boots on the porch and Bjorn walked in, it was all Rune could do to keep from cheering.

Einar looked up from eating. "What happened?"

"I was last in line, and he almost told me to leave the load and come back in the morning, but he changed his mind, marked our logs, and then unloaded. I learned a lot watching those men. I asked, and we could cut ours in fifteen-foot lengths to make the logs easier to handle."

"Ja, depends on the mill."

That night in bed, Rune admitted his concern to Signe. "I was about to take Rosie and ride out to find him."

"If you hadn't, I would have, or sent Knute. I think today Bjorn became a man." Pride glowed through her words.

Each day they got better at loading, so Bjorn got home earlier from the second load. One day they were able to load the sledge with a third load and park it by the barn for an early morning start.

They had several warmer days, but when it turned cold again, Einar seemed to relax. In spite of two or three loads a day, there still seemed to be no dent in the number of logs left to haul.

"Tomorrow you leave before full dawn," Einar told Bjorn, "so we can do four loads. We will try a load with four of the smaller logs. Or five." He shook his head.

"Is that many safe for this sledge?" Rune asked.

"We need taller steel posts on the sledge and can only do it with smaller logs."

What could happen to shift the load? It wasn't like Bjorn would be racing or anything careless. Even if the horses spooked at something, they would not be able to run away hitched to the loaded sledge. *Stop finding things to worry about,* Rune ordered himself. Einar was treating Bjorn like a man, even if he was only sixteen.

Lord, please keep my son safe, he prayed that night. *Keep us all safe, accidents happen so easily. Thank you for the many ways you bless us.*

He hugged Signe close. "Someday soon, we will have our own house," he murmured in her ear. This would be the first house they had ever owned. He'd dreamed of a log cabin, but since that was not really feasible, a farmhouse would be perfect. Even if they had so little furniture. They could use tree rounds for seats.

The next morning, Einar was his usual grumpy self. "Knute, you come right out to the woods when you get home." He glared at Signe. "Haul branches."

Knute looked to his mor, who shook her head before he could even ask.

Bjorn ate before he went to the barn and hitched the team to the sledge. The horses threw themselves into their collars repeatedly, but the sledge did not move.

"Frozen." Einar motioned Bjorn down and took the reins, turning the team off to the side. He slapped the lines hard and yelled at the same time. "Hup! Move! Get on there!" At the third try, the jerk broke the sledge runners free. After straightening the team and pulling forward a length, he stopped them and handed Bjorn the lines. "Let 'em rest a few minutes to catch their breath, and then get going."

One night a couple weeks later, with the pattern of three loads hauled one day and two the next, Bjorn got home long after dark again. Knute took care of the horses, taking time to brush them down and feed them extra oats.

Einar had already gone to bed when Knute returned to the house. "Far."

Rune looked up from writing a letter at the table. "Ja."

"I think the horses are losing weight. I could feel their ribs when I brushed them."

"I will check them in the morning. Horses need rest just like humans." And they could break down just like humans if driven too hard.

The next morning at the breakfast table, Rune turned to Einar. "I think the horses need more feed. They are losing weight. How about if Bjorn takes a measure of oats along for each of them to eat while waiting in line to unload?"

Einar stared at Rune, then shifted his gaze to Knute. "You figured that out?"

Knute nodded. "Ja, I could feel their ribs when I brushed them. I give them oats and plenty of hay." He looked to his far, who nodded.

"Good." Einar pushed his chair back and headed for the coatrack and out the door.

All three of the boys stared at their far, eyes wide.

Rune nodded. "Good is right. You are all doing a great job. And taking good care of the animals is both wise and compassionate. We depend on them, and it is our job to take care of them."

"And each other," Signe murmured under her breath, but not so low that Rune couldn't hear it.

For the next three days in a row, they woke to icicles dripping and the snow melting enough to slide off the roofs in big chunks, whomping onto the drifts below. When one small avalanche happened during breakfast, Einar muttered an imprecation and glared at the window. "Keeps up like this, and we won't get many more logs hauled in."

Rune looked at him. "But we've not hauled any of mine yet."

"You think I don't know that? How many logs you got ready?"

Rune thought a bit. "Fifteen, I think."

"You think? Good grief, man, don't you keep count?"

"We got fourteen, Far. One still to limb." Bjorn pushed back his chair. "Let's get this first load out."

"We got a full moon tonight. Work late, cut a couple of the downed ones into lengths," Einar suggested.

Rune looked at Signe and gave a slight shake of his head. She glared at him but settled back without saying anything. Out loud anyway. "We do what we have to do," he said quietly as Einar stormed out the door.

That night after supper, Bjorn turned to Einar. "Today a man came up to me and asked if we had a lot of logs to haul yet. Said he got his all in and could help us."

"Nei. I don't need any help. What doesn't get hauled this year, I will haul early next. He just wants to cheat me."

"But —"

"No buts about it. I said nei, and that is it."

Bjorn looked at his far.

Rune shrugged and shook his head. *I will go talk with him,* he promised himself. *If I can pay him with a couple of logs, I will have help to get ours in. Einar, I will never under-*

stand you, cutting off your nose to spite your face.

The next day, he handed Bjorn a folded piece of paper. "Give this note to that man if you see him."

"You're going to hire him?"

"I want to. If he can come out Sunday morning, we'll go look at our logs."

"Onkel Einar?"

"He'll be out in the woods. But he will most likely yell when he hears I decided to do this." Rune shrugged. "So be it." *Lord, I sure hope I have made the right decision.*

Chapter 10

Holding the dinner basket, Rune watched Bjorn pull the gelding's tail through the crupper, finishing up the harnessing. The boys were right; the horses had both lost condition. And here came a brace of fine Belgians up the road, pulling a light sledge. The fight was about to begin.

Einar came out of the shed with a handful of axes and stopped cold. "Who's that?"

"Oskar Kielund." Rune kept his voice soft. "He's going to help me load logs today."

As Rune had predicted, Einar yelled. "I told you I wasn't going to hire him!"

"*I* hired him. *My* logs."

Bjorn froze in his tracks and stared open-mouthed at the two men.

Einar stood a moment, fury oozing out all over him. "Send him away and get on the sledge like you're supposed to." He turned away and waved an arm at Bjorn. "Boy, get on there. We have work to do."

Bjorn didn't move.

Rune dipped his head toward the approaching team. "Come."

Bjorn hesitated, watching Einar, then ran over to Mr. Kielund's sledge and jumped up on it. Rune felt a little swish of pride that the boy chose obedience to his far over fear.

"You go with that scoundrel, and you don't need to come back to this house, do you understand?" Einar hollered. "You're gone, you and your whole lazy family!"

Rune kept his voice level. "We will discuss it tonight." He climbed up on the sledge behind Mr. Kielund, bringing the dinner basket with him.

The fellow clucked to his team and turned them aside, heading toward Rune's land. "My sister Mildred knows the Strands. She said he might blow up. She's good at reading people, y'know?"

"Apparently." Rune turned to watch Einar as they slid over the frozen ground. He was shaking his fist and yelling, but Rune could no longer make out words. "Months ago, my wife, Signe, did some calculations and showed that we had more than worked out the terms of our indenture. He fumes and blusters, but he has no financial or legal hold on us anymore."

Bjorn braced himself beside Rune. "You have a mighty fine team, Mr. Kielund. They're the biggest horses I ever saw, and in really good flesh. Almost fat, even."

Mr. Kielund chuckled. "They're Belgians, lad. There's blond Belgians and roan Belgians, y'know? And that's not fat. It's all muscle. They work hard and eat hearty, these two." He pointed ahead. "Them the logs?"

Rune smiled. "Them's the logs." *His* logs.

Mr. Kielund pulled in beside the pile, jumped down, and began pulling rope and pulleys and hooks off his sledge. He had obviously done this many times. He smiled at Bjorn. "That fellow called you 'boy,' but I bet that's not your name."

"Bjorn Carlson, sir."

"Bjorn, I'm Oskar." Mr. Kielund extended a hand, so Bjorn shook it. "You're a pretty good hand with horses. How about you unhitch that mare? Her name is Petunia, and we'll use her to roll the logs up onto the sledge."

Elated, Bjorn pulled Petunia's lines free and unhooked her singletree.

Mr. Kielund was a pro at this. Within moments, it seemed, they had a chain around the nearest log and a pulley system set up. Bjorn hooked the singletree into a heavy steel ring, and Mr. Kielund urged his Petunia forward.

The log tilted a bit and rolled onto the sledge. Mr. Kielund used a pole with a hook and spearpoint to arrange it just so.

Bjorn wagged his head. "That was sure quick. What is that tool?" He pointed to the pole.

"It's a peavey. Real handy for making a log do what you tell it to."

Bjorn laughed.

Just as quickly, they loaded a second log. Mr. Kielund chained them down. "I'll take these two out and be back. I charge by the log, not the load. Two is plenty for the horses to handle."

"Then have a bite to eat first." Rune broke open the dinner basket and handed Mr. Kielund a sandwich.

Mr. Kielund sat down beside a log and started on his sandwich as Rune poured coffee. "Fresh bread! Really good bread. And the ham is excellent. Your wife's a fine cook, Mr. Carlson."

"That she is."

Mr. Kielund chose a pickle and munched for a moment. "Yes sir, a fine cook. She doesn't happen to sell these pickles, does she?"

"No, she doesn't." But what a great idea

that was. Rune could build her a cold frame for starting cucumbers early. In fact, he ought to do that anyway. He would build a cold frame on the south side of Einar's house. Gerd could use a cold frame too.

As Mr. Kielund drove off with the logs, Bjorn watched, wistful. "He sure knows how to do it, Far. And he doesn't overwork his horses. Onkel Einar works his horses too hard, I think."

"I think you are right. You have learned a lot from Onkel Einar, but you are also learning what not to do. I'm pleased." He drained his coffee and stood up. "It's probably unwise to go to the house with Einar so angry. Wait for him to simmer down. Let's use the time here to take down one more tree."

"Sure!" Bjorn hopped up. "Far, you think we can buy a peavey?"

"Letters, Mor!" Leif leaped up the steps later that afternoon. "One for us and one for Onkel Einar." He burst through the door waving them and looked around. "Where is Tante Gerd?"

"She and Kirstin are taking a nap," Signe said.

He shrugged and made a face. "Sorry." His grin returned as he handed her the letter. “Oops, almost forgot. Knute needs something to eat.”

She gave him a sandwich, and he dashed back out the door, pausing to shut it carefully.

Signe shook her head and smiled at the same time. Oh, to be young like that again. Studying the letters, she realized they were both from Nilda. Guilt beating her about the head and shoulders, she propped the one for Einar against the empty bowl in the center of the table. She slit the other envelope with her fingernail as she pulled out a chair and sat.

Dear Brother Rune and my still best friend Signe,

Signe sniffed and rolled her lips together. Such a simple thing to make her teary-eyed already.

We are so excited. My temporary job with Mrs. Sieverson turned into full-time when her regular assistant, Matilde, decided to live with an aunt in Malmo. Ivar got a small job too, and we could afford his ticket at last. The tickets have arrived, and I take them out almost daily to make sure the dream is coming true.

I really am coming to Amerika. I should make myself write this in English, but it would be a very short letter. We have been following your advice, and both Ivar and I are taking English lessons from an old gentleman up the road who lived in Amerika for five years. He finally decided he would rather live in Norway after his wife and their two children died in a house fire in the middle of the winter. That is such a tragic story, and he has never really become himself again. But he agreed to teach us, and we go three times a week, and he gives us homework. So we are all learning to speak English. Are you not amazed?

Since Ivar promised Mor he would make sure she gets to Amerika, she goes with us for lessons too. Mor is doing her best, but she cannot make Far want to ever go there nor learn the language. He says Norwegian he is, and Norwegian he will remain until the day he dies. He will be buried here next to his far and mor and the other relatives in the home plot. I know that is a rather depressing thought, but it has not deterred the rest of us from dreaming, including Mor.

We are packing the trunks, and I am including the list we are working from, so if you can think of something else, you better write back quickly.

Again Signe sniffed.

"Is something wrong?" Gerd asked, gently closing the door behind her. "Kirstin is still sleeping, so I banked pillows around her so she can't tumble off."

"Nei, just a letter from Nilda and a list of the things they are packing in their trunks." She motioned to the letter on the table. "That is for you both, I think. Would you like to hear this one?"

Gerd stepped to the stove. "Coffee will be ready in a minute." Waving a hand to signal *go ahead,* she stuck a couple more pieces of wood in the stove and pulled the pot to the hottest place. "Uff da, I slept too long."

Signe shook her head and returned to her reading, continuing out loud. " 'We are arriving in Duluth on May the twenty-ninth and will take the train to Blackduck. And then I will see your dear faces. I know the boys have grown so much, and the baby — oh, I am so excited. Please greet everyone from those of us at home and know we think about you and pray for you every day. Your sister and friend, Nilda Carlson.' "

She went back and read the first part aloud to Gerd, then laid the letter aside.

The air seemed so heavy. She knew why. Rune and Einar would both come back this evening. She had heard the terrible argument that morning, except that Rune did not argue. He simply stated what he would do, and then he did it. She thought how stubborn those two both were and wondered if her family would have a roof over their heads tonight.

Kirstin was making noise in the other room, so Signe brought her to the kitchen. She was very wet, of course, so Signe changed her and set her to nursing.

Gerd spoke. "I should have started bread last night."

Signe frowned. "We still have yeast, don't we?"

"Ja, but that will be the last."

"Go ahead and use it. I will add yeast to the list for the boys. Anything else for the list? We have butter we can send along."

"Good."

"Gerd, do you know where to pick chokecherries?"

Gerd nodded. "If we take the horse, I will be able to show you. Maybe we will get enough strawberries from the garden to make jam, if they made it through the winter. Did you see any raspberry bushes out there last summer? One year I got juneberries too." She wagged her head gently. "So many berries grow in the areas logged off a few years ago."

"We used lingonberries at home." Signe glanced down at her daughter, who grinned up at her, milk leaking out the side of her mouth. "You're just playing now, you silly. I think you are ready for porridge, my girl." Tucking herself back together, she sat Kirstin on her lap, and at the healthy burp, shook her head. "Uff da, such manners." Kirstin waved her fist and chortled to her mor, her two gleaming white bottom teeth flashing bright. "I know, you. Showing off those teeth. You bite me again, and you will end up eating from a spoon." She stood and turned to hand the baby to Gerd.

The door slammed open. Einar glared at her. "Are you packed? You're leaving, you know."

"I heard the argument this morning." She did not answer the question he asked.

"You lazy, selfish people have disobeyed me for the last time. Pack your things, or I send you off without them."

Gerd stood up, casually walked over to Signe, and handed her the baby. Just as quietly and casually, she walked over to Einar and stood immediately in front of him, nose to nose. "I live in this house too. They will live here until their house is built because I want them to. Signe helps me; there is so much I cannot do yet. I need her. You need the men, and they work hard for you, for long hours. So you are just going to have to stuff that abominable, haughty pride back into its tiny box in your heart and *shut up*!"

She walked over to Signe, took the baby back, and quietly sat down.

Einar's face turned purple. His mouth worked, but no sound came out. He wheeled and slammed out the door.

Gert muttered, "Prideful, thick-headed old goat."

There were tears in her eyes.

CHAPTER 11

Two days later, they woke to the song of spring, icicles dripping from the roof. Signe lay in bed for a few extra breaths just to listen. "You hear that?" she asked Rune.

"Ja, perhaps it will stay this time." He threw back the covers and dressed, still buttoning his shirt as he disappeared down the stairs to start the fire.

By the time Signe was dressed, Kirstin gurgled at her. Scooping her up, she called to the boys as she went downstairs. April already, and even though dawn came earlier, they still woke when dawn was only a trace on the horizon. At least the boys could get to the barn without stumbling in the darkness.

Rune nodded to Signe as she laid the baby down to change her. He settled the stove lids back in place and adjusted the damper. "Do you need anything from the well house?"

"Ja, that last slab of bacon and the jug of buttermilk. We have enough eggs for bacon, eggs, and pancakes, for a change."

The boys, their eyes still heavy with sleep, slouched out the door, headed for the barn. Einar strode out the door with nary a word, in spite of her "good morning."

Signe refused to let the way he acted bother her anymore, so she greeted him anyway. Someday he would have to give in. "Kill them with kindness" had been one of her mor's favorite sayings.

By the time the men and boys trooped back inside, a stack of pancakes waited in the oven, and the bacon took up the warming oven. Signe cracked eggs in the frying pan. "Only two eggs each this morning so everyone gets some," she announced as the guys took their chairs.

Gerd, pouring the coffee, nudged Einar's shoulder, earning a glare for her efforts. She glared right back and filled Rune's cup.

"Tante Gerd, I can drink my coffee black now," Knute told her.

"The cream is in the pitcher," she said after filling his cup the usual halfway.

Leif grinned at her and held out his cup, which was already half full of cream and a hefty teaspoon of sugar. "Takk."

"You are welcome," Gerd said in English.

Signe had not been practicing her English enough.

She slid the eggs onto a plate and passed it around the table. When it came to Einar, he hesitated, took only two, and passed it on to Rune. He ate without a word. Signe loaded more pancakes on a platter, and for a change he did not put half the platter on his plate. *Tante Gerd, you are one wise woman. Maybe he can be taught after all.*

As always, Einar finished wolfing down his breakfast and poked Bjorn as he stood up. "You're done. Go to work."

Bjorn looked sadly at his plate, only half emptied.

"Finish your breakfast," Rune said quietly.

With gusto, Bjorn shoveled in the eggs and bacon, then hurried out the door with his pancakes in his hand.

Signe wagged her head and refilled Rune's cup. "How is the arrangement going?"

"All right. Yesterday I sent Bjorn back to help Einar while Oskar and I loaded logs. Bjorn says Einar was grumpy but did not abuse him. I warned Bjorn never to say, 'But Mr. Kielund does whatever-it-is.' They got two loads to the railhead — that's six logs."

"Do you know how many loads he took on the day you and Bjorn were not there?"

Rune smiled. "Bjorn keeps count. Only one."

Gerd plunked the big dinner basket down beside him. "I put extra snacks in for Mr. Kielund. He seems to like to eat."

"He loves to eat homecooking, especially your cooking, both of you. He lives alone and doesn't like to cook."

"So he's not married." Gerd sat down with a cup of coffee.

"His wife died in November. Pneumonia. Two children."

Signe's heart lurched. "Oh, I so wish we could invite him to dinner. But that would never work."

Gerd nodded sadly. "I agree. Einar is still too angry. Not that he would ever invite someone to dinner under any circumstance. Rune, how many logs do you have to move yet?"

"Only four. He will be done today."

Signe smiled. "Hiring Mr. Kielund, then, was a godsend."

"It was. And I think he will be a good friend." Rune picked up the basket and left.

Signe untied Kirstin from her seat in the rocker and put the baby on her lap. Kirstin waved her feet and fists, grinning from ear to ear when she saw Gerd.

"She is becoming quite a talker," Gerd

said after taking the baby and conversing with her.

"Ja, that she is. I don't remember the boys being so lively. She notices everything." Signe finished two sandwiches for Bjorn and poured the warmed coffee into a jar for him. At the jingle of the harness, she threw her shawl around her shoulders and headed outside to hand the sack up to him. "Here's your dinner, in case you get stuck in long lines. Thanks to Gerd."

"Takk. Good thing the lines at the yard aren't always so long now." He secured his sack and flapped the lines to signal the team forward.

Signe waved and, tucking her arms around her waist, watched him head down the lane. *Lord God, please keep him safe.*

The snow level dropped every day.

With Rune and Bjorn both working with Einar, they were able to take three loads a day. But Bjorn announced at supper one evening, "I don't think we can do any more loads. I almost didn't make it there today. The main road is near to bare, and it gets soft wherever the sun hits it."

Einar grimaced. "Woulda had more logs out if I'd had the help I needed."

And we would not have had nearly enough to pay for our house. Once in a while, Signe knew, Rune regretted crossing Einar and hiring Oskar. Neither of them liked friction. But now she was very glad he had. "Is this typical for Minnesota?"

"Ja, some years. Some we've had snow in June. But once the frost starts to leave the ground, the roads become impassable in places. Sometimes weeks before wagons can be used again." He pushed back from the table. "We'll start blasting stumps soon as we can dig down to plant the dynamite."

"Shame we can't blast a hole for the cellar," Rune thought aloud.

Einar snorted and headed out the door.

The nights still froze, but the days grew warm. Two days later, it rained.

"It is Sunday today." Signe sighed as she watched the rain drip off the eaves. "How I wish we could go to church."

Rune shrugged and finished his pancakes. "Roads just aren't passable for either sledge or wheels. It's a muddy mess out there."

"I know. So what are you going to do?"

"Take out a couple more trees so we can build our house where we really wanted to, a bit beyond where it was already cleared."

"Are you leaving any trees for shade?"

He blinked at her. "I guess I could."

"I know which one," Bjorn said. "I'll mark

it. Deciduous trees will work better for shade." He looked at Signe with a smile. "We can find some birch saplings, too, and maybe a maple. Plant them anywhere you want."

Gerd looked hopeful. "I would like a shade tree here by this house too."

Bjorn nodded. "We can do that."

"A cottonwood grows the fastest." Rune pushed back his chair. "Soon as the ground thaws, we will do that."

Gerd nodded to the boys. "I will even bake you cookies in exchange."

"Today?" Leif grinned at her.

"There's no trees yet."

"Payment in advance?"

Gerd shook her head, but surely that was a twinkle in her eye. "We shall see."

"I'm sorry to say this, but that stack of wood on the porch is nearly gone." Signe hated to have to ask.

"We will do that today too," Rune assured her.

"Takk." She knew Rune would prefer working in the shop, but all the other work had to come first. "Leif, how about bringing up a basket of shavings? They make the house smell good, besides being a great fire starter."

Gerd nodded. "When you get some cedar

shavings, we can put them in bags in the trunks and cupboards. They keep moths away."

"Far said we will have cedar shakes for the roof on the house. Me and Knute get to split them." Leif slid his arms into his coat sleeves. "Oh, Mor? Mr. Jahnson wants to come out to visit you and Far. He said he visits all the families of his pupils."

Signe gulped. Her gaze darted to Gerd. Would Einar try to drive him off too?

Chapter 12

"Stop your fussing, everything looks very nice." Gerd jiggled Kirstin on her hip and made her chortle. Nothing could be as contagious as a baby's laughter.

"But it's the boys' teacher. The place should look decent." Signe's trepidation lifted as she grinned back at her daughter.

The sound of horse hooves splocking in the mud made her suck in another breath. It wasn't as if she didn't know who was coming. The boys had told her about Mr. Jahnson. If he was as good a teacher as they described, her boys were fortunate to have him. Even though Knute would rather be here working or out in the woods, he still seemed to be doing well at school. Leif loved every moment of it.

She answered the knock at the front door. The steps were now free of snow and ice, so they could use that door again. She made sure her face wore a smile as she pulled the door open. It still stuck a bit, but Rune had worked on it for some time. "Good afternoon, Mr. Jahnson. Welcome." Signe spoke her English carefully.

"Mrs. Carlson?" He held his hat to his chest.

"Ja, come right in." She stepped back and beckoned him inside. Taller than Rune and some rounder, he seemed to fill the doorway. Stepping back, she held out a hand. "May I take your coat and hat? It is much warmer in the kitchen." She hung them on the coatrack by the door and led the way to the kitchen. "As I said in my note, my husband and the boys are all out working in the woods until near dark. Hopefully we'll be able to return to church now that the roads are more passable."

"I was hoping to meet Mr. Carlson too, but I do understand. Work has to come first when the weather cooperates."

As they entered the kitchen, Gerd nodded and jiggled Kirstin, who eyed the stranger with a bushy mustache. First the baby hid her face in Gerd's shoulder, then looked at him again and screwed her face into a scowl that turned to a whimper. She reached out her arms for her mor, who took her immediately.

"Sorry. Mr. Jahnson, this is Mrs. Strand.

Gerd Strand." As they both murmured the proper responses, Signe swayed Kirstin from side to side. "Please sit down, and we will have a cup of coffee and dried-apple pie."

He took the chair she indicated. "Dried-apple pie, really? My mother used to make that, brings back good memories. You didn't need to go to so much bother. I apologize it has taken me so long to come to meet you. Today Mr. Larsson is teaching, so I am free."

"I am glad you are here. The boys say you are German."

He nodded. "On my mother's side. I spoke German growing up. That makes it easier to understand those who speak Norwegian. Did you know that your Leif has a knack for learning languages?"

"I know he has picked up English faster than any of us. Even on the ship, he did."

While Signe sat talking with Mr. Jahnson, Gerd took Kirstin and settled her in for a nap. After setting the pieces of pie on the table, along with a pitcher of thick cream, she filled the coffee cups and set them around. "There is sugar for your coffee too, if you want."

"No, thanks. I take mine black. I'm glad you are going to join us."

"Takk."

Signe sucked in a bunch of courage to ask, "Are both of our boys doing well?"

Mr. Jahnson nodded. "I am glad to say they are. I think Knute would rather be somewhere else, but he is one of my better math students. I know Mr. Larsson, the man who teaches them English, is pleased too." He savored another bite of pie. "Let me give you an example of a problem I posed to the upper grades. I asked them how many board feet of lumber could be cut from a thirty-foot log. Knute looked at me for a moment and raised his hand. What size boards, he asked. That was the kind of answer I wanted. No one could figure out board feet without more information. I want my students to not only love to learn but be able to think for themselves." He forked the last bite of pie into his mouth. "Do you have any questions you would like to ask me?"

"I am curious. Are there many other immigrant children who do not speak good English?"

"Several, but they are in the lower grades. I thought we might have to keep your boys back a grade, but it wasn't long before I knew that was not necessary. History and literature are their hardest, of course, because they involve so much reading on their own and understanding what they have read. Again, Mr. Larsson helps with that."

"So they are not failing?"

"Not at all, but they both spend more time on their homework than others do. They both do well in Latin, and young as he is, Leif is tackling Greek. He said his teacher in Norway started him on it." He shook his head when Gerd offered to fill his coffee cup again. "Thank you, but I need to be on my way in a few minutes." He pushed his chair back and stood. "I hope I can meet Mr. Carlson soon, and thank you again for the delicious pie."

Signe stood to walk him to the door. "Are you any relation to the family who owns the lumber mill and yards?"

"That is my father and uncle. Grandfather started it all."

"And you are teaching school?" Gerd gave him a puzzled look.

"Both my brothers excel in the lumber business, so I had the freedom to do what I wanted." He smiled. "And I wanted to teach."

She nodded. "I see."

When Signe returned from seeing the teacher out, Gerd seemed to be fretting. "He didn't say what he wanted from us."

"He wants to meet all the parents, Knute said."

"No, he wants something more. They always want something."

"Now you sound like Onkel Einar."

"Sometimes he is right." Gerd paused and looked at Signe. "At least he was in the past."

Signe often wondered how much of the discord between the Strands and the surrounding community was because of Einar's attitude. But did it really matter what came first? That was all behind them now. At least in her own mind. If Einar learned of the teacher visit, he would most likely not be happy. Inhaling what she hoped was courage, she smiled at Gerd. "It seems to me that Mr. Jahnson was just doing his job, and since the boys seem to be doing well at school without complaints, what if we add dumplings to the leftover stew, and I go down in the cellar and see if I can find any jars of corn to make scalloped corn like my mor used to?"

"Are there any beet pickles left?"

"I'll see."

Signe lit a lantern and hung on to the rail as she walked down the narrow stairs to the cellar. Soon the snow would be gone from the outside door, and she could begin to clean this out. Holding her lantern high, she inspected the dwindling number of jars on the shelves. Next year she would be sure to make more beet pickles for Gerd. Finding none, she took a quart jar of corn and one of carrots back up the stairs. There was still one jar of peas. Good thing they had canned lots of green beans and dried plenty too. This year she would plant more corn and dry some of that. With Nilda here to help, they could make the garden larger.

Back upstairs, she found Gerd rocking Kirstin, who was reaching up with one finger until Gerd nibbled on the end of it and made Kirstin giggle. What a happy sight.

Right on time, the boys trotted into the yard, and both came through the door. "Look, the sun has not gone down yet. The days are getting longer." Leif set their dinner buckets on the counter. He slung another sack off his shoulder. "Homework."

Kirstin waved her arms at them and spoke her baby language. Both boys smiled at Gerd and grinned and made baby noises back at their baby sister. She reached out, waving her arms.

"Nei, can't pick you up right now. I got to head for the woods." Knute let her grab his finger but when she tried to chew on it, he pulled back. He waved at her, took the sandwich Signe held out to him, and headed outside to ride down to the woods.

Leif knelt beside Gerd's knees and took Kirstin's hands in his to clap them together. "See, you can do that." As soon as he let go, she reached for him with both arms.

"Go ahead," Gerd told him. "I think she can tell when it is time for you to come home. See how happy she is?"

Leif scooped her up in his arms and jogged her around the kitchen on his hip. Kirstin laughed, told him something, and grabbed his hair with her other fist. "Ouch, that hurts." He untangled her fist and bounced her up and down again. "Pretty soon you can ride on my shoulders, baby." He handed her back to Gerd. "Gotta go do chores. Mor, when will she be big enough to ride in the wagon?"

"About the same time it warms up enough out there. She is sitting up and getting stronger all the time."

He waved at her, sandwich in his other hand, and asked over his shoulder, "Need anything from the well house?"

"Nei, but we need wood in the box."

"You always do." He wolfed down his sandwich, carried in a couple armloads of wood, and headed back out.

Dusk had nearly given in to dark when the men came in from the woods. Signe watched as they stopped at the barn. Einar parked the wagon by the machine shop to unload the tools before Bjorn unhitched the team, drove them back to the barn, and took off their harnesses. They had moved the wagon bed from sledge runners to wheels that morning, a sure sign of spring.

Spring, though, was arriving in bits and pieces. Snow was still piled on the north sides of all the buildings, but parts of the pasture and the lanes were drying up, with green sprouting where the sun had melted the snow.

Signe heard the clunk and scrape of boots on the porch. "Bring in wood," she called as the door opened.

Einar still refused to answer her greeting, and he did not bring in an armload of firewood.

"Supper in about ten minutes," Gerd announced.

When everyone was washed and seated at the table, Gerd and Signe removed the stew with dumplings from the oven and the scalloped corn from the warming oven. Sliced bread and butter along with glasses of milk for the boys were already on the table.

"Let's have grace," Rune said as he did every night.

Einar sat still until he finished, then

reached for the bread plate. "Who was here today?"

Signe and Gerd exchanged a look, and Signe shook her head. How did he know someone had been there? She filled his plate and passed it around to him, since the pots were too hot to pass.

He growled this time. "Who was here today?"

"Mr. Jahnson, the schoolteacher. He makes calls on all the families of his students."

Einar slammed his fist on the table. "How many times do I have to tell you, no one is to come here!" His angry voice made Kirstin wrinkle up her face and whimper.

Signe picked her up and started the swaying waltz of comforting. "Shh, shh, all is well."

"All is not well! I don't want anyone coming here, and you all know that."

"Onkel Einar —" Signe started, but with a slashing hand, he cut her off.

"Enough!"

Kirstin broke into a full, red-faced cry.

"Let's just finish our supper, and we can talk about this later." Rune spoke softly but clearly.

"Nei! This is still my house and as long as you live here, you will all do as I say." He tried to nail Signe with his glare, but she kept her attention on the rigid baby in her arms, who had a voice louder than Einar's. Perhaps someone could outyell him.

Gerd planted her hands on her hips and met him glare for glare. "Einar Strand, this is my house too, and I live in it all day and night. And I like having company, and I *will* have company. If you would rather sleep in the barn, so be it."

Everyone stared at her, mouths hanging open. This was the second time she had opposed him. Einar shoved his chair back, pushing the table enough to topple Leif's glass of milk and send it spreading across the table. He stomped out.

"Put a slice of bread in the spilled milk and let it soak up." Gerd sat back down. "Now we will finish our supper in peace."

Chapter 13

Simmering inside did not feel good at all.

"You have to let go of this," Rune said to her several nights later. "His bark is always worse than his bite."

"Gerd says the same thing. I know God says to not hold on to anger, but . . ." She rolled her head from side to side on the pillow. "I am so looking forward to having our own home. It cannot happen soon enough." She clung to his hand, which lifted hers to his mouth. His gentle kiss brought tears that leaked into her ears. "Is he like that when you are out in the woods?"

"Not as much."

"Then why does he hate me so? I do my best to be pleasant, but nothing ever seems to make a difference."

"At least he does not mistreat the boys, even though Leif is so frightened of him."

"No, only me."

"Have you asked Gerd about this?"

"Nei, I hate to make her feel bad. She has enough to bear. I know she works in spite of pain. I see it in her eyes. Kirstin is the delight of her life."

At the sound of Rune's gentle breathing drifting into sleep, Signe lay beside him, watching the moon paint square patterns on the floor. The part she had read in the Bible that morning said to give thanks for all things. How was she supposed to thank God for Einar Strand? For the way he acted? Surely God didn't really mean that. She could be grateful for the house they lived in, for Gerd, that was easy.

Be thankful. Full of thanks. That made no sense at all.

Spring thaws in Minnesota are pretty much like the spring thaw in Norway, Rune mused to himself. The tract of land — *his* tract of land! — inched ever closer to spring. Every day, bit by bit, bare ground showed through the snow, followed by green shoots that appeared like magic. Mud followed, but that meant the ground was thawing. Thawing ground led to plowing the garden and corn fields and digging out their cellar.

Rune marked the boundaries of his cellar with stakes, double-checking that the angles were exact, and he and his boys spent every spare moment digging the frost-free soil off so that the sun could warm the next layer.

Then came a task Rune was not sure he wanted to tackle.

"We'll start dynamiting stumps today," Einar announced at the breakfast table.

Bjorn grinned at his far. This would be a new experience.

Rune asked, "Start with the line along the hayfield?"

Einar nodded.

"Can't we stay?" Knute glared down at the table when Rune shook his head.

"There are plenty of stumps to clear. You'll get your chance." Rune nodded to his boys. Leif looked relieved; Rune knew that the farther he could stay from Einar, the happier he was.

Bjorn harnessed the horses as Rune and Einar loaded tools and hooks, pulleys and cables, the garden spade, and a couple of large garden trowels. Einar put three old axes into the wagon, axes that would never be properly sharp again, but Rune held his peace.

When Einar set the crate of dynamite sticks in the wagon bed, Rune's peace shattered.

Einar might be crotchety and unreasonable, but he was careful out in the woods.

Rune should trust that Einar would put safety first.

But he couldn't.

The leaf springs on Einar's wagon box were old and tired and had lost half their bow, so the wagon bounced at every rough spot in the track. The ruts were soft mud in the sun and still mostly frozen in the shade, making the wagon jostle wildly when it moved from mud to hard ground to mud to hard ground. Rune winced at every jounce. When the wagon bucked over a thick stick in the track, he broke out in a cold sweat. All he could think about was a huge gaping hole where he, Einar, Bjorn, the wagon, and maybe even the horses had been moments before.

As they rode out into the stump field, the ground softened, but now the numerous tree roots made the wagon bounce. Rune could not settle his intense foreboding.

Einar drew the horses to a halt and explained, pointing, "We'll start here. Pull these, drag them to a pile there, then burn the pile. We can spread the ashes across the meadow. Good fertilizer." He got down, picked up one of the dull axes, and walked over to a huge stump. "Cut the surface roots first."

He slammed the dull ax into the ground,

and it bounced. Ah — now Rune understood. The ax had struck a root. Einar chopped at it from an angle. When the ax sank deeper into the spring dirt, he found another root and started chopping.

How clever! Chopping into dirt and clay dulled an ax quickly. So they might as well use tools that didn't matter.

Bjorn had figured out the process just as Rune had, and Rune felt a happy little surge of pride. What a fine son! They cut the roots on four stumps. Then Einar shouldered his ax and walked off toward the wagon, so Rune and Bjorn followed.

When Einar pried the lid off the crate of dynamite, Rune broke out in a cold sweat again. Now the nightmare would begin.

Einar stuck a trowel in his belt and scooped up as many sticks as his two hands would hold. "Bring a shovel."

He walked back to the first stump they had chopped around. He took the shovel from Bjorn and dug deep beside the stump. Rune noticed how dark the soil was at the surface and how quickly it changed into pale clay and gravel. In fact, the soil was very much like most of the lowlands in Norway.

Rune took the shovel when Einar stopped digging. On his hands and knees, Einar used his trowel to dig down under the stump. He forced several sticks of dynamite down as deep under it as he could get them, then stood up and snapped at Bjorn, "Go get the reel of fuse."

He dug a deep hole alongside the next stump and handed the shovel to Rune. "Dig out the next one."

When all the dynamite had been nestled in place under the four stumps, Einar positioned his fuse as Rune held the reel. Rune had trouble keeping up, as Einar kept yanking on the fuse, demanding more. Grinning, Bjorn stepped in beside Rune with an ax and ran the ax handle through the center hole of the reel. Of course! In spite of his extreme fear and tension, Rune cackled out loud. He gripped the ax on either side of the reel, using it as an axle. The reel spun freely. Rune backed up as Bjorn played out fuse to meet Einar's needs.

Did Einar notice how quickly the operation was going now? Apparently not. Rune could see no change in his face or scowl. Much less did Einar notice the excellent improvement Bjorn had figured out. But then, wasn't that always how Einar was?

When Einar stood up from attaching the fuse at the fourth stump, he barked, "Leave the wagon there and unhitch the horses, boy. Take them to that chokecherry at the far end and tie 'em up good."

Rune felt better instantly. At least his son would be well away from danger.

But no. Bjorn led the horses at a trot out to the chokecherry and then came running back as Einar laid his fuse out along the ground and stopped beside the wagon.

"This is far enough."

Rune licked his lips. "Are you sure? We seem kind of close yet."

"It's far enough." Einar lit the fuse. It took three matches to get the fuse to catch, but suddenly it sputtered and sparkled brightly. As Rune's heart pounded in his chest, the brilliant, hissing little flame moved swiftly down the line of laid fuse.

It reached the first stump.

Boom! But it wasn't so much a *boom* as it was a *bwahp,* or maybe the world's biggest shotgun being fired, or —

Bjorn whooped with surprise and joy as the stump lifted, trembling, in the midst of a cloud of dirt and stones. It dropped back at an angle as earth rained down all around it.

The burning fuse reached the second stump. *Boom!* Not just *boom,* but *boom-boom,* for the third stump exploded simultaneously. Dirt and stones were blown treetop high, and some of them landed so close that you could hear them hit the ground. Rune was convinced now that they were not nearly far enough away. A sudden wave of dirty air smacked him in the face; his ears rang.

BOOM! Einar had set the fourth stump with two sticks more than the others, and it went off with a horrific explosion. Earth and rocks and splintered wood blasted upward and outward in all directions. Rune could feel the ground vibrate beneath the soles of his boots. He had never been so terrified.

Stones rained down, and the three of them buried their heads in their forearms. Poor Bjorn! He must be terrified. But no, he was laughing boisterously.

Whunk! A rock the size of a chicken landed on the wagon and punched a hole through the wagonbed. Einar swore. Rune stood aghast. If that rock had landed on one of them, it could have killed them. Suddenly he realized that the rock had missed the crate of dynamite sticks by only a foot or two. Had that rock landed on the dynamite . . .

He was terrified and horrified and wildly angry all at once. Einar could have killed them all!

Einar didn't seem concerned. He dragged

ropes and pulleys out of the wagon and ordered, "Boy, fetch the horses up."

Bjorn stood, staring raptly at the stumps as the dirt cloud slowly thinned.

Einar snarled at Bjorn. "Boy! I told you to do something. Do it!"

Bjorn did not move or look at Einar. It was as if he hadn't heard.

As if he hadn't heard! Rune's sense of dread before was nothing compared to his anger and terror now. Bjorn hadn't heard!

Einar swatted Bjorn's arm with the back of his hand, and Bjorn wheeled, wide-eyed. "Quit mooning around! I said, get the horses!"

"No!" Rune roared. "Bjorn, say your name."

Now the boy looked terrified. "What? What did you say? Far! I can almost not hear you at all. It's like you are very far away!"

Rune shouted and pointed. "Go to the house. Now!"

Einar shouted just as angrily, "No! I said get back to work! Go get the horses!"

Bjorn stood trembling for a moment, but thank God he knew better than to disobey his far. He turned and took off running toward the house.

Einar wheeled on Rune. "We need him to

handle the horses while we're pulling the stumps. He's just faking it so he won't have to work."

"He loves this work, and he is not faking. That lightning strike last year deafened him, but he got his hearing back. Let us pray to God that it returns again. One thing is for sure, he will never again be near where we are blasting. Never! His ears are too damaged."

Einar suddenly smirked. "Very well. If that lazy boy doesn't want to work, we're pulling the other one out of school. You understand? We need someone on the horses."

Rune's fury was past containing. "I cannot make you stop disrespecting my Signe. I cannot stop you from misusing me. But by God in heaven, you will *not* destroy my boys!"

Chapter 14

Nilda stared and clutched her bag. She had seen pictures. She had read books. Nothing prepared her for this. "Ivar, this steamship is *huge*! And black. And . . . it's frightening." She stood on a cement pier gazing at the ship they would be on for the next eight days.

"Want to turn around and go home?" Ivar did not seem awed at all.

She ignored his comment. "Is it true that the bigger the ship is, the smoother it rides?"

"That's what I heard. Well, let's go." He started forward.

Nilda followed him, along with hundreds of other people, as they funneled in a long line up a steeply sloping ramp. The ramp hung out over water but did not move the least bit. That was encouraging. She stepped aboard the first ship she had ever been on.

The signs were all in English. That was encouraging also, since she and Ivar had been studying English so intently. An arrow pointed down to Deck 2. She and Ivar joined the milling crowd of voyagers descending the stairs. Their tickets both said 2A. Apparently they would have to live and sleep in the same room for eight days.

After squeezing down a narrow corridor, they found 2A. Ivar stopped in the doorway. "It's a bunkhouse."

Nilda gaped. "We had more room up at the seter, and we thought that was crowded." Two levels of bunk beds lined the walls on each side. All the lower bunks were already taken.

"Over here." Ivar shoved his way to an outside wall, threw his shoulder bag onto an upper bunk, and quickly guarded the next one over.

Nilda threw her bag up onto it. "Do you think they might run out of bunks?"

"There don't seem to be many empties left. I want to go find the dining hall."

"I want to find the women's toilet."

So they went exploring. They found the dining area in about the middle of the ship, and then the toilets. The women's was on one side of the center aisle, the men's on the other. Nilda stepped inside a windowless room with a row of porcelain thrones that you flushed with a bucket of seawater.

Was there no privacy? A single electric lightbulb burned in the middle of the room, leaving it very dark at the perimeter. That would be her privacy. She went to a commode as far from the feeble light in the middle as possible.

A girl beside her was just standing up, her task finished. "You don't flush for everything," she said. "Just solids. I was asked to spread the word. There is a sign outside the door, but nobody reads it."

"Ah. Takk." On her way out, Nilda told three other women of the rule.

She and Ivar also found a lounge area with chairs, where you could read a newspaper or book. But where would one get a newspaper at sea? They returned to 2A.

Ivar headed for the stairs. "I want to see us cast off."

But at the top of the stairs, a steward stopped him. "Steerage passengers are not permitted on this deck."

So Ivar and Nilda had to watch from a small round window in 2A as the ship was untied from its moorings. The window was very near water level, and you could hear the engines throbbing and growling. Slowly, very slowly, the ship moved away from the pier.

Nilda was on her way to Amerika! She was

leaving everything behind. Mor and Far, of course, but also all her friends, all her cousins, Johann and Solveig, Mrs. Sieverson. . . . Her eyes burned, and she began to weep.

She heard Ivar exclaim, "We're out in the channel. Look! We're on the wrong side of the ship to see the islands, but we can watch the coast all the way out to Tungenes, I think."

She blew her nose and squeezed in beside Ivar to watch the coast of Norway move past.

"This means," Ivar explained, "that we're on the port side. Used to be *larboard* but now it's called *port*. Remember? Our English instructor did a whole lesson on ships."

"And you recall every detail, I see."

The boat was sailing along quite smoothly. *Let's hope it stays that way.*

Ivar's immediate dream came true when dinnertime finally arrived. The meal was soup and bread. Was there coffee? No. Just tea. Was sugar available? Yes, here were sugar cubes in a strange bowl that was wide and flat on the bottom.

When they returned to 2A, Nilda stopped to read a huge list of rules posted beside the door in both English and Norwegian. They could go out on deck only at certain hours. They could not smoke tobacco or burn candles while on board. They had to help with serving meals on certain days. They must remain modestly dressed at all times and display proper deportment. Only English would be spoken for announcements. What, for pity's sake, was *proper deportment*?

Late in the afternoon, they lost sight of the coast completely. Now what would she do? She had brought a bit of knitting, but that would be completed quickly. She had brought a book in Norwegian and one in English. Once those were read . . .

"Ivar, did you bring the Norwegian-English dictionary?"

"Nei, I left it for Mor so she can work on her English. I figure we'll be able to buy one easy enough in Amerika."

True; that was probably a good decision. Still, it left her feeling strangely empty. She got out her knitting, studied it a moment, and put it away again. She was going to be dreadfully bored.

Ivar was stretched out in his bunk, but his feet hung over the edge. How long was her bunk? She and Ivar were not tall, but they were both a bit longer than their beds. And what was this at the head end? It looked like a window box or planter. Oh, you could put your things in it. She tried it out. Her books fit nicely. The steep-walled sides would prevent them from falling on her head at night, should the ship lurch.

The next day went smoothly. Breakfast was porridge. Dinner was soup and bread. Supper was soup and bread. The soup had no meat and no taste. The porridge suffered similarly. Seven days left. Nilda feared it was going to be a long seven days.

At breakfast on the second full day at sea, she fell into a conversation with a girl her age who seemed to be traveling alone. The very first words the young woman spoke were, "I'm bored."

"Oh, so am I! My name is Nilda."

The girl brightened. "I'm Bekka. Want to play cards?"

"I'm sorry. I don't know how."

"We'll start with something simple." Bekka pulled a pack of cards from her bag. Her nimble fingers shuffled them quickly.

Nilda was intrigued by the soft churring sound they made. She knew men in the public houses sometimes played cards, but not women. But then, she had never been in a public house, so maybe women did too. This might be interesting.

"The object of this game is to get rid of all your cards first. Your opponents then count up the sum of their remaining cards — face cards are ten points. The first score to reach 500 marks the end of the game. And is the loser, obviously."

They played a practice hand, with all cards facing up on the table, as Becca showed how cards were matched and melded and explained some of the strategy. Nilda quickly grasped the concept and could see that playing cards was a wonderful time spender.

Bekka dealt, and Nilda examined her hand. She chose a card to —

"What do you two think you are doing?" A stern, gaunt woman glared down at them. "Playing cards is entirely inappropriate for young ladies. Not to mention turning the dining area into a den of iniquity. Give me those cards!" She reached for them, but Bekka snatched them away and stuffed them in her bag. Nilda dumped her hand of cards into her own bag.

Bekka's voice rang firm and clear. "You will *not* confiscate my possessions!"

The woman did not lose her glare. "Then do not let me see them again. It is unladylike! Go back to your rooms."

"Good idea." Bekka stood up, so Nilda did too. They started toward the front of the ship. "I'm in 2A. Where are you?"

"In 2A as well. On the port side." She

used the word Ivar had taught her and hoped he had remembered correctly.

"The side with windows! I tried for a window, but I came aboard too late. Perhaps, if there is something to see, I can look out your window now and then." She paused at the big rules list by the door. "I didn't read all this. Is there anything on here about playing cards, do you know?"

"I read them, and there is not. She was talking about being unladylike. Maybe this would be covered under *proper deportment.*"

Bekka snorted. "If we are bound by proper deportment, I am bound for the brig. I can see that now." She stopped in the middle of the bunkroom. "First we need a thundermug. You know, a chamber pot."

"There!" Nilda brought out the pot under Ivar's bunk.

"And a flat surface. Ah. I know." Bekka hurried outside. Moments later she returned with a large sign saying OUT OF ORDER. "This should do nicely." She turned the sign upside down and set it on the chamber pot. She sat crosslegged on the floor at their "table." "Our den of iniquity. Deal over again, please."

Laughing, Nilda sat on the floor opposite her new friend and they pulled out their cards, counting them to make certain. Apparently a complete deck was fifty-two cards. The morning sped by. Boredom was banished. This would be a wonderful voyage!

That evening Nilda noticed motion in the ship from waves for the first time. As she and Ivar walked to ship's center for supper, a steward shouted something from the far end of the dining area.

Nilda looked at Ivar. "I could not understand him. What did he say?"

He shook his head. "Something about loose items. I couldn't tell."

The ship was now moving enough that their soup sloshed slightly in their bowls. That was not difficult, of course; it was pretty watery soup.

The ship was rocking even harder when they went to bed that night. Sometime in the darkness, Nilda suddenly felt a need to throw up. She had just made it to the hall when her stomach decided to send everything back. Almost losing her balance, she leaned against the wall. What should she do? She could not just walk away and leave this. She needed a mop or something. The women's toilets would surely have a mop and bucket. Or she could use a bucket of seawater to rinse it away.

When she entered the women's toilet, a

dozen other women knelt at the commodes, all losing their stomachs. Some toilets served two people at once.

What a horrid, terrible mess! Surely the ship would stop rocking soon.

Nilda lost her stomach again. A few minutes later, she experienced what her mor called "dry heaves." There was nothing left to lose, but her stomach was bent upon emptying itself anyway. She lay down on the floor, wretched and retching, and prayed for the night to end as the floor heaved up and down.

"Miss? Miss." Someone was shaking Nilda's shoulder. She opened her eyes. A woman in a long white apron and white nurse's cap was kneeling beside her. "Miss, you must go back to your bed. I will help you. Come."

"I don't . . . I should . . ." It was hard to think. Nilda struggled to her feet. "I need a mop and bucket. I made a mess, uh, in the hall."

"You and many others. Our crews are cleaning up the hallways."

Nilda needed the woman's support, her knees were so shaky. She gripped the nurse's arm. "Is it night or day?" She could not tell in that windowless room.

"Morning, but breakfast is not served

yet." She was speaking Norwegian.

"I really do not care for breakfast." That was an understatement.

They entered 2A, and the nurse helped Nilda into her bunk. The nurse put a strange bottle with a coned lid, almost like a baby's bottle, into Nilda's book rack. "This is water. You are very dehydrated, and dehydration not only makes you feel sicker, it can kill you if it goes too far. Take a mouthful and swallow it a tiny bit at a time so that your body can absorb it."

"My stomach will just send it back."

"Not if the sips are small enough. Please do this."

"Ja, I will. Ma'am?"

"Yes?" The ship was lurching so much that the nurse had to hold on to Nilda's bunk.

"I read in a book that when ships were fighting in naval wars, they simply threw dead bodies over the side. To get them out of the way. When I die, will you throw my body overboard?"

"Nei. At the end of the voyage, we have to account for every person on the passenger manifest. But if you keep sipping, you will not die."

"I'm beginning to believe it might be preferable."

But the nurse had left.

Nilda put some water in her mouth. It tasted bad, but probably her mouth itself tasted bad. She drank trickling amounts and realized that she actually was very thirsty.

Where was Ivar? His bunk was empty. Surely not at breakfast. On the other hand, he had a robust appetite. Perhaps he was. She dozed and sipped and retched, but nothing came up. The ship rolled so wildly that she was being thrown in all directions.

Sometime during the day, she made another trip to the bathroom and returned without collapsing. Ivar was still not back, but she felt so weak she couldn't rouse herself enough to go look for him.

Her water had been replenished as she slept. She sipped some more and slept some more. She was beginning to fear the nightmare would never end. That night was just as miserable as the one before had been. But toward morning, the ship seemed to be lurching less violently. Or perhaps it was simply her fond wishes making it seem less.

Around noon, she made herself get up. She must find out about Ivar. Was he so sick he had died? The thought chilled her through and through. She should have done this yesterday. She remembered seeing a map of the vessel's decks somewhere. Then she thought of an easier way. She asked a steward in the dining area, "Where is the infirmary, please?"

He directed her to Deck 1. She went down the stairs from 2 to 1. Signs directed her to a door. She entered.

"You're up!"

She wheeled. Ivar! She ran to him and wrapped him in a bear hug. "Where have you been? You were not in your bunk, ever."

"When I got sick, you were not in your bunk, so I came down to the infirmary for treatment, expecting to find you here. They gave me a medicine that helped me enough that I could work here."

"You were working in the infirmary?"

"Ja, I still am. Several of their orderlies were so sick they couldn't help, and they needed lots of orderlies; just about everyone on the ship was ill, including some of the nurses. So I told them I would gladly help."

She released her hug and stepped back to look at him, gripping his arms. "Ivar Carlson, you are more a man than I imagined. I am proud of you."

He shrugged, but he was grinning broadly. "At least I did not have to help in the galley."

CHAPTER 15

Two more weeks, and Nilda will be here.

Signe felt like dancing. Until she began to think about all she had to get done before Nilda arrived. She heaved a sigh. May, and the spring cleaning was not even finished yet, let alone the garden in.

"What is bothering you?" Gerd asked, swaying from side to side to make Kirstin's eyes drift closed. Gerd looked down at the baby in her arms. "I think she must be teething again. That's the only time she really fusses."

"There's so much to do."

"Signe, Nilda and Ivar are coming here to work, to help us, both in the house and outside. You do not have to have it all done before they come."

Signe blinked. "Takk. Takk for the reminder." She sucked in a deep breath and felt her shoulders drop from her earlobes. Another breath. "Less than two weeks until school is out. One horse cannot pull that plow or disc, can she?"

"Nei. But perhaps while they are blasting, the team would be available. Have you driven a team and plow before?"

Signe shook her head. "But it cannot be too hard."

"Much easier with the newer plow, but ask Rune. Come to think of it, he will probably be plowing the fields anyway."

That night, Signe and Rune sat in the kitchen talking after the others had gone to bed. "Could you please work up the garden before you start on the fields?" she asked.

He looked up from reading his verses for the day and rubbed his eyes. "It is getting nearly impossible to read this any longer. Some days seem better than others but . . ." He blinked. "Ja, I will plow tomorrow. We are going to church on Sunday, even though I hate to take a day from digging the cellar."

"Have you blasted out enough stumps?"

"There will never be enough until all the big trees are gone and the land is all clear. With Ivar here, we will make more progress. I plan to leave a couple standing on our land. A grove of hardwoods at the south line would be something to think about."

"Sugar maples? I dreamed we would have

birch trees up by our house." Not that either of them had much time to dream, but . . .

He gave her a half smile, and there was a faraway look to his eyes. "After the house and well house, I want to build a wood shop. I believe making skis could be something to bring in money when the big trees are gone. Farming is good, but making furniture can be a good wintertime living." He turned to look through the wall in the direction of their future home. "Shame we have to come back right after church, but that cellar is critical so we can raise the house in June. I've been thinking that I would like to make our house two full stories with an attic. We might have enough to pay for the lumber to do that." He stretched his arms over his head and twisted from side to side. "Morning comes sooner than I am ready."

Sunday morning, Signe observed that getting out of the house to get to church on time was easier now that the sun came up earlier. Bjorn had the horse hitched and the wagon by the door in plenty of time.

"You could leave the baby here with me," Gerd offered.

"Takk, but this way you get some time off."

Gerd rolled her eyes. "I will start dinner,

and then I was thinking about a dress for her. I have not done any smocking for years, and that pink gingham will do nicely."

"Mor, we're going to be late." The call came from the smaller wagon that Rosie could pull. Einar had the team hitched to the plow and was already out in the field.

When they were finally under way, Signe drew in a deep breath of spring morning. Gerd should have come with them. Perhaps by next Sunday, Signe would be able to talk her into it.

At church, Mrs. Benson met them at the door. "Oh, I am so glad to see you." After talking with Kirstin, she locked her arm through Signe's. "You come sit with us." She looked at Rune. "How are things going?"

"Trying to get the cellar dug so we can start the house in June."

"Won't a house of your own be wonderful?" She patted Kirstin's cheek and this time received a smile. "She is growing so fast."

"My brother and sister will be here in a couple of weeks," Rune added.

"Oh, folks from home. I can't wait to meet them." The organ invited the last of the stragglers to the sanctuary. "Come, Mr. Benson has saved the row for you."

Signe sat down with a sigh and let the music wash over her. Mr. Larsson, from the school, had a way with the organ. Such a talented man, both a teacher and a musician. Shame that none of her boys, nor she or Rune, played an instrument. Her far had played the fiddle. She should have asked him to teach one of the boys.

Reverend Skarstead took his place at the front and raised his hands. "Come, let us worship our Lord with our opening hymn, 'Holy, Holy, Holy.' " The organist pumped his feet, and the familiar song filled the room.

Signe closed her eyes, the better to hear the words and tamp them into her mind to come back to when she needed them. "Lord God almighty." *Help me remember you are indeed the mighty God.* "Ever more shall be." *Not just today, but every day and every moment of every day.* "Though the darkness hide thee." *Lord, help me to always look for thee and thy face.* "Though the eye of sinful man, thy glory may not see."

Kirstin wiggled in her arms. Signe shifted her daughter and swayed in time to the music. The harmony on the "amen" must be what heaven would sound like when she got there.

If you get there. That little voice that

always sought to bring her discontent and fear. It even followed her through the church doors.

When they were seated again, Signe snuggled Kirstin close and swayed just enough to calm her. At least she would not be demanding to be fed during the service.

"Today we read Luke 13:10–17, concerning the travels of Jesus and the miracles He performed everywhere He went.

"Jesus was teaching in the synagogue — in church, like we are here — and a woman came in who was so bent over that she could not straighten herself to look anyone in the face, let alone see Jesus. She was always looking down, had been for many years. And yet she came to worship, because that is what a good Jew does on the Sabbath. The men worshiped on one side, and the women and the children on the other." He paused and looked around at his congregation. "We are privileged in that we get to worship as families. I see all ages here, and that is as it should be. When I think of that poor suffering woman and the terrible pain she must have endured, I marvel that she came anyway." He paused and looked around. "She came anyway. So often situations happen to keep us from worship. You are ready to leave, and the cows get out.

One of the children comes in bleeding from a slight accident, or someone starts throwing up. All these parts of life that seem to occur especially on Sunday morning to keep us from worship. During the winter, the weather is a factor, making it impossible for us to get here. During the spring, it is planting, summer and fall, harvest. All things that need to be done, have to be done." He nodded. "Life is just that way.

"Yet God ordained that on the seventh day, we should rest, like He did. And if God needed to rest, what about us? Is showing up for worship a form of rest? Is doing something different on Sunday afternoon a form of rest? I know, I am full of questions today, and none of them have easy answers. But . . ." He held up his index finger and waited. "But learning to listen for His answers, His guidance, can help us develop the wisdom to choose wisely the things we will do. As farmers and loggers, we live by the seasons. And while the land rests under snow, we are out cutting trees. Hard, hard work. But when we show up, God blesses us. Just as Jesus did with that woman. Jesus healed her so she could stand straight, and she went out rejoicing and singing praises. So when we put God first, and that is a lifelong lesson, He blesses us for showing up. He gives us rest and healing, and we find joy in His will. Amen."

Signe felt Leif leaning against her and Kirstin asleep in her arms, so she stayed seated when the others stood. *Lord God, help me to show up. Here, especially, even when it isn't easy.*

After the benediction, Signe gathered up her things, careful not to wake the baby in her arms.

Mr. Benson shook Rune's hand. "Good to see you. How are things going out there?"

"I've learned how to dynamite stumps. Good thing, since there is only a forest more of them to deal with."

"Ah, so true. Wrestling with the big trees and turning the land into farmland is not a dream for the faint of heart." Mr. Benson smiled at Leif and Knute. "You boys are nearly out of school, aren't you?"

"Ja, then we can help dig out our cellar even more."

"Good, so you've started on your house?"

Rune nodded. "We have. There's never enough time to do everything, though."

"Ja, that is true. Could you use a hand with the cellar digging?"

Rune stared at him, and Signe could almost see the visions of a rampaging Einar stomping through his mind. "Well, of course."

"Your place is beyond the home farm, right?"

"Right. We have a path now across the field behind the barn."

Mr. Benson smiled. "I'll see what I can do. Maybe if we get you some help, you'll have more time to be part of our church family. Won't have to run off so fast."

Rune nodded. "Takk. I'm sure you'll hear us back there. Signe can point out the path."

Reverend Skarstead stood by the door, greeting folks as they filed out. "Good to see you, Mr. and Mrs. Carlson." He looked at Bjorn. "Now you are . . . ?"

"Bjorn Carlson, sir. I work with Onkel Einar out in the woods during the week and at our place on Sunday."

Her middle son piped up. "I'm Knute, and this is my little brother, Leif."

"Seems to me, I heard you like to go fishing," the reverend said.

Knute grinned. "Yes, sir. Hunting too."

"A man after my own heart. You know my son, Olaf, from school."

"Oh, ja, Olaf. He is very good at Red Rover."

"He says exactly the same of you. Next time we go fishing, we'll see if you can't come too."

"Takk, sir."

In the wagon on the way home, Knute said, "That Reverend Skarstead, he's pretty nice, huh?"

"Ja, he is." Rune clucked the horse into a trot. "Let's get on home, Rosie. We've got work to do."

Later, Signe and Leif worked out in the garden, digging around the raspberry bushes that had sent up lot of shoots. "Soon as your far plows and discs this, we can start planting," she told him.

She shaded her eyes with her hand at the sound of horses coming up the lane. *Mr. Benson really is coming to help. And he brought three other men with him!* When she had mentioned to Gerd that some men might come to help dig the cellar, the older woman had snorted and shaken her head, as always, doubting everyone's intentions.

"Leif, you go with them to show the way," Signe said, and he dashed out of the garden.

Mr. Benson waved to her. "My wife said she would try to come out one day this week."

"Takk. And takk for coming too. Just follow Leif."

"Come on, son, you can ride with me."

The four men rode on out to the hole in the ground, and Signe turned back to the raspberry bushes, her heart lightened by the act of friendship.

Rune stopped shoveling when he heard horses approaching. "They really did come to help." He took off his hat to wipe his forehead with the back of his arm. "Good to see you," he called to Mr. Benson.

"Not sure if you've met all these men, but it's about time." Mr. Benson waited for Leif to slide off his horse, then dismounted. "Looks like we got our work cut out for us."

He introduced the others and, shovels in hand, they all jumped down into the hole, not deep enough yet that they couldn't throw the dirt out. They spaced themselves out so as not to get in each other's way and fell to digging. Dirt flew up and over the growing piles. When someone hit a rock, they dug around it, and several men got together to hoist it over the edge. Less than two feet down, they hit dense clay and gravel. Rune sent Bjorn and Knute to the shop for fence post diggers, a mattock, and a pickaxe. One of the men had brought a pickaxe too. They took turns loosening the gravel so it could be shoveled out.

"You're going to need the wheelbarrow and a ramp for the middle section," Mr. Benson said to Rune.

"Sooner than I thought, thanks to all of you." Rune wiped the sweat from his face.

"Mor sent coffee and water," Leif said, toting two jugs to the edge of the cellar hole. He set them on one of the mounds of earth. "What are we going to do with all this dirt?" he asked.

Good question. Rune would have to think about that.

After the brief break, the men returned to digging, slower now but still making progress, until one of the men announced he had to go home to do chores. Another said the same, and with Rune's heartfelt thanks ringing in their ears, the two men rode out. Leif and Knute headed up to the barn to do the same; the other four kept on.

Rune kept watch on Einar, who was plowing the cornfield. Dread made him dig harder. If Einar came over here and ordered these men away — wait. He could not. This was Rune's land, not Einar's. Still, he could raise a nasty fuss. Just the thought of that . . . *Lord, please keep him out there.*

Sometime later, Mr. Benson checked his pocket watch. "I think we need to hang it up for today. I know you've got a lot to go, but there's progress." He stretched his arms and shoulders. "Reminds me that digging uses different muscles. Hope you got a good bottle of liniment, but then, you've been working in the woods." He stared across the field at Einar. "Planting corn?"

Rune nodded. "I cannot begin to thank you for your help."

"Will try to get back again." Mr. Benson mounted his horse. "Your Bjorn is a good worker."

"Ja, he is. Smart, too."

Rune and Bjorn dug until they saw Einar heading for the barn and the setting sun painting clouds in the west. Gathering up their tools, they trudged up to the shop and put them away. Rune clapped a hand on his son's shoulder. "Hopefully we can get some more done tomorrow night."

Rune and Bjorn both loaded up with wood for the kitchen stove and dumped it in the woodbox in the kitchen.

"Einar, you know where any more downed or dead trees are?" Rune asked. "About done with that last one."

"The boys can start sawing up the bigger branches from those earlier stacks. Can't burn again until next winter."

"Will that be dry enough for stove wood?"

He nodded. "And there's a birch west of your property."

"Saw those limbs by the stacks?" Bjorn asked.

Einar nodded. "Bow saw will work. No sense loading 'em on a wagon."

"Supper's on." Gerd set chicken and dumplings on the table and waited while the men and boys took their places.

Rune breathed a sigh of relief that Einar seemed normal, not about to blow like he'd expected. "Let's have grace." Together they repeated the grace in Norwegian, and at the *amen,* Einar reached for the bowl of biscuits. He dished up his plate and ate without a word.

Rune gave Signe a raised-eyebrows look. Her return smile made all the hard work worthwhile.

Bjorn asked, "Far, what if we used dynamite to help dig the cellar? That should make a hole."

"Ja, blow it up!" Knute said. The boys looked at each other and chuckled.

Einar slammed his palm down on the table. "That dynamite is no joke!" His voice exploded, sending the laughter into hiding.

Kirstin answered with a piercing shriek.

Gerd glared at her husband. "Now see what you've done! Scared the baby!"

Einar glared but said nothing. Apparently he was no more interested in babies than he was in children or kittens or life.

Chapter 16

"We're almost there." Nilda turned to Ivar, who stood beside her at the deck rail.

He shook his head. "I have to pinch myself to be sure this is real."

The ship on which they were crossing the Great Lakes to Duluth, Minnesota, had bucked winds, but nothing like those on their Atlantic crossing. Nilda had gained a new appreciation for the power of wind and water that could toss a huge ship around like a toy.

A man on the other side of Ivar pointed to a lighthouse on the southern shore. The light was not shining, as it was daytime, but the stubby white tower and its red roof still showed prominently, guiding ships away from the rocks. They had seen such beauty when they sailed close to the lake shores, but mostly they steamed out far enough to feel like they might still be on the ocean.

Almost there. Such magical words. The announcement that they were two hours from Duluth had come a bit earlier, bringing her to the rail where Ivar had spent most of the voyage.

"I think I could be happy working on a ship like this." He smiled at her over his shoulder.

"Doing what?"

"There are a lot of men working to keep this ship moving. Not like it used to be with sails, but still."

Nilda sniffed. "Well, it's a good thing you have a job to go to. You always said you wanted to be a lumberjack."

"But I'd never been on a big ship before. A fishing boat is far different. And I really enjoyed that work as an orderly on the ocean steamer. Something else I'd love to do." Ivar had spent one summer aboard a relative's boat, fishing off the northern Norwegian coast. Their onkel had asked him to come back again this year because he was a hard worker, but Ivar said he was going to Amerika instead. "I heard there are fishing boats out of Duluth," he said to the man next to him.

"Ja, good fishing in the Great Lakes," the man replied, "but from what I heard, the storms can be killers of both boats and men in these waters. Even big cargo ships like those hauling timber or iron ore sometimes end up on the bottom of the lake."

"Hard to believe on a day like today," Ivar said. The sun winked on the swells, and a breeze brought smells of land and sea and coal smoke.

Nilda asked the man, "You came on the same ship we did, right?"

"Ja, that was a nightmare to end all nightmares. I don't ever want to make that voyage again. I come to Amerika to stay." Since they were all speaking Norwegian, the conversation was easy.

"What are you going to do when you land?" Ivar asked.

"Work for a relative in his lumberyard."

"Oh, where?"

"Place called Blackduck."

"That's where we're going." Nilda smiled at him. "I know we've not been formally introduced, but this is my brother Ivar Carlson, and I am Miss Nilda Carlson. We're joining our brother and his family, who work for an onkel somewhere near Blackduck."

The man took off his hat, the breeze immediately lifting his hair and dropping a hank down his forehead. "I am Petter Thorvaldson, from near Bergen." He put out his hand. "I am glad to meet you both."

Nilda noticed his crinkly blue eyes, square chin, and mouth rimmed by smile-made creases. Taller than Ivar by only an inch or so, he had broader shoulders and hands calloused by hard work. She bit back her first question and tried to rephrase it. "You are the first of your family to emigrate?"

"I am. In Norway, I worked on a fishing boat and helped my far on our mountain farm."

Ivar grinned. "Me, too. Did you like fishing?"

"Not particularly, but it was work. Mor always said to be grateful for any honest work. But when I saw a man washed overboard, I decided I would rather work on land if I can."

He did not mention a wife and children. Nilda tucked that knowledge away for future reference.

Sea gulls and huge, low-flying white birds caught her attention. When one of the white birds dove straight down into the water, she pointed for Ivar to look. The bird popped back up to the surface with a fish in his bill, which he swallowed with one gulp. Broad wings spread and flapped him back up to skim the waves again.

"What kind of bird is that?"

"A pelican," Petter answered. "You saw

that big pouch under his beak? He can hold a whole lot of fish before he needs to swallow."

"I've never seen anything like that." Ivar was openmouthed.

They watched as several more pelicans dove, gulped, and flapped aloft again. Sea gulls screeched overhead and floated on the surface of the water.

"Must be a bait ball," Petter said as the pelicans wheeled and skimmed back. "A huge cluster of small fish will gather in one spot, swimming in a tight knot. Even when sea birds pick off some of them, most of them are safe." He pointed to the stern of the ship, where seagulls circled and screamed, fighting each other for the scraps dumped from the galley. "That is always fun to watch. Sea gulls are such scavengers."

The hills and piers of Duluth hove into view. Cargo ships, fishing boats, and tugs with barges of iron ore, logs, and finished lumber lined the piers, some waiting out in the bay for a place to dock.

The engines slowed their rumble and brought the ship to a stop about half a mile out. "We will be docking within the hour," a voice announced. "Be ready to disembark from the main deck. Your baggage will be unloaded from the hold and can be claimed on the pier."

Nilda felt shivers run up and down her spine. They were almost to Duluth. How far away was the train station? And how would they transport their big trunks to the train?

"Do you have baggage?" Petter asked.

"We do, several trunks and a wooden crate," Ivar said.

"I would be glad to help you, since we're both heading to the train. I only have one case and a shoulder pack."

Nilda smiled her gratitude. "Takk. I heard someone say there are wagoners and draymen to hire."

"I will ask."

Nilda nodded in thanks and pleasure. Surely a train ride would give them a chance to get to know Petter better.

They were all huffing by the time they had pushed the four-wheeled station cart from the pier to the train station. Nilda carried the carpetbags she and Ivar had used on the ship, just in case they needed something from them. All their letters and ticket information were in her reticule.

The next train to Blackduck would be in two hours. They parked the cart and sank down on the benches in front of the station.

Dark clouds rolled in and hid the sun,

bringing with them wind strong enough to tug at her hat. Nilda clapped her hand on top of it in case the hat pins slipped out. After three drops of rain as a prelude, the downpour hit.

"Get inside before you are soaked," Ivar told her. He grabbed the carpetbags and pushed through the doorway of the station. The pounding of rain on the roof sounded more like thunder than falling rain.

"Our trunks," Nilda said, peering at their car through a window.

"They should be able to withstand a rainstorm."

"But what if they leak and everything gets wet?"

"Better them than us."

"Come on, I'll help you." Petter stood and settled his hat more firmly on his head. Ivar groaned but got to his feet.

"I'll hold the door," Nilda said.

She pulled one side of the double door inward. The two men shoved the cart through the door and then stood in the doorway, watching the rain.

Thunder boomed right over them, lightning jagging the sky at almost the same moment. A pine tree at the west end of the station exploded, showering burning branches and needles on the platform and across the tracks. Within minutes, the downpour had drowned out even that fire.

"That was close," said the clerk who had been behind the ticket window. "Took the tree instead of the train station. Thought we'd be hightailing it out of here for sure. Where you folks bound for?"

"Blackduck."

"You all have your tickets?"

Nilda patted her reticule and Petter his chest pocket.

"Good, good. Blackduck your destination?"

"It is mine," Petter answered.

"Nei, we go on to Benson's Corner." Nilda and Ivar spoke at almost the same time.

"You're going to spend the night in Blackduck, then. The next train to Red Lake that stops in Benson's Corner doesn't leave until morning."

Nilda groaned, and Ivar heaved a sigh. "Takk, I guess."

"They don't have a hotel there, but there's an inn of sorts. And some households take in paying guests."

As if we had money to spend on a night in a hotel. Nilda looked at her trunk. There were two quilts in there. Sleeping on hard benches in the Blackduck station would be better than on the floor.

"I could go to my cousin's house and see if they have room," Petter offered.

"Have you ever met your cousin?" Nilda asked.

"Not since I was very young, but his mor is my favorite tante. He is ten years or more older than I am."

The incoming train whistle made them pause.

"That will be the train you want." The railroad man headed for his office. "The baggage car is next to the caboose. You all have a good trip now."

When the train screeched to a stop, they pushed the luggage cart out into the downpour. Nilda followed, but the conductor waved her over to the steps leading to the passenger car. Once inside, she found two seats facing each other and sank into one. Her coat was wet clear through, and her hat dripped rainwater down her face.

"Oh, dear, here let me help you." An older woman in the seat behind her stood and helped Nilda take off her coat. "Do you have a sweater or anything else to put on so you don't catch your death of a chill?"

"Nei." *Death of a chill.* Nilda had no idea what the woman was talking about. She and Ivar may have taken lessons in English, but obviously they would need many more. She smiled at the lady, unpinned her hat, and dropped it on the seat.

Ivar and Petter came up the steps, and the conductor called "all aboard." The train shrieked and screeched as it eased forward, picking up speed with every turn of the wheels.

"Sir, do you have any towels or blankets for these young people, to dry them off?" the older lady asked the conductor.

"Not that I know of."

She turned to Ivar and Petter. "You two, get your coats off and hang them over one of the seat backs." She might be aging, with her silver hair in a bun, but she knew how to give orders — and clearly expected to be obeyed. She looked back at the conductor. "Well, are you going to go check?"

"Yes, madam."

"Here." She put her black wool coat around Nilda's shoulders.

"But I'll get it wet," Nilda protested.

"That coat has been wet before and getting wet again won't hurt it."

Nilda could pick up most of what the woman said. She had a great deal of trouble separating out the words, even though the lady did not speak rapidly.

As the train picked up speed, a draft blew

down the aisle, making Nilda wish she could take off her wool stockings and tuck her feet under her skirt, which had been protected by her coat. It was May, but right now it felt like winter was trying to repossess the land.

The older woman frowned at Ivar and Petter. "And you young men, even your shirts are wet."

"No worry, we will dry. Takk for your concern," Ivar said.

When the conductor returned with several dish towels, the lady *tsk*ed in disapproval. "That is all you could find?"

"Sorry, madam."

She handed each of them a towel. "Dry your hair and what you can, and then we are going to the dining car for a pot of hot coffee." She looked at the conductor. "The dining car is open, I take it?"

"Yes, ma'am." He checked his watch. "Or at least it will be in a few minutes. There will be an announcement."

The woman looked at Nilda. "You might want to go to the women's restroom and see if you can brush your hair dryer, then put it up again. Then we shall have our coffee."

Nilda dug into her carpetbag. "Ja. Please, I don't know what to call you."

"I am Mrs. Schoenleber."

Nilda introduced the three of them. "We truly appreciate your help."

But why are you doing this? Obviously the woman was wealthy. The quality of the wool and the cut of the coat hanging on Nilda's shoulders said that, if nothing else did. Mrs. Schoenleber's suit was tastefully accented with jet beads, and a cameo brooch at the high collar said "money." Her hat, with its elegant black feather and fine veil, perched on her roll of silver hair, said so even more clearly.

Nilda had seen women dressed like this on the steamship, but only from a distance, as their quarters were on the upper deck, not down on the lower decks. Why was this woman helping emigrants like them?

The dining car opening was announced, though Nilda caught only a few of the words. Mrs. Schoenleber herded the three of them down the aisle and through the doors connecting the two cars.

"Well, good afternoon, Mrs. Schoenleber," said the steward in the dining car. "Where would you like to be seated?"

Ivar and Nilda exchanged looks. The people on the train knew her name, who she was.

"There will be fine. We will have a pot of

coffee immediately and then we will see about what else. These young people need to be warmed up."

"Yes, madam." He seated them and stood a menu in front of each. "Your coffee will be right here. Do any of you take cream or sugar?"

They started to shake their heads, but Mrs. Schoenleber intervened. "Just bring them, thank you."

The dining car was so elegant. Blindingly white tablecloths and napkins, a small vase with a pink flower in the metal rack that held silver salt and pepper shakers, and polished silverware at each place setting — so many genteel touches. The food here must cost a fortune. How would Nilda and Ivar pay for this?

"Now then," Mrs. Schoenleber said, "as soon as we are served, you can tell me about yourselves and where you are going."

A waiter set cups and saucers at each place and then filled each cup full of steaming coffee.

Mrs. Schoenleber perused the menu. "Bring us a plate of these hors d'oeuvres and one of fruit. And then we'll see." She closed her menu and handed it to the waiter without looking. "Now, I take it you were on the ship that docked early this afternoon.

Did they serve you dinner first?"

Ivar nodded. "Ja, we had soup and bread."

"But you could eat a sandwich or something now?" She looked from Petter to Ivar. "Are you three related?"

They all shook their heads.

"We met on the ship just this morning," Nilda answered when it seemed the two men were more interested in their coffee. "Ivar is my younger brother, and we are going to work for an onkel near Benson's Corner."

Petter added, "I have come to work for my cousin, who manages a lumberyard in Blackduck."

Mrs. Schoenleber nodded and looked at Nilda. "And so you will continue on the train to Benson's Corner?"

"Ja, tomorrow morning." Nilda felt the hot coffee warm her both inside and out as she cradled the cup in her hands.

"And where will you spend the night? Pardon me if I seem meddlesome. I am accused of that often."

Nilda and Ivar looked at each other. "Uh, at the train station. The next train leaves in the morning."

"That's what I thought." Mrs. Schoenleber looked up with a smile when two platters of delicacies were placed before them.

"If you could bring us a platter of sandwiches also?"

"Right away, madam. Any preference?"

"Oh, roast beef will be fine. And make sure there is plenty of meat between those slices of bread."

"Yes, madam."

"I-I don't want to sound ungrateful, but . . ." Nilda started.

Ivar finished the sentence. "We do not have enough money to pay for this."

"Of course you do not. You traveled in steerage. The food here has already been paid for. So just eat and make an old woman happy." Mrs. Schoenleber smiled at them. "I do not have many younger people in my life anymore, and I enjoy feeding hungry young men. I want you all to feel welcome in this new land of yours, so please don't leave any food on the platters." She raised a hand, and the waiter was right there, even though many of the other tables were filling. "More coffee, please."

She picked up a morsel of some sort from the plate that held the hors d'oeuvres and took a bite. "Ah, they do have a fine baker on this train. Now, to get back to business. I have rooms at my home that need to be used. I cannot bear the thought of you sleeping at the train station. So we will leave your luggage in storage at the station, and you shall come home with me. My butler will make sure you are back at the station in time for the train in the morning." She clasped her hands on the table, her rings glinting in the lights of the dining car. "Any questions?"

Her butler! Nilda had never met a person who employed a butler. "But . . ."

"Surely you don't want to deprive this old woman of the pleasure of your company tonight."

What have we gotten into? Nilda thought. *Is she an angel or what?*

The men seemed to have no trouble accepting free food, and after her involuntary fast on that ocean voyage, food tasted mighty good to Nilda also. She was uncertain about American customs and how they differed from Norwegian politeness, but apparently the offer of food here was to be accepted. Courtesy demanded it. And so she ate a delicious beef sandwich with fruit and warm, fragrant coffee. *Welcome to Amerika!*

The train arrived at Blackduck late in the day. Petter started to give them his goodbyes, but Mrs. Schoenleber would hear nothing of it.

"Nonsense, young man. It's far too late to be wandering around town, trying to find a cousin you barely know. Leave your baggage here and stay at my house with your friends. There will be time enough tomorrow to settle in to your new home."

Petter tried to protest but soon gave up. He gave Nilda and Ivar a sheepish shrug and did as Mrs. Schoenleber said. Nilda bit her lip to quell a smile. She didn't think he'd had much choice. Once Mrs. Schoenleber decided on something, she seemed to get it.

Mrs. Schoenleber marched into the station to speak to the agent about storing their luggage.

"She acts like she owns the railroad," Petter muttered.

"She sure is forceful," Ivar agreed.

The boys went off to gather the trunks while Nilda held the carpetbags.

A stately carriage arrived, drawn by four horses. The rain had stopped, so the driver folded back the two leather bowtops that kept the interior dry. Two seats, each large enough to comfortably serve two or three people, faced each other. Were all Americans so rich?

Mrs. Schoenleber came marching out of the station. "Thank you, George," she said to the carriage driver. It was hers!

Ivar and Petter returned with the trunks,

and the station agent came out to take possession of them.

Mrs. Schoenleber nodded. "We're on our way. Hop in." She waved a hand toward the carriage.

The driver gave Mrs. Schoenleber a hand in, then did the same for Nilda just as elegantly. The men climbed in the other side. The driver cracked his whip, and the well-matched team of four horses moved forward as one.

"If I may, ma'am, what sort of carriage is this?" Petter asked.

"It is a landau, very common in this country. In fact, the president, Ulysses S. Grant, had a landau built especially for him."

They arrived at a fine mansion, but by now, Nilda expected nothing less. George helped the ladies down, and all went inside. The interior, like the outside, was the kind of place kings lived in. They dined at a long table, the four of them clustered at one end. Then they sat in a large room furnished with leather chairs and a huge stone fireplace, drinking brandy from odd, round snifters.

Mrs. Schoenleber had all sorts of questions, and Petter had some too. Nilda simply could not get comfortable immersed in such luxury, and her English left much to be desired. But the evening went well anyway.

There were apparently many guest rooms; Nilda, Ivar, and Petter each had a room of their own. As Mrs. Schoenleber had promised, a tall, stolid, humorless fellow named Charles, her butler, woke them in the morning and led them down to a sumptuous breakfast of poached eggs, ham, melon, and toast.

"Mrs. Schoenleber is otherwise occupied," Charles explained, "so I shall conduct you to the station." He led them out front, where George, the landau, and the four horses were waiting.

Nilda told Ivar, "That good night's sleep has really refreshed me. Things look much cheerier today."

Ivar smiled. "It doesn't hurt that it was cloudy yesterday and the sun is out today."

As they rolled into the station, Nilda dug down into her bag for the stubby little pencil she carried. She tore the title page out of one of her books and passed both across to the butler. "Please, Mr. Charles, may I have a mailing address? I want to send Mrs. Schoenleber a note of gratitude. This was a wonderful rest during our trip, and so generous of her."

His long, stolid face melted into a smile.

"Miss Carlson, nothing would please Mrs. Schoenleber more." He printed her name and address on the paper.

Petter asked, "Why did she do this? I mean, all of this?"

Charles hesitated and licked his lips.

"We will tell no one else," Petter assured him. "But we would like to know."

The train was coming. Nilda could hear it in the distance.

"You know what Schoenleber means?" Charles asked.

"Beautiful life?" Petter guessed.

"Yes. And Mr. and Mrs. Schoenleber had a beautiful life. Very comfortable financially, as you see, and five children, all of whom were bright and handsome. One year they were visiting a friend and business associate in southern Minnesota. A rainstorm in the night spawned a tornado, destroying the house they were in. The business associate, Mr. Schoenleber, and the children all died. She never got over it. She likes to surround herself with young people like you, people who are the age her children would have been."

Nilda felt tears burning her eyes.

Petter asked, "What business, may I ask?"

"She has just returned from a business trip. She owns the majority interest in this railroad."

Petter smiled. "That explains much. Thank you."

Charles left the travelers in the station agent's care, climbed up beside George in the carriage box, and the landau rolled away.

Ivar watched the train pull to a halt. "You know what I liked best about that mansion?"

"What?" Nilda asked.

"The floor didn't move. At all."

CHAPTER 17

"The train arrives at ten thirty. You go pick them up." Einar threw the orders over his shoulder at Signe as he headed out the door.

Signe turned to Knute and Leif. "You boys better hurry, then, since I will need the horse." *He could have mentioned this earlier,* she muttered inside. She caught Rune's look of caution and nodded.

The boys grabbed their dinner pails and ran out the door. "Tante Nilda and Onkel Ivar are coming!" Leif shouted, and both boys cheered.

Signe took the cup of coffee Gerd handed her.

Gerd waved a hand. "Sit down, and we will have breakfast."

Rune set his coffee cup in the steaming dishpan. "Bjorn and I will be dynamiting a few more stumps. Days like today, we sure could use another team of horses."

"Einar says the same thing." Gerd crossed

to the stove and pulled the big pan forward.

"Bjorn!" Signe stopped her son as he was following his far out the door. "Do you have your ear protection?"

He grinned and waved his fur earmuffs. "Ja, Mor. I have these, and lots of cotton in my pocket to wad into my ears. Takk."

"Good." Signe waved him out the door. "I so wish he wasn't helping with the dynamiting. Not just because of the danger. His ears."

Gerd broke eggs into the pan. "That first day of blasting, when Rune sent him home, he said his ears started getting better as soon as he was in the quiet. And his hearing was almost completely returned by bedtime. I agree that it would be best if he got nowhere near the noise, but by plugging his ears with cotton and then covering them with those heavy earmuffs, he seems to be getting along all right."

"But in the long term. What about twenty years from now? Will his hearing be forever affected?"

"No one knows. Only God knows."

Signe's thoughts shifted. Gerd had just expressed trust in God, at least to an extent. That was good news!

Her thoughts shifted again. "Rune mentioned getting another team. And if we have our own farm, we'll have to buy stock. Perhaps I should mention that to Mrs. Benson. Where does one buy livestock around here?"

Gerd shrugged. "Most people raise up their own. We should have bred our mare, but Rosie is too old now." She slid the scrambled eggs onto Signe's plate. "Pick up a newspaper at the store. Might be an ad there. Einar mentioned Red Lake one time, someone up there breeding heavy horses. Good thing Garborg down the road has a bull and a boar."

Kirstin waved both arms from her seat in the rocker. She'd already figured out that she could make it rock by moving forward and back, which made her chortle. Signe had tied a string from arm to arm of the chair and hung some spoons from it to entertain her. Drool running down her chin, Kirstin slapped the spoons together to make noise.

"I will feed her just before I leave. Is the train usually on time?"

Gerd shrugged. "No idea. I never paid attention. But when the wind is just right, you can hear the whistle."

With bread rising, ham and beans simmering in the oven, and Kirstin fed and put down for her nap, Signe gathered her list.

The sound of a stump exploding was so common now that they could almost ignore it.

Rune harnessed Rosie and drove her and the cart up to the back porch. He helped his wife up to the seat and smiled at her. "Tonight we celebrate."

Signe grinned back. "I'm so excited I can hardly sit still. So many things to do, and all needing doing right now."

"Don't forget the paper. Reading some news will be good for a change."

"Knowing Nilda, she will bring all kinds of news."

It was all she could do not to flick the reins and make Rosie pick up the pace from a slow jog to a fast trot. Swallows were dipping mud out of a puddle left from the last rain. Soon all the barns would have swallow nests under the eaves. A killdeer called and ran down the road, dragging one wing to draw them away from her nest in the grass.

Signe sucked in a deep breath of spring and felt joy flood clear to her fingertips. Their first spring in Minnesota, and they were to celebrate it with family arriving. Knute had reminded her that only ten days remained of the school year. The shades of green around her could only be dreamed up by God, some so bright they hurt her winter eyes. She inhaled again and closed her eyes to try to identify all the scents that made up spring. Overturned earth, green things growing, something blooming sweet, someone cleaning out their barn or spreading manure on a field, and pine trees emitting their own perfume.

She stopped Rosie by the railing at the store and climbed down. She could hear children laughing and calling, so it must be recess time at the school. Shouted commands drifted from the stacks of logs being loaded onto flat rail cars to be hauled to the lumber mills up around Red Lake and beyond.

"Good morning," Mrs. Benson called as soon as Signe opened the door. "Isn't this a perfect spring day? Do you have time for a cup of coffee?"

Signe returned the greeting and the smile. "I have some things to get, including a newspaper and information, and when the train comes, our family will be here."

"That is so exciting. Come, let's have coffee on the back porch. I've been thinking of putting rocking chairs on the front porch. Make people take some time to enjoy the world around them." She checked the clock. "Half an hour until the train gets here. Enough time for coffee and to catch up.

How is that sweet baby girl of yours doing?"

Signe followed her through the storeroom and out back, where a big maple tree was still leafing out. The swing that Leif had so enjoyed still hung from the lower branch.

"You sit there, and I'll bring the coffee out." Mrs. Benson pointed to the chairs by a round table dappled by sun through the branches.

Signe sat with her eyes closed, experiencing spring with her other senses. Between tending Kirstin, planting the garden, keeping the house, and feeding ravenously hungry men, she never had time to just sit like this and — and what? Experience.

"Shade trees sure make a difference around a house, don't they?" Signe smiled as her hostess brought out the serving tray. "I promised Gerd I would plant several around her house. She asked for a birch, just like I am going to plant by my house." She eyed the plate of cookies and wrapped her hands around a coffee cup. "This must be close to what heaven is like."

"I think so too. Good thing you came by to remind me to stop and let the sun drive away the cold of winter. Sometimes it seems to settle deep into my bones and makes it hard to get warm." Mrs. Benson sat down and pushed the plate closer to Signe. "I just baked these this morning, and I'm so glad you came to enjoy them with me. My grandma's ginger cookies."

Signe dunked her crisp cookie in her coffee and closed her eyes, the better to appreciate the flavors. "This is so good."

"I wish we could get together more often like this. Women need to spend time with each other. I sure hope you and Gerd will come to our Ladies Aid group. It will help you get to know some of the others."

That reminded Signe. "We can't thank Mr. Benson enough for bringing the others out to help dig our cellar. Rune was so grateful for the progress they made."

"That's what neighbors do for each other. He had me rub liniment on his back that night." Mrs. Benson laughed. "He said you have a right nice place to put your house. Shame you don't have a lake on that property. Did Knute get to go fishing with the reverend and his boys?"

"One time. He sure loves to hunt and fish. His snares keep us in rabbit." Signe reached for another cookie. "Do you know anyone who has a team of horses for sale?"

Mrs. Benson shook her head. "Not off hand. The mister would know more than I. We'll ask him. You might check that board by the door. Sometimes people post notes there when they have a need or something to sell. I saw one for a litter of puppies."

"Really? The boys would love to have a dog."

"How are the cats doing?"

"No mice dare invade our house, but neither one of them is much interested in being a barn cat. I take them down to hunt, and they show up on the back porch after a while. I think one of them is going to have kittens."

After a few more quiet moments, Mrs. Benson set down her coffee cup. "How about I fill your order while you go to the platform and pick up your family? I'm looking forward to meeting them."

"I will." Signe stood and stretched. "Takk for the coffee."

"I'll send some cookies home for those boys of yours, if you don't mind."

"Mind?" Signe's eyebrows arched. "They will be delighted."

Waving good-bye, she backed the horse and cart away from the store and drove over to the station south of the loading area for logs. The train whistle sounded far down the tracks, and Rosie flicked her ears.

Signe could not bear to sit still, so she climbed down and stroked Rosie's neck and ears while she waited. When the train whistled again, Rosie laid back her ears and snorted.

"Easy, you've been here before," Signe soothed. "That monster is not going to come after you."

Perhaps she should have tied the horse to the hitching rail nearby, but comforting her kept Signe's hands busy. Another blast of the whistle, and Rosie tried backing up. Ears flat against her head, she reared enough to get both front feet in the air, but Signe gripped an ear and grasped the lines just below the bit. She kept up a singsong voice, saying soothing nonsense syllables.

Steam blew out the screeching wheels, and the monster finally halted. Rosie shook her head, snorted, stamped one more time, and settled down with a puff of breath, now that the train no longer personally threatened her.

Signe watched the three passenger cars and finally saw the conductor help a young woman down the steps. When she reached the platform, she turned to thank him. A young man followed right behind her, handing the conductor two carpetbags as he stepped down.

Signe waved and called their names, not daring to leave Rosie in case something frightened her again.

"Signe!" Sun glinted off the gold streaks in Nilda's crown of hair as she lifted her skirts and dashed across the wide boards of the platform to throw her arms around Signe.

Rosie tossed her head and pulled away again.

"Oh, I scared the horse. Sorry." Nilda hugged Signe again, and then, keeping one arm around Signe's waist, held out her other hand for Rosie to sniff. "What a good horse you are." She heaved a sigh. "I am so grateful to be here. Oh, Signe, I didn't think we would ever make it. This train ride from Blackduck seemed as long as the one from Duluth."

Ivar set their carpetbags down and grinned at Signe. "We made it. We finally made it." He looked around. "I hope we can fit our trunks and crate into that little cart." He returned her hug and looked down the train to the baggage car, where dollies of boxes, crates, and trunks were being unloaded. "We better get down there to load before the train leaves. It doesn't stop long."

Since several others had gotten off the train too, the baggage was still unloading.

"They must have supplies for others around here too," Ivar said, eyeing the large pile of crates being offloaded from the train.

"Probably for the store," Signe said. "There's a mail pouch, oh, and a bundle of newspapers."

Mr. Benson drove up with a wagon, and the railway men started moving boxes and crates to that. "You want some help, Mrs. Carlson?" he called.

"Takk." She started to lead Rosie to that end of the platform, but Ivar took over.

"We'll toss those bags on top last," he said.

"I have supplies to pick up at the store too," Signe told him. "The three of us on the seat will be tight."

"Who cares?" Nilda said. "Oh, Signe, this has been such a long year since you and Rune left. I have missed you dreadfully."

Signe nodded. "I learned that homesickness is not a joke. I cried too many tears to count, I missed you all so much. Things are good now, but one of these days I will tell you what was really going on here. I could not bear to write it all in my letters. I never have liked whiners." The two women locked arms and followed the horse and cart.

"Tante Gerd is taking care of the baby?" Nilda asked.

"Ja. As far as she's concerned, the sun rises and sets on Kirstin. She is like the jewel to all of us. Leif especially loves to make her giggle. No one can keep a straight face when she gets going." Other than Einar, but Signe did not mention him. No sense dimming a perfect day.

"You want me to drive?" Ivar asked after helping them up to the seat.

"If you want. If we give Rosie her head, she will take us home. The boys ride her to school every morning." Signe smiled around the tears forming in her eyes. "I cannot begin to tell you how happy I am to have you here. Family from home, my best friend, let alone sister-in-law."

Nilda winked. "Don't forget Ivar. I had to chase all the girls away from him on the ship. That baby face of his caught lots of attention."

Ivar rolled his eyes, but in spite of himself, red crept up his neck. He shook his head. "Not that my *older* sister would exaggerate or any such thing."

Nilda shivered. "The voyage over was so bad, everyone was puking their guts out and wondering if they were going to die from seasickness."

Ivar nodded in agreement. "One old man and a baby did die. They buried them at sea after the storm let up. That was so sad."

At the store, Signe introduced Nilda and Ivar to Mrs. Benson, who invited them for coffee. "I made fresh ginger cookies this morning. In fact, I am sending some home for the boys. Your nephews are becoming fine young men."

"Takk, but I think we will get on home," Signe said.

"I understand." Mrs. Benson handed up several bags. "Tell Gerd that is the last of the yarn for a while. Your newspaper and some mail are here too." She patted Nilda's knee. "I will be out to see you soon." To Signe, she asked, "Do you have any butter or eggs to send with the boys? I don't know what we will do when school is out. They have been our errand runners."

"I'll check our stores at home," Signe said. "Let me know when Ladies Aid meets. Perhaps we can break away for a while. Especially after the garden is planted. But at least we will see you in church."

"True, I am always grateful the store closes on Sundays." Mrs. Benson stepped back. "So glad to meet you, Miss Carlson. Mister too." She waved as Ivar turned the horse and cart toward home. Rosie picked up her hooves immediately in spite of the load she was hauling.

Signe and Nilda chattered away, exchanging family news.

"Do you know many of these neighbors?"

Ivar asked when there was a slight lull.

Signe shook her head. "You have to understand something. Onkel Einar drove away all the neighbors, ordered them all off his land some time ago. He is a stubborn man, and all he can really think about is cutting down the big trees so he can clear the land for farming. Selling the logs is the income for the farm."

"What happens when it is all logged off?"

"Who knows?" She decided not to go into the conflict they'd had with him regarding paying off the tickets and earning wages. Maybe he had learned some lessons in how to treat people.

"Rune mentioned in one letter that Einar seems to have it in for you," Nilda said.

"Ja, he blames me for everything. I'm hoping he is at least polite with you. He knows now that when Rune takes a stand, he will do what he says he will do. Einar figured all the boys would be home working, but Rune told him no, our boys would be in school. Bjorn was old enough to make a choice, and he would rather work out in the woods than anything." Signe took a breath. "Ah, so much has happened here this year. I am so grateful that Gerd has gotten much of her health back. She was bedbound when we got here, but now she is able to help with the cooking and the wash, and she has knitting needles in her hands all the time unless she is taking care of Kirstin. I think our baby gets all the love that Gerd did not know she had to give."

"How wonderful."

"She saved my life and Kirstin's too, not that she would ever admit that." Signe nodded and patted Nilda's hands. "Enough about us, what has been going on at home?"

"We had enough food to eat this winter, but mostly because we live on a farm. Last year was the first year I did not go up to the seter but worked for other people around town to bring in some money. Mor keeps slamming that loom and is able to sell some of her rugs." Nilda glanced over her shoulder. "Wait until you see all we brought. Good thing you are building a new house. From the sounds of Gerd's house, there isn't room there for everything."

Ivar tightened the lines as Rosie picked up her pace. "Sorry, girl, you don't need to work up a sweat like that."

"Ja, the boys get home a lot faster in the afternoon than they get to school in the morning."

"I cannot believe how big this country is." Ivar shook his head. "Those days on the Great Lakes, and then from Duluth to here.

I looked on a map, and Minnesota is kind of right in the middle of Amerika. I did not realize North Dakota was so far away."

Nilda nodded. "Ivar really wants to go to Blessing to find work there with Tante Ingeborg."

Ivar added, "But we are here now, and here we will be for at least a year until we pay off Nilda's debt to Onkel Einar."

"We all managed to buy Ivar's ticket, so he is not beholden to Onkel Einar," Nilda explained.

Signe nodded. "Good for you. But there is plenty of work for you here, and I know Onkel Einar is looking forward to another hand in the woods. The more trees he ships, the better."

And I will make sure he pays you a decent wage. She wondered who she could ask about what the going rate was for lumberjacks. She knew Einar and Ivar had already come to terms, but that didn't mean Einar wouldn't try to back out in some way if Ivar upset him.

One moment she was so thrilled Nilda and Ivar were here, the next she dreaded what could be ahead. But at least she and her family would be in a house of their own before the end of summer.

If all went well.

Chapter 18

The house looked smaller than what Nilda had pictured in her mind. It looked teeny compared to the Schoenleber home. But the Schoenleber mansion had felt like a museum, not a home, empty of family. And that made all the difference.

She glanced at Ivar to see if he was surprised too. Nothing showed on his face; usually she could figure out what he was thinking, but not now. The barn sat some ways back from the house with a windmill and well house in between. A man was disking with a team in a field off to the west. The field looked to be several acres in size.

An explosion from near the wood line sent debris into the air and shocked their ears.

Signe explained, "Rune and Bjorn are dynamiting stumps, the quickest way to get them out."

"That's Onkel Einar out with the team then?" Nilda asked.

"Ja, he's getting the field ready to plant corn. Rune plowed and disked the garden the other day. We're making it bigger this year — more potatoes and sweet corn, especially."

"Where are Knute and Leif?"

"School won't be out for another week. They get home around four and usually start chores. They take care of the livestock and the chickens."

Ivar pointed ahead. "Look at the size of those pines. Was it still solid woods when Onkel Einar bought this land?"

"No, the family that homesteaded it had already cleared these front acres. He built the buildings and almost doubled the pasture land. We hay a good part of that too."

"Two cows out there?" Ivar asked, squinting toward the pasture.

Signe nodded. "Ja, and a steer from last year. The heifer had her calf about a month ago, so it is still in the barn. The yearling must be lying down. Leif takes care of the chickens, and Knute the pigs. Two sows and two gilts will be farrowing. We hope to trade a couple of weaner pigs for a young boar." She pointed to the front door of the house with its stoop entry. "We'll bring your trunks in there to the parlor. Probably the crate will have to be stored in the shop for now."

"So what first?" Nilda asked.

"We'll tie Rosie up by the back door until someone comes to help unload. Come and meet Tante Gerd."

"And Kirstin." Nilda nudged Signe. "She's the important one." She grinned at Ivar. "Here we go," she whispered. *Here we go.*

The kitchen door stood open, and through the screen door they could hear a baby giggling and a woman talking with her.

Nilda asked, "Is she always that happy?"

"Pretty much. Unless she's hungry, and then cover your ears." Signe held open the screen door. "We're here," she announced.

Gerd, with Kirstin on her hip, greeted them. "Welcome. Come in, come in. I saved dinner for you."

Signe made the introductions. "Nilda and Ivar, meet Tante Gerd and, of course, our Kirstin."

Gerd nodded. "Glad you are here safely. Welcome to Minnesota. Do you want to speak Norwegian or English?"

Nilda exchanged a look with Ivar. He nodded. "Norwegian is far easier yet. Takk."

So this is the Gerd I've heard so much about. She's smaller than I thought and looks far older than Mor said she was. Must be from being so ill. Nilda smiled. "Takk. I heard that you have been knitting for everyone. Mor said she remembered how you love to knit. We brought some yarn for you."

Gerd's eyes lit up. "Leif and I have been wanting to get some sheep. Maybe soon we can make our own yarn."

Nilda hid a smile. Gerd would be pleased when she saw what Nilda and Ivar had brought with them in the crate.

Knute and Leif came slamming into the house.

"Onkel Ivar, you finally got here!" Knute grinned up at him.

"You've grown a foot since I saw you," Ivar said.

Knute looked down. "No, I only have two, same as always."

Ivar rolled his eyes and knocked Knute's hat off, ruffling his hair. "And you too, Leif. My goodness, I hardly recognize you."

Leif stood for the obligatory hair ruffling. "Guess what! You can help us with the chores."

"Leif, Knute, why are you home so early?" Signe's eyebrows flattened out. "Did you skip school?"

"Nei, we told Mr. Jahnson our family from Norway had arrived on the train, and he said since we had our work done, we could leave early."

Signe shook her head. "All right. Now, regarding chores. Give them one night to settle in. Why don't you two get the supplies for the house out of the cart and then drive around to the front to unload the trunks?"

Ivar followed Leif and Knute out the back door. Both boys stared at the cart. "You brought a lot of stuff," Knute said.

"Wait until you see," Ivar assured them.

Leif dragged a bag of oats off of the wagon. "Good thing we got oats again. Onkel Einar bagged up most of what was left to seed the field."

Knute set bags and brown-wrapped packages on the kitchen table. "Come on, Leif. There is more."

Out at the cart, Ivar pointed. "Leif, you take those bags in, and Knute and I will meet you at the front door. I think we can haul these trunks inside."

In minutes they had the trunks in the parlor and were headed for the shop to leave the crate.

"What's in the crate?" Leif asked.

Ivar grinned. "I'm not telling until we open it."

Leif pointed to the long building on the

right. "The shop started out as a machine shed, but Far got Onkel Einar to let him close part of it in for the winter so we could work there. Onkel Einar had the sharpening wheel in that three-sided building. Far said he couldn't believe Onkel Einar sharpened axes and saws in there during the winter. He made sure a stove could heat it. We added more later."

"So this is where Rune is making skis?"

"Ja, and furniture, and Onkel Einar works on the machinery and keeping the saws and axes sharp." Leif ran to open the door while Knute and Ivar wrestled the crate off the cart and lugged it inside.

"Looks like a good place to work. That stove must have really made a difference."

"Far made sure. There are the skis over there. We ran out of time to finish them this year. Did you know skis take a long time to make?"

"Ja, that's why not many people make them."

They closed the door, and Leif drove the wagon to the barn. Ivar and Knute carried in the sacks of oats, and Leif unhitched Rosie and lifted off the harness.

"I can't reach the team yet," Leif explained, "but Rosie is just enough smaller. She's a good horse. Would you believe she is twenty years old? She works hard too." He stroked the old mare's shoulder. "We better put her in the corral for now so she can't drink."

The boys introduced Ivar to the rest of the animals, showed him the well house and the smoke house, and returned to the house to leap up the back porch.

"You ever set dynamite?" Knute asked.

"Nei. No need of it in Norway."

"Far will teach you. Bjorn really likes blowing up stumps. We bring the bigger chunks of stumps up to the house and burn the rest. Wait until you see a big tree crash." Knute held the door open.

"Sit down, sit down." Gerd pointed to a chair. "We did not wait for you, as you can see." She retrieved the last of the dishes from the warming oven and set them by Ivar's plate. "Help yourself." She shook her head at the boys. "You can have the leftover corn bread and glasses of milk." She handed them each a plate and set two glasses on the table. "Knute, did you check your snares today?"

"Not yet," he said around a mouthful of corn bread. "But I will right away. You want to come with me, Onkel Ivar?"

"Ja. Might we have fried rabbit for supper?"

"If there are two in the snares. Must be about time to move them farther out again. Knute tries to keep the rabbits from grazing on the garden. We need a dog to chase them away." Leif drained his milk glass and wiped his milk mustache off with the back of his hand, earning a frown from Signe. "I saw an ad for puppies on the wall at the store."

"If there were no rabbits around, what would we eat?" Signe asked.

Gerd shook her head. "There are always plenty of rabbits around. Bjorn has brought in a couple deer too and a goose last fall. This year the smokehouse was going most of the time with pork and venison."

"Do you like to go fishing?" Knute asked Ivar.

"Ja, I do. But not out on a fishing boat on the North Sea."

"You did that?" Both boys wore round eyes.

Knute said, "I went with the Reverend Skarstead and the Bergens one Sunday, but the fish weren't biting much yet. There was still ice on the lake."

"How far away?"

"A mile or so to the west. Onkel Einar says there are lakes all around us, but he says fishing is a waste of time."

Nilda and Ivar swapped raised eyebrows.

"There aren't a lot of lake or stream fish left near our home in Norway," he said. "Fried fish sounds almost as good as fried rabbit."

Bjorn and Rune greeted the others from the door.

"You boys better get some wood in that box," Rune said as he crossed the kitchen to greet his younger sister and brother. He smiled. "I was beginning to think you'd never get here."

"He's as bad as the boys at waiting." Signe swayed from side to side with Kirstin, who waved her arms at her far.

"Who is this man with you?" Nilda asked, grinning at Bjorn. "Is there something in the air here that turns a boy into a man in a year?"

"Not in the air, but with an axe and a crosscut saw." Bjorn's neck was turning red, moving up to his cheeks.

"Ah, but I can still make you blush." Nilda gave him a hug in spite of his embarrassment. "So you chose to work in the woods rather than finish school?"

"Ja, but Far and Mor were not happy about it. Onkel Einar has taught me a lot."

"Well, good." Ivar grinned. "Now he can teach me."

Knute and Leif each dumped an armload

in the woodbox and went back out for more. Leif made sure the door did not slam with a grin at Tante Gerd.

"That coffee still hot?" Rune asked.

Gerd pulled the pot over on the stove. "In a minute. I'll make more for supper."

Rune sat down at the table with the others. "What are we having for supper?"

"Fried rabbit if the snares are full, otherwise the last of the ham." Gerd fetched a cup from the cupboard.

"Oh." Knute looked at Onkel Ivar. "You want to come?"

He glanced at Rune and shrugged, then followed Knute out the door.

Listening to the banter between the men, Nilda's mind flashed back to Tilly, one of her girlfriends in school, who had always said that men were all alike, only wanting one thing. That was how she described the kind of boy Dreng was. But she was so wrong. She thought of Petter, from the ship. He was about Dreng's age, but he was so pleasant, and mature, and clever. And most of all, Nilda had never once felt worried or uncomfortable in his presence. So all men were not like that. In fact, nearly all the men Nilda had met were polite and . . . well, safe.

Rune and Bjorn were telling her about getting their logs hauled to the railroad. Imagine cutting enough trees to pay for building a house! And now they were talking about a man named Oskar, whom Rune had hired to help haul logs. Even this Oskar, apparently widowed recently, sounded like a perfectly decent fellow.

Was all of northern Minnesota populated by eligible, polite, interesting young men? Deep inside, Nilda laughed at herself. *Silly girl! But I do want to be married and have a family, especially here in Amerika.*

She answered Rune's questions about home while he and Bjorn drank their coffee. Gerd poured the last of it into their cups, and Signe took the pot to the sink to wash and fill it with cold water. She added ground coffee, using up the last of that tin.

"I'll grind more," Nilda said. "Just show me where things are."

Signe shook her head. "Today, at least, you should still be a guest."

"I have been lazing around since we left home."

Her sister-in-law laughed. "All right. The coffee beans are in a tin up on the third pantry shelf on the right. And the grinder is next to it. I grind quite a bit at a time, as we go through it so fast."

"But it is real coffee, not mixed with roasted grain to make it go further?"

"Ja, real coffee."

"No wonder it was so good."

When Ivar and the two boys returned with three rabbits, Signe nodded. "One in every snare?"

"Nei, I set four snares this time. One is only half grown." Knute dug a knife out of the drawer and tested the sharpness with a finger. Without saying another word, he dug out the whetstone, spit on it, and set to sharpening.

Ivar looked at his brother, nodding while his eyes crinkled. "You got two knives? We can get done faster."

Later, with the three rabbit carcasses in cold salt water, Rune, Bjorn, and Ivar returned to blowing stumps, while Knute and Leif left to start chores. Signe nursed the baby and put her down to sleep, all the while she and Nilda talked. Nilda had brought out her knitting, and Gerd was nodding over hers.

"If you would like to take a nap, Tante Gerd, now would be a good time." Signe paused in setting out the ingredients for sour cream cookies. "I'm going to show Nilda the cellar and the well house, and Kirstin should sleep for a while."

Gerd heaved a sigh. "Ja, I s'pose so. I keep hoping that one of these days I'll be able to work through the day like I used to."

"True, but look how much better you are doing."

"Ja, thanks to you." Shaking her head, Gerd looked at Nilda. "Only by the grace of God and General Signe. I will take you up on the nap. Make yourself at home." Gerd shut the bedroom door behind her.

Since Kirstin was sleeping, Signe showed off the well house and smokehouse, and they ended the small tour in the cellar. "We are down to rationing jars of canned goods. We ran out of jams and jellies a month or so ago, and you can see what we have left of the pickles. Good thing I canned small potatoes, because the fresh ones were looking pretty sad at the end. I wanted to keep some for seed, but Mrs. Benson assured me they would have seed potatoes at the store. That's what is in that basket. I'm going to plant a lot more this year."

"Is this soil deep enough for potatoes?"

"We go down as far as we can, then heap compost over the hills to keep them from getting sunburned. Learning to garden here is different than at home."

Back in the kitchen, with the smell of coffee filling the room, Signe poured two cups and moved a cookie plate within reach. They'd just sat down when Kirstin made her first waking noises. She squeaked and squirmed, talked to her fingers a bit, and when her voice took on an insistent note, Signe retrieved her from her bed and brought her to the table. "You ready to go to your tante Nilda now?" Signe held Kirstin up and kissed her cheek.

Nilda held up her arms while Kirstin studied her, then leaned closer to her mor.

"Not yet, eh, little one?" Signe murmured gently. "But soon. Let me nurse her, and then we can cut up the rabbits."

"I will cut up the meat while you nurse her, and then we can brown it and let it finish in the oven?"

"I made noodles and dried them a few weeks ago, so we can have those with gravy and the canned corn we brought up and biscuits."

"And cookies." Nilda took another off the plate.

Supper was ready to be put on the table as the sun sank toward the horizon. The men and boys all came in together, Ivar making the boys laugh and Rune enjoying the banter. The man who must be Einar wore a scowl.

Rune motioned to Nilda. "Onkel Einar,

I'd like you to meet my sister, Nilda Carlson."

" 'Bout time you got here."

Nilda glanced at Rune and saw that Signe and Gerd were both observing the floor. Laughter left the room. "Takk for purchasing my ticket so I could come to Amerika. Mor sends her greetings."

Einar grunted and made his way around the table to his chair.

The others washed their hands and took their places while Signe and Nilda set the serving platter and bowls on the table.

"Ivar, you sit over there between Leif and Knute." Rune waited for them all to be seated. "Let's say our grace together tonight. *I Jesu navn går vi til bords. . . .*"

One by one, the others joined in and finished with the *amen.*

Einar filled his plate and set to shoveling in the food as if he'd not eaten in a week.

Nilda sat next to Signe. Forks scraping on plates, someone asking for more biscuits, another asking for the salt. Einar filled his plate again, ate, mopped the plate with a biscuit half, pushed back his chair and, setting his hat on his head, strode out the door.

Rune and the boys settled back in their chairs, and a sigh of relief floated to the ceiling.

"Can I have more milk?" Leif asked.

Knute passed the pitcher. "Mor, do we have to go to school tomorrow?"

Signe gave him a look. "Ja, you do."

"I told you." Leif made a face at Knute, who shielded himself behind Ivar.

Signe retrieved Kirstin from the rocking chair where she'd been tied in and settled her on her lap. She mashed a noodle in the gravy and spooned a bit into the baby's mouth. Kirstin gummed the strange substance around, then pushed it out to run down her chin.

Signe wiped off her face. "You're just not excited about solid food yet, are you?" She looked across the table. "If you are done eating, pass your plates around, and we'll get the cookies."

Gerd brought a plate piled high with cookies from the pantry and passed them around.

Nilda laid a hand on Signe's shoulder. "I'll get the coffee."

"Takk."

"Can we have coffee too?" Knute asked.

Ivar nudged him. "You're too young to drink coffee."

"Not the way Mor makes it."

"Like our mor used to?" Ivar looked at Signe, who nodded. "All right, we'll all have coffee and cookies and toast our new life in Amerika." He watched until everyone had their drink and cookie in hand, then he raised his cup over his head. "God bless our life here in Minnesota of Amerika. *Skål.*"

"Is Onkel Einar always like that?" Nilda asked under her breath.

Signe rolled her eyes. "Ja, pretty much."

"Uff da."

Chapter 19

Nilda watched as Einar pushed his chair back from the breakfast table and stood up. "Rune, you take over the team today. Ivar, you and Bjorn come with me."

Rune asked, "What about the stumps?"

"Go back to that tomorrow. Should be able to start seeding tomorrow. After dinner I'm going to look at that team." Einar headed for the door.

Rune nodded. "We can blast stumps then. The boys can pick up pieces when they get home."

Einar paused. "How much dynamite is left?"

"Quarter of the box."

"How many to blow at your place?"

"Six, ten."

"Keep out that many sticks."

Nilda listened to the exchange. Every word that left Einar's lips sounded angry. Everyone back home was soft-spoken. Nilda resisted the urge to shake her head. How would she ever get used to this?

Bjorn and Ivar followed Einar out the door. "I'll hitch up the team," Bjorn threw over his shoulder.

"Now that was a surprise." Still at the table, Rune stacked his dirty dishes.

"What?" Nilda asked.

"He's going to look at a team of horses that's for sale. I sure hope he can get it. Ours need a rest." He rose from the table. "You going to start planting the garden today?"

"Ja, potatoes first. And peas. It'd be good if the boys could help us instead."

Rune nodded and smiled at his sister. "Welcome to the way we live."

Nilda followed him out onto the porch. "Is this usual for Onkel Einar?"

"Ja, why?"

"I know you hinted at his way in your letters, but I just wondered." She looked out over the fields. "It's pretty flat here, compared to home."

"Ja, and no mountains on the horizon. Open land, once the big trees are gone. If I let myself think of the mountains or life in Norway, I get homesick. Signe had a real hard time with that, but then, Gerd was not as she is now."

Nilda watched him go. Her brother had aged in the year he was here, but there was something in him that she had not seen in Norway. She'd have to think on that to figure it out.

Signe joined her on the porch. "I'll get the basket of seed potatoes. We should have cut them up last night."

They cut the potatoes into chunks, making sure there were two eyes in every piece. With Nilda carrying the potato sacks and Signe bringing two hoes and her gardening basket, in which were two stakes strung with twine to mark the rows, they headed for the garden.

"When we got here," Signe said, "the weeds had taken over the garden, so we had to weed really carefully. I have no idea how Einar planted the garden last spring, not with taking care of Gerd and the house too. You cannot believe how filthy this place was. And overrun by mice."

"But now you have cats."

"Ja, he was not happy about that either. One of the many things he holds against me. He does not like cats in the house."

"But he didn't mind mice?" Nilda shuddered. "I hate mice in the house." She shaded her eyes with her hand. "You don't have anyone living close by."

"Nei, but we finally met some of the neighbors at church. To the west are the Garborgs. The boys know their children from school." She handed one of the stakes to Nilda. "You take this end down to where the plowed land ends and sink it in the dirt so we can mark straight rows. We'll plant till we run out of potatoes. I'll dig the hole, you drop in the seed, and push the dirt back over it with your foot."

The potato planting went quickly. They moved the stakes over and switched off between hoeing and burying potato chunks.

"If it weren't for Gerd, Kirstin would be in a sling on my back, helping her mor plant. This sure goes faster with two people."

"Do people stop to have coffee around here?" Nilda leaned on the handle of the hoe and used her apron to wipe the sweat off her face. "Where is that wind you've talked about?"

"Let's set the stakes for the first row of peas and at least get a drink of water."

They walked to the house and met Gerd at the doorway.

The older woman smiled. "I was just coming to call you for coffee. And Kirstin is fussy and nuzzling for her mor."

"Good timing. Potatoes are in, peas by

dinner." Signe put the pea seeds in a large bowl and poured water on them.

Nilda pondered this new life as the women sipped coffee and discussed planting beans soon. The soil here was as rich as any she'd known in Norway, and flatter. *It is so much easier to plant a garden that isn't sloping. And look at the size of this garden.* There was even an unplanted berm around it, as if there were so much land that you could afford to let a strip lie idle. Wouldn't it be lovely to plant flowers on that berm?

By the time the men came in for dinner, Nilda was cleaning and sharpening the hoes, and Signe was feeding Kirstin again.

Nilda and Signe had finished the early crops of potatoes, peas, lettuce, and greens and were working on the second row of beans when the boys came up the lane, the little horse under them as eager to get home as they were. They hollered and waved before Leif bailed off with the dinner pails and Knute let their horse loose in the corral. The little mare immediately trotted to a sandy hollow spot and rolled from side to side, kicking her legs in the air. Knute made his way, whistling, up to the garden gate.

Nilda grinned at him. "You two sure are fortunate to have a horse to ride back and forth to school."

"I know. Onkel Einar wanted us to get home faster so we could get more work done here. Leif and I do all the daily farm chores so the others can be out felling the big trees."

"They cut and split most of the wood for the stove too." Signe set her garden basket at the base of the gate post. "Let's go have coffee. I imagine a certain someone will think it time to eat too."

Knute nodded. "Then Leif and I better cut up that tree and get to splitting. You are about out of wood."

Nilda clapped a hand on his shoulder. "How was school?"

"Almost done." He turned to walk between them toward the house. "They have a big party on the last day, which is two days from now. All kinds of races and such. Sometimes the parents come too."

"Do you want us to come?" Signe asked.

He shook his head. "You don't need to. I'd just as soon get home as fast as I can. Jason Bergson said they even have ice cream on the last day and prizes for the races."

They mounted the stairs to the porch, where there was no longer a stack of firewood along the wall.

"I can split wood too." Nilda looked at

Signe. "It would not be my first time, you know."

"I know. You split wood, and I'll churn the butter. We can plant more in the garden tomorrow."

"Mor, did I tell you we have a broody hen?" In the kitchen, Leif grinned around a mouthful of cookie and a milk mustache.

"How many eggs under her?" Gerd asked.

"I'll check. How many do you want?"

"Ten, at least. We need fryers and pullets both."

"Isn't it early for a hen to be setting?" Nilda asked as she dried her hands after washing the garden soil off them.

"A bit, but it will be warm in three weeks when they hatch. Some of those hens are getting up in years and will end in the stew pot this year. We need a younger rooster too."

"How come you don't have a dog here?" Nilda caught the raised eyebrow from Signe. Figuring she already knew the answer, she watched Gerd.

"Einar doesn't . . ."

Nilda nodded. "Ja, I see."

"But he got used to the cats," Gerd continued, "and even he admitted cats in the barn would be good, and I think it's about time we had a dog here too. Help keep away the varmints."

Knute pushed back his chair. "I'll check the snares now, and then we need to start sawing."

Nilda nodded at Leif. "Come on, show me where things are, and we can start."

Leif hopped up from the table and they went outside. "Mor said we should wear gloves so we don't get blisters."

"Good idea. Where might I find them?"

"In a box on the shelf on the porch. During the winter we keep it behind the stove to dry things out. I'll get them for you." He scampered to the porch and leaped off the edge a moment later. "This one has a hole but they should work."

Nilda pulled on the gloves and grabbed one end of the crosscut saw. Sawing wood felt good on her shoulder muscles and made her quickly realize the need for leather gloves. She had winter hands, and the garden hoe had already started a blister.

"Remember," Leif warned, "pull, don't push."

"Takk." She grinned at him. "You know your stuff."

He set the saw at the end of the tree trunk that rested on two sawbucks. "You pull."

They got into a rhythm after only a couple of bucklings and reminders, and soon the first spool dropped to the ground. They grabbed the trunk and hauled it forward to give them another fifteen-inch length, then set to sawing again.

When Knute arrived after hanging two rabbit carcasses on the porch hooks, he rolled the first spool to the chopping block and set it on top. With one swing, he nearly buried the ax head in the center. Wiggling it free, he swung the ax again, and the two halves split apart.

Nilda watched him out of the corner of her eye while she sawed. The blade buckled. "Oops." She looked at Leif, who shook his head.

"Onkel Einar says if we break a blade, we have to buy a new one."

One more mark against "Onkel" Einar.

"What happens when we run out of tree here?" she asked.

"We need to find another one. When school is out, Knute and I get to go cut up branches from the big trees to use for the stove. Onkel Einar was going to burn them all, but it seemed such a waste."

"Now you sound like your far. He has always been careful not to waste things. Remember, in Norway we don't have all these trees to cut for firewood. So we were very careful not to waste anything."

They had just moved the chopping block closer to the rounds when they heard the jangle of a team coming up the lane. Looking up, Nilda saw Einar and Bjorn driving a team with two other horses trotting behind on leads.

"Onkel Einer got another team." The boys grinned at her. Then kept on splitting, one on the second chopping block.

"Where are we going to stack all this?" Nilda asked. She nudged Leif. "Let's take a quick break and go see the new horses."

Einar drove the team down to the barn, where he and Bjorn unharnessed their team. Bjorn led their horses to the corral while Einar started harnessing the new team.

Nilda and the boys stood off to the side, admiring the new team. Rune and Ivar walked up with their tools slung in a sack on their backs and joined them.

"You finished with the stumps?" Einar asked.

Rune nodded. "Even those on my land."

"Got some time yet. I'll hitch these two to the disk and see how they do in the field."

Bjorn stepped in beside Einar and held the crupper while he adjusted the tugs. "That's not what the fellow said, Onkel Einar. He said hitch one of ours to a new one for a week or so until they get used to the work and the place. Settle them. This is the first they've ever left their farm."

"You saying I can't handle a team, boy?"

"No sir. Just saying what he said; they're trained to pull, but they're green."

"Not you, and not some stranger going to tell me what to do." Einar walked the new team over to the disk.

Bjorn shrugged and hooked the tugs in.

"Good-looking team," Rune commented. "Big, good muscle, bulky."

"The mare is pregnant." Einar settled himself onto the metal seat of the disk and flipped the lines. The horse on the right did a sidle dance and snorted, but his teammate started forward at the second flip of the lines and a barked order.

Then a gust of wind caught Nilda's apron and flapped it.

The horse on the right jumped forward, half rearing, and the other bolted into a gallop.

"Whoa, whoa!" Einar yelled, hauling back on the lines with all his might. The disk tipped one way and then the other. Einar flew off backward, landing on his back with a horrible grinding thump. The lines flew free, then wrapped around the disk seat.

Ivar and Bjorn ran for the team. Rune and Nilda leaped to Einar's side.

Rune knelt next to him. "Einar!"
No response.
"He's breathing." Nilda said from his other side. "Check his head — is he bleeding?"
Rune felt the back of the man's head. But when he drew his hand out, there was no blood. "One spot feels rather soft. Most likely right where he hit. Einar, can you hear me?"
Still no response.
Nilda felt his neck and pinched both hands.
"What the — ?" Einar muttered but the words were still clear. He jerked his hands away from Nilda. "What happened?" He blinked and blinked again. "What — where — ?"
"Just lie still," Rune urged, "let's see if anything is broken."
"Nei, I can . . ." Einar started to raise his head but let it fall back down, saved by Rune's arm, which cushioned him.
"Lie still! Don't be a fool."
Nilda stared at her brother. She'd never heard him use that forceful of a tone before.
Einar groaned but did as he was told.
Nilda looked up to see Ivar and Bjorn leading the new team, still dragging the disk, back to the barn. The horses' ears and

the whites of their eyes told of their fright. They jigged in place but were settling as they walked.

"Tell me when something hurts." Rune lifted each of Einar's arms and legs and bent them. "The hip?"

"Ja. My head."

"How bad is he?" Signe softly asked from Rune's side. Nilda hadn't heard her come from the house.

"No broken bones that I can find. But he plowed dirt with his head."

"Bleeding?"

"Not that I can find."

"Einar, can you see me?" Signe asked.

His eyes fluttered twice, then opened. "Ja."

She held up her hand. "How many fingers do you see?"

"Three. No time for games." He groaned again. "Help me up."

Rune laid a hand on his shoulder. "Not yet."

A string of expletives filled the air.

"Just listen," Rune said, getting forceful again. "If you have broken bones in your neck or back, you could make the injury far worse, so just give us some time."

Signe looked up. "Knute, go get the rocking chair from the house and a quilt. Leif, get a horse blanket from the barn."

Ivar knelt beside Nilda. "The team is in the corral. We let the others out to pasture. How will we move him?"

"I will walk," Einar growled.

Rune kept a hand on his shoulder, just in case.

Signe looked up. "We can carry him in the chair if he cannot walk. Or we will carry him using the horse blanket and a quilt."

"I can walk." Einar stared up at Nilda. "This is all her fault!"

Chapter 20

Signe asked Einar, "Do you want to sit in the chair or lie on the quilt?"

"I will walk." Einar dug his elbows into the dirt and tried to raise his head. He fell back with a groan.

Keep it up and you'll make yourself worse, Nilda thought.

Rune heaved a sigh and leaned closer to Einar's ear. "You can let us help you, or you can lie here through the night. You make the choice."

Einar groaned.

"Head wounds are dangerous," Signe said softly. "It hasn't split the skin yet, but if he bangs it again and there is a crack in the skull, I don't know how bad it could be. People die from injuries like this."

Einar swore again.

Rune barked, "Einar Strand, you will not treat my wife like that. If you want, you can lie here and I will go get the doctor. Or we can take you into the house and to your bed, where you can be comfortable and we can see how you do." He looked at Ivar. "Last winter we had to haul him to the kitchen after he collapsed in the snow. We used horse blankets to get him into the wagon and to the house."

Einar held out a hand. "Help me up."

Ivar took his hand and set his feet. "On three."

Rune planted his boots on either side of Einar's head and nodded. Between the two men and Signe, they got Einar sitting up. His chin rested on his chest.

"How do you feel?" Signe asked.

"Dizzy."

Rune braced his knees against Einar's back and turned to the boys. "You go get the chores done. Bjorn, we might need you here. Signe?"

"I'd like to get him to the house, but let me look at his head now that I can see."

Rune kept his knees against Einar's back, bracing him. Einar started to slip to the side. "Bjorn, here!" Bjorn leaped to his far's side. "Hold him up."

With gentle fingertips, Signe felt around the swiftly growing duck egg on the back of his head. "There's a scuff, an abrasion, but the bones did not move or feel mushy." She brushed some of the mud from his hair. "Good thing the ground is so soft. He's lucky he didn't break his neck. I wish we had ice or snow to put on it."

"How do you think we should move him?" Nilda asked, kneeling next to her.

"Seems the blanket would be easiest. We have enough muscles for all the corners now."

Rune nodded. "Einar, I am going to ease you back down. Then we'll get the blanket under you."

Signe rolled one of the quilts to cushion Einar's head, and he groaned when his head sank into the quilt rather than the ground.

They were all panting by the time they had carried Einar to the house, taking turns on the blanket corners. Gerd met them at the bottom of the steps.

"He's a big man," Nilda muttered, her arms aching.

They carried him to the bed, where Gerd had thrown back the covers and laid an old sheet across the mattress.

"Dumb fool," she muttered as she unlaced his boots and set them beneath the bed. "What could a doctor do that we can't?" she asked Signe.

"What do you have for pain?"

"Willow bark. He used up what was left

of the medicine the doctor gave us for Bjorn when he cut his hand. We could send Bjorn to town to get more."

"Any whiskey?" Ivar asked.

"Nei."

Einar muttered something unintelligible. His groans, however, were distinct — and not pleasant.

Rune ordered, "Bjorn, saddle Rosie and go to Benson's. See if they have any . . . any . . ."

"Laudanum." Signe filled in for him. "Or whiskey. That would work too. If they have both, fine."

"What if they don't have any?" Bjorn asked.

"Then go to the doctor in Blackduck," Rune said.

Gerd dug in the dresser and brought back some bills. "Pay with this."

Bjorn ran out the door.

"Onkel Einar, we're going to roll you on your side so I can clean the back of your head." Signe ignored his muttering.

"You want an infection too?" Gerd asked, shaking her head. "What got into you?"

Einar yelped when they rolled him slightly onto his side. Signe slid a towel underneath his head and, taking the pan of water Nilda handed her, set about cleaning the injury with a cloth. Nilda dumped the pan of dirty water and brought more.

Once the mud was cleaned off, Signe parted his wet hair with her fingertips to see how bad the lump at the base of his skull was. Nilda peered over her shoulder. It had grown both higher and wider but seemed more of a scrape than a bleeding cut. Signe laid his head back down, ignoring the groan that sounded like another expletive. "Gerd, that liniment you have, that has alcohol in it, right?"

Gerd shrugged. "I can look at the bottle. He can't drink it."

"I know, but it could disinfect the wound. All that mud and dirt. If I wash it good with that . . ."

"It's going to sting like fire," Nilda offered.

Gerd returned with the bottle of brown liquid and handed it to Signe, all the while shaking her head. Out in the kitchen, Kirstin progressed from fits of whimpering to full-blown demand.

"Let me finish that. You go take care of that hungry baby." Nilda took the bottle of liniment and the cloth from her sister-in-law, who went straight to her daughter. "Gerd, you want to hold his head?" Nilda leaned closer to Einar's ear. "This is going to burn."

He muttered what sounded like an assent.

She soaked the cloth and laid it against the deep scrape. Einar clamped his teeth and jerked his head away when she reapplied the cloth after soaking it again. "I am going to hold this here to let it sink in." When she felt him relax the slightest, she laid his head down on the cloth and stepped back. "Can you open your eyes?" His eyes fluttered open. "I'm going to open them further with my fingers."

"What for?"

"To see if they match. When my brother hit his head badly, the doctor said if the pupils match in size, the wound is not severe." She checked each eye. "Almost the same. Your head is going to hurt a lot. And you might be dizzy. The doctor told my brother to take it easy until the dizziness passed."

Einar slitted his eyes at her, but then closed them immediately. He started to raise his head but groaned and flopped back.

Nilda turned to Gerd. "How long before Bjorn can be back here?"

"Soon, if they have something at Benson's Corner. Otherwise it will be several hours. You can't push that old horse too hard, or she might collapse." Gerd looked at her husband. A snore moved his lips. She motioned to the door. Out in the kitchen, she said softly, "If he would just do what you say, but he is so stubborn."

Signe and Nilda exchanged looks that did not need words. Signe put her clothing back together and laid Kirstin on the chest to change her, blowing on her tummy and making her giggle.

Nilda laughed. "She is such a happy baby."

"Ja, that she is. Not getting fed when she says she is ready is about the only thing that makes her cranky."

"That and teething." Gerd started to set the table. "Wait until the boys come in, she gets so excited."

By the time Rune and the boys came in from chores, supper was ready.

"Smells good in here." Ivar nudged Knute. "You did a good job getting rabbit for supper."

"I might need to move the snares again. Bjorn was hoping to get another deer, but I would rather go fishing."

"Do you ever hunt squirrels? I read there are a lot of squirrels here, and ducks and geese."

Knute shrugged. "We haven't used the shotgun to get birds. Bjorn is the best shot."

They all sat down at the table. Knute

looked from Einar's empty chair to his mor and cocked his eyebrows.

"He's sleeping right now, the best thing he can be doing." Signe and Nilda set the platter of food and bowls on the table.

"Is he hurt bad?" Leif asked.

"Could be a lot worse, but he should get better soon."

Supper without Einar was far different. The boys got Ivar talking about people they knew in Norway and what had gone on there since they left. He made them laugh with a story about trying to teach a pony to pull a cart, leaving Nilda shaking her head.

"He does stretch things just a bit." Nilda grinned at her younger brother.

"That's why he is a storyteller and I am not." Rune passed the plate of biscuits around again.

Knute looked up at some sound he had heard. "Bjorn is back."

A minute later, they heard boots on the porch, and Bjorn pulled open the screen door. "Mrs. Benson sent what she had. The store doesn't carry much medicine." He handed Signe a bottle. "She said she hopes he feels better soon."

Knute pushed back his chair. "I'll take care of Rosie."

"Cookies for dessert," Gerd told him.

"I know. I'll hurry."

While Bjorn and the others finished their supper, Signe took a spoon and the bottle to the bedroom, and Nilda followed.

"Onkel Einar." When he didn't respond, Signe shook his shoulder. "I brought you some medicine."

Nilda fetched a glass of water. "Let's pour some in this. It'll be easier to take."

"Onkel Einar, you must wake up and drink this," Signe insisted.

The snoring stopped, and his eyes fluttered open. "What?" No matter the pain, the growl did not leave his voice.

"I'm going to lift you enough so you can drink." Nilda slid her arm behind his shoulders.

Signe put the glass to his lips and helped him drink the liquid. She wiped his chin with a towel after Nilda laid him back down. "That should ease the pain. We will bring you something to eat when you are ready."

He mumbled something but slipped back into sleep as they watched.

The others spent the evening talking around the table, laughing, doing away with the cookies, and drinking coffee or milk or a combination thereof. After the boys went to bed, the five adults kept talking, with Gerd mostly listening. Nilda and Signe washed and put away the dishes as if they had not had an entire year apart. When they tried to feed Einar, he shook his head, then groaned and slid back into sleep.

Gerd left them to go to bed, and the four kept on.

A while later, Nilda asked, "So, has he always been careless?"

"No, but he thinks he knows more than anyone else. He works harder than anyone I know, but he always has to be right." Rune shook his head.

"Seems more like mean to me." Nilda looked at Signe.

"He's a different man in the woods. He has taught me and Bjorn so much about lumbering. He built, although he had help for a time, all the buildings on this land. But after he ordered everyone off his place, he was working alone. Had we not come when we did, I am sure Gerd would have died, but Signe refused to let her do that." Rune smiled at his wife. "She slipped past Gerd's anger and got her back to where she is now. Signe carried the heaviest burden here."

Nilda reached across the table and patted Signe's hand. "You always have been such a hard worker."

"But here it was without gratitude from

either of them," Rune said.

"But remember, Gerd saved mine and Kirstin's lives." Signe trapped a yawn with her hand.

Nilda echoed the yawn. "I'll stay downstairs tonight, so I can hear if Einar needs anything."

"I will too." Ivar said. The yawn was making its way around the circle.

"Einar was planning on seeding corn tomorrow," Rune said.

"He probably won't be able to stand yet by the morning. If he tries without help, he will most likely fall." Nilda looked at her older brother. "Another dose of laudanum will probably see him through the night."

Signe picked Kirstin up from her downstairs bed and carried her upstairs. "Good night, everyone."

Nilda and Ivar set up pallets in the parlor, and she fell asleep before she could even turn over. Sometime during the night, she felt one of the cats curl up in the bend of her knees. The purring sent her right back to sleep.

She woke to the creak of stairs as Rune made his way down to the kitchen. She lay there a few minutes more, enjoying the rattle of the stove lids. What a good brother she had, to start the stove in the morning.

She threw back the cover and was just standing when she heard a thud from the other bedroom.

Gerd called, "Rune?"

Nilda and Rune found Einar on the floor, groaning but not moving.

"You think he forgot?" Nilda asked.

Gerd, sitting up in bed, snorted. "Or more likely figured he knew better. Who knows."

"Einar, we are helping you up. Can you hear me?" Rune asked.

"Not deaf."

"I know, but you need help to stand. Ready?"

The muttering didn't sound like he believed them.

"Here, let me help." Ivar took Nilda's place. On three, he and Rune hoisted Einar up to sit on the edge of the bed. He swayed to one side, but they kept him from falling. "Lie back now, and we'll help with your legs."

"Ain't no cripple."

"Keep him sitting while I get the laudanum." When Nilda held the glass to his mouth, Einar drank without being prompted.

"Got to seed that field." The words slid apart and slurred before he lay flat again.

"We'll see to that," Rune assured him.

Back in the kitchen, Nilda refilled the coffeepot while Rune started the stove. When Ivar came back inside from visiting the outhouse, his bare feet wet from the dew, he nodded and smiled at his brother. "No mountains, but it sure is beautiful out there. Will the boys go to school today?"

"Ja." Rune cocked his head. "That's them on the stairs."

"You want to milk this morning?" Knute asked Ivar when he entered the kitchen.

"I guess I can." Ivar flexed his hands. "I don't think they forgot something that important." He followed Knute and Leif out the door.

"So what are the plans for the day?" Bjorn asked.

Rune replied, "I'll do the seeding. You and Ivar clean up from the blasting. I'm going to pair the two teams like that man said, so that if one wants to bolt, the other will hold steady. If Einar had done what the man suggested, he'd be out planting corn right now. We'll put one team on the seeder, and you can hook the others up to the wagon to haul whatever wood can be used up to the house. Then I'm thinking to start plowing that section we've already cleared. It'd be good if we can plant hay or oats there." He glanced toward the bedroom door. "If Einar would only tell me what he wants in advance rather than barking out orders at the table, I could follow his plans as well."

Signe held Kirstin on her hip as she entered the kitchen. "That was Einar that hit the floor, right?" She shook her head at Rune's nod.

The men and boys trooped out to handle the morning chores, and Nilda made her morning outhouse trip.

"What a glorious morning," she said to Signe when she came back in. "You heard the birds singing?"

"Ja, that was robins and probably a thrush. They're back now."

"Lovely. Signe, what do you want me to do first?"

"Start the oatmeal, which is on the third shelf in the pantry, in the bigger tins. We'll have fried eggs and the last of the ham. Then we can set dried beans to cook on the hambone for supper."

Nilda felt her mouth start to water. "You eat well here."

"Ja, we do. I will start bread from the sourdough after breakfast." She turned to smile at her daughter. "You'd think she knew how to talk the way she carries on."

"She probably wishes you knew what she is trying to say." Nilda fetched the oatmeal tin and pumped water into the kettle Signe set out. "We won't be eating porridge?"

"Oatmeal here is different than porridge at home. Thick and served with cream and brown sugar."

"Perhaps you better show me."

Signe scooped out several cups of oatmeal. "This is enough. Add salt too. I wait until the water is near to boiling." She set the ham on the table and sliced off the remaining meat into a skillet with fat from the drippings can on the shelf behind the stove. "Not as much as usual, but this ham sure has gone a long way."

Still tucking up the twist of her long hair, Gerd joined them in the kitchen. "Sorry I slept so long."

"Did he do all right during the night?"

"Must have, his snoring seemed normal. I woke when he hit the floor, but you and Rune were there before I could move, so I didn't. Takk." She nodded at Nilda and reached for her apron. "Hard to believe that I went back to sleep."

After the boys left for school and the men for the fields, the three women sat down for another cup of coffee.

"Your second morning in Minnesota," Signe said.

"Yesterday sure was an eventful day."

Nilda glanced toward the bedroom. "I hope he sleeps much of today."

"Who knows," Gerd said with a slow shake of her head. "I hope he listens for a change."

"He might pay a price if he doesn't." Nilda heaved a sigh. "Men can be so stubborn, and some are more stubborn than others."

"Ja." Gerd stared down at her coffee. "Some are."

Chapter 21

"That laudanum works pretty well," Rune said at supper that night.

"Whenever he started to grumble, I gave him some more," Signe answered.

"Best thing for him." Gerd glanced toward the bedroom.

Best thing for us. Signe didn't say what she was thinking. She'd made sure Einar had something to eat, groggy or not, and was relieved when he went right back to sleep. At least he was not trying to get up and falling down. "Anyone want more ham and beans?"

"Should I try to feed him?" Gerd asked.

"We will after supper."

"Any more cookies?" Leif asked.

"You all go work out in the garden, and I will make some pudding for dessert." Gerd pushed her chair back. "Kirstin and I will, that is." She leaned over the rocker and untied the sash that kept the grinning little girl from falling on the floor.

"I could take her outside in the sling." Signe thought a moment. "We need to figure out a way for her to ride in the wagon."

Gerd looked toward the bedroom when Einar grumbled, and sighed. "Signe, you and the others go out to the garden. I will make sure Einar has some supper."

She smiled. "You need not worry about him."

Gerd rolled her eyes. "Hardheaded as he is, he most likely thought he'd be back outside today. By tomorrow he will be yelling."

Signe picked up her daughter, who gurgled in delight. Kissing the round little face, she wrapped the sling around Kirstin and settled her in front, looking out. "There now, we'll see how long this lasts."

Gerd stared at her, nodding slowly. "If we cut holes in that sling for her legs . . . I will work on that tomorrow."

Nilda announced, "I will do the dishes. The rest of you get out of here."

"Yes, ma'am!" Ivar and the boys headed outside, while Rune held the door for Signe.

"I think we should move the rocker outside onto the porch, and you and Kirstin can sit and enjoy the sun setting." He tickled his daughter's cheek, and she reached for his hand, always ready to chew on fingers.

"Let's see if we can finish the planting," Signe said. "That would make me much happier than sitting down right now."

When dusk had darkened so they could no longer see the garden rows and Kirstin was soundly sleeping in the sling, they made their way back to the house.

"Wash your hands, and we can take the pudding out onto the porch to eat. There is coffee or buttermilk to drink." Nilda held the jug of buttermilk above the glasses. "Who wants what? Gerd, you first."

Gerd pulled back, shaking her head. "Nei. Not me."

Leif stopped in front of her. "You want coffee or buttermilk? I will bring it out for you."

"C-coffee."

Knute picked up one of the bowls and a spoon. Ivar picked up a chair. "Come, show me where you want to sit."

Signe nodded as the others surrounded Gerd and eased her toward the door. She sputtered all the way out, and Signe felt her heart fill at her boys' kindness.

Snores reverberated from the bedroom as Rune and Bjorn brought out two more chairs. "All the men can sit on the steps or floor."

When they were all settled outside, both cats followed Signe, still carrying the sleeping baby, out to the porch and found a lap to purr in. Signe leaned her head against the back of the rocking chair. Surely this was a little bit of heaven come down for them all.

A red-gold line still marked the horizon as the evening star stepped out and beamed down at them. A breeze lifted hair and kissed cheeks.

"Did you finish the planting?" Gerd asked while spoons scraped bowls and one of the boys went back in the house for more buttermilk.

"Corn, beans, and squash are in. Along with the lettuce and most of the beets. Cucumbers and dill to do yet. Oh, and that second planting of corn, but I want to wait until this one is up first." Signe rocked gently. "Takk to everyone."

"We brought some more seeds. Perhaps tomorrow we can unpack the crate." Nilda looked at her older brother. "You finished planting the oats?"

"Ja." Rune sipped his coffee. "Einar had that seeder working perfectly, far as I could tell, but we'll know for sure when it comes up." He tipped his chair back on two legs, then thumped it back down when Signe cleared her throat. "Once the corn is in, we'll move the cows and horses over to the smaller pasture so that field can grow up for hay."

Lightning forked and flickered to the north.

"Heat lightning," Rune said softly to Ivar's nudge. "Not unusual here. Doesn't necessarily mean rain, but that would be fine now. Water the oats in good."

Signe sighed with pleasure. "And the garden."

"I am getting up for breakfast," Einar announced the next morning when Rune went in to help him.

"Let's see how you do."

"And no more of that — that —"

"Laudanum. If you say so. Do you need help getting dressed?"

Einar glared at him. "No!"

Rune shrugged.

Signe watched the interchange from the door. What an impossible man. She nodded at Rune's questioning look.

"Get out," Einar growled.

"Ah, no," Rune said calmly but firmly. "I am waiting to see how you do. Head injuries are nothing to fool around with."

Einar swung his legs over the side of the bed and pushed himself upright. "See, I am fine. Get out now."

"You are a big man, and if you fall, you are not easy to pick up."

Einar tried staring him down, but Rune just stood there.

Signe swelled with pride over the way her husband was handling the situation. Poor Gerd had to put up with Einar all these years. No wonder she had aged and gotten sick.

Signe started to turn around but stopped when Einar pushed up with his arms and attempted to stand. He sank back onto the bed, sweat breaking out on his forehead. He blinked repeatedly, attempting to focus. "G-get me a chair. Must be that stuff you made me drink."

Signe brought a chair from the kitchen and set it beside the bed.

"Your fault, that . . ." A string of expletives followed her back to the door.

"Einar Carlson, you may not talk to my wife that way. She has done all she can — we all have — to help you. But now you are on your own." Rune headed to the door and smiled at Signe. "Let's have breakfast. We have a lot of work to do."

She smiled back and laid her hand on his cheek. "Takk." What would it take to make that man . . . She knew there were no answers.

"Last day of school tomorrow!" Knute shouted over his shoulder as he and Leif headed out the door. "We get out early today too."

"Takk for filling the woodbox." She turned back to the kitchen.

"You ready for breakfast?" Gerd asked from the stove.

Signe glanced toward the bedroom door. "Did someone take his breakfast to him?"

"I will after we eat." Gerd broke more eggs into the frying pan. The boiler steamed on the stove, awaiting the first load of clothes. Kirstin gurgled as she rocked her chair.

Rune looked at Bjorn. "Do we have enough firewood?"

He shrugged. "I don't know. That's Knute and Leif's job."

Rune stared at him.

Bjorn looked down at the table. "I'll go check." He pushed his chair back and headed out the door.

"So what's for today?" Ivar glanced at his older brother but had a hard time keeping a straight face.

"You and Bjorn get the team hitched to

the plow. I'll do that, and the two of you can plant corn. There's about an acre out there that is ready."

"Will that be enough?"

"Probably not, but we are out of cleared land. Einar had planned on seeding the new field to corn. So that is what we will do, as soon as we get it plowed and disked."

Bjorn dumped another armful in the woodbox. "We need to chop wood too."

Rune drained his coffee. "I thought to feed Einar, but . . ."

"He's snoring again," Gerd reported.

"I'll make sure he gets some breakfast." Nilda glared at the doorway. "How bad do you think he is hurt?"

"I wish I knew." Signe shook her head and smiled at Gerd, who set the plate of eggs and fried cornmeal on the table.

"He is always worse than a bear with a ripped paw if he gets hurt." Gerd sat down, then started to rise.

Nilda put a hand on her shoulder. "I'll get the coffee."

"You come get me if he falls or causes trouble," Rune said as the men left the kitchen. "I'll be plowing that new section."

Signe nodded. "Ja. If we need to."

A few minutes later, Nilda finished her coffee and set the rest of the dishes in the pan steaming on the stove. "My brother has changed a lot in this year."

"Ja, he has."

After breakfast, Signe stirred the first load of sheets into the broiler, then showed Nilda how to get the washing machine ready. Together they took turns cranking, then running the clothes through the wringer to rinse.

"I like this machine a whole lot." Nilda admired the wringer. "Never dreamed of such a thing."

"Ja, Gerd says Einar brought this back from Blackduck one time." Signe lifted the clothes basket. "Gerd, would you like to hang these up?"

"I would." She took the basket and headed for the clothesline.

"Now that she can do it, she so enjoys hanging clean clothes on the line," Signe murmured to Nilda.

With the two of them cranking and stirring and Gerd hanging, and the wind and sun doing their drying job, the sheets were dry before the fourth load could be hung.

When Einar woke up, Nilda took a tray in to him, and between the two of them, she and Signe helped him sit up to eat.

"Are you feeling dizzy or sick to your stomach?" Signe asked.

He glared at her. "Ja." He looked down at the tray. When he lifted the toasted bread with a fried egg on top, his hand shook so hard that he had trouble finding his mouth. The egg fell on his chest.

"I will help you," Signe said.

Einar shook his head. "Gerd." He used his other hand to assist the first.

Signe left the room to find Gerd tucking Kirstin into her downstairs bed. "I think he wants you to help him."

"Really? All right."

Nilda returned to doing the wash, but Signe hovered in the bedroom doorway, just in case.

Gerd stopped beside her husband. "So you want me to help you." She scooped up the egg with a spoon and held it to his mouth. He scowled furiously, but he ate it. She asked, "How is your head?"

"I've got to get up. Too much to do." He leaned forward as if to try standing again, but fell back with a groan.

"You want more to eat?"

"Nei. I want to get up."

"More medicine?"

He started to shake his head and instead swallowed and closed his eyes.

"Coffee?"

"Ja."

"I am going to put some laudanum in his coffee," Signe whispered when Gerd brought the tray out.

"Ja, good idea." Gerd took the cup back in and held it so he could drink it without spilling.

He blinked. "Light too bright."

"Then close your eyes."

"Got to get up."

"Here, finish this, perhaps you will feel better later."

He sipped the rest of the coffee, and within a few minutes, the snoring resumed. Gerd picked up the tray and, shaking her head, returned to the kitchen.

"Should we send for a doctor?" Signe asked.

"If you want. But I think he will say we must wait to see what will happen. That he needs to rest so his head can heal." Nilda laid a hand on Gerd's shoulder. "We went through this with a neighbor. One of those things that take time. If it were winter, we could put ice or snow around his head to take away the swelling, but that bump is not as bad as it was."

Gerd nodded slowly. "Ja, he is so hard-headed. Perhaps right now that is a good thing."

"I think so."

"I will bring in the things that are dry."

Signe and Nilda ran the final load of laundry through the machine and the rinse. "That does it," Nilda said.

"We'll make egg sandwiches from the ones I boiled last night. I'll get them from the well house. Perhaps Gerd would like to peel them."

Signe paused on the edge of the back porch. She could see the two older boys out planting corn, and once she rounded the corner of the house, she saw Rune plowing the cleared land. Einar should have been disking with the other team. "Lord, help us. Help him," she whispered as she reached the well house and unlatched the door.

Cool air flowed over her. The milk pans needed skimming, and they had more than enough cream to churn butter. Even after all Gerd had used for the egg and cream pudding last night. She picked up the bowl of eggs and returned to the house. She would skim the pans after dinner and have Bjorn carry the full churn to the back porch.

"Tonight we will unpack the crate," Ivar announced after they had eaten dinner. He looked to Rune. "If that is all right with you?"

"Of course. Leif was asking me about it this morning."

"Can we work on our cellar tonight?" Bjorn asked. "We should be able to finish planting the corn this afternoon."

Rune smiled. "Sounds like a busy evening. When the boys get home, they can take over the corn planting, and you two could start digging. I'm hitching the other team to the disc." He looked at Gerd. "I will help Onkel Einar sit in the chair, if he will let me."

"If he wakes enough."

That evening, when dusk shut down the digging, they gathered in the machine shop with the doors wide open to let the evening breeze blow out the heat of the day. Using a crowbar, Ivar lifted the boards of the crate, making the nails screech, so the boys could pull it apart.

"Look, Mor, a loom!" Knute pulled on another board, then dug a sliver out of his finger with his teeth. "Ouch."

Signe lifted the lamp higher so they could see. "A loom like Gunlaug's. And we have no room to put it together."

"But we will when our house is done." Rune unwrapped layers of wool from the loom. "And here you have wool to spin."

"But no spinning wheel." Signe sighed.

"Oh? You think so?" Nilda said with a twinkle in her eye.

"I will make you a spinning wheel," Rune

told Signe.

"Ah, Rune, look here." Ivar pulled another package apart. "You just have to put it together."

Nilda clapped her hands in delight when Signe covered her cheeks with her hands and the tears flowed. "I wanted to tell you so badly, but Ivar made me promise not to ruin the surprise. There is room in the parlor for a spinning wheel."

"Gerd will be so pleased. She said we needed to buy sheep next year so we have wool. Mrs. Benson just doesn't keep enough yarn in stock. Oh, I wish she were down here."

"I'll go get her." Leif started for the door.

Signe shook her head. "She won't leave Einar by himself."

"Then I will stay there," Leif bravely volunteered, despite his fear of Einar.

"That's kind of you, but she knows what a spinning wheel looks like. We will tell her." Signe stroked the smooth wheel. "Who made this?"

"Far did, last winter after you left," Nilda said. "He said someone else would go to Amerika eventually and could carry it. Mor said to tell you that you must think of her when spinning and then weaving. She made those rugs wrapped around the spinning wheel for your new house."

"Our new house." Signe held one of the rugs in her lap, stroking the warp and woof. "She has always made such beautiful rugs."

Rune stepped behind her and laid his hands on her shoulders. "We better dig faster. And this Sunday we will celebrate the baptism of our Kirstin with her tante and onkel there to be her godparents."

"Will Onkel Einar be better enough that Tante Gerd can come too?" Leif asked.

Rune shrugged. "We can only hope and pray for that. Only God knows some things."

"Leave it to Onkel Einar," Knute muttered under his breath.

Signe heard him, but what could she say? For she had thought the same thing.

Chapter 22

"Aren't you coming?" Leif gave Gerd a hopeful look.

She shook her head. "It is better this way."

He nodded. "I know, someone has to stay here with Onkel Einar." He looked at Signe. "I've never seen a baptism before."

"That's 'cause you were the baby." Knute made a face at him.

"We all wish you were coming, Tante Gerd," Leif said, ignoring his brother.

"I will have dinner ready." She glanced toward the bedroom, where Einar had resumed snoring after she had taken him breakfast. "It's better when he is asleep."

Signe nodded. They had put the laudanum in his coffee again, anything to keep him from being so restless and angry. She scooped Kirstin up and followed the others out the door.

"What a glorious day," Nilda said after they were all loaded in the wagon.

Rune clucked the team forward. "Makes it easy to smile." He pointed out the other farms as they trotted past.

Mrs. Benson met them at the church door. "We haven't had a baptism here since I do not know when." She held her arms out to the smiling baby. For a change, Kirstin leaned toward her, her tiny fist planted firmly in her mouth. She kicked her legs. Mrs. Benson kissed her cheek and cuddled her close. "She is growing so fast."

Mr. Benson joined them, reaching to shake Rune's hand. Rune introduced him to Nilda and Ivar.

"Glad to have you here in Minnesota," Mr. Benson said. "I think you'll find life a bit different here than in Norway."

"We have already found that to be true, sir," Ivar said with a smile.

The organ began the prelude, inviting the congregation to the sanctuary. Reverend Skarstead joined them, shaking hands and welcoming the newcomers.

"You have any questions about the ceremony?" He looked at each of them. When they shook their heads, he nodded. "She might cry and fuss a bit, but don't let that bother you, all right? And you'll be sitting in the front row." At their nods, he smiled again.

"We'll be sitting right behind you." Mrs. Benson handed Kirstin back to her mor. "And how is Mr. Strand?"

"Up and down." Signe looked to Nilda, who shrugged.

When the four of them rose to join Reverend Skarstead at the baptismal font, Kirstin sat in her mor's arms, but when Signe tipped her to her back, she grumbled. When the water was patted onto her head, she screwed up her face and tried to pull away. The third time, she let out a wail that could be heard clear back to the farm. After the blessing, Signe lifted her whimpering daughter to her shoulder. Reverend Skarstead smiled at her and nodded.

After the prayer, they filed back to their seats, and the service continued.

Leif patted his baby sister's hand and made a face at her that caught her attention and shut off the tears. Signe sucked in a deep breath and jiggled her daughter in her arms. She knew she should not be embarrassed, but what a howl. Some people in the congregation had chuckled a bit, and Mrs. Benson patted her shoulder. Nilda nudged her and smiled, her eyes dancing while she tried not to laugh.

After the closing hymn and the benediction, Signe detected a certain smell. Kirstin definitely needed her diaper changed. "Excuse us." She made her way down the side aisle and, with Mrs. Benson running interference for her, headed for the women's room.

"She sure knows how to get attention, doesn't she?" Mrs. Benson smiled down at Kirstin, who waved her fist at her from the table where Signe had laid her blanket.

"At least it did not happen when she was being baptized." Signe wiped her daughter clean again and dusted her with talcum. She dug a clean soaker out of her bag and slid it over the diaper. "Now you are set to go, little one." Kirstin gurgled back at her.

They climbed the stairs back to the narthex, where people were greeting the reverend as they filed out the door. Signe glanced up to catch a venomous glare from one woman and her husband. She tried to smile and nod, but her face refused to cooperate. Nilda nudged her side, having seen the nasty looks as well, and Signe turned to her and just shrugged. One of these days, she would have to sit Mrs. Benson down and learn the whole story behind the hatred she saw in some people. She knew it had to do with Onkel Einar.

"Thank you for bringing your charming baby daughter to us for her baptism."

Reverend Skarstead smiled at Signe and Rune as he shook their hands. "Baptizing babies is one of my favorite parts of being a pastor. I know all of you take very seriously your commitment to raise her in the faith and the church."

Rune nodded. "Thank you, sir."

"Did I hear that you are digging a cellar for a new house?"

"Yes, sir, we are."

"When you are ready to raise the house, some of us will come to help. Mr. Benson will let us know when you are ready."

Signe watched her husband try to find something to say. Some of the men had come to help dig the cellar, and that had so surprised him. But now this. Even when they had to put up with Einar's venom.

"Takk, tusen takk." Rune shook the reverend's hand again and cleared his throat. "Thank you. I will let him know."

Reverend Skarstead leaned a bit closer. "Rune Carlson, I want you to understand me. This church is part of God's family — we all are — and helping each other is part of the family, in spite of past actions or the actions of some people. I believe that is why God stresses the importance of forgiveness." He nodded. "Perhaps I need to preach and teach more on the subject of forgiveness.

But talking about it is easy. It is the living of it that is hard."

"Yes, sir. Thank you."

In the wagon going home, Ivar asked, "We going to dig more today?"

"I could help too," Nilda offered.

Rune nodded, smiling. "Ja, we are, we sure are."

Signe and Nilda grinned at each other. Kirstin squirmed in Signe's arms, reaching for Leif and chattering at him.

Gerd had dinner all ready to set on the table when they got home. "I already fed Einar. I think he feels some better today." She took Kirstin, who was reaching for her. "Did that man pour water on your head, little one? I hope you gave him your most winning smile." She looked at Signe, who was shaking her head. "She didn't like it?"

"Ah, not exactly, and she let everyone know her feelings." Signe glanced at Nilda, who rolled her eyes.

"That she did. Very clearly." Nilda reached for an apron and tied it around her waist.

Signe suggested, "You might need to change her again, so while you do that, I will put dinner on the table. You boys go change into your work clothes so we can eat and get to digging."

When they were gathered at the table,

Rune bowed his head and waited for the others. "Thank you, Lord, for this baby you have given us. Thank you that we could have her baptized today in a church that is beginning to feel like home. Thank you for bringing us to this country and this place, for Gerd and Einar, and that Nilda and Ivar arrived here safely. Thank you for the house we are building, for work we can do to build a home here. Bless this food and bless this day. Amen."

Signe sniffed and noticed that Gerd did too. *Thank you, Lord, not only for bringing Gerd back but for making her stronger and now such a part of our family. She is more like a grandma to the boys.* She paused in her thoughts, heaved a sigh, and added, *And thank you for Einar too.*

Sometime later, when Kirstin and Gerd were napping, Signe saw that Einar's eyes were open. "Can I get you anything?" she asked.

"That chair." He pointed to the chair Gerd had sat in so often when Signe was working to get her stronger.

"Of course." When she added, "Be glad to," she surprised even herself. She set the chair beside the bed. "I could help you."

His glare told her what he thought of that idea.

"Would you like some coffee and cake when you are seated?" She knew his growl meant yes, so she chose to leave the room rather than argue. She returned with a tray for the coffee and spice cake Gerd had baked in honor of the baptismal day. A fork lay beside the cake.

Einar's hand shook so severely that he almost dropped it until he grasped it with both hands. His right hand seemed so much weaker than the left. Wishing she had watched him move to the chair, she started to ask about the weakness, but his glare sent her out of the room instead.

What a mean, nasty person. Served him right.

And is he not one of My children?

Signe almost looked to see if someone else was in the kitchen, the voice had seemed so clear. Her sigh seemed to come from her ankles. *I guess. I don't think I can forgive him.* She thought a moment. *But do I want to?* She had to sit down. *Be honest,* her reasonable side whispered.

Lord, how do I forgive him when he keeps hurting those I love, let alone me? And now this, all because he is so sure he knows everything better than anyone else. And we all must pay for his stubbornness.

Silence can be very uncomfortable.

An even deeper sigh inched its way up, followed by a tear. *Does it make any sense to say I am trying?* Right now she wished Reverend Skarstead were here to answer her questions. Telling Einar that she forgave him would make him . . . She stopped to think. He would yell at her and wake Gerd and Kirstin. Or he would just glare at her, which always made her feel nailed to the wall. Or . . . ? A mental image of him lunging at her made her shiver.

Was she afraid of Einar Strand? Another question that stopped her mid-thought.

Ja. Ja, she was. If his temper got out of control . . . Reminders of the winter fiasco made her shudder again. And always, his actions either wounded or made life harder for the others. Especially Gerd. Even though she would get furious with him, he was her husband, and even if she didn't love him now, she had at one time. Then again, had she, or was this a marriage of convenience that was still that?

Signe rubbed her forehead. Was she getting a headache from all this thinking? All over forgiveness. Something she should be able to just *do.*

A crash from the bedroom jerked her to her feet. An expletive made her stop at the door. Einar had not fallen. The tray lay on the floor, leftover coffee spreading over the painted floorboards. Kirstin set up a howl, jerked awake by the noise.

"What happened? Is Kirstin all right?" Gerd was heading for the baby before she was fully awake, and she had to pause to get her balance.

Signe caught her before she hit the floor. Once Gerd was steady, Signe patted her arm, and Gerd headed for Kirstin.

Einar yelled at Signe and pointed at the tray.

Instead of forgiving, Signe exploded. Without thinking, praying, or breathing, Signe stomped to a stop just out of Einar's reach. "If you would think about someone other than yourself for a change, then life —"

She stopped. She did not pick up his tray. She did not offer to help him.

She left the room, left his roaring, and slammed the door shut behind her. Gritting her teeth, she nodded at Gerd, who already had Kirstin comforted, and shoved open the screen door, ignoring the slam of it behind her. At the garden she picked up a hoe and attacked the weeds between the hills of already sprouting potatoes. She chopped at the ground until forced to catch her breath.

Somehow the thought of using the hoe on Einar made her sad as the anger had seeped out of her sometime in the hoeing. *Lord, you asked me to forgive that man, and here I wanted to wound him, to pay him back.* She wiped away the tears she'd not even been aware of. How could such a wonderful, special day sink to this so easily?

Chapter 23

"But I could spend the day digging out the cellar or helping the boys cut firewood," Nilda protested.

"I know," Signe replied, "but this is the last meeting of the year, and I would love to go. And even more so, I want you to come with me."

Nilda glanced at Gerd, who mouthed *Go.* "Who will help with Einar?"

Gerd declared firmly, "I will take care of Einar. After all, he is the man I married. He is my responsibility, not yours."

"I know! You come too, we take Kirstin, and we let Einar fend for himself until the others come up for dinner, which we will have waiting for them." Nilda grinned from one ear to the other.

Gerd shook her head. "I am afraid that would only cause more problems. I will stay here, play with our baby, and feed all the men. You two go and have a good time. The work always waits for us." She patted Nilda's arm. "Please. That would make me very happy. Perhaps I will be able to go along another day. Ladies Aid will always be there."

Nilda tipped her head back and closed her eyes. "All right. But if himself in there finds out, he'll threaten to send me back to Norway. He's done it before, and he'll do it again."

Later, when the two women were seated on the wagon box and ready to trot down the lane, Signe paused to ask, "If he really could send you back, what would you do?" She flipped the reins over Rosie's back and looked at Nilda.

"I would go work for someone else. I am not returning to Norway, and you can be sure he would not order Ivar to leave. Onkel Einar might think he can order me around, but once I stepped off that land, he would no longer be my master."

Signe nodded. "Glad to hear that." She inhaled a deep breath scented by growing fields and flowers blooming along the roadside, a whiff of horse, and a tiny trace of a skunk that had visited during the night. "I feel light as a butterfly. Just us together, without any of the others. Do you know how many years it has been since we had time together like this — alone?"

"Too many." Nilda stared at the farms as they trotted past. "Einar has done well, hasn't he?"

"Ja, but at the cost of no friends or neighbors who come to visit."

"You said he forbade everyone from coming on his land, so he did that himself."

"And made life all the harder for Gerd. She refuses to talk about getting weaker and sicker, but I don't think he ever really looked at her or realized how sick she was until he found her on the floor one day."

"Either she hid things very well, or he really doesn't care about anyone, just getting the work done."

"I'd much rather hope it was the first."

"Ja, me too."

When they reached the turn in the road at Benson's store, Mrs. Benson came from her house behind the store. Basket over her arm, she waved at them. "Good wonderful morning!"

Signe waved back. "You want a ride?"

"That's okay, meet you there. Did you bring little Miss Kirstin?"

"No, she stayed home with Gerd."

"Oh, sad, she is the sweetest baby ever."

"Takk."

Signe turned into the road beside the church that led to the school and the three or four houses beyond that. Nilda climbed down first and tied Rosie to a hitching rail in the shade of a maple tree by the church. A buggy and a trap were already tied there. They retrieved their baskets of food and a few pieces of fabric for the quilting, along with needles and thread, and joined Mrs. Benson at the front steps.

"We meet down in the basement, but outside would sure be more pleasant on a day like today. Perhaps we can bring our dinners out here."

Signe paused on the steps, a wave of apprehension freezing her feet in place. *What if — no, just keep going,* she ordered herself. She followed Mrs. Benson into the narthex, which seemed dim after the brilliance outside.

Laughter and chatter floated up from those gathered.

"Good morning, everyone." Mrs. Benson smiled.

"Good morning, Elmira," sang out one of the women's voices. "Now we can get started."

"We have two new members this morning." Mrs. Benson turned and nodded to Signe and Nilda. "I know you have met some of our church women, Signe, and now you will meet more of our group." She took Signe's arm and led her to the tables that had been pushed together to make a big square, with chairs all around and the quilting supplies in the middle. "Ladies, meet Mrs. Rune Carlson, Signe, and her sister-in-law, Nilda Carlson, recently arrived from Norway. Signe's baby was baptized last Sunday, and I know some of you put baby things in a box for her last fall. Her little one is the sweetest baby imaginable. Now, Signe, you know Mrs. Jungkavn, our midwife, and Mrs. Engelbrett, who nursed little Kirstin when you were so ill."

Signe nodded. "I can never thank either of you enough."

"Our real pay is knowing both you and that baby are well and thriving. That was too close for comfort." Mrs. Benson nodded again. "That Kirstin, she waits for no one." She turned to the others. "See, God answered our prayers again."

A murmur and smiles drifted around the table, and Signe started to relax.

But then a woman on the other side of the table pushed back her chair. "I cannot do this." She gathered her things and headed for the stairs and out the door, leaving everyone blinking.

Signe watched, openmouthed. "What did I — ?"

"You did nothing, Signe. This happened long before you came here."

"But there is no need for her to leave. I mean, I — we can go back to the farm."

Mrs. Jungkavn shook her head. "Please, Mrs. Carlson, join us. There is nothing you or any of us can do about the past. We are glad to have you here. Come, let's continue."

"Who was that?" Nilda whispered to Signe.

"Mrs. Olavson," she replied. "She hates us, for some reason."

Nilda move closer to Signe.

I just want to go home, Signe thought. *Why will no one ever tell us what really happened? Surely Einar didn't kill someone or something, did he?*

"This is Mrs. Solum." Mrs. Benson continued around the table, then turned to Signe and Nilda. "We will have a test after dinner to see how many names you remember."

Nilda smiled. "That will be interesting."

The women chuckled, and the heavy feeling was banished, sent up the stairs after Mrs. Olavson.

After the brief meeting and a devotion,

Mrs. Torsing, who was in charge of the quilting, assigned all the jobs, and everyone set to their tasks, some sorting, some cutting, others piecing, and the remainders hand stitching.

"We trade off after dinner," the woman next to Signe said. She smiled at Nilda across the table. "I am Kara Tolefson, Nilda. What part of Norway did you come from?"

"Valders region," Nilda answered the question asked in Norwegian. "I am trying to learn English. We were told we needed to do that, so my younger brother Ivar and I tried. We didn't get too far."

"Mr. Larsson, who teaches at the school and plays the organ at church, will be teaching a weekly class this summer. He grew up speaking German but learned Norwegian, so he knows how hard it is to learn a language."

"But you speak Norwegian?"

"I learned both growing up, thanks to my Norwegian mor and German father. They met in the lumber camps, and now he works for one of the big companies. I grew up south of Blackduck. My husband and I live in the white house right across from the school."

Signe looked at Nilda. "English classes! We could both go. Or you could come home and teach me what you learned." She turned back to Mrs. Tolefson. "Do you know when the class starts?"

"On Wednesday at seven in the evening here at the church."

"We will be here." Signe did not bother to check with Nilda. "Perhaps Ivar will come too."

"Maybe, but he was learning faster than I was anyway," Nilda said. "Leif said he would teach me, remember."

They enjoyed their dinner outside, cleaned up, and switched to different assignments, and all too soon, three o'clock arrived. Some of the ladies took pieces to work on at home, but Signe shook her head when Nilda reached for a packet.

She whispered in Nilda's ear. "Right now we have more than enough to work on at the house. We can make up for it next fall when we can use Gerd's sewing machine."

Nilda nodded and collected the empty bowls in which they had brought biscuits and egg salad.

"Do you still have pickles in your cellar?" Mrs. Benson asked Signe.

"Not anymore."

"Then you take the rest of this jar. I have more at home." She thrust a quart jar of bread-and-butter pickles into Signe's hands.

"You are so generous. I have nothing to give back."

"I hope you will have eggs and butter for the store soon, but I know you are all so busy out there, what with Einar down and you trying to get ready for the house-raising. And our delivery boys are at home too." Mrs. Benson paused.

Signe smiled. "Ja, we will have more soon. I should have churned yesterday."

"How is Einar doing?"

"Getting stronger, but really slowly. He is not a patient man."

"So that slows him down or causes setbacks," Nilda said firmly.

Mrs. Benson shook her head. "I understand. Well, you tell those boys that the cookie jar is full if they can get to the store."

"I will."

Mrs. Benson raised a finger. "Oh, and don't you worry about feeding the men when they raise your house. We women will bring all the food and make a party out of it, just like a good, old-fashioned barn raising, only this time a house. Mr. Benson said we should be able to get it all framed and ready to roof on a Saturday and to get a good part of the roof done after church on Sunday."

Signe clapped her mouth closed. "Is that

possible? A two-story house?"

"You just watch."

"But . . . but Einar . . ."

"Make no nevermind about him. We might cross his land, but we won't stay on it. He'll just have to learn that we take care of our own, and you are part of our church now. I'm sorry, but we should have been there before."

Signe rested a hand on Mrs. Benson's arm. "You were, remember?"

"I know, but I was shaking in my boots. As long as he was out in the woods . . . Gerd needed help, and we let her down. It's hard to forgive myself for that."

"But —"

"What she means is thank you," Nilda said with a grin. "Come on, Signe, let's get going before they send the boys to look for us."

Driving home, Signe kept shaking her head.

On the wagon seat beside her, Nilda watched her. "All right, what is bothering you?"

"Well, first Mrs. Olavson storming out like that, but then all the others, so warm and welcoming . . . I — I didn't expect that, is all."

"It surprised me too, but then, I am new

here. And I still don't know half of their names." Nilda smiled. "It was sometimes hard to get a word in edgewise with Mrs. Benson. And yet, they were all so cheerful and generous. I was starting to fear that everyone in Amerika would be like Onkel Einar. Someday I want to hear what really happened with him and whoever and whatever."

"I tried to get Gerd to tell me, but she just shook her head. Whatever it was, she had no part in it." Signe drew Rosie back to a walk. The old mare wanted to be home as much as Signe did.

"Not intentionally, anyway."

Signe grimaced. "I would like the past to be in the past."

"Sometimes, as Mor would say, you have to pick off the scab to let the festered wound heal."

The clip clop of hooves, the warning of a crow, and a dog barking were the only sounds for a while.

"I was going to check on the board at the store to see if anyone has puppies," Signe said. "A dog would be helpful."

"And more cats in the barn."

"I have a feeling that is going to be taken care of soon. The orange tabby is looking fat."

Nilda giggled. "A tomcat found her, eh?"

"Or she has been eating far more than Gra. Besides, she does not mind the barn anymore. And why else would she be hunting?"

"Perhaps she will have a litter in Einar's pants on the floor one night."

A laugh burst from Signe. "Nilda Carlson, you have an evil mind. Those cats know better than to get near him."

"Cats have been known to get even."

The two were still laughing when they stopped Rosie at the back porch.

Nilda hopped down. "I'll unhitch her and bring the churn to the house. Need anything else from the well house?"

Signe shrugged. "I'll ask Gerd." She could hear Kirstin starting to fuss from the doorway.

"Just in time," Gerd said. She set the stove lid back in place and turned to Signe.

Signe could hear Einar grumbling from the bedroom. "Nilda is bringing the churn from the well house. Need anything else?"

Gerd shook her head. "Not right now. You take care of Kirstin. She has been such a good girl." She glanced at the bedroom and shook her head, but only slightly. She sighed.

"Why don't you let Nilda take care of

him? You take a cup of coffee out on the porch and sit for a bit. In fact, pour two cups of coffee, and Kirstin and I will join you out there." Signe laid a hand on Gerd's shoulder. "Please."

The muttering continued. Signe scooped her daughter up in her arms and kissed her head. "Tante Gerd says you have been a good girl." She nuzzled her baby's rosy cheek. "I know what you would like. You need dry diapers first?" She checked. "Here we go."

"Coffee will be hot in a minute or two," Gerd said.

"Gerd!"

The order from the bedroom made Gerd close her eyes. "I will be there in a minute," she said.

Nilda called from the porch, "I'm putting the churn out here."

Kirstin nuzzled her mor's chest, whimpering. "Yes, baby, yes." Signe joined Nilda on the porch. "Gerd is bringing coffee out. Will you please see to Einar?"

"De-lighted." Nilda's eyebrows wiggled. "Here, let me bring out the rocking chair for you."

"Gerd!" Einar yelled.

"Be there in a minute," Nilda called back. She brought out the chair and set it down for Signe and her questing baby.

"I hear Nilda. Not her. I want Gerd," Einar growled.

Gerd started toward the bedroom, but Nilda motioned her to the porch. "He can yell at me just fine. You go sit out there for a few minutes at least. Keep Signe and Kirstin company." When Gerd reached for the coffeepot, Nilda shook her head. "Please, let me. I'll take him some too."

"Takk." Gerd went outside without arguing.

This wore her out today, Signe thought as Kirstin settled in to nurse. She flipped a piece of old sheet over her shoulder. Gerd sank down on the porch bench and leaned up against the wall.

"Has he been like this all day?" Signe asked.

Shaking her head, Gerd took the cup of coffee Nilda held out. "He slept most of the morning, I fixed him a tray, and Rune got him settled with it. Then he slept some more and decided to sit in the chair. He did really well with it right by the bed like that. Then when he heard you two come home, he started in."

Kirstin made her usual nursing noises, but Signe and Gerd listened to the conversation happening in the bedroom through the open window.

"I brought you coffee, Onkel Einar," Nilda said.

"Where'd you go?"

"Signe and I went to Ladies Aid."

"I paid your way for you to work here, not go off to church!" His voice rose on every word.

"Be careful, your coffee's spilling."

Einar roared.

Gerd started to stand, but Signe waved her back down.

"Now look what you've done," Nilda chided. "Coffee all over the bed and your head is killing you. No, you are not falling to the floor."

They heard her grunt. The bedsprings shrieked. Einar groaned.

"You just never seem to learn, do you?" Nilda chided. "Laudanum or not? I'll get it for you. You know, if you would let us help you, you just might get better faster."

Signe and Gerd both shook their heads.

CHAPTER 24

Nilda glared at her younger brother. "But you said you would go."

"Finishing the cellar is more important right now."

"Then I will come and help dig."

"You two go to the class. Then you can teach me." Ivar grinned at her. "This way you can catch up with me."

Exasperated, Nilda turned to her older brother. "Rune."

"There isn't room in the hole for another shoveler. We all take turns pushing the wheelbarrows up the ramp now. I should have devised something else to haul the dirt out."

Nilda listened for a moment. Had Einar's snoring changed tempo? While he was now able to walk a few steps, the headaches forced him to lie down again. More than a week had passed since his accident, and he was a long way from being himself.

"Maybe we better stay here with Gerd," Nilda said.

"No, you two go." Gerd made a shooing motion with her free hand. "Supper and the dishes are done, and Kirstin and I are going out on the porch to rock in the evening breeze. We like this time of day. Don't we, little one?" She paused to jiggle the baby on her hip. "Go now, or you will be late."

While the others headed for the new cellar, Nilda and Signe climbed up into the wagon and clucked Rosie into a trot down the lane.

"Stubborn Norwegians," Nilda muttered under her breath.

When they arrived at the church, several other horses and wagons were already tied to the hitching rail. Nilda shuddered. "We should not have come, I know it."

"We are here now, so come on." Signe climbed down and tied up the horse. The two women followed the sounds of talking and joined the others in the front pews.

"Welcome." The man who must be the teacher, Mr. Larsson, smiled around at those gathered. "I am glad you are here. Since this is a beginners class, no one from last summer is here, but someone told me these sessions gave him enough help to be able to carry on decent conversations. I hope to do the same for you. Let me introduce myself. I am Fritz Larsson. Most of you know me as the man playing the organ in church on Sunday. Some of your children have been students of mine. I speak both German and Norwegian because of my parents. I grew up in a village near Stuttgart, and while my pa wanted me to go into lumber, all I ever wanted to do was teach at a school and play the organ in a church. Here, I have both."

Nilda felt like turning around to see who he was smiling at, but when Signe nudged her, she shook her head.

"He keeps looking at you," Signe whispered.

"Nei. He is looking at everybody."

"Mrs. Carlson," Mr. Larsson said, "your sons have been in our classes. Would you please tell us where you came from and when?"

Signe stood. "I am Mrs. Rune Carlson, and we came from Valders, Norway, last June to help some relatives on their farm."

Nilda noticed she did not mention the name Einar Strand.

Mr. Larsson smiled. "Thank you. And would you please introduce the woman next to you?"

Nilda swallowed the block in her throat as

she stood up. "I am Nilda Carlson; her husband is my older brother. My younger brother, Ivar, and I came several weeks ago. We took some lessons in English but not enough." She sat back down and watched and listened while the six other people in the room introduced themselves.

Mr. Larsson nodded. "Now I will explain how I run this class. I will give you a list of words and phrases that you can study during the week, and we will review and answer questions the following week. Halfway through our class time each week, we will switch into speaking only English." He looked around the group. "We will keep it simple, and we are not in a hurry. You will enjoy the class more if you do the homework each week. Each class builds on the week before."

Every time Nilda glanced up, it seemed like the teacher was looking right at her. Was her hair falling down, or was there a smudge of dirt on her face? He was tall, six foot or more, and comely. Not overly handsome, but not plain either, with a wide forehead and hair that waved slightly away from his face. His eyes were his best feature. Amber with crinkles at the edges and thick dark eyelashes and brows. *Kind* was the word that kept coming to her mind. His hands did not know hard manual work, but those long slender fingers could make the organ sing and dance.

Handsome was no longer a draw for her anyway, not after that handsome devil at home. Like her mor often said, sometimes evil came in pretty packages.

"Are there any questions?" Mr. Larsson looked around the room.

Without quite realizing what she was doing, Nilda raised her hand like a good pupil. When he nodded, she asked, "What made you want to teach school?"

He half smiled. "I love learning, and I want to help children do the same. God gave us marvelous minds, and learning to use them takes a lifetime. Helping others makes life worth living." He shook his head like a dog coming up out of the creek. "Sorry, I get carried away at times." He looked around the group. "Anyone else?"

"Do you teach music classes too?" Nilda blurted.

"Not at the moment, but one never knows what God has in mind." He nodded. "All right, I am going to say a phrase in Norwegian and then in English. Please repeat after me. 'Gud dag.' 'Good day.' " When he repeated a phrase, they did likewise. He led them through several more, all the while nodding and smiling encouragement. "Many of those words most of you already knew. They are on the list for this week. Now, let's count together, first in Norwegian, then in English."

They then did the days of the week and the months of the year, followed by identifying body parts and clothes and things around them.

Dusk had dimmed the sky when he raised his hands. "We are done for tonight. Take your papers with you, and I will see you all next week. Thank you for coming."

Nilda and Signe stood along with the others as they slipped back into Norwegian to discuss the class.

"I was surprised I understood most of what he said, more than I expected," the woman in front of them said. "This was good."

"Ja, that it was." Nilda stretched her neck and shoulders. She'd forgotten what being in a class felt like.

Mr. Larsson stopped in front of them. "Mrs. Carlson, you have learned a lot, I think, in the year you have been here. I know your boys picked up the language quickly. Did they happen to mention that they were each supposed to check out books to read over the summer?"

Signe rolled her eyes. "Not that I recall, and I did not see any books come home."

"Not surprising." He sent Nilda a side glance while he spoke to Signe. "We have shelves of books at the school. They could come get some on Sunday after church. Or I can choose several and send them home with you."

"Perhaps that would be best."

"Good, I hoped you'd say that." He leaned down and picked up three books. "They can start with these."

Signe smiled up at him. "Takk, er, thank you."

He turned to Nilda. "I'm glad to meet you, Miss Carlson. Welcome to our community."

"Takk." She caught herself. "Thank you."

"May I suggest you all speak English at your house? The boys will enjoy it too."

"We shall see."

Halfway home, Nilda swatted a persistent mosquito and chuckled. "Do you think we can do that, speak English, only English?"

"I think our conversations will be mighty short. But I would like Kirstin to grow up with both languages. The teacher said he spoke Norwegian and German and now English, and that is a good thing." Signe paused and chuckled. "I think you caught his eye, though."

Nilda nudged her with an elbow. "I think matchmaking does not become you."

"We shall see."

Nilda flicked the reins over Rosie's back. Thinking of Mr. Larsson brought back thoughts of that lech, Dreng Nygaard. Not a good thing. She had hoped she'd left him behind, but it seemed he still dogged her steps.

They reached home just as the evening star stepped out in the western sky. A light breeze lifted tendrils of hair and the horse's mane.

Knute stepped down from the porch where the rest of the family were all sitting. "I'll put Rosie away." He took up the lines and headed for the barn.

"Thank you. We're supposed to talk only English from now on." Signe stopped at the steps and turned her head, listening to night sounds. Nilda paused to do the same. Crickets, a bird's call, the whine of mosquitoes. An owl hooted as it flapped past the house, and bats dipped and darted. "I love evenings like this."

"Ja, me too. Though I think I should take up smoking a pipe to help keep the mosquitoes away." Rune tipped his chair back against the wall. "We are nearly finished with the digging."

"Do you have the timbers to frame the cellar?" Ivar asked.

"Nei. Got to go to the lumberyard." Rune patted the bench. "Come, Signe, sit yourself."

She settled beside him. "Where's Gerd?"

"Over here. In the dark." A chuckle announced her location.

As Signe sat down beside Rune, Nilda joined the boys on the steps.

"So how was your class?" Ivar asked.

"Like Signe said, we are supposed to only talk English around here," Nilda said with mock sternness.

Rune shrugged. "We can try."

Gerd's voice drifted from the dark. "At the beginning of the day when we are refreshed, ja. At the end of the day when we are weary, nei. Too much work."

Leif popped from the steps. "Hooray for Tante Gerd!"

"How did Einar do tonight?" Nilda asked.

"Sat in his chair for a while, seemed a bit better." Gerd's voice sounded tired. Knute came up from the barn and sat on the floor at his far's feet.

Signe leaned toward Knute. "Mr. Larsson sent you boys a present. What's this about you supposed to be reading this summer, and you were to bring books home?"

Knute shrugged. "We musta forgotten."

"To make up for that, he sent books home for you. Wasn't that nice of him?"

"Uh-huh."

"I have three, and I expect you each to read one chapter every evening. You finish one book and start on the next."

"But, Mor . . ."

"What?"

"They're in English."

"Good, you can read to me then."

"And me," Tante Gerd chimed in.

Knute nudged Leif. "You think Onkel Einar would like us to read to him?"

Leif's snort could be heard clear to the barn. He quickly changed the subject. "Far, did you check the gilts? I think they're getting close." Since they'd kept the two young gilts from the year before, they now had four hogs farrowing.

"Want to do it now?" Rune asked.

"Maybe we should."

While Rune and Leif ambled to the barn, the others picked up chairs and went back in the house. Nilda heard Einar snoring in the bedroom. Good. Ivar, Bjorn, and Knute said their goodnights and went up the stairs, laughing about something. Kirstin snuggled into her mor's arms to be carried upstairs as well.

Gerd started toward the bedroom but stopped. "I think I will sleep on a pallet in the parlor tonight."

Nilda looked at her. Even in the light from the kerosene lamp, she could see how tired Gerd looked.

Signe asked, "Is he worse at night?"

"Nei, not worse, but he thrashes around and mutters, and I don't sleep very well."

"I know, you come upstairs with me, and Rune will sleep by the bed in your room in case Einar needs something."

"I — I don't . . ."

"If it is the stairs, I will help you," Nilda said softly. "That is what we are here for, to help you." She put the emphasis on the last word.

"I — I'm j-just tired."

"How long since you've had a decent rest in the afternoon?" Nilda whispered.

"I lie down, but . . ."

"How about we help him out to the porch in the afternoon tomorrow, and you take your nap when Kirstin does?" Nilda suggested.

"We shall see. But takk, I will sleep upstairs, just for tonight."

■ ■ ■ ■

The next morning Nilda woke early and, grabbing her clothes, tiptoed down the stairs to dress in the parlor. When she entered the kitchen to start the stove, Rune was there already. "You got in here before me," she said.

"No wonder Gerd wanted to sleep upstairs. I can usually sleep through anything, but I was up with him a couple of times." Rune was building the fire while he talked. "He is so angry at not being able to be out felling those trees. The boys and I will go out there today just to try to calm him down."

"How are the gilts?"

"One had eight, the other wasn't quite ready." He took a match from the holder on the wall behind the stove and lit the shavings, adding more wood when the kindling caught.

"I'll be right back." Nilda paused at the edge of the porch to inhale the morning. Walking barefoot through the dewy grass made her want to skip, which she did, and dance, which she didn't. The outhouse needed lime again, so she hurried.

She was setting the kettle on the quickly

heating part of the stove when Signe came in, tying her apron.

"Sorry, I did not even hear you get up," Signe said. "Gerd and Kirstin are both still sleeping. I told the boys to dress downstairs and let them sleep. Poor Gerd, she was so terribly tired."

The boys trailed through the kitchen, heading for chores.

At breakfast, Leif announced they now had fifteen baby pigs and two sows left to deliver. "If we can keep them all alive, we'll have lots to sell come fall."

"Far, can we go out to the big trees today?" Bjorn asked.

"You think you two can handle that big crosscut?" The twinkle in his eye let them know Rune was teasing. "Ja, I told your mor last night we would be doing that. I will tell Einar too, so maybe he can quit worrying so much."

"How come he is so mean to Tante Gerd?" Leif asked.

"What are you talking about?" Rune asked.

"Well, you were all at the cellar, and I came back to check on the sows. I could hear him yelling at her clear to the barn. He was calling her names, even." A frown wrinkled Leif's forehead. "He made Kirstin cry too."

"She will not be left alone with him again." Nilda spoke softly, but those who knew her knew she could be formidable.

Rune's eyebrows raised. "Still have that temper, eh?"

"If you only knew," Ivar muttered into his cornmeal mush.

Nilda gave her younger brother a look that made her older brother chuckle.

"Gerd!" The order came from the bedroom.

Rune waved the women back and headed for the bedroom.

Nilda heard Rune speak in a determined voice without yelling, but she knew she would not want to cross him when he used that voice. "Einar Strand, listen to me and listen well. If you want any more of your trees cut before you can get out there again, you will *not* yell or roar at Gerd, Nilda, or Signe. We are going out to the woods today, but we will not go back if I hear you have been yelling at them again. They are doing their best for you, and you will keep a civil tongue." He paused. "Do you understand me?"

Einar started to growl but stopped.

Nilda smiled into her hand. This was a new side of her brother that had come about since he left Norway. He had always been so quiet. She nodded at Signe. Yes, the two of them were in agreement, just like all those years as best friends.

Gerd hurried into the kitchen. "I-I'm sorry, why didn't you wake me?" She cocked her head and turned around.

"You sit down and eat, I will go get her." Signe patted Gerd's shoulder as she went by.

"I will!" Leif was up the stairs before Signe got to them. In a minute or so, he carried his grinning baby sister into the kitchen. "She sure is wet." He dodged Kirstin's questing fingers and handed her to Signe.

Kirstin babbled at him and her mor.

"You slept so long, no wonder you are so happy." Signe changed her while the others ate their breakfast, then sat down and touched a spoon of milky mush to her daughter's mouth. Kirstin tongued it around before shoving it out again.

"Put a bit more brown sugar on it," Gerd suggested. "She should be hungry."

"Oh, she is hungry all right, but cornmeal is not her idea of what to eat," Signe said.

"She does okay with oatmeal, though."

"When I cook it to death and mash it." Signe added a bit more brown sugar and repeated the feeding. Kirstin mouthed it, some dribbling down her chin, and finally swallowed.

"Good girl," Leif said from across the table.

Kirstin looked at him and waved her fist.

"Two down," Rune announced when the men returned at noon. "Leif is at the barn. The remaining gilt has had her first baby."

"So he will be staying there?" Nilda asked.

"Yes." He nodded toward the bedroom and dropped his voice. "How is he?"

"Quiet. Got him up in a chair for a bit, then back down. I offered that you and the boys will help him to the rocker out on the porch before you go back to the woods."

"Good."

"Ivar learns really fast," Bjorn said between bites.

"The teeth on that big saw are different than the crosscut we had at home, but better I think. Trading off, we dropped one earlier, then just did another before we came to eat." Ivar flexed his shoulders. "I cannot believe how big those trees are. I mean, when you are right there on the end of the saw, they are huge!"

Nilda set another bowl of rabbit and beans on the table and dished up more corn bread. "Perhaps tomorrow you will want dinner out there?"

"We'll see."

After dinner, Rune and Ivar went into the bedroom. "You ready to go out on the porch?" Rune asked Einar.

Nilda moved to the door to watch and listen.

Einar nodded. He swung his legs to the side of the bed and slowly pushed himself up to standing.

Rune smiled. "Good. Now we can walk with one of us on each side of you. Put your arms over our shoulders."

"The chair." Einar nodded to the one by the bed.

"Bjorn, you bring that chair behind us."

Half carrying, half walking him, they got the big man through the kitchen and out to the rocking chair on the porch, where they let him down slowly while he puffed and panted as if he'd been running.

"You all right?" Rune asked.

"Ja." Einar rested against the back of the chair.

Nilda watched from the doorway. "Can Signe and I get him back in?"

"In a couple hours I'll come back. After we fell the next one," Rune said.

A while later, Gerd took a bowl of beans

and a cup of coffee out to Einar on a tray. "I am lying down with Kirstin. Do you need anything else?"

"Water."

She brought him a glass, along with a plate of cookies. "To go with your coffee."

Nilda thought she heard him mutter something about wasting time baking cookies, but she wasn't sure. She nodded as the realization hit her. The only way he would be happy was if they were all out felling and limbing trees.

She turned to Signe. "He'd even have Kirstin out dragging branches if she could walk."

Gerd shook her head and rolled her eyes at the joke.

Later that afternoon, Nilda heard Leif out on the porch. The last time she had checked, Einar had been sleeping in the chair.

"Onkel Einar, we have eighteen piglets. That gilt rolled on one, but the others are all under their corner. Just think, eighteen, and two more sows to go."

"Killed one, eh?"

"Sorry." Leif came in the house, shaking his head. "I thought eighteen was pretty good."

"It is." Nilda handed him a cookie. "You are a good animal husbandman."

The next time she checked on Einar, he was asleep again. *Thank you, Lord, for small favors.*

"I'm going out to weed for a while," she announced. "Signe, you too?"

"Ja, be right there. Let me tell Gerd."

They were mopping their faces with their aprons after hoeing for an hour when they heard a roar from the porch.

"I need help!"

They both took off for the house at a run.

He shook his fist at them. "I got to get up and —"

"Hold on!" Signe yelled.

But before they could get to him, Einar pushed himself upright and fell forward, flat on his face.

Chapter 25

The next morning, Rune and the women stared down at Einar, sleeping again after breakfast and a dose of laudanum. They had carried him from the porch to the bed the night before, and Rune had spent the night on a pallet next to the bed. Einar had awakened with garbled speech, his usual hostility, and definite weakness in his right side.

"We will have someone with him at all times. That's all we can do," Signe said.

"I will stay with him," Gerd answered.

Rune shook his head. "No, we will take turns. Leif needs to stay near the barn to watch the pigs, so he can do turns here too. The other three boys will go back to limbing and cleaning up brush out in the forest. They can cut firewood too. I have told them to leave the standing trees until I get back."

"You will have the lumberyard deliver the lumber for the house?" Signe asked.

"Ja. I will bring back what we need for the cellar, so I should be back by early afternoon, if I start right now." He looked at each of the women. "If he starts to get agitated . . ."

"He should sleep for three or four hours with what I gave him," Nilda said. "You might buy some more laudanum while you are in Blackduck. We have enough for one more dose."

"I will hurry." He shook his head. "If only he would listen to others."

"He never will." Gerd wagged her head. "Never has, never will."

"We'll do what we can. If he starts flailing those long arms, you just get out of his way," Rune urged them. "If he gets agitated and falls out of bed, let him lie there until either the boys come back or I do. I do not want one of you to get hurt."

All three women nodded in response.

"We could tie him down." Gerd gave Rune a questioning look. "Feet and hands. We've got some sheeting we could rip into strips."

"The laudanum should be enough," Nilda said. "When we bring him coffee for dinner, I will give him a bit more."

"Tie him if you must, but do not try to keep him from falling, and do not argue with him. He might be calmer when he wakes, but he might be worse." Rune thought a moment. "Maybe I better stay here."

"I could go order the lumber, since you have the sizes and amounts all written out," Signe volunteered. "Or Nilda could."

"And when they start asking you questions about the structure of the house, or do we want this instead of that . . ." He shook his head. "And paying for it. I do not have enough money to pay for it all at once, and I can almost guarantee they do not accept installments from women."

Nilda shook her head. "Shame, isn't it?"

Gerd stared Rune right in the eyes. "I — we would help pay for it."

"Nei! No!" Rune said, then caught himself. "Tante Gerd, I would do business with you, but not Einar. Not ever again. My house has to be bought and paid for by me. I appreciate your offer, but please understand why I am saying this."

Gerd reached for his hand. "I do understand, but you all mean far more to me than money. If I have it, I want to share it with you."

Signe sniffed. "Gerd . . ."

Rune felt overwhelmed too, but he had two women to thank God for. *Thank you, Lord. I asked for a family here, and you have given us one with Gerd and now Nilda and Ivar.*

Signe let the tears drip. Easier than fighting them, no doubt.

Rune laid his hands on Gerd's shoulders. "Thank you. I cannot begin to tell you how much this means to me and to Signe and to our boys too." He blew out a breath. "Now I will be on my way and home again as soon as I can." He started to the door. "Remember, Ivar and Bjorn are strong as full-grown men if you need them."

"Here. Take the eggs and butter with you for Benson's." Signe handed him the baskets she had packed.

He gave her a swift kiss on the cheek. "Be careful, hear me?"

He climbed up on the wagon that had become the flatbed used to haul the hay, waved to the women, and set the team at a trot down the lane. The boys had the other team out in the woods, so Rosie was alone with the cows in the pasture.

He waved at Mrs. Benson, sitting out on the store's porch, as he turned the corner toward Blackduck. Drawing the team to a halt, he called, "I brought you eggs and butter. I'm going to order the lumber for the house today. Can I get you anything?"

"Wonderful. Wait just a moment." She disappeared into the store, so Rune climbed down and carried the baskets Signe had given him to the front porch and set them in the shade.

"Here." Mrs. Benson handed him a bag. "Some to take home, and some to eat on the way. Holler when you get back, and I might have something else to send. Should the mister round up the crew?"

"Not yet. We need to get the cellar framed so the foundation is ready to set the house right on it. We are going to have a celebration for certain when this house is ready to move into."

"That we will. A real party. How is Mr. Strand doing?"

"Worse. He fell again. Can't get it into his head that he needs time to recuperate. Just because he's not bleeding and nothing's broken." Rune shook his head. "Takk for asking."

"Can any of us help?"

"Not that I can think of." He peeked in the bag and grinned at her when he saw the cookies. "For me?"

"I know Leif and Knute especially like those too."

"I will share. Lord bless you, Mrs. Benson. You are a true friend. Oh, wait a moment. Do you have any laudanum?"

"I do, order came in just yesterday. I'll have it ready for you when you get back."

"Good, saves me a stop in Blackduck."

"Takk for these." She picked up the baskets.

Nibbling on the two cookies he'd allowed himself, he took the next five miles at a slow jog to keep from wearing the horses out. They'd been hitching the teams the way the former owner had suggested, one of Einar's old team paired with one of the green team. Probably he should have hitched up the other team too, but they'd not driven the four together yet.

Sweat streaked the horses' shoulders as he turned into the lumberyard. He drew them to a stop in the shade, swung down, made sure all his papers along with a good part of the cash he had saved were in the packet stuffed in his shirt, and strode toward the office. If only he knew things were safe at home, he could enjoy this long-dreamed-of day, rather than needing to hurry home.

"Good to see you again, Mr. Carlson," Mr. Hechstrom greeted from behind the counter. "How did those skis work out? You get them finished?"

"Not yet, but they will be for this winter. I sure have learned a lot."

"Trial and error can be pretty good teachers. How can I help you today?"

Rune took the papers out of his shirt front. "I'm here to order the lumber for my house."

"Well, good for you. Congratulations are in order. Hang on." Mr. Hechstrom called to the back. "Petter, you come out here and run the front while I help this man?"

A young man jogged out of the warehouse bay, his face sweaty. "Yes sir, Mr. Hechstrom."

"Mr. Carlson, here —"

"Rune Carlson." Rune failed to mention anything about Einar Strand. He'd learned that the name Strand could bring out bad feelings.

"Okay, Rune, this is my nephew, Petter Thorvaldson."

When the two shook hands, the young man asked, "Carlson! Are you the Carlson that Miss Nilda Carlson and her brother Ivar came to help?"

"I'm their older brother. My wife and I came last year to help our relatives."

"Well, I'll be snookered. I heard a lot about you and your wife and, what, three boys and a baby girl? From Valders, Norway, and Ivar was going to help fell the big trees, and Miss Carlson was so looking forward to seeing her best friend again. We got to know each other pretty well. How are they?"

Rune smiled at the young man's enthusiasm. "Ivar took the other end of a crosscut saw yesterday for the first time, and we brought down three trees. His shoulders were pretty sore last night."

Petter grinned from ear to ear. "Well, I am so glad to meet you. Greet them from me, please."

"I will. If you make it out our way, I know they will be glad to see you again too. They talked of you like friends."

Mr. Hechstrom nodded. "Perhaps Petter can drive one of the loads. He's told us a lot about his friends from the ship." He pointed toward a door along the back wall. "Come to my office, and let's put your order together."

Rune took the chair Mr. Hechstrom indicated.

"You want something to drink? Coffee, cold water?"

"Ja, both would be good. My team is in the shade, so they should be good for a while."

Mr. Hechstrom called for someone to bring the drinks and then sat in the other chair. On the desk in front of him were tablets and pencils, along with pen and ink. "Now, tell me about your house plans."

"I drew them out, much as I was able. I was trying to estimate how much lumber I'd need, but I know this is nowhere near accurate. I was going to build a one-and-a-half story, but I decided we better go with two full stories." He pushed the papers over to the other man. "You might have this already figured out, but we need a real second floor, not just an attic like at Einar's house."

Mr. Hechstrom nodded, leafing from page to page of Rune's drawings. Probably in his eyes, the plans were laughingly crude. He nodded. "Pretty standard farmhouse style. Good. This what you've dug for the cellar?"

"Ja. Today I need to take home posts and joists and whatever else I need to frame that in so it will be ready for the rest."

"You got some helpers?"

"My brother and two sons, but the men of the church have said we are going to have a house-raising."

"That the Lutheran church at Benson's Corner?"

Rune nodded.

"Those are good people there, some real good carpenters too. This house'll go up real fast. They know how to do it, raising walls and such. Good for you." Mr. Hechstrom pulled a list of materials out of the drawer under the table. "How about this: We load your wagon today with the cellar materials like you said, then I get an estimate together and come out to your place so we can make sure we have at least most of it. I will include roofing and siding and doors and windows. We'll deliver the framing supplies first, and the roofing and remaining supplies when you are ready for them."

"Sounds good. Can we talk about money?"

"If you want. Tell you what I have done plenty of times. You tell me how much you can pay now, and then we'll divide the rest up into payments, due when the trees are sold. I figure that is what you will use to pay with."

Rune stared at the man across the desk. "You would do that?"

"Well, yes, unless you would rather go through the bank. I figure you got enough trees out there to pay off your house in the next year or so."

"We are not talking Einar's trees here, but those on my five acres."

"How many acres already cleared?"

"About one and a half."

"And the rest is white pine?"

"Mostly."

"You got enough timber to pay for more than this house, even with furnishing it. You agree?"

"Ja, but what if something happens and . . ."

"And you can't pay?"

Rune nodded.

Mr. Hechstrom smiled. "I know accidents happen. Sometimes sickness too. But I'm gambling that if you can't cut trees any more, your sons and brother will take over and make it happen. You Norskies are like that."

"In spite of . . . ?" Rune hated to bring up Einar's name.

Mr. Hechstrom leaned forward. "Rune Carlson, I am a pretty good judge of character, and you got plenty of it. You can't always choose your relatives, but you can choose your friends and those you do business with. I've worked with you some already, and I've heard really good things from others. So you give me the money you have today and go frame your basement. I will write you a receipt that says what you have is paid on account. This is all legal and frequently done." He extended his hand across the desk.

Rune took it and nodded before shaking. "Takk. While they are loading, can I water my team?"

Mr. Hechstrom nodded. "You want to come have dinner with the wife and me?"

"Sometime, but not today. I need to get back. Thank you, again."

Rune watered his horses, and as soon as the lumber and nails were loaded, he pointed the team toward home. He let them rest once before Benson's Corner and again while he retrieved the baskets, one with several packets in it.

"The laudanum is there along with some other things I figured you could use," Mrs. Benson explained. "Greet them all from me, please. Perhaps I can get out there for a visit before that sweet baby is down and crawling."

"She gets up on all fours now and rocks back and forth but hasn't quite got the idea she can crawl forward. Leif keeps encouraging her."

When he arrived home, he left the team hitched in the shade and strode to the house. Leif joined him.

"We got two more babies, but she is done now," he reported. "They all nursed, I made sure."

"You and Knute are mighty good with the animals." Rune ruffled Leif's hair. "How were things at the house?"

"Onkel Einar has slept, mostly. Bjorn helped him sit up to eat dinner."

"Good. How'd the guys do in the woods?"

"Bjorn said they got two of the trees limbed and the branches stacked. They should be ready for the next one by the time you get there."

The kitchen was empty when he entered, but he could hear Signe and Nilda down in the cellar. He set the baskets from Mrs. Benson on the table. "There's some cookies there, but make sure there are enough left for everyone else too."

"You can take some out when you go to the trees." Leif dug out two cookies and headed back out the door to check on his piglets.

Signe came up from the cellar. "I thought I heard you here. How did it go?"

"Better than you can believe. I'll tell you all tonight at supper." He pointed to the baskets. "Mrs. Benson said to tell you takk for the butter and eggs. She had ordered laudanum, so that is there, along with some other things she thought you could use."

"Leave it to Mrs. Benson. A jar of honey. Ginger cookies — oh, and three peppermint sticks. Leif didn't find those, eh?" Signe smiled.

"What about . . . ?" Rune nodded toward

the bedroom.

"Been pretty docile so far. He let the boys help him sit up and move to the edge of the bed. He didn't make an effort to move to the chair. Nilda doctored his coffee like she said." She brushed a strand of hair out of her face. "It's nice and cool down there in the cellar. We got it about all cleaned out. The cat helped. The orange tabby must have found a secret place to have her babies, but Gra dispatched a couple of mice when we found a nest. It's a good thing Leif was at the barn. He'd have wanted to keep the babies."

Rune smiled. Yes, that was his boy, all right. "I'll drive the lumber out to the house, and Leif can unharness the team and let them into the pasture. We'll probably unload the wagon on our way up for supper."

As he headed for the barn again, he stared out over the fields. The sprouting oats cast a green haze out to the west. The cows were lying down under the one shade tree. What a peaceful scene.

"You think you can get the harnesses hung up?" Rune asked Leif as he drove the wagon out to the big hole.

Leif gave him a patient look. "You want me to come out to the woods?"

"I know you want to, but I really need someone here who can run fast to get us in case something happens with Einar."

Leif nodded, then grinned at his far. "I should get an extra peppermint stick for staying here."

Rune laughed. "You take that up with the others."

"What they don't know can't hurt 'em."

Rune chuckled as he headed farther out into the woods, where he could hear two axes thudding into branches. He swung the bag of cookies in one hand and realized he was grinning like a child with a peppermint stick. He had paid money down on his own house. He and Signe were landowners and would soon have a house of their own. All in one year. Only in America. In spite of what a mean old man Onkel Einar was, they owed him a debt of gratitude for bringing them over.

He stopped at the edge of the clearing to watch the three boys at work and to inhale the fragrance of cut pine. The other team nodded in the shade. There were two new piles of branches, and the earliest piles of branches were now neatly stacked in stove lengths, ready to haul to the house. Einar had been all set to burn those piles, but Leif and Knute insisted that would make good firewood — and they were right.

He called to the boys and raised the cookie bag over his head.

The three planted their axes in a branch near them, and while they weren't running to meet him, they weren't staggering either. They all sat on or leaned against the wagon to drink water kept cool in the shade and devour the cookies.

They felled the second tree at the beginning hush of dusk. All fell silent until one branch that caught on another tree crashed to the ground.

"Two trees today, in spite of my being gone. You've done well," Rune said.

Ivar stretched. "Shame Onkel Einar isn't out here to appreciate this."

Bjorn snorted and shook his head at Ivar. "All he'd say is, 'Shoulda had three. You didn't limb them yet, don't just stand around.' "

Rune watched his son's face. Bjorn wasn't angry or critical, he was just stating the facts. And he was so right.

"Perhaps tomorrow we can do four . . ." Ivar joked.

"Or maybe six." Knute looked at his far with a grin.

"Bring Nilda out here," Ivar added. "She is good with an ax and could do the limbing with Knute here."

Ivar grabbed the axes, and Rune and Bjorn brought the saw. Bjorn hitched up the team and drove the wagon over to one of the stacks of wood for the stove. They loaded the pile into the wagon and hauled the wood up to the house to dump in a pile to be split.

That night at supper, Rune looked at Nilda. "I met a friend of yours today. He works at the lumberyard, says he came over on the ship with you."

Her eyes went wide. "*Petter?* Petter Thorvaldson?"

"That's the one. He was real glad to hear about the two of you. Mr. Hechstrom says he could be one of the drivers to deliver the lumber, so we might see him here soon."

Ivar waggled his eyebrows at his sister, and Nilda threw a dish towel at him — and laughed.

"This house needs more laughter," Gerd said softly. "It really does."

CHAPTER 26

"Why — you — here?" Einar glared at Rune. "Get — in — woods."

"Your speech is much better today." Rune stood by the bed. "Would you like to sit in the chair?"

"Nei!" Einar pointed toward the woods with a trembling hand.

"I warned you that if you can't be polite to those who are trying to help you get better, I will stay here at the house. I will go out in the woods when I can trust you to be decent here. If you would cooperate with them, you might be out in the woods sooner."

Signe and Nilda listened from the doorway. Signe shook her head. "Won't happen. I don't think he *can* be polite."

Rune nodded. "I'm afraid I agree with you. But he wants those trees down mighty bad. So, Onkel Einar, one way to get stronger again is to get up and sit in this chair for a while."

Einar glared knives at Rune, but slowly he swung his legs over the edge of the bed and sat up, panting. Rune held out his hand to help, but Einar batted it away. He clamped a hand on the arm of the chair.

Signe retrieved Gerd's cane from the pantry and brought it to Einar. "This might make it easier." The look she received for her efforts might have withered a weaker woman, but she met him eye to eye. "To help you get stronger, faster."

He eyed the chair, the cane, and Rune, then grabbed the cane with one hand and the chair with the other and heaved himself to his feet. He stood swaying, steadied, and then turned enough to sit in the chair.

Signe felt like clapping.

"Do you promise to be polite? If you will, I will return at dinnertime. If there is a problem, Leif will come for me, and I will stay here." Rune waited. "I know you are a man of your word. If you agree, I know you will do it."

Einar nodded.

"Then I will see you at dinnertime."

In the kitchen, Rune beckoned the three women to come out on the porch. "I'm concerned about him having that cane if he goes berserk again. He could really hurt someone with it, so be careful."

"Takk." Gerd shook her head. "I should be the one taking care of him."

"Why?"

"I married him."

Rune squeezed her shoulder. "Gerd, we are your family, and we will take care of each other as we need to. You took care of Signe and Kirstin, remember?"

"Ja, but . . ."

"Leif can run fast if need be. Keep that in mind." He looked at Signe and Nilda, who both nodded. He nodded in return and headed down the steps to join the others in the woods.

Nilda stood agape. "I have never in my life heard my brother string so many words, and such wise words, together at one time. I wish Mor could see and hear this. She would be so proud of him. Not that she would let anyone know, but I have watched her eyes gleam, and I know what she is thinking."

Signe felt her eyes get moist. "Talking like this makes me miss her even more. Ivar says that one day he will send them tickets, but I know your far will never come to Amerika. He is adamant, and I don't remember in all the years of knowing him that he ever changed his mind, once he locked on something."

"I know." Nilda heaved a sigh. "I do not want to be like that. Nor like Onkel Einar."

Gerd carried Kirstin on her hip now, since she was getting so big and so busy. "Yesterday she found a beetle on the floor and scooted her quilt over to pick it up."

"And it went directly into her mouth?" Signe said, shaking her head.

"I got it before she did." Gerd jiggled the baby up and down to make her giggle. "I need to sew her some shifts for the hot weather."

"And a sunbonnet so she can come out in the garden with us?"

"Ja, I even have a pattern and some of that gingham left. Perhaps I can do that this afternoon. Right now we need to put the boiler on the stove and wash diapers." Gerd handed Kirstin to her mor. "I better check on Einar, see if he is ready to go back to bed. Remember when you had to drag me out of bed?" She glanced at Nilda. "This Signe, she can be mighty tough when she chooses to be. She decided I was going to get back on my feet, and that was that."

"But she better stay out of reach of that bear in there. No matter how tough she is, he is bigger and stronger." Nilda fetched the broiler from its nail on the wall and set it in the sink. Pumping water to fill it, she looked out the window. "I want to be out in that garden before it gets too hot."

"I will do the diapers," Signe said, "you go out in the garden, and Gerd, you go sew for our baby girl."

Gerd went to check on Einar. "He is back in bed and sleeping."

At least he's quiet, Signe thought as she rinsed out the diapers and stirred them into the hot soapy water. A cake might be good for dinner — no, gingerbread. She found herself humming as she stirred the ingredients together. Gingerbread was Rune's favorite. They had plenty of cream to whip for topping.

"Two trees," Knute announced when the men came through the door at dinnertime. "What smells so good?" He spied the pan on the table. "Of course, gingerbread."

The kitchen went from quiet and peaceful to laughter and ruckus. Bjorn picked up his baby sister and set her on his shoulders. She clamped her fingers in his hair, making him flinch.

"You be careful with her. Knute, don't let her fall backward." The three of them paraded around the table, a baby chortle making everyone laugh.

Rune went to Einar immediately, and Signe followed in case he needed help.

"All right," Rune said, "let's get you back up again, and you might enjoy sitting at the window. See the outside."

Einar rumbled and grumbled, but he did as instructed. "Quiet," he whispered as he stood. "Tell them quiet."

Rune nodded. "The noise makes the pain worse?"

"Ja." Together the three of them walked to the window, and Rune moved the chair into place. Once Einar was seated, Rune and Signe left to settle the others down.

"Oh, sorry." The boys quieted immediately. Signe took her daughter and tied her into the rocking chair. The gingerbread disappeared nearly as quickly as she put it on their plates and spooned whipped cream on top.

"Now that was fine." Rune patted his belly. "Leif, how are your babies doing?"

"All still alive. Daisy is going to have hers next. She is starting to nest."

"We need more farrowing stalls at this rate. We could turn the horse stalls into pig pens for now. Take some of that scrap lumber and nail boards across the ends. Ivar, how good are you with building something like that?"

"Had to at home at times. I can measure and cut boards and pound nails."

"So can we," Bjorn offered. "And sharpen saw blades. Onkel Einar usually does that."

"We better do that tonight rather than working on the cellar. Let me get Einar back to bed, and we'll return to the woods."

Rune stood up, and Signe did the same. "I'll help you."

"Let me take that tray," Rune said as he entered the bedroom and bent over Einar, "and we'll get you back to bed. You want to try walking around the room first?"

"Nei. So tired."

"A little more each day will get you stronger again. If you were out in the woods with us, we could do three, four trees a day — easy. Those boys are getting better and better with the axes and saws." Rune waited for Einar to stand, handing him the cane to walk with. "We'll do this again when I get home."

Seeing that Einar was calm and Rune had everything under control, Signe went out to the porch. She rinsed and wrung out the diapers, then hung them on the line to flap in the breeze.

She looked up to see a hawk circling against the blue. "Don't you even think of stealing our chickens." Just that morning one of the brooding hens came off her nest with a flock of eight chicks, so Signe and Leif had moved them to another small, fenced pen with a nesting box. Three other hens were setting. They were having babies all over the place, much to Leif's delight. Since Knute had gone to help in the woods, all the responsibility for the farm animals had shifted to Leif and the women.

Signe watched the hawk fly away before heading back into the house.

That evening, Nilda helped Leif milk the cows so that when the others trooped in from the woods, all of the farm chores were done. They had just finished supper when they heard a horse and wagon coming down the lane.

Nilda was doing the dishes and Signe was changing Kirstin as Rune and Knute stepped out on the back porch. Nilda heard Rune's strong voice say, "Welcome, come on in. Good to see you. Hey, Ivar, Nilda, come on out here. There are some folks who will be right glad to see you."

What?

Nilda went outside, wiping her hands on a dishtowel. "Who . . . ?" She stopped in her tracks at the sight of Petter hopping down from the wagon. "Why, Mr. Thorvaldson. I am delighted to see you. Ivar, come here!" The two men shook hands, and Nilda motioned them to the benches and chairs against the house. "Sit down, sit down, I'll bring the coffee right out." Back inside, she whispered to Signe, "Remember that young man from the ship that we told you about? He is here! Came out with his uncle from the lumberyard."

Signe smiled. "It's a shame we ate all the gingerbread. You could take out a plate of cookies, though."

"Does my hair look all right?" Nilda tucked a stray strand back where it belonged before pulling the coffeepot forward and dishing up the cookies. "He said he would come find us, but I didn't really think he would." She stopped. "I'm dithering, aren't I?"

Signe's smile had turned knowing. "A bit, but that's all right."

Signe lit the lamp and set it where Gerd was sewing on the machine. As Nilda picked up the tray to serve the coffee, Signe was scooping up her daughter, who already wore the sleepy look that said she was not long for the day. Often Signe took Kirstin out to the rocking chair on the porch, and they enjoyed the evening breeze. Would she come out here with the others? Signe turned toward the stairs. Apparently not.

As Nilda carried out the tray, the man who had been introduced as Mr. Hechstrom was saying, "How about we drive out to look at your place before it gets dark?"

"Fine by me. These young people can visit while we're gone." Rune climbed up on the wagon seat with the lumber man and motioned to the lane past the barn that led toward the clearing near the woods. Their trap rattled away down the rough lane.

"So how is your job going with your uncle?" Ivar asked Petter.

"He is teaching me the ways of running a lumberyard, filling orders, waiting on customers, that kind of thing. I would rather be out in the woods, but he needs the help, and Tante Soren treats me like one of her sons. They had three boys, but one died a few years ago. One works for the railroad, and the other is married and lives in Minneapolis. They did not want to work in the lumberyard. But Onkel said business slows down in the winter, and if I want to go be a lumberjack, fine, just so I come back in the spring."

Ivar asked, "Did you do much lumbering in Norway?"

"Nei. The lumberyard runs its own mill, and I work on that. But out in the woods?

That's where I'd rather be. I want to learn how to do it all well."

Nilda asked, "Have you heard from home?" *Do you have any news from Norway?*

"Ja, my brother and sister both want to come, so I am saving for their tickets. They are too."

Nilda smiled. "Sounds like us last year."

Signe came outside without the baby. Kirstin must have fallen asleep. And since Onkel Einar was not yelling, he was probably asleep as well. Signe asked their guest, "Are you taking English classes?"

"Nei, but I'm picking up a lot from work. I hear there is going to be a house-raising as soon as you are ready. Do you mind if I come help? We are closed on Sundays."

Nilda grinned. "You think we would turn down a pair of willing hands?'

"You never know. I mean, I've heard rumors." Petter looked away.

"About Onkel Einar. Ja, we know." Nilda shrugged. "But right now he is laid up from an accident." Ivar snorted, but she ignored him. "It will be better when we can move to the new house."

Petter and Ivar chatted on, but Nilda found herself thinking surprising thoughts. A strong young lad who wanted to learn lumbering, and Onkel Einar's woodlot, and . . .

They heard the jingle of harness and hooves clopping before Mr. Hechstrom stopped his horse by the house.

"You want to come in for coffee?" Rune asked as he climbed off the trap.

"I better get on home. You've got the copy of the contract, so we'll start hauling the lumber out so as to be ready when you are." Mr. Hechstrom called, "Come along, Petter, we need to get on home."

Petter climbed nimbly up over a wheel and into the seat. "I'll see you again soon."

Nilda had the feeling he was speaking more to her than to Ivar, but Ivar answered, "Perhaps you can stay for dinner or supper when you deliver the lumber. Meet the rest of the family."

"Perhaps." Petter settled into the trap beside his uncle, and the two of them waved as they trotted down the lane.

"What a nice surprise." Nilda watched the trap disappear into the evening.

"Maybe he would want to work here in the winter?" Ivar asked.

"You think Onkel Einar would pay a real crew what they are worth?" Nilda asked. "Real crews expect to be properly paid, not to give away their labor because of family ties."

Ivar looked at her in the dim light from the doorway. "You never know what will happen between now and then. You just never know."

Chapter 27

Dear Mor,

Thank you for your letter. I have to apologize for not writing more often since we arrived. Life here is full of challenges as we try to keep up with the regular summer work, and now they are working on Rune's house whenever possible. I'm not sure if I told you that Onkel Einar had an accident with a new team of horses hitched to the disc. He injured his head in the fall, and he is very angry that he cannot be out cutting down the big trees.

Nilda felt like saying a lot more, but she wanted to get the letter in the mail the next day when she and Signe went to Benson's Corner for their language class. The thought of the class made her tap the end of the pencil on her chin. Signe had been teasing her that Mr. Larsson spent a good part of the class looking at her. Surely that wasn't so, but it did make Nilda watch him more closely, so that their glances often intersected. Strange.

She returned to her letter.

Ivar is helping in so many different ways. I did not realize how very adaptable he can be. He and Bjorn have become a good team, both in the woods and on the farm, while Knute spends his time with both, along with taking charge of splitting wood for the kitchen stove. Leif is busy taking care of the farrowing sows, their babies, the hens and chicks, and his baby sister. I wish you could see her laugh and wiggle when he comes near. She has a lot to say, if only we could understand her.

Tante Gerd is able to do more around the house all the time. One day she even went out to the garden to pick lettuce for supper. I think she misses being outside. She set Kirstin in the wagon and brought her along.

Rune and Signe will have a wonderful, big house when it is finished. People from the church have promised to come help with the house-raising, in spite of

Onkel Einar telling everyone to stay off his land. I still have no idea where all his anger has come from. It might be easier if I understood what is behind it all. Rune and Signe do not know either, but they are making friends at church and in the community.

I still long for the mountains at home, the seter, and all our family. How I wish you and Far would come here. Norway might as well be in another world. How is your garden doing this year? What is happening with the newlyweds? Uff da. Now I am getting more homesick than ever.

Oh, we will set up the loom at the new house when it is built. And Tante Gerd said we would get a small flock of sheep before fall. Leif is so excited that we will have lambs next spring. More babies for him to take care of.

Remember the young man that we met on the ship that I wrote about? He works in Blackduck at the lumberyard. He and Ivar were talking about working in a logging camp this winter. Ivar would get paid extra if he took one of our teams to work there too. They have not talked with Onkel Einar yet, though. There is plenty of time to talk about that before they would leave. I am sure Bjorn would want to go along too, but he is needed here. They are felling more trees with Ivar here even though Onkel Einar is laid up.

This letter is growing into a book, so I will stop now. Greet everyone for me, for us. I am not the only one who dreams of home, although this place is becoming home too. Please write soon, and I shall try to do better.

Your loving daughter and the rest of the family here,

Nilda Carlson

She folded the pages and tucked them into an envelope. Writing the address on the front led to wiping away a tear. In spite of sniffing and swallowing, more tears followed. She laid her head on her arms, and let both tears and thoughts flow. She'd never see her family again, never hold the babies born, inhale the fragrance of home, trek in the mountains, hear the spring freshets leaping down the creek beds, card the wool, spin and weave with her mor.

She cried for a while without making noise so as not to wake the others who needed their sleep so badly. Carefully, she stood and stepped outside onto the porch. Sink-ing down on the steps, she stared up at the stars arching across the azure sky, the same stars she had seen at home, but which somehow seemed closer there. She wiped her eyes on her apron. Fireflies danced, a cricket sang, and the breeze kissed her cheeks, drying the tears. She inhaled the fragrance of turned earth in the garden, the faint touch of pine, the barnyard and chicken coop, and sighed.

Pushing herself up to her bare feet, she ambled to the outhouse, then returned to tiptoe up the stairs and slip into bed without waking anyone else.

"Are you all right?" Signe's whisper tickled her ear.

"Ja." *I will be by morning.*

A verse floated through her mind. *"Weeping endures for the night, but joy comes in the morning."* Surely this was true and always would be.

Late the next afternoon, she and Signe hitched Rosie to the cart and trotted down the lane to attend their language class. Since they had missed the last one, they practiced their lesson from the week before all the way to the church. Not that they hadn't practiced during the days, but some things needed more time.

Signe stumbled over a phrase, then repeated it three times. "I am not very good at this," she moaned.

Nilda clucked Rosie into a slow trot. "You're doing fine, better than some of the others."

A picture of Mr. Larsson at the front of the class leaped into her mind. *Don't be silly,* she told herself. *Why would he ever be interested in me?*

"Do you have the letters?" Signe asked.

"Ja." Nilda patted the bag on the seat between them. "And the grocery list to give to Mrs. Benson. Good thing she doesn't close early in the evening." Only the clip-clop of trotting hooves rose with the dust of the road.

When they entered the sanctuary of the church, six other students were talking with Mr. Larsson. When he heard them enter, he looked up with a smile that widened when he saw who they were.

"Welcome back. We were about to start."

"Takk." Nilda and Signe slid into the pew behind the others.

The teacher handed each of them a sheet of vocabulary words and phrases. "I'm sorry, I should have given you these on Sunday."

Nilda took the paper. His smile sparkled in his eyes, and she smiled back. He certainly had nice eyes, something she had noticed before. "T-takk."

The students were laughing more this evening, even when they stumbled on their responses. Nilda and Signe joined in, Signe nudging her when she caught Mr. Larsson smiling at Nilda.

"I told you so," Signe whispered.

Nilda felt like fanning her face as the heat rose up her neck. Good thing they were sitting behind the others instead of in a circle like they had before.

"Thank you all for coming," Mr. Larsson said at the end of the class. "And for working hard at learning English. I have a couple of short stories I would like you to read. You won't know all the words, but I think you will understand anyway. I would like them back at the end of our sessions so I can use them with the next beginning class."

"Will we continue into the fall?" one of the two men asked.

"Yes, until it gets dark too early for those who come farther." Mr. Larsson looked at Nilda again. "I am thinking of having a Saturday class until the snow makes things difficult. The longer we can go, the more quickly you will become comfortable speaking English. Please use your new vocabulary when you are talking at home. That is not easy, I know, but that is why we will be working more on phrases and conversation. In another two weeks, we will speak only English during our class time.

Nilda rolled her eyes along with the groans of the others. Signe sent her a look of near panic.

"Now, please, you will do fine. We will keep our conversations simple, using words and phrases you have learned. You will have a good time, really. Tonight we will say our farewells in English." Mr. Larsson switched to English and repeated what he had just said. "Good night, and I will see you next week. Now repeat that with me."

They did, and then said the same to each other as they walked down the aisle and out the door.

Signe and Nilda paused on the steps. "Look at the sunset." Nilda pointed to the bands of brilliant oranges and reds fading to lavender and pinks on the flat clouds above.

"Those are cirrus clouds," Mr. Larsson said behind them. Then he said the same in English.

"Cirrus?"

"Yes. That word stays the same." He nodded to them, and they repeated the words with him.

Nilda gazed up at the sky. "It's so . . . *vakker.*"

"Yes, beautiful." Mr. Larsson looked right at her.

"Ah, ah . . ." Nilda fumbled for words.

"Thank you." Signe's grin made Nilda want to poke her, but instead she headed for the horse and cart. Since when was she shy and tongue-tied like that? *Nilda, my girl, behave yourself. You've had men smile at you before. What is so different now?*

Signe hummed on the way home as if she had not a care in the world.

They were just turning into their lane when Nilda finally huffed. "I do not want to hear another word about this."

"About what?" If innocence had a face, it was Signe's.

Chapter 28

Leif burst into the clearing in the woods where the men were working. "Far, come quick, Onkel Einar fell."

Rune called Bjorn to take his place on the crosscut saw. "You and Ivar finish this. Come for dinner at noon if I am not back. Knute, keep on limbing the tree you are on."

Rune caught up with Leif, who had started back to the house. The two of them jogged all the way, and Rune had a hard time catching his breath by the time they reached the steps to the porch.

Nilda met him at the door. "I don't think he's hurt badly, because he is awake and furious that we won't help him get up."

"How did it happen?"

"I was walking with him to the chair by the window, and he stumbled. He tried to grab me, but I couldn't stop his fall."

"Any idea why he stumbled?" When she didn't answer, Rune turned to look at her.

She heaved a sigh. "He wanted Gerd to help him, but I couldn't let her do that, or they might both go down. He wasn't angry until he stumbled. Well, he was still Einar, but he was not yelling at me."

"I told you —"

"Rune, he actually asked for help."

"Miracles do happen," Rune muttered as he crossed the bedroom to the man swearing into the floorboards. "All right, Einar, let's get you up."

"Tried walking to the window, and look what happened." He pounded his fist on the floor. Another string of expletives followed.

"Okay, let's get you up on your hands and knees."

"What, you want me to-to crawl over there?"

"Not a bad idea, really, but I was going to bring the chair here so you can use it to help you."

"Just get the chair."

Nilda plunked the chair down beside him. Rune held it steady as Einar gripped the seat, dragged his uncooperative legs under him, and made it up. He twisted to sit, but he kept his eyes closed, barely shaking his head. "Will this dizziness ever go away?" The pauses between each word showed that though his speech had improved, it was not by many degrees.

Rune wisely kept his mouth shut. "The window or the bed?" he asked softly after an extended period of silence.

"Bed." When Einar was settled back against the pillows, he glared at Rune. "Go back to the woods, I — won't yell at that Nilda. No need to send for you." The effort to talk cost him, Rune could tell.

"It is almost dinnertime. The boys will be up to eat soon, and I will go back with them."

"How — how many trees?"

"Two down. Two more this afternoon."

Einar groaned. "I should be out there."

"As soon as you are strong enough."

"Walk out to porch after dinner."

"We'll see how you feel."

Einar declined dinner, but for a cup of coffee and a piece of bread. Nilda slipped some laudanum into the coffee at Rune's suggestion.

"I will help him out to the porch when we come back to the house," he said.

"What if he wakes up and insists?"

"Do not try to stop him, but don't help him either. I know that is hard-hearted, but the three of you should not have to pay for his stubborn mistakes."

The boys came in from the woods for their meal, and Leif hopped up from the table as soon as he finished eating. "Got to get back to the barn. Daisy is going to start having her babies any time now." He jumped down the steps and ran for the barn.

Knute headed for the woodpile to bring in an armload. "We need to split wood tonight too."

Nilda waved him off. "You get out to the woods. I'll take care of the woodpile here."

"Well, I'll be," Rune purred. "And here I was going to ask you to come and start limbing or dragging branches."

Nilda smirked at him. "I'm thinking about that."

"Not really." Rune gave her a *big brother is right* look.

Nilda smiled with a wide-eyed look of innocence. "We'll see," she called out over her shoulder.

Ivar clapped his older brother on the back. "You might not want to order her around. She has a stubborn streak two feet wide, or so Mor says. Come on, let's go knock down a couple more big trees."

When they returned, Leif and Nilda had the chores done, Einar was seated in the rocking chair on the porch, and supper was ready. Split wood not only filled the woodbox but lay in a neat stack by the chopping block.

"Kirstin likes the sound of wood chopping," Signe said with a smile. "Put her right to sleep."

"She could hear it clear in here?" Rune asked.

"No, she was on the porch in her rocking chair."

"I see. Is it about time for Einar to come in?"

"Ask if he wants his supper out there. I'll bring him a tray."

Rune got a *yes* from Einar, which was unusual, so he took out a tray with chicken and dumplings, bread and butter, and coffee and got him set up. When the rest of them had finished eating, he found Einar asleep with his chin on his chest, but the plate was clean. After getting him back to bed, Rune and his crew headed for their new home's cellar.

"We're going to need eight flat rocks to go under the vertical posts, so Knute, you and Leif take the horse and wagon to the rock piles and search some out. There are a couple in that pile behind the machine shed, I know, and two more piles out on the southwestern corner of the hay field. I'd go there first. The flatter the better, but we can flatten them with a chisel if we need to."

The boys climbed up on the wagon seat and urged the horse out to the hayfield. They knew where the rock pile was, since they had thrown many of the rocks on it. Dusk was dimming the land when they returned with six.

Rune and the others had hauled the posts and joists down into the hole and were measuring and sawing two-by-tens into twelve-foot lengths on the saw horses. Rune looked over the rock collection the boys threw down into the hole.

"Pretty good. We need two more, and then find a few more just in case."

Other than Einar's snoring, all was quiet at the house when they trudged up the steps later that evening.

"Daisy had thirteen babies," Leif told Gerd, who was sitting out on the porch in the soft evening air.

"Does she have that many teats?"

"No, only twelve, but I made sure the little one nursed too."

"Onkel Einar would tell you to knock the runt on the head and throw it on the manure pile."

"But why would I do that?" Horror squeaked his voice.

"The runt never does well and takes away

nourishment from the others."

Leif turned to Rune. "Far!"

"My far used to say the same thing," Rune said, "but we hand-raised more than a few runts through the years. If you can get them to nurse from a bottle, they might make it."

Leif relaxed. "Can I try that?"

"Help the small one get to a teat for these first days of colostrum, and then you can switch it to cow's milk on a bottle. It'll be a gamble, but sometimes you win."

"But more often you lose. Aren't twenty-six babies with another sow to farrow, enough?" Gerd's voice came gently from the darkness.

"I still want to try," Leif said stubbornly, and Gerd patted his arm.

Rune swatted at a persistent mosquito. "Let's get to bed, woodsmen. The morning will be here before we know it."

Three days later, Signe stared at the tired faces around the breakfast table. "You can't keep working so many hours. You all look like you should just go back to bed."

As if on cue, Rune yawned. "The day after tomorrow is Sunday. We'll go to church, and then I want the boys to go fishing. I've been dreaming of having fried fish for supper."

Knute nearly leaped out his chair. "You

mean it?"

"I hear there's a lake not far from here. Can we fish off the banks?" Ivar asked.

"The Garborgs have a rowboat; they said we can use it. We can ask them at church." Knute's excitement lit up the table.

"What will you use for fishing gear?" Signe asked.

"I've got three willow poles, but only two hooks."

She smiled. "I'm going to take butter and eggs to Benson's. Surely they would have hooks and line, maybe even corks."

"What are you going to do, Far?" Bjorn asked.

"I'm going to work in the cellar."

Bjorn straightened. "Me, too."

"I thought you'd want to go fishing."

"I prefer hunting." Bjorn shrugged.

Rune turned to Ivar. "He brought down two deer this last year. Between his hunting and Knute's rabbit snares, we've had meat most of the year."

"I could help you in the cellar," Ivar offered.

"I know, but Knute and Leif love to fish, and —"

"So do you, Far," Leif piped up. "Besides, who will check on my babies?"

"I will," Gerd said firmly. "I should have

been down to the barn more by now anyway. Seeing piglets and chicks" — she wagged her head — "best part of farming. That was always my responsibility, and here you are doing such a good job with it."

Leif smiled. "But you have Kirstin to take care of now."

Gerd nodded. "Ja, she is even better than baby pigs and chicks."

"Next summer she can come to the barn with me."

Signe rolled her eyes. She could just picture her little daughter playing in the dirt or the straw. "We shall see."

"Help me down the steps!"

The order came Saturday evening as the men were returning from working in the cellar. Caught unaware, Rune blurted, "Why now?"

"Because I need help, and you just got here." Even Einar's bark was weaker.

Ivar leaped the porch stairs and offered his arm. "Do you have your cane?"

"Ja."

"Then here we go."

"Wait, I can help too." Bjorn stopped on the first step. "Use my shoulder."

Rune felt himself grinning from ear to ear. These were indeed young men to be proud of. Ivar clasped Einar's hand and arm, and together they took one step down. Bjorn braced himself as the older man's hand clamped down on his shoulder. The three of them paused to let Einar blow out a breath. One more step, and then the final one to the ground.

"You want to sit or walk?" Ivar asked.

"Sit on the steps."

Both young men hovered, ready to help as Einar used his cane and an extended arm to lower himself to the middle step and sit with a grunt.

Rune felt like applauding but knew better. "You are a great deal stronger, Onkel. I know it is hard work."

"Next week, out in the woods."

Sitting on the porch, Rune could hear the June bugs slamming against the screens. A mosquito buzzed his ears. Crickets sang in the darkening dusk.

"The fireflies are out." Leif pointed to a dancing dot above the path to the outhouse. And then another. "How come they only come out at night?"

"Some things like the day, and some like the dark. Besides, how could they see one another's lights when the sun is out?"

"Mor brought back hooks, lines, and corks," Knute reported. "She said there is a card about puppies on the board at the store."

"Don't need a dog here," Einar almost barked, but not quite.

"Why not?" Knute asked, making Rune nearly choke.

"Dogs kill chickens and chase sheep."

"We don't have sheep."

"The women want sheep. Got that spinning wheel and loom now."

Rune reminded himself to breathe. Shock did that at times.

"Rugs might bring in some money," Einar mused.

Swallowing a snort could make one cough. Rune covered his mouth and cleared his throat.

"Help me up."

"To walk or back inside?" Ivar asked.

"Back up." Einar shook his head. "Might not make it if I walk a ways first."

"Can you believe that?" Rune whispered as he and Signe mounted the stairs to bed.

"We could hear him through the screen door. I thought Gerd was going to choke on her coffee."

"You were drinking coffee and didn't bring us any?"

"Didn't want to interrupt."

Rune's chuckle danced softly through the

darkness.

That night a rainstorm struck with only a smatter of warning before the deluge tried to pound the roof in on top of them. When the thunder crashed right above them, Kirstin woke with a shriek that matched the wind.

"Is she all right?" Nilda asked, raising her voice to be heard over the tumult.

Signe was already picking up her wailing daughter. "Shhhhh." She stroked her baby's back and spread kisses mixed with murmurs over her cheeks and forehead, swaying all the while.

Rune mumbled, "You okay?" before joining the boys as they slept on in spite of the uproar.

A few minutes later, when the storm had blown over, Signe whispered, "Nilda, you still awake?"

"Sort of."

"Come on, let's go sit on the porch."

"Are you crazy?"

"Possibly." Signe could only hear rather than see Nilda in the black of the room. Together they felt for the stairs with their feet and padded down. Dark as the house was, the darkness outside seemed to glow. Rainwater still gurgled through the down spouts and sang into the rain barrels. A breeze blew a few sprinkles into their faces as they sank down into the porch chairs.

Signe inhaled. "Nothing smells as wonderful as a rain-washed garden."

"If it were daylight, I would have been out in it, washing my hair," Nilda said.

"I know. I thought of that too." Signe tipped her head back. "One day when there are trees by the house, the rain perfume will be even more healing." Kirstin wriggled in her arms and then sighed herself back to sleep. "I could sleep out here in the coolness."

"If we had porch screens, you really could. I saw them in a magazine."

"When did you see a magazine like that?"

"On the ship."

They sat outside for a few more minutes, then silently crept back up to their beds.

In the morning on the way to church, they detoured around mud puddles. Some trees were down, and a creek rushed by at the top of its banks.

"It really rained hard last night, huh?" Ivar looked to Rune.

"Seems so. Guess we slept through most of it."

The two women in the bed of the wagon swapped smiles. "The fish should be biting well," Signe called up to them.

Ivar smacked his lips. "Mmm, fish for supper."

"We could probably catch more fish if we went now," Knute added.

Rune shook his head. "Sorry, son, church comes first."

"Did you go look in the new cellar?" Ivar asked Rune.

"Nei. If there is water in it, which is most likely, I will either work in spite of it or drag my feet through the mud it has left behind. I wish we could put up concrete walls and floor, but not this year. Some river gravel would be good down there in the meantime."

After church, Mr. Benson greeted Rune and Signe and asked, "We going to be raising a house on Saturday?"

Rune nodded. "We'll be ready."

"Good to hear." Benson clapped him on the shoulder. "When are they delivering the lumber and supplies? I'd have thought they'd have done so by now."

"Starting tomorrow. After that storm last night, we'd have had some wet wood."

"True. Good thing the roads will dry up quickly. I'll let the others know. We'll be there bright and early on Saturday."

"Have you mentioned the house-raising

to Mr. Strand yet?" Reverend Skarstead asked when they were shaking hands at the open door.

"The rest of us have talked about getting the house done, but not to him directly, no," Signe said.

"You might want to, to keep him from coming out after us with a shotgun. Folks don't take too kindly to that."

"Yes, sir, we will take care of it," Rune said. "I don't think he'll be up to much, even by then. Although he walked down and up the porch steps last night with the help of Ivar and Bjorn. He was nearly pleasant about it too."

"Now that is good news. I've been praying for him. I'll keep on it." The reverend turned to Signe. "Now don't you worry about feeding that crew on Saturday. The women will take care of that. Part of the package."

"How will we ever repay you all?" Signe asked.

"You don't. You just pass it on when someone else is in need."

On the way home, the boys could talk of nothing but going fishing. The puddles in the road were already half gone. And Signe could not get Einar out of her mind. What if he did threaten all their new friends with a gun? Would he possibly do more than just threaten?

CHAPTER 29

Signe stepped out on the porch. "What are you doing?"

Rune looked up from the two-by-four he had laid across two sawhorses. "Building railings for Einar so he can get up and down the porch stairs more easily."

Bjorn brought him the measuring stick and the saw. Together they measured the length needed.

"Do we need three posts, or is two enough?" Bjorn asked.

"Two should be fine. The top one nailed into the porch and the other onto the last step, high enough so he needn't bend over."

Signe watched her two men work as a well-trained team. They seemed to read each other's minds as they measured and cut boards. Railings on these porch stairs would be good for all of them, especially Gerd. Strange how she thought of Gerd as an old woman when in reality she was only ten years older than Signe.

She could hear Gerd murmuring to Kirstin and the baby answering with her own little noises that were progressing from gurgles to real sounds. When they laid her on a quilt on the floor, she delighted in finding and catching her toes and feet, and playing with her hands, moving her fingers and grabbing for anything in sight. Gerd's joy in the baby made Signe's heart sing with thankfulness.

"Where's Onkel Einar?" she asked as she returned to the kitchen, inhaling the rich odor of baking chicken.

"Sleeping in the chair in front of the window."

"With all that hammering?"

Gerd shook her head. "He can sleep through anything, more so since the accident."

"I think I'll go weed and hill the potatoes."

"Better take a can of kerosene. I think the bugs are there already. Just think, soon we'll have new peas and perhaps tiny potatoes to cream. Nothing tastes better than peas right from the garden."

"Or in the garden. Peas are best when shelled and eaten in the garden. Leif said there are almost blossoms."

Signe put on a sunbonnet and headed for

the machine shed, where the barrel of kerosene rested on a rack. She opened the spigot and drained a couple of inches into the can that waited on the shelf beside the barrel. It was a shame Leif wasn't here; he had eagle eyes when it came to spotting bugs on the plants. She sure hoped the boys were catching fish. They'd save the baked chicken for tomorrow.

Once she'd finished the potatoes, she picked lettuce leaves off the quickly growing plants. Gerd's recipe for a dressing of vinegar, sugar, and cream over baby lettuce leaves was as good as dessert.

Rune and Bjorn waved to her on their way out to the new cellar. Her sunbonnet hanging down her back, Signe lifted her face to the cooling breeze. Swallows dipped for mud in the pigpen where Leif kept a corner wet for the hogs in the heat. Building their nests up under the eaves of the barn took a lot of mud and hard work.

Signe wiped the dripping perspiration from her face with the edge of her apron. Good thing they had planted a long row of lettuce, or they'd not have enough for supper yet.

She met Nilda at the doorway. "Where you going?"

"Out to help Rune. I sure wish I had a

pair of pants like the men. It would be much easier to work out there in pants."

Signe smiled. "I remember cousin Ingeborg decided to work in pants when she and Kaaren were widowed in North Dakota and Ingeborg worked the fields to prove up her homestead. Kaaren wrote more letters home than she did. I never forgot that story. Remember how your mor told us and was so horrified?"

"Ja, Ingeborg did what was necessary. That's where Ivar really wanted to go to work, in Blessing. He said that the last time a letter came from them, asking for workers, he was too young to go."

Signe wanted to go with Nilda to see the new cellar but knew she needed to stay here in case Onkel Einar needed help, even though Rune had made her promise she would not help him walk or get within reach of his cane. How sad to have to think about something like that.

"Gerd!" The order thundered from the bedroom.

"Ja, coming."

"Help me!"

Signe shook her head at the older woman as she entered the house. "I will." *I can duck faster than you can.* She stopped in the bedroom doorway. "How can I help you?"

Einar had moved himself back to bed at some point. "I want Gerd."

"Gerd is busy. How can I help you?"

"I am going out to the porch. Did Rune bring up the saw to sharpen?"

"I believe so. I'll be right back." She checked the porch and returned. "Ja, he did. The files are there too."

"Help me!" He pushed himself to his feet, teetered a moment, but steadied himself.

"I will walk with you, but you must do it yourself."

He glared at her, thumped his cane on the floor, and slowly shuffled around the end of the bed. Signe stepped back as he neared the door, earning herself another glare.

"Can you at least hold the door open?" he growled.

Do you ever say please? She nodded without answering.

He stumped through the doorway while she held the screen door open. He stopped and stared at the new railings. "Well, I'll be. . . ."

Please, Lord, don't let him start down those steps. Please.

Einar shuffled to his chair and lowered himself into it with a sigh. After a moment, he reached for the file and the long crosscut saw they used to fell the big trees.

The sound of the file was almost reassuring as Signe returned to the kitchen. The pan of baked chicken sat on the table, and she shook her head at Gerd.

The older woman huffed. "I know you don't want me lifting heavy things, but really, that pan is not that heavy. I washed the lettuce, and I will cook the canned potatoes, our last two jars, later."

Signe turned when she heard the boys shout for her and headed back to the porch.

"You better sharpen the knives, we got fish for supper!" Knute crowed. All three of them held up strings of fish. "We got perch and bass and even sunfish. Ivar says we'll fillet them by the house and bury all the fish heads and skins between the corn rows."

Signe got out two slender knives and set to sharpening them on the whetstone.

"They can use the tall bench in the shade. That's where I butchered chickens and such." Gerd shook her head, an almost-smile peeking out. "I wish they could show their far."

"He will enjoy eating them fried more than seeing the stringers." Signe checked the sharpness of the blades and, taking the whetstone along, went out to get them set up. Leif carried the dishpan.

"I caught the biggest one," he told her.

That night, fishing stories bounced around the table. It was a good thing Onkel Einar had eaten outside and gone to bed, because the jollity in the kitchen would have earned them all orders to shut up.

"Mr. Garborg was real happy for us," Knute said. "He said the fish have really been biting lately. The missus even smoked some of the bigger ones."

The boys' words tumbled and bumped over each other, leaving Signe with smiles and laughter. How wonderful to see her family having such a grand time, in spite of the grumpy man in the other room. He roared at them to be quiet once, but the hilarity dimmed only momentarily. Perhaps just enough time for him to fall asleep.

The first wagons delivering lumber for the new house arrived late on Monday morning, pulled by teams of four horses. Leif ran to tell Rune and the others, who trotted over to help the drivers unload the wagons. The drivers turned down an offer of dinner and drove directly back to Blackduck.

"How many loads will there be, Far?" Leif asked as they sat at the dinner table.

"I am not sure, but they said they would load the wagons again today and be here earlier tomorrow."

"We will have sandwiches for them tomorrow." Signe had started bread that morning. With the new yeast from Benson's, they no longer had to start the sourdough the night before.

"What are you doing?" Nilda's near shout an hour later brought Signe running to the back door.

"I am going down the steps," Einar barked.

"But what if — ?" Nilda stopped, giving a glare that matched his, and grabbed the ax to split wood. Keeping one eye on Einar slowed down the slam of the ax splitting rounds on the chopping block.

Signe breathed a sigh of relief when Einar reached the bottom of the steps and stood firm on the ground. She held her breath again when he turned and started back up the stairs. If only Rune were here in case he fell again.

"No fool like an old fool," Gerd muttered behind her. "You can't tell him anything, so don't waste your breath."

When Einar set to sharpening the saw, Signe sighed again. "Onkel Einar, you want a cup of coffee?"

"I will take it to him. He might poke you with his cane." Gerd did as she said and came back shaking her head. "At least he feels he is doing something. That might settle him down some."

By Wednesday, all the framing lumber was stacked near the cellar. Every evening, Rune and the boys slaved to get the cellar posts and ceiling joists in place. They finished Friday night.

"Tomorrow we lay the flooring at dawn." Rune looked haggard, aging before her eyes with the hours they put in every day.

"I will help Leif with the chores in the morning so you can all get started." Nilda looked to Signe. "They said not to worry about food . . ."

"But we can bake those three rabbits Knute brought in and serve them with noodles," Signe said.

Gerd swayed with Kirstin in her arms. "You and me, we'll take care of the house, right, baby?" She kissed the baby's fists and cheek, getting her hair pulled in reply. Untangling her hair from the grasping fists, she and Kirstin both made happy noises.

Rune roused everyone before the sun yellowed the sky. He ignored Einar's early mutterings that soon escalated into threats. After a hurried breakfast, he took his crew out to the house. Einar moved to the porch to start on the other saw.

"And keep track of what everyone is doing," Gerd muttered.

When the wagons started arriving for the house-raising, Einar stood on the edge of the porch, muttering and glaring.

Please, Lord, keep him from scaring away these wonderful people who are coming to help us. Signe saw four wagons drive past the house and down the lane to the piles of lumber where Rune and the boys were laying down flooring as fast as they could.

Leif harnessed Rosie to the cart and drove up to the house. "Far said to fill the cream cans with water for the workers."

They pumped and hauled buckets of water to fill the cream cans, and Leif waved as he drove off again.

"What will we use as tables for the food?" Signe asked.

"The sawhorses with boards laid over them and set up down there. I'm sure the women will arrive about eleven thirty," Gerd answered. "At least that's the way it was the day we raised this house."

"You had helpers?"

"Ja, that was before Einar . . . well, got so angry." Gerd did not look at her.

"I hope someday you will tell us the entire story. Perhaps then we can understand better."

"We'll see."

They were just loading their dinner contributions into the cart when they saw two wagons coming down the lane. Mrs. Benson waved from the first one. "We'll follow you," she shouted.

When they arrived at the new house, some of the men were turning the saw horses into tables, while others kept on hammering. Three walls had been lifted and nailed in place on the subflooring for the first floor, long boards bracing the framing, and the fourth was being assembled on the ground, almost ready to be raised in turn.

Signe paused after stepping down from the cart and stared at the house rising from the hole. "It is real," she whispered. "We really are going to have a home of our own." She nudged Nilda. "Look who's here." She nodded to the young men up on the ladders, both Petter Thorvaldson from the lumberyard and Fritz Larsson, the schoolteacher and organist. They both waved at Nilda.

Nilda waved back and turned to help carry over the food. Within minutes, the women flocked around the table, uncovering dishes, sticking big spoons in bowls and wooden spoons in pots, and laying out a stack of plates.

Mrs. Benson banged a big metal spoon on

a pot to get everyone's attention and nodded to Nilda, who hollered, "Dinner is served."

The hammering ceased immediately, men scurried down ladders, and Reverend Skarstead raised his arms. "Let us pray." He paused for silence and then began. "Lord God, heavenly Father, we are gathered here in your name to create a home for Rune and his family. We thank you for the privilege of building a new house, for getting to know each other better as we work together. Bless this home and this food to our bodies. Lord Jesus, we give you all the praise and glory. In your precious name." He paused, and the *amen* rolled across the building site.

Laughing, the men jostled for the line and started heaping their plates full.

As Signe dipped water from the milk cans into the men's cups, she kept an eye on the long table of food and the people both serving and eating it. She could not help but notice how Mr. Larsson and Petter Thorvaldson lingered by Nilda as she cut big slabs of bread. They were both grinning broadly, though she could not hear what they were saying to Nilda.

"You know, Signe," Mrs. Benson whispered, "I think two of the young men here are more than a little aware of our Nilda."

Signe shook her head. "She and Mr. Thorvaldson became friends on the ship coming over. She was glad to see him again, but nothing else. At least, I don't think so. And Mr. Larsson, he teaches our boys. And the English class for adults." She didn't mention that she had noticed his interest in Nilda at class.

Mrs. Benson shrugged. "All I can say is that this is the first barn or house-raising that Mr. Larsson has ever attended. He is usually practicing the organ on Saturdays for church the next day. Just something I noticed. And besides, both of them are hovering around her like bees around the only buttercup."

Signe watched Nilda carry the coffeepot around and refill cups. She was laughing at a comment from one of the men, the sun glinting off her deep golden hair, which was getting more sun-streaked as the summer continued. Nilda was indeed having a good time. Her laugh rang out again, making those around her smile.

And to think they had been best friends for so many years and were now here in America, living in the same house and working together. Signe had never dreamed something this wonderful could happen.

"Where is that sweet little daughter of

yours?" one of the women asked.

"Tante Gerd is taking care of her at the house."

"She is growing up so fast. It's been so long since I had a baby around that I forget what one can be like." Mrs. Benson glanced up. "I better go cut the pies and cakes so the men can get back to work. Don't you worry about tomorrow. Most of the workers will have dinner at home before coming here, and we will bring food for an afternoon break. Mr. Benson said they should be able to set the ridge board in place and most of the rafters, maybe even the roofing boards. Doing two full floors like this is a big difference from something like the Strand house."

"It looks huge already."

After dinner, the men went back to work, and the women cleaned up the dinner things, each retrieving the items she'd brought to wash at home. Nilda and Signe helped load the wagons and waved them off.

"So this is the way they do things here in Minnesota." Nilda dusted her hands together. "Some neighborly, that's for sure."

Together they loaded the cream cans along with their things in the cart, drove it up to the house, unloaded, refilled the cream cans with water, and Leif took them back to the building site.

On their way to the house, Signe nudged Nilda. "You seemed to be having a fine time with your two gentleman helpers. Although I'm not sure they were real friendly to each other."

Nilda stopped and stared at her. "What?" Her brow wrinkled. "Who?" But her cheeks were reddening as she spoke.

"You know, Mr. Larsson and Mr. Thorvaldson."

"They were just being polite."

Signe nodded. "Of course. However, even Mrs. Benson commented on them hovering around you like honey bees."

"Signe Carlson, I never —" Nilda clamped her fists on her hips.

Signe snorted. "Just thought I'd mention it. I think it's kind of fun."

Nilda shook her head. "Perhaps Gerd will have the coffee on."

As the shadows lengthened, some of the men left to do chores at home. Einar stood on the back porch and yelled at every wagon that went by, waving his fist in the air. "And don't come back! Stay off my land."

Some stayed on until dusk made it too dark to pound nails any longer. Mr. Benson was one of the last to leave. "Many of us will be back tomorrow after church. And I know a few who might drop by when they can find the time later. You'll be able to move into your new house sooner than you think."

Rune shook his hand. "We can never thank you enough."

"That's all right. Good things happen when neighbors help each other. Far as I can see, that's the way God wants us to live, helping each other." Mr. Benson looked toward the other house. "It's a shame Einar can't let go of the past. He always was rather stern but still a good man."

"Seems there are a few other people with the same problem, holding on to the past."

"Yep, there are. Downright shame." Mr. Benson waved as he drove out.

A shotgun blast split the air.

Rune spun around and raced toward the house. "Einar Strand, what on earth were you thinking?" he yelled once he was in earshot.

Einar tried to turn, staggered, and grabbed for the porch post, his shotgun clattering to the ground. "I can shoot any time I want. Be glad I shot in the air as a warning."

Rune felt his jaw drop before he strode up to the porch. What in the world? He forced himself to slow down and swallow at least some of the words he wanted to bellow. "These people are helping build our house, you know that!"

"He was on my land, and he knows I do not want anyone on my land."

"Einar Strand, have all these falls gone to your head?" Rune leaned over and picked up the shotgun.

"Gimme that!"

Rune bit back the "come and get it" comment that almost made it out of his mouth. All he needed right now was for Einar to go down again. Weary did not begin to describe his leaden feet and fuzzy mind. Surely he misunderstood what Einar had just done. But the weight of the gun in his hand told him otherwise.

"Give me that gun," Einar repeated.

Rune ignored him, instead going inside and hanging the gun on the hooks above the bedroom door. He shot Signe a sad look and kept on going up the stairs to bed. He could hear the boys breathing in the gentle air. How they could sleep through all that noise was beyond him, but gratitude helped blur anger's edges.

Lord, give me patience, he prayed as he drifted off.

Chapter 30

Morning came before anyone was ready to meet the new day. Rune fought his heavy eyes, blinking in the dimness. The cooling breeze that announced dawn came through the window. He breathed in deep, praying for the energy to get through this day. *Lord, what do we do about Einar? What if he had aimed that gun at someone?* Thankfully it was the shotgun, which would never reach that far, but if he was crazy enough to shoot at all, would he be tempted to use the rifle?

Rune pulled on his pants and slid the suspenders over his shoulders. He had to move the rifle. In the barn or machine shed would have to work. Since Signe and Nilda had already gone downstairs, he roused the boys and pulled on his boots. He paused, looking around the slope-roofed attic and nodding. Einar would not search up here. He had to do this without Gerd knowing so she would not give it away.

Walking carefully down the stairs, he looked above the back door. Good, the rifle hung just where Bjorn had put it, with the shotgun over the bedroom door. He lifted the rifle down and, after the boys went out the door, took it upstairs and laid it against a wall back under the slant of the roof.

They were a quiet group on the way to church that morning. But they were all there, and that counted for something. While the house called them to come work, church called softly with the promise of worship. God was answering their prayers so far beyond what Rune had asked for.

Mr. Benson met him at the door. "Good morning, Rune."

"Mr. Benson."

"My name is Josef. Joe."

"Ja, takk, but I have to apologize for Einar."

"I wanted to talk about that. If I were you —"

"You would hide the guns?"

"Yes."

"I hid the rifle but not the shotgun. The wagons are too far away, and he did shoot up in the air."

"I would not take chances." Benson looked directly into Rune's eyes. "I am concerned for all of you."

Rune felt his mouth open and close and then stay open. Slowly his head wagged as if with a mind of its own. He tried to form words, but they would not come. Surely Einar wouldn't — couldn't . . .

Rune closed his eyes and nodded. "Yes, sir." *Lord God, protect us, please.* Surely Onkel Einar would not do such a thing. Even his thoughts couldn't form all the words.

He sat through worship in a daze.

When they stood for the benediction, Signe studied him, concern written all over her face. "What?" she whispered.

"Tell you later."

Organ music followed them out the doors, and several men shook hands with Rune, saying they'd see him a bit later.

"I'm so sorry I cannot come help today," Reverend Skarstead said at the doorway. "I have my other parish to take care of too."

Rune shook his head. "I know that, and I cannot say enough thank-yous for your help yesterday and for encouraging so many others to come. I have never in my life seen so much work accomplished in so little time. Unbelievable."

"By the grace of God, Rune. Grace of God."

Rune loaded his family into the wagon and set the horses to a trot until the women called, "Enough, we are bouncing like balls back here."

"Sorry, just a bit excited to get home." But how could he hide the shotgun without Einar noticing?

Einar was sitting on the porch, sharpening a saw. He shook his head. "Waste of good time."

Rune gritted his teeth and went into the kitchen without saying a word.

Gerd looked up at him and said for his ears only, "Don't let him make you mad. His bark is always worse than his bite."

"I hope to God so. What if — ?" Rune shook his head. "Can we eat right away?"

"Sit down, we will have food on the table by the time everyone is seated." Gerd reached up and patted his cheek. "Like you said, all will be well."

Her words reverberated in his head as he wolfed down his dinner. The boys leaped up to follow him out the door, Leif grabbing another biscuit on his way past the basket.

By the time the other men arrived, they had the tools all laid out again and leftover pieces of lumber tossed into a pile away from the sawhorses. The cream cans of water sat in the shade of the nearest tree to keep them cool. The crew was smaller than the day before but started to work with a will. Most of them finished framing in the second floor, including the plate around the top of the framed walls. Several others started measuring and cutting the rafters. Knute and Leif were the go-fers, doing anything that was called for.

Rune marveled at how well these men worked. They hammered in temporary scaffolding to stand upon as they anchored the posts that would support the ridgebeam. A shout went up when the beam settled into place. By afternoon, they were raising rafters and nailing them into position. Nail by nail, the structure looked more like a house.

Thank you, Lord. Thank you, God.

But even with as much progress as they made, and working till dusk, they were not able to get all the rafters in place.

"Sorry, Rune. We hoped to get further." Joe Benson shook his head. "I'll be back tomorrow. Got to get that roof on before it rains again."

"You can't do that." Rune shook his head. "Next Saturday would be great."

"Yes, I can, and so can a couple of others."

But I need to be out in the woods or — no. Einar would just have to be angry. This was more important than another tree or two.

"We will all be out here. I cannot thank you enough."

"Far!" Leif came running up, panting.

Rune shook his head. "In a minute."

"No, Far, Onkel Einar is missing."

Rune turned to face his son fully. "Einar is missing? He can't walk that far."

"Tante Gerd sent me." Leif could hardly talk around his puffing.

Joe Benson turned and yelled to the last few men getting in their wagons. "Einar Strand is missing."

The four of them gathered around, looking to Rune.

"He can't have gotten far," Rune said. "We'll search the farm buildings first. I'll go talk with Gerd, see what happened."

They loaded up the wagons and drove to the barn, Rune heading to the house while the others fanned out.

Gerd stood in the kitchen, her apron clutched tightly in her hands. "I — I — he was out on the porch, and — and I was busy in the house — and Signe took coffee out to him, and — and he was gone." She blinked often, but a tear escaped in spite of her efforts. "Nilda and Signe are out looking for him. Rune, where could he have gone?"

"The shotgun?"

Gerd looked up, as did Rune. The gun was not on the hooks. "Out on the porch, I guess," she said.

"No, it isn't," Nilda said from the doorway. "He is not anywhere around the buildings."

Signe came in behind her.

"Gerd, you stay here with Kirstin and Leif, just in case he comes back," Rune instructed, "then Leif can come let us know."

"I will help search," Nilda said with a look that brooked no argument.

Rune turned to the door. "I'll go talk with the others. We will need lanterns soon."

"I'll refill the lanterns from the barrel." Signe followed them outside.

"He's not in any of these buildings nor outside of them," Benson said when they gathered by the porch.

Rune turned to his sons. "Knute, go see if any of the horses are missing." He darted off.

The men talked among themselves. "He had that head injury. . . ."

"Maybe he's gone crazy?"

"Ja, remember the gunshot yesterday?"

"Not looking good."

"You think he'd go down the lane to the road?" one asked.

Rune shook his head. "I have no idea, but as obsessed as he is with the big trees, I would think the woods are more likely. But how could he get there? He must be fallen someplace. Let's fan out and go through the pasture toward where we cut down the trees. It's all I can think of. He can't have gotten far. He is just too weak."

Signe handed three lanterns to the search party as they passed the machine shed. "Should we follow with the wagon?"

Knute ran up to them. "Far, Rosie is missing and so is the cart."

"The harness?" Rune asked.

"How else could he use the cart?"

"How could he harness Rosie to the cart?"

"If he is really as weak as you say, how could he do anything?" one of the men asked. He shook his head and spat on the ground. "You got to admit, he always has been devious."

Einar couldn't have faked his weakness, Rune knew that for certain. "Maybe, but he has a will of iron when he really wants something. Let's go."

A couple of the men headed out to search the hay, oat, and corn fields while the rest of them strode down the lane to the big woods standing dark sentinel ahead.

"Einar! Einar! Einar Strand!" Rune could

hear the others calling as they searched. They spread out when they reached the stacks of cut wood and piles of branches. Dusk had slipped in among the trees, cutting down on visibility.

Rune cupped his hands around his mouth and bellowed, "Einar! Einar, where are you?"

"Up ahead, isn't that the horse and cart?" Bjorn tore off to make sure. "He's not here!" One man brought over a lantern. "Far, the shotgun is here."

"Okay. Takk." At least Einar had not shot someone else or himself. Rune realized he'd been thinking that. But the Einar he knew would never shoot himself, at least not on purpose.

The men kept walking and calling, holding the lanterns high as darkness overtook the forest.

Ivar, Bjorn, and Knute forged ahead.

"Rune, over here! Bring a lantern!" Ivar's voice echoed through the dark.

The men thrashed through the downed limbs and branches and stood in a half circle at the base of one of the big trees. With the lanterns lifted high, they could see Einar crumpled on the ground, his cane to the side, his ax handle still in one hand.

"Is he alive?" someone asked.

Rune knelt beside the still form and felt for a pulse at the side of his neck. Shaking his head, he whispered, "I think he's been gone for some time. Even with the heat, he is getting cold."

"Let's turn him over and straighten him out while we can," Joe Benson suggested.

Rune's head kept wagging. *Einar Strand, you died doing what you lived for, at the foot of a big tree.* He glanced up to see a slash on the tree trunk. He pointed. "See that?"

Bjorn held the lantern closer. "He hit it once. Chopped at it. Far, he was so weak, how could he do this?"

"Pure ornery willpower," another man answered.

Several of them laid the body straight, and Rune closed the staring eyes. *Onkel Einar, it didn't need to end this way. You could have . . .* Eyes shut and one hand on Einar's shoulder, all Rune could even think was, *Dear God.* He swallowed against the shock.

Joe Benson said softly, "Must have been his heart that took him. No blood anywhere."

Rune agreed. "Or apoplexy. With all those falls, he had a couple of strokes, we think." He patted Leif's shoulder as the boy clung to his side.

"Darn fool," someone else muttered.

"Let's get him back to the cart."

Together, four of the men lifted Einar while Bjorn and Knute held the lanterns, and they stumbled and staggered their way through the branches and detritus of fallen trees back to the cart, where they laid him in the bed.

Rune blew out a sigh that carried all the ache in his soul with it. Now he had to tell Gerd. Whoever would have thought Einar's story would end like this?

Chapter 31

"We will bury him at the foot of one of those big trees he was so obsessed with." Dry-eyed, Gerd stared blankly at her coffee mug, her face cut out of stone.

"Ja, Gerd, if that's what you want," Rune said with a nod. "I know just the one, where his grave will not be disturbed."

"In the morning."

Signe couldn't help her shock. "Don't you want to — to prepare him?" she asked.

Gerd shook her head. "Bury him the way he lived, boots and all." She stopped. "I guess we should wrap him in a sheet." Looking to Rune, she continued, "You want to read some words over him?"

"I — I thought to bring out Reverend Skarstead."

"Makes no sense. Einar despised the man and all he stands for."

Signe laid a hand on Gerd's arm. "Are you sure? I mean, sure of what he believed?"

"All he wanted was to fell trees."

"To earn money for this farm and for us to live here," Rune added softly.

"I think he hated those trees." It was as if she'd not heard him.

Signe stared at the woman caught in the circle of lamplight. The young ones had gone to bed, leaving the adults around the table. Ivar had included himself with the younger set and gone upstairs to sleep. "Hated the trees? That's what he lived for."

"He wanted to farm, but the trees were in the way."

"But . . ." Rune shook his head. "I guess that is not important anymore, is it? He did what he did."

"And now I —" Gerd looked at each of them. "*We* get to clean up the mess." Her head wagged as if too heavy for her shoulders. "Takk." She pushed herself up from the table and made her slow way to the bedroom, stopping in the doorway. "The best thing he ever did was bring all of you here. The very best." She stepped into the bedroom and shut the door behind her.

"I feel guilty leaving his body out there in the cart." Rune gazed down at the table. "At least I put it in the machine shop. I mean, what if a wild animal . . . ?"

Signe sniffed. "But this is her choice, and

we need to help her all we can." She covered his restless hand with her own. *Lord, help this man of mine to do the best thing. This is all so strange.*

On the other side of him, Nilda covered his other hand. "And you, my brother. You do not need to carry this load all alone. We are here, and God said He never leaves us, so He must be here too."

"But she doesn't even want Reverend Skarstead to conduct a simple ceremony. Will she regret that someday?" He shook his head. "I — I'm not qualified to do that."

Nilda and Signe looked at each other. "Do we need to tell the sheriff or someone that he died?" Signe asked.

"Joe Benson said he would tell the reverend and the sheriff."

"So then what?"

Rune shoved back his chair, arms rigid on the table edge. "Now we go to bed. Tomorrow will be a new day. We will bury him as Gerd requested, I will read a passage and say a few words, and may God rest his soul."

Halfway through the night, Rune sat up and rubbed his head.

Oh, my husband. Signe sat up beside him. "What is it?"

"You go back to sleep. I am going to the machine shed."

"Why?"

"I need to make a marker until we can carve a headstone."

"I see." She lay back down. "Be careful." Unsure why she had said that, she drifted back to sleep.

Breakfast was subdued. Even Kirstin was quiet, as if she recognized the gravity of the morning. Rune and the boys left to do the chores.

"Gerd, is there something special we can do for you today?" Signe asked.

Gerd looked up from her cup of coffee, shaking her head. "Not that I can think of. We will do what we have to do, and then we will go on with our day. I thought to bake cookies for the boys. They really like my cookies. If you would like to help me clean my bedroom, that would be good."

"Then that is what we will do." Nilda nodded. "We could start on that now while you bake cookies. If that is all right with you."

Gerd looked from one to the other, then leaned slightly forward. "Listen to me. Yes, I am sad today, not only because Einar died this way, but because he chose to live the way he did. That is sad." She paused for a deep breath that seemed to catch in her throat. "He missed out on the important things of life, and he made me miss them too. I think I almost hated him at times for the way . . . the way he treated people. But thanks to him, I now have my family around me, and I will not live that way of his ever again." She looked at each of them and grasped their hands. "I — I wish he . . ."

Kirstin's baby babble was the only sound in the room until Gra wrapped herself around their legs, her plaintive meow a counterpoint to the baby music.

Gerd spoke each word distinctly. "I wish he could have known this." She squeezed their hands again and shook her head slowly from side to side. "That is the saddest part of all."

"That tree over there." Rune pointed to a thirty-foot white pine west of their new home. Einar had deemed it too small to cut for sale. Someday there would be pasture or planted fields around it. It seemed appropriate that Einar would rest in the shade of a pine tree.

Bjorn stopped the team, and they all climbed out to drag the pick and shovels from the wagon bed. Rune paced off the plot, digging in a mark at the corners with his heel.

"Let's see if two people can dig at once." Rune started in the middle and hit a rock just under the surface. "I'll move back here. Bjorn, see if you can dislodge that rock."

While the boys worked on the rock, Rune moved to the head of the grave and dug in at the line. The rock proved to be larger than he had expected, so when they rolled the stone away, they had a sizable hole already. As soon as sweat started down one face, they switched diggers, and someone else would use the pick to loosen the dirt. The rock pile grew.

"We'll pile these stones on top to keep any wild animals from digging him up," Rune said.

"What animal would dig this deep?" Ivar wiped the sweat from his face with his shirt-tails.

"Just not taking chances."

When the hole reached the six-foot mark, Rune helped pull Bjorn out of it. "You all did a fine job."

They paused to stare down into the hole. Leif leaned his head on Rune's arm. Rune didn't say *let's get this over with* aloud, but the words crowded his mind. Cruel as Einar had been, Rune had realized long ago that he could not carry bitterness at the treatment they had received.

He looked at Leif, who was staring down into the grave. "What is it, son?"

"I never saw him smile." A tear trickled down Leif's cheek. He looked up at Rune. "Maybe Tante Gerd will smile more now."

"Knowing you, Leif, I am sure you will help her smile. Let's go back to the house."

"I don't think he liked us much."

Knute laid a hand on his younger brother's shoulder. "Onkel Einar didn't like anybody."

At the machine shed, Knute whistled for Rosie, the only horse that came when called. The other horses dropped their heads and went back to grazing, and Knute had to go to them with the bridles and bring the old team to the barn. Leif led Rosie to the rail by the barn, and Bjorn settled the harness on her back. Together they hitched her to the cart, which still held Einar's body.

Ivar drove the team to the house, so the women — Signe carrying Kirstin, and Gerd, the sheet — could climb into the wagon bed. Without a word, they followed the cart to the grave site.

Stiff as the tree above them, with her arms locked across her middle, Gerd stared into the hole. Signe, eyes closed, her prayers for peace bombarding the heavens, gently swayed her sleeping daughter. Nilda stood on the other side of Gerd, blinking back tears as she gently patted the older woman's shoulder.

A crow flew by and settled at the top of the pine tree, an overseer in black.

A slight breeze lifted a lock of Signe's hair as she listened to the men lower the body into its resting place. Leif came to stand beside her and leaned into her for comfort. His sniffs brought on more of her own. *Dear God, please.* She could think of nothing else to say.

Rune took his place at the head of the grave and opened the Bible that Nilda handed him. The rustle of dirt sliding into the hole was drowned out by the warning calls of more crows in the trees, the loudest at the top of the sheltering pine.

" 'The Lord is my shepherd, I shall not want.' " Rune's voice stilled the crows, and the words calmed the hearts of those around him. " 'He maketh me lie down in green pastures and leadeth me beside still waters.' " He paused and cleared his throat. " 'He-he restoreth my soul.' " Knute shifted beside him. Rune stumbled again on. " 'Yea though I walk through the valley of the shadow of death . . .' "

Signe chewed on her bottom lip, eyes swimming with tears, as she watched and heard her husband struggle with the reading. *I will fear no evil, for thou art with me* floated in her mind as the quiet stretched. Poor Rune. *Help him please, Lord God.*

" 'For thou art with me, thy rod and thy staff, they comfort me.' " Rune's voice grew stronger and more sure. " 'Thou prepares a table before me in the presence of mine enemies, thou annointest my head with oil, my cup runneth over.' "

First Signe and then, one by one, the others joined Rune in reciting the psalm. " 'Surely goodness and mercy will follow me all the days of my life. And I will dwell in the house of the Lord forever.' "

Rune paused.

Nilda used her apron to wipe her eyes.

"Amen. I pray you rest in peace, Onkel Einar. Thank you for bringing us to Amerika and teaching us how to fell the big pines. For giving us a home. I hope we do you honor as we continue with what you started." Rune looked around at his family. "Do any of you want to say something?" When they all shook their heads, he bent down and picked up a handful of dirt to sprinkle in the grave. "Einar Strand, you have fallen like one of your big pines. Dust to dust, may our Lord have mercy upon us all. Amen."

Leif looked up at his mor. "Is Onkel Einar up in heaven now?"

Signe caught Rune's sad look. "I hope so, son. I hope so."

After Rune tossed in the first shovelful, Ivar and Bjorn took up shovels too, and the grave began to fill. Rune picked up the hammer and a board to which he'd nailed sharpened legs. The hammer's thud drove the sign solidly into the ground. He had chipped the name *Einar Strand* and the date on it. When finished, he stepped back and nodded.

Leif slipped his hand into Gerd's and smiled up at her. "I smelled the cookies."

"Ja, I baked them for you boys especially."

"But we will all have cookies, and then we can have dinner?"

Gerd frowned. "Shouldn't dinner come first?"

He hung his head. "I guess."

"But not today."

"Takk." He squeezed her hand, his grin beatific.

They walked to the wagon, where Nilda helped Gerd up to the seat. "No sitting in back for you today, Tante Gerd."

Leif climbed up on the seat. "Far said I could drive." He turned the team in a circle and headed back to the farmstead.

They'd gone only a short distance when Gerd asked him to stop. She turned in her seat and looked back at where the others were piling rocks on the mounded grave. Then, shaking her head, she turned back. "We probably need to put a fence around that sometime."

Back at the house, they found a frosted cake, a basket of rolls, a jar of honey, and a jar of pickles on the table. On the stove, which had been fed, sat a pot of stew, set back to heat but not burn.

"Would you look at that?" Gerd looked around the room. "Who do you suppose . . . ?"

"Oh, I have a feeling about who's behind this. Bless that woman's heart." Signe laid an arm around Gerd's shoulders. "I think she plans to make sure you feel like part of this community."

"Mrs. Benson?"

"Ja. She probably recruited help, but I am sure she's behind it."

"Einar never had a good word about her. Well, not about anyone, really. Hmm."

After the late dinner courtesy of Mrs. Benson, the men and boys all headed for the new house, and the women returned to the bedroom. The thin mattress now hung on the clothesline, the dust beaten out of it, along with the summer blanket. The curtains and sheets awaited the washing machine.

Nilda finished washing the bed frame and Signe the windows. "Let's do the dresser next," Nilda suggested. "Gerd, where do you want me to put the clothes?"

"We'll keep Einar's things for the others, and I'll stack mine on the chairs and put them back when the drawers are dry again. I think I'll take the drawers out onto the porch to wash them."

Gerd brought the chair from the window closer and pulled open the top drawer. Tossing the holey socks, handkerchiefs, and a stocking hat she had knit for Einar years ago in a pile by the door, she set a small box and some papers on top of the dresser, often shaking her head. A deerskin pouch that jingled joined the box. Long johns, drawers, and another pair of pants, along with three folded shirts were added to the pile. She placed her clean underthings on the chair and heaved a sigh, then moved to the next drawer.

"Let me carry those out." Nilda lifted a drawer in each hand.

As she headed out of the room, Gerd yelped. "Wait!"

"What?"

Eyes wide, Gerd pointed to the bottom of

one of the drawers. "I never saw that before."

"What is it?" Nilda bent over and dug at the paper glued to the wood. When it came away, she handed it to Gerd.

Gerd held the sheet of paper in her hand for a moment. "I think it is time for coffee. While it heats, we will look through all that." She nodded to the collection on top of the dresser, then scooped it all into her apron and dumped it on the kitchen table.

Nilda hauled the drawers to the porch while Signe wrapped a cloth around the broom and dusted the ceiling and walls, driving out a couple of spiders in the process.

"We need to do the wash tomorrow." Nilda pumped herself a glass of water and leaned against the sink counter to drink it. "And take what's left of the stew and milk to the well house."

"After we go through this." Gerd shoved wood into the stove and opened the damper on the chimney so the fire would heat the coffee more quickly.

Baby babbling announced that Kirstin had awakened. Instead of getting demanding, she waved her feet in the air, trying to catch them with pudgy hands.

When they were seated, coffee and cookies in front of them, Gerd sucked in a deep breath and reached for the box first. "Einar kept his cash in here and in the pouch." Opening the lid, she lifted out a pile of paper money and handed it to Signe. "You count that, please, and Nilda, the pouch of coins." At their nods, she lifted out folded papers, envelopes, and a small leather bound ledger. She sorted through the papers, making a pile of letters, one of bills, and another of receipts.

"One hundred and two dollars," Signe reported.

"Twelve dollars in change plus four silver dollars, for sixteen dollars and forty-five cents," Nilda added.

Gerd nodded. "This is what we buy groceries and other supplies with until we sell the trees next spring."

"Can trees be sold in the fall?" Signe asked.

"Ja, but it is far better to haul them in the winter while the ground is frozen and skids can be used in the snow."

"Are there any other bills to pay?"

Gerd flipped through another stack. "These are all paid for now. But we will get cash for selling weaner pigs now, and in the fall, butchered hogs."

"And logs if we need to."

"Ja. But what we do need, we can put on the account at Benson's. Your butter and eggs help with that bill, you know." Gerd eyed the packet that had been glued to the bottom of the drawer. "The old fox."

"Any idea what is in it?" Signe pushed the plate of cookies nearer to Gerd. The baby noises were changing from happy to hungry. "I better see to little miss over there before she turns louder."

Bending over the baby bed, Signe received a grin that crinkled baby eyes and moisted her own. "You sure are having fun with those toesies." She took hold of one little foot and moved it in a circle. Kirstin kicked with the other and waved her hands. A stream of definite sounds made it seem like she was carrying on a conversation. Signe picked up her daughter, and the two of them chattered back and forth as she changed the diaper and settled into the rocker to nurse her. "Well, look at that. Two teeth. Where did you find those? I tell you, you better be careful with those teeth, or your mor will take away the fountain here."

With Kirstin settled, Signe laid her head back on the chair. How could so much happen in so little time? She thought of something her mor said often. *"Life can change in the blink of an eye, and most times we have no control over it."* It certainly had.

"Well, I'll be. . . ."

Gerd's whisper snapped Signe's eyes open again. "What?"

Gerd and Nilda were staring at each other. "There's five hundred dollars here. I never knew he had that. It must be from the sale of logs, but why hide it like this?"

"How long do you think it has been there?" Nilda pointed at the faded paper.

Gerd fanned the money out in her hand. "I have no idea. But I know one thing. This could pay off what you owe on your house."

Signe smiled while shaking her head. "Rune will never go for that."

"There are always ways to get around stubborn." Gerd pushed her chair back from the table and closed the box lid with all the money and papers inside. "Let's get that bedroom done so we can start supper. Not that we have to cook much, thanks to Mrs. Benson."

With that, Gerd took a pan of hot, soapy water out onto the porch to wash the drawers.

Nilda and Signe swept the floor and wiped down the inside and outside of the chest of drawers. "Let's move it over so we can sweep and scrub this part of the floor too." Together they hefted the dresser and moved it several feet along the wall. Signe swept while Nilda went for a bucket of hot soapy water to scrub the floor.

"Gerd, I think you better come here," Signe called.

"Just a minute, nearly done."

"Okay, but . . ."

Nilda set the bucket, brush, and rags on the floor. "What is that?"

"Maybe nothing, but I have a sneaky notion. What if . . . ?"

Gerd came into the room, wiping her hands on her apron. "Now what?"

Signe pointed to a short floor board that had warped enough to raise on one end. "You ever noticed that before?"

"No. We'd better get it nailed down."

Signe knelt and tried to lift the board with her fingertips. "Get me a knife, please." Nilda slapped one into her hand. After prying up the board, Signe stared down into the dark hole. "There is a box down here, a metal box." She looked up at Gerd. "It seems Einar left another surprise for you."

Chapter 32

"Do you have any idea where the key might be?" Nilda asked after they set the metal box on the kitchen table.

Gerd fingered the padlock, shaking her head. "I have no idea, but a saw will take care of that."

"Or some really strong cutters. But where would we find those?" Nilda asked.

"Only in the machine shed. Seems to me this might be worth calling Rune for help," Signe said.

Gerd shook her head. "It has waited this long. Another few hours won't make any difference. I've been thinking . . . it seems like the contract would have been with those other papers."

"The contract?"

"From when we bought this place. Einar always kept his papers in that drawer, not that we have very many." She shook her head again. "Strange. I wonder where that could have gone."

They finished scrubbing the bedroom floor, and when it had dried, they put the bedroom back to rights. Signe could tell that Gerd was worrying over the whereabouts of the contract.

"Perhaps the contract is in that metal box. That might make sense."

"Perhaps." Gerd rested her hands on her hips as she looked around the room. "Takk for all your help. Such a difference."

"A rug by your bed would look nice and feel good on your feet in the morning," Signe suggested.

Gerd shrugged. "I braided a rag rug one time. I think Einar burned it after he tripped over it." She spoke without rancor. "Perhaps I shall buy some pretty material to make new curtains, brighten it up some. If you like, we could move Kirstin's bed in here."

"Rune said one of these days he is going to make another rocker. Just think, you might have one too after we move into the new house."

Gerd nodded and sighed. "I will miss my little one." She straightened. "But Nilda and Ivar will still be here. That is a good thing."

"We will be here as usual." Signe smiled at Gerd. "And we aren't far away."

Leif and Knute leaped up onto the porch

steps and burst into the kitchen. "Time to start chores. You need anything from the well house?"

"That's all right, I'll get it," Signe told them. "I need to skim pans anyway."

The sun was floating toward the horizon when she stepped out of the well house with the crock of buttermilk in her arm. She paused to look across the western fields and let the hint of evening breeze kiss her cheeks. *Lord God, such beauty, even if there are no mountains.* Smiling to herself, she strode back to the house, pausing when she heard a horse and buggy coming down the lane.

"Who can that be?" Gerd asked from the chair on the porch, where she sat with the baby sleeping in her arms.

"Reverend Skarstead, I think." Signe waved and carried the crock into the house to set on the counter. On her way out, she added, "I think we'll make dumplings to go with the stew for supper. Perhaps he would like to join us."

"Hello, Mrs. Carlson," Reverend Skarstead called. "I hope you have time for a visitor."

Signe smiled. "For you, always. Rune and the boys are down at the new house."

"I figured. How about I head on down

there to see how the house is going? Then we can talk?"

"Of course. We will set you a place at the table."

"You needn't —"

"Ja, we do."

When the men and boys trooped through the door a while later, supper was ready to dish up.

"That will be, or rather, is becoming some house," Reverend Skarstead said with a nod to the ladies. "We will have to have a real celebration when you move over there." He dried his hands and stopped next to Gerd. "Thank you for having me in your home."

"I am the one to be thanking you." She wiped her hand on her apron and held it out. "The order to stay off this land was buried with Einar, along with all the anger and hate. Please, make yourself at home here with us."

"I hope this means you will join your family in church?"

"Ja, I will."

Signe and Nilda smiled at each other with matching sighs.

When everyone was seated, Rune asked the reverend to say the blessing.

Skarstead smiled around the table. "That is my privilege. Takk. Thank you, Lord, for this family, this home, this food. We thank you for the new house and pray your grace and mercy upon us all. In Christ's name, amen."

As Signe poured the coffee, she could not stop smiling. To think that Reverend Skarstead was having supper with them. Was it he who brought this sense of peace to the house or . . . ? *Just be thankful,* she told herself.

"I know it is getting late, but before you go, could I please ask you a couple of questions?" Rune asked.

"Of course?"

"I — we are curious as to what happened all those years ago to cause the hate and animosity."

Skarstead nodded. "Actually, the Bensons know more details than I do, but . . ." He looked to Gerd. "May I continue, Mrs. Strand?"

Gerd nodded.

"Please add anything you want." He cleared his throat. "When Einar lived in Blackduck, he was looking for a place in this area to purchase. When Joe Benson heard that, he brought Einar here, where a cousin of his had died and his widow wanted to return to Norway with her children. Einar offered to purchase this land with tickets to return to Norway as the down payment. I — I'm not sure what the exact amount and stipulations were, but he agreed to pay the remainder in installments, most likely when he sold logs." He glanced at Gerd, who nodded. "But the controversy began when the Bensons received one letter and then several others saying Einar had never sent any further payments."

Gerd's mouth dropped open. "Are — are you sure?"

He nodded. "It seems that way. The Bensons were furious and came out here to try to settle this, but Einar drove them away before they could even talk." He looked at Gerd, who sat like stone. His voice softened. "You did not know that?"

"B-but he told me two or three times that he had sent another payment. He went to Blackduck to do so. We built this house after the shack she had lived in burned down. They had started the barn before the husband died, so Einar finished that first. Several men came to help with both buildings. But after that . . ."

"Do you have the contract?" the reverend asked.

"I thought so, but it is not with his papers."

"Today we found a locked metal box

beneath the floor." Signe leaned forward. "But we have no idea where the key might be."

Gerd shook her head. "The contract was not in the drawer with his papers or the cash box. I'll get it to show you." She returned from the bedroom with both boxes in hand.

Rune inspected the metal box. "A padlock like this can be sawed open." He looked at Ivar. "Could you please get that small saw down in the machine shed? On the wall of the bench? You'll need a lantern."

Ivar nodded. "Be right back."

"More coffee anyone?" When everyone shook their head, Signe sat back down. "Are you all right, Tante Gerd?"

Gerd stared at her. "He was such an honest man when I married him. What happened?"

"Looks to me like he got greedy. I'm sorry, Mrs. Strand. So very sorry." Skarstead leaned forward. "Are you all right?"

A sigh that ached of anguish made her close her eyes. "I will be."

Ivar returned with the saw, a hammer, and a screwdriver. "There is more than one way to break a lock."

"The voice of experience?" Rune asked.

"Not telling." Ivar applied the saw to the metal, but when it didn't appear to be a quick process, he picked up the hammer and screwdriver and pried the box apart at the hinges.

They all stared at the contents. A fat leather pouch that clanked, a small stack of receipts tied together with string, and several letters addressed to Einar, along with another plain envelope. A thick one.

Rune laid everything out on the table. "You want me to open them?" he asked softly.

Gerd touched the blank envelope. "This one."

Rune pulled the papers out of the envelope and unfolded them, then leaned closer to the lamp to read it aloud. It spelled out the details of the contract.

"Ja, that is what he told me." Gerd sniffed. "I — I thought he offered a good way to help them. She seemed so lost and homesick, and this made it possible for her to go home. Einar bought the tickets and gave them to her. Once they left, we moved in right away and got to work. Einar — well, we both were hard workers. And so pleased to have a place of our own." She glanced slowly around the kitchen, pausing at the door to the bedroom where Kirstin was now asleep in her bed. She pointed to the two envelopes addressed to Einar. "Please read those."

Rune did so; both were pleas for the remainder owed. Gerd's head started shaking again, as if of its own accord. Only the sound of the June bugs banging on the screen door and an errant mosquito broke the silence. As if none of them were breathing.

Gerd straightened her back and raised her chin. "I will pay her what is due — with interest. Whatever it takes, I will make it right. If I can't pay it all right now, I will finish when we sell the logs next winter."

"God bless you, Mrs. Strand. Would you like help with this?" the reverend asked.

"If you mean with money, no thank you. If you mean getting this sent to her, yes."

"How about if tomorrow I bring Mr. and Mrs. Benson out, and between us all, we make sure this happens." Skarstead looked at the contract again. "Are you sure you have enough cash to cover a bank draft for this amount?"

"How much is it?" Gerd nodded to Signe, who opened the cigar box and the leather pouches and removed the money.

"Never have I seen such prosperity in cleaning a bedroom," Signe quipped.

Rune rolled his eyes, Nilda rolled her lips,

and Reverend Skarstead cleared his throat as if to stop a cough.

"Well?" Gerd said. "Start counting."

Though Signe and Nilda had counted the money earlier, they laid the bills out in stacks of a hundred dollars and recounted the coins into stacks as well, just to be sure. Reverend Skarstead tallied up the columns.

"You have enough here, I think. If you send her the money owed and interest at two percent, the total will be, uh . . ." His pencil scratched as he wrote it all out.

They all stared in shock at the final amount.

"You won't have much left," Signe said.

"I will have enough to pay off the other house and get through the months till we sell logs again."

Rune bristled. "No, Tante Gerd, no. We will pay for our own house."

Her eyes narrowed. "We shall see on that." She nodded again. "And we will buy a small flock of sheep." She looked directly at Rune again. "There will be no more contracts around here."

Nilda snorted. Signe coughed.

Ivar threw back his head and laughed. "If I were you, Reverend Skarstead, Rune, and the rest of you, I would just do like she says. They don't say Norwegians are stubborn for nothing."

A few minutes later, after a parting prayer and good-byes on the porch, Ivar untied Skarstead's horse and backed him up enough to turn the buggy around. "Sorry, we never thought to take care of your horse. Takk, sir, you have been a wonderful help."

"Good thing we have a near full moon tonight. No chance of us stumbling along." Skarstead looked at those on the porch. "I will see you tomorrow afternoon, most likely, Mrs. Strand, and we will get this all taken care of."

"You won't tell anyone else, will you?" Gerd asked.

"No, only those necessary."

That night in bed, Rune reached for Signe's hand. "Did all of this really happen in one day?"

"I think so."

"I can't let her pay off our house."

"I would not try to stop her." Signe could hear his sigh, but that was the last thing she heard that night.

In the morning at breakfast, Gerd announced, "I expect you to work on your house and all the farming duties until fall. Then you can start felling trees again."

"But . . . but . . ." Rune tried to stare her

down — and utterly failed. "We'll see."

That afternoon, Reverend Skarstead rolled in, accompanied by the Bensons and a young man.

The women hastily removed their aprons and hung them behind the stove. "Come in, come in," called Signe. "Leif, go fetch your far." He left the woodpile and darted away.

The fragrance of fresh gingerbread greeted their guests as they entered the kitchen, where a tablecloth decorated the big oak table.

"This is Mr. Ellis Carnes from Blackduck. He is an attorney with a firm that specializes in contracts and international affairs." Reverend Skarstead then introduced them all around, and the men moved to the chairs around the table.

"Where is that sweet little Kirstin? Surely she's not napping." Mrs. Benson's smile dimmed. "She is, isn't she?"

Gerd nodded. "Ja, but we moved her bed into my bedroom. She'll be up soon."

"Guess I will have to wait." Mrs. Benson held out a basket. "Just a few things I thought you could use."

"Takk, and also for all the food yesterday. We found a full meal on the table when we came back from . . ." Signe paused and continued with a slight nod. "You were and are most thoughtful."

Mrs. Benson nodded. "You are welcome. I treasure your friendship. And, Mrs. Strand" — she took Gerd's hand in hers — "the Lord be with you."

Gerd raised her chin and blinked quickly. "Takk. You have been so very good to us, in spite of — of everything."

While the women had discussed using the parlor for this meeting, Gerd had insisted on the kitchen, where there was more room. "Please, be seated. If you like, we could have our coffee before the business."

The three men nodded. "Nothing beats gingerbread." Mr. Benson smiled at Gerd. "I'm sorry for all you've gone through."

Gerd nodded. "Takk for helping search for Einar."

They all looked toward the door when they heard Rune's boots on the step. He paused for only an instant when he entered the kitchen and saw the table. "Thank you for coming so quickly. It will be good to be done with all this." He shook the hands of each of the men and nodded at Mr. Carnes.

Nilda poured the coffee, and Signe set out the gingerbread drizzled with hard sauce. "Help yourselves, please."

They talked about the house-raising and the weather as the dessert and coffee disappeared. When the visitors had declined more coffee and cake, Reverend Skarstead rested his arms on the table. "Let us begin. I explained your plans to Mr. Carnes, so I think we all know what you want, Mrs. Strand. Have you changed your mind on anything? You can, you know."

Gerd shook her head. "No, not at all. I want this done and finished."

"But you realize that by paying out everything at once, you will leave yourself without much cash for the next several months?"

"I have been without before, and now I have all this to be thankful for and family to help me. What more do I really need?"

"Well said," Mr. Carnes commented. "Thanks to Reverend Skarstead, I took the liberty of drawing up some papers. Since he said the cash is all right here, after you sign these" — he motioned to the papers in front of him — "I will purchase a bank draft and mail this to the family in Norway. You will have copies of everything." He slid several sheets over to her. "Please read these — Mr. Carlson too, if you desire — and then sign on the lines. Do you have any questions?"

Gerd looked to Rune and Reverend Skarstead. When they nodded, she read the pages, dipped the pen they had brought into the ink, and signed her name. "Strange, these are the first legal papers I have ever signed. Einar did all that." She laid her hand atop the pages. "Do you want Rune to sign them too?"

"Only if you want him to."

"Yes, I do." She gave the papers and pen to Rune, who read and signed them before handing them to Mr. Carnes.

"Anything else?" Gerd asked. When the attorney shook his head, she nodded. "Then I feel we are finished here. Thank you for your time. What do I owe you, Mr. Carnes?"

"Not a dime."

"Surely —" When he shook his head, she nodded. "So be it." Pushing her chair back, she stood erect. "If you would like more coffee . . . ?"

When they all stood, Mrs. Benson turned to Signe. "Are your boys, especially Leif, nearby?"

"I heard wood being chopped, so I know he is here."

"I have something for him, for all of them." She looked to Mr. Benson, who headed out the door.

"What?" Signe asked.

"Please, I want to give them this. I hope it will be all right. Let's go outside."

Mr. Benson lifted a basket from the rear of the buggy. A small whine gave away the occupant. He called Leif over and handed the basket to him. "We heard you've been wanting one of these."

Knute skidded around the corner of the house and joined them. He stared at the basket. "What is it?"

Wearing a face-splitting grin, Leif set the basket down, opened the bouncing lid, and lifted out a white puppy with brown and black spots. His eyes stretched even wider. Holding the puppy up, he stared at his far. "Really, can we keep him?"

"Ja, you now have a puppy. And one of these days he — or is it a she?" Rune looked to Mr. Benson.

"A he."

Leif cuddled the puppy, which squirmed to lick his entire face at once, as well as under his chin. "We have a puppy, we really have a puppy. Thank you!" He nodded to Mr. Benson. "Thank you. I promise to take good care of him."

"He needs a name." Knute took the offered puppy and got his face cleaned too. Both boys giggled.

"Thank you, for all you have done." Rune shook hands with all three men. "Beyond measure. Thank you."

After they waved the guests off down the lane, Rune turned to Gerd. "See what you have now? Not only a farm but good friends. And more to come."

"And right now, a heart of peace." She shook her head slowly. "Whoever could have dreamed up anything like this?" She took the puppy Leif offered her and tried to keep it from licking her chin.

"Can you watch him while we do chores?" Leif asked.

Gerd's lips twitched. "Ja, I think I can watch a puppy."

"Good. Come on, Knute, let's get at it." Leif paused, giving the older boys a pleading look.

Bjorn and Ivar rolled their eyes. "Yes, we will help so we can get back to the new house quicker." The four of them headed off to the well house to grab the milking pails, load the cream can in the wagon, and take them to the barn.

"I think we might just take the evening off." Rune blew out his cheeks and tipped his head back to stretch out his neck. He then rolled his head from side to side. "Reverend Skarstead had no idea when he talked about hope on Sunday that all this would happen so immediately. And yet God did. You know, hope does not disappoint us. Our God is a God of hope. We hope for what we do not see." He huffed a breath.

"I've been thinking on that."

Signe looked at her husband. "I was just hoping to see our house begun, and look how far it got."

"Way beyond what you hoped for." Rune nodded, eyebrows arching a question.

"For years I hoped and dreamed of coming to Amerika, and here I am." Nilda looked out over the fields to the west, where the sun was sliding to the horizon. She raised her chin and closed her eyes to feel the first breath of an evening breeze. "Can you feel it?"

Signe and Rune copied her, nodding. Rune whispered, "A breath with the dawn and another in the settling of the day."

"Surely today, this that we feel, is the breath of hope. Hope for tomorrow and all the days after. Hope that comes in spite of sorrow." Signe looked at Gerd, who was now sitting with the puppy in her apron. "Hope for new beginnings?"

"Ja, and I have one right here. Never thought I'd have a dog again, but here he is. Ouch, sharp teeth."

Nilda locked her arms around one knee and rocked back against the step above. "I always dreamed of having a baby girl to name Hope, and another Grace. I love those names, those words. You said 'breath of hope,' Signe. We need to make a sign out of that and put it above the door at your new house, to remind us all, every day."

"And one here too. I thought I had no hope at all, and now look." Gerd nodded slowly, as if imprinting the words on her heart. "Makes a lovely name for a little girl, and when she grows up too." She smiled and nodded at Nilda. "Perhaps you better hope for a good husband first."

"Tante Gerd!"

Their chuckles lifted on the evening breeze and swirled heavenward.

ABOUT THE AUTHOR

Lauraine Snelling is the award-winning author of over 70 books, fiction and nonfiction, for adults and young adults. Her books have sold over 5 million copies. Besides writing books and articles, she teaches at writers' conferences across the country. She and her husband make their home in Tehachapi, California, with basset hound Sir Winston and their "three girls," big golden hens.

The employees of Thorndike Press hope you have enjoyed this Large Print book. All our Thorndike, Wheeler, and Kennebec Large Print titles are designed for easy reading, and all our books are made to last. Other Thorndike Press Large Print books are available at your library, through selected bookstores, or directly from us.

For information about titles, please call:
(800) 223-1244

or visit our website at:
gale.com/thorndike

To share your comments, please write:

Publisher
Thorndike Press
10 Water St., Suite 310
Waterville, ME 04901

By Death Possessed

by Roger Ormerod

BY DEATH POSSESSED
TIME TO KILL
THE SILENCE OF THE NIGHT
FULL FURY
A SPOONFUL OF LUGER
SEALED WITH A LOVING KILL
THE COLOUR OF FEAR
A GLIMPSE OF DEATH
TOO LATE FOR THE FUNERAL
THIS MURDER COME TO MIND
A DIP INTO MURDER
THE WEIGHT OF EVIDENCE
THE BRIGHT FACE OF DANGER
THE AMNESIA TRAP
CART BEFORE THE HEARSE
MORE DEAD THAN ALIVE
DOUBLE TAKE
ONE DEATHLESS HOUR
FACE VALUE
SEEING RED
DEAD RINGER
STILL LIFE WITH PISTOL
A DEATH TO REMEMBER
AN ALIBI TOO SOON
THE SECOND JEOPARDY
AN OPEN WINDOW

By Death Possessed

ROGER ORMEROD

A CRIME CLUB BOOK
DOUBLEDAY
NEW YORK LONDON TORONTO SYDNEY AUCKLAND

A CRIME CLUB BOOK
PUBLISHED BY DOUBLEDAY
a division of Bantam Doubleday Dell Publishing Group, Inc.
666 Fifth Avenue, New York, New York 10103

DOUBLEDAY and the portrayal of a man with a gun
are trademarks of Doubleday, a division of
Bantam Doubleday Dell Publishing Group, Inc.

All of the characters in this book are fictitious,
and any resemblance to actual persons, living or dead,
is purely coincidental.

Library of Congress Cataloging-in-Publication Data
Ormerod, Roger.
By death possessed.
"A Crime Club book."
I. Title.
PR6065.R688B9 1989 823'.914 88-33559

ISBN 0-385-24993-4

PRINTED IN THE UNITED STATES OF AMERICA
JULY 1989
FIRST EDITION IN THE UNITED STATES OF AMERICA
OG

By Death Possessed

1

I might have known he would be there, peering disdainfully over shoulders and strolling around with that rolling gait of his, as though to claim as much space as possible. My son. You wouldn't guess it, I hope, with that up-tilted little nose and the sneer he'd been experimenting with. Tatty, disorganized, contempt oozing from him; my son, Aleric: nineteen years of solid and inflexible loutishness. This was exactly the setting in which he excelled—an Antiques Road Show. There he could treat the excited throng to one undiluted dose of his practised disdain. Their precious possessions, which they'd brought to display to the experts, were nothing more than out-dated rubbish to him.

I tried not to catch his eye, but it never works. He spotted me before the door swung shut behind me, and pushed his way through.

"Hiya, Pop!" His little eyes fell on the package under my arm. "You ain't brought The Picture! Never! You've got a cheek."

The noise was appalling. The hall was large and echoing, and the swirling crowds made my head swim. For a moment I felt lost. Aleric always did that to me, denigrating everything I ever did. I didn't answer. Suddenly I felt ashamed at having brought along The Picture.

It had possessed capitals ever since my marriage, my fault I suppose for having given it too much importance. But it was important to me. My father had passed it on, with the implied suggestion that his mother had painted it, though he hadn't seemed certain about that. It was twenty by sixteen inches, on canvas on stretchers, and in a rather poor frame. I hadn't even been certain whether to be proud of it. Certainly I liked to look at it, but was it really Grannie's work? The subject was a country cottage, early morning, the sun dappling the walls through the leaves of a tree. You could feel that sun on your cheek and see the dapples moving to a slight breeze through the leaves. And it was mine, you see. The initials, an A and an F superimposed, could well have been my grandmother's. It was dated 1910, and she had been Angelina Foote at that time. I knew that, but not much more about it.

I stood there like a fool, suddenly convinced that I should turn about and retreat. But I was trapped. A man, dapper and placid in the chaos, touched my arm.

"A painting, is it? You want Dr. Dennis, over there on the right."

As Aleric at the same time told me his mother would be mad, me bringing The Painting, I was caught between the two speeches, not really registering either.

"Come on!" he said, grabbing my arm. "This is gonna be great. Wait till you get an eyeful of this picture expert."

I don't know why crowds part to allow his progress, but they always do. It's probably because he exudes the certainty that they will. There were protests and nasty remarks, aimed at me of course, and suddenly I was in a short queue, well towards the head of it, and when I looked round in apology all I saw were tentative smiles and nods. Already there was an air of expectancy, that here was a man of importance bearing, in now-torn newspaper, something special.

Aleric was no longer with me. Then I spotted him, large ears and tip-tilted nose reaching over a shoulder in the spectator group. (Where *had* he got that nose from?) I looked away quickly, and it was only then that my eyes fell on Dr. Dennis. Dr. Margaret Dennis, I learned later. I don't know what she was a doctor of, but the title clearly merited a suit: straight skirt, large-lapelled jacket with the shoulders cut wide, and the white shirt and stringy black tie of the almost obligatory uniform. But none of this hid the fact that she was a woman, every inch of her, out where she should go out, in where she should go in, every contour shouting out that there was a female body inside all that, yearning to get out. There was a feeling stirring inside me that I hadn't felt for years, and I realized she was enthralling me with an exposition on the various imitators of John Sell Cotman. Art is not a subject that has ever seized me with enthusiasm. As a professional photographer, my concern has always been for how things look. Was the photograph balanced, appealing, and did it make its point? There appeared to be rather more than that to art.

She was working at a small table with a couple of easels at her shoulder. To one side a TV camera was spying on the proceedings. I assumed they were recording everything for later editing, and suddenly seized by a fit of stage fright, I prayed that my bit would be cut.

Then I was into it before I was emotionally prepared, tearing at the wrapping, determined not to waste one second of the precious time of this splendid doctor of whatever it was. Numbly, I handed it over. The camera eye leered at me. It's strange that photographers so rarely experience the frightening side of the lens. I wondered how I would manage to register the correct amount of delight—or disappointment as appropriate—when the fatal decision was made on the value of The Painting.

"Well!" she said. "What have we here?"

She placed it on one of the easels. Her voice, close to, had been a soft and liquid burr. Now I was hearing nothing of the background din. There had been a momentary relaxation of her on-camera smile as her hazel eyes fell on my offering, a pucker of her delicately moulded lips, a blink, a nod. Then she'd recovered, standing back from the easel with one finger to her lips and taking what seemed to me a devil of a time on the scrutiny.

"It's very dirty," she observed at last. She swivelled her head at me. "I bet it's been hanging in a living-room—and you smoke . . ."

I inclined my head, patting the pipe in my pocket. My mouth had gone dry, my teeth felt sore, and I didn't think my lips would unseal again. She nodded severely and turned back to it.

"Of course, since he's become famous there have been dozens of copiers. Only six have survived, you know, so, from a rarity value alone, the prices have rocketed. He sold six before he died. That would be in 1917. He enlisted in the French army, a *poilou,* and was killed in the trenches. This is really a very good fake though. Where did you get it?"

I coughed to clear my throat. "Who?" I croaked.

"Pardon?"

"Who are you talking about?" I asked, shaking the hair out of my eyes.

"Frederick Ashe, of course: 1887 to 1917. British. Really post-Impressionist, but the style is pure French Impressionism. This is remarkably good, I must say. The brush strokes have all the power and confidence of Frederick Ashe. Where did you get it?"

"My father," I whispered. The way she was talking, I was beginning to feel like a crook. Fake indeed! "From his mother."

She turned and considered me with some severity. I realized she was only an inch short of me, which would make her five feet nine. Her make-up was subdued and perfect. Well, it would be, wouldn't it, she being an art expert. Behind her eyes she was making calculations, assessing my age, probably within a month of my true forty-one. They're good at ages, these people. She wouldn't need to carbon-date me.

"But that would make it . . ." Her voice faded away.

I could appreciate her difficulty. She had already hinted that this Frederick Ashe, of whom I'd never heard, had become collectable, and therefore worth forging, only in recent years, and here was I claiming it had been painted in my grandmother's days.

Abruptly she turned away, and snatched the canvas from the easel, turning it over, examining the deterioration to the back of the picture, fingering the wooden stretchers. What she discovered seemed to upset her.

"But of course," she said to herself in exoneration, "it's always possible to obtain a canvas of the correct period. Your grandmother?" she threw at me.

I nodded. There seemed nothing to say.

She turned the canvas back, licked her finger, and wiped it across the lower right-hand corner. The superimposed initials and date appeared:

A 1910

"Not just a fake," she said fiercely. "A forgery. It's even got his signature. An F and an A overlapping. Nineteen-ten," she said. "He went to France in 1910."

"So he painted it in England," I suggested, helping her out.

"I can't believe that."

"It's always looked very English to me." I was feeling more relaxed, probably encouraged by her uncertainty. "The cottage, I mean."

"It must be a forgery. Well worth the effort—the last genuine Ashe fetched eighteen thousand at auction."

At that I gulped. Then recovered. After all, it wasn't a Frederick Ashe, it was a Grannie Angelina.

"It's not F.A.," I ventured, before she took it too far. "And it can't be a forgery."

"Why not?" she demanded.

"If the existing six genuine Frederick Ashes were sold in Paris and he didn't go there till 1910, it'd be a bit stupid to forge one and date it before he sold any abroad. You'd at least have the sense to date it around 1913, I'd have thought."

She considered me again. I might look stupid, but I do like logic, and that seemed logical to me. Her eyebrows lifted delicately, not disturbing the smooth, high forehead. "Very well." She was brisk, turning back to the painting and attacking it with her licked thumb, her tongue flicking out vigorously. Portions of the original colours began to appear, and indeed it *had* become dirty. I resolved to treat it to a toothbrush and washing-up liquid when I got it home.

"They're his colours," she declared. "This yellow. Surely it's his yellow! You'd never be able to match . . . And the chairoscuro! This play of light on the wall! The shadows in the doorway—the luminosity! But it *must* be a Frederick Ashe. Oh dear Lord, a seventh! They'll go wild at Christie's."

"It's not," I said quietly, "a Frederick Ashe."

"What?" She didn't turn.

"It's not F.A. It's A.F."

Then she swung round. "What are you saying?"

I twisted my head and looked into the camera, making it a statement for posterity. "I said it's not F.A., it's A.F. My grandmother. Angelina Foote."

"Nonsense."

I shrugged. I think I smiled. "My father gave it to me. He was under the impression that his mother painted it."

"Under the impression?"

"That's what he said."

She took a deep breath. "Have you got it insured?"

"No."

"Then I'd advise you to do so. To a value of around twenty thousand pounds."

It was at this point I was supposed to register shocked delight. I regret to say that I laughed. "Gerraway," I said. "It's my grannie's."

"It's a pity, then, you can't ask her," she said, her voice acid. Who could blame her, being laughed at in front of the camera? "I'll stake my reputation on the fact that it's a genuine Frederick Ashe." She mentally added a number of years to my age. "If she was alive, your grandmother would agree, though how she got hold of it . . ."

"Oh, but she is. Alive, I mean. Around ninety-five, but alive. Maybe I'll take your advice, and go and ask her."

"You do that, Mr. . . ."

"Hine," I said. "Tony Hine."

"Very well, Mr. Hine." She reached into a shoulder bag which had been sitting on the floor between the easels and produced a small wallet, extracted a business card, and handed it to me. "And when you've discovered the facts—the provenance, we call it—I'd be very pleased if you'd contact me again. Any time."

I took it, and slid it into my jacket breast pocket, producing one of my own with the same two fingers.

"Thank you," she said. "A photographer? Hmm!" Was there disapproval there? She leaned closer. This was for my ear alone. "Guard it with your life," she whispered.

Then she was all teeth and encouragement for an old dear behind me who was presenting a tightly rolled canvas I could hear crackling as it was forcibly straightened out.

I looked round for Aleric. When I wanted him—pretty rarely, I must admit—he was never on hand. Now I did, but he'd gone. Dr. Dennis had impressed me. Guard it with my life? She must have been certain that I was carrying a seventh, and unknown, Frederick Ashe. No doubt he'd painted dozens in his life, short as it had been, and apart from the known six the rest had been assumed to be lost. So perhaps I really was carrying something very valuable. Nah! It was Grannie's. How else could she have given it to my father? The art lady was mistaken, put it like that.

Nevertheless, I would have felt more comfortable with Aleric at my shoulder. All right, so he was moronic, obstinate, and unpredictable, but he was six feet of bone and muscle and heavy boots and hard fists. You have to exploit what you have available, and heaven help us, my wife and I had been presented with this. So I would have liked to encourage him in a little exploitation of his abilities. Trust him to disappear.

Hugging the canvas close, now without wrapping because I'd been too confused to collect it up, I sidled towards the door. I'm usually inconspicuous. I vanish into backgrounds, an ability that can be useful to a photographer. It didn't help me then. A hand touched my shoulder and a hoarse voice said, "Got a minute?"

I turned. He was a weasel of a man, smelling strongly of tobacco and something else less pleasant, draped in tattered cast-offs and with a battered cap over one ear.

"Not really," I said.

"Five thousand," he said. "On the nail. Used fifties."

I had never met anyone who spoke in terms of fifties, plural. And *used* fifties suggested a close acquaintance with such wonders.

"No," I said.

"Six."

"Sod off," I said.

He shrugged, and melted into the crowds.

But he'd done something for me. Probably he was a man who followed these Antiques Road Shows around, pockets packed with used fifties, in search of quick bargains. His offer indicated confidence in the abilities of Dr. Dennis. He, to the tune of six thousand, was prepared to back her judgement. This disconcerted me.

A woman held open the door for me. Fresh evening air brushed my face. I smiled my thanks. She slid a card into my breast pocket, her fingers like claws, her eyes meeting mine with obdurate impersonality. "Insurance," she whispered hoarsely. "Give me a ring. Any time." She smelt of violets.

I nodded and headed for my Mini, hoping it would start reasonably quickly. I wanted to get away from there, to think, to decide on my attitude. The impulse to take The Painting along for appraisal had been urgent. Somewhere in the back of my mind must have been lurking an uncertainty about the history of it, and the opportunity had presented itself. So why, you ask, hadn't I thought of going to ask my grandmother? Well, to tell you the truth, I hadn't visited her for over twenty years—not since, just before I married Evelyn, I drove her to Wiltshire to show her off to Grannie, and for some reason the two women had hated each other on sight. Grannie Angelina had at that time been over seventy, an age when the restraining of one's opinions had become an effort not worth making. She had expressed herself on my choice of a wife in precise terms, as though Evelyn had not been in the same room. The journey back had been strained. The fact that Grannie turned out to be pretty accurate in her assessment didn't help at all. So I'd refrained from visiting her only from a sense of loyalty to Evelyn, but I'd refrained for too long. Now it would be embarrassing to visit, particularly if I used the painting as an excuse, thus indicating self-interest. Yet clearly such a visit had now become urgent and imperative.

All these things I intended to consider on the way home, but the time for that had disappeared when my car finally started. The garage had spoken about a new starter motor, but I really had to get a zoom lens for my Olympus, so . . . I'd discovered that I could get action by first striking the starter with a spanner, which entailed lying on my back in a dark car park—it *always* didn't start in the dark—and bashing away blindly.

When I got to my feet, there was a tweedy gentleman with a tweedy moustache watching me with interest, his business card already in his fingers.

"Security," he said. "Give me a ring. Doors and windows. Direct alarm to the nearest cop-shop. Satisfaction guaranteed." He nodded and stood back as I climbed into the car. It started. He waved me goodbye.

Heavens, I thought, I couldn't *afford* to own a valuable painting. It was like winning a Rolls-Royce in a raffle; you'd have to sell it in order to have enough money to run it. But I didn't own a valuable painting, did I! I owned the same old picture I always had, an Angelina Foote, worth nothing more than its sentimental value to me. But unfortunately . . . ah, there was the snag . . . unfortunately, the clever Dr. Margaret Dennis had broadcast the general idea that I was the owner of a unique and previously unknown Frederick Ashe. If that hall had contained insurance touts, tatters, and security buffs, then there was a good chance it had also had its share of crooks and ruffians, eyes and ears well open for the useful snatch.

I peered into the rearview mirror. Nothing was following me.

The canvas sat on the passenger's seat. It hadn't changed. All that had changed was my life, and that by the strange coincidence of the initials: F.A. and A.F. No, more than that . . . the coincidence of the matching style, if Grannie Angelina *had* painted the picture. Two coincidences were too much to accept. It had to be a Frederick Ashe. My scalp tingled. Around twenty thousand pounds sat on the seat beside me.

Then why wasn't I delighted, excited, panting to get home and share the joy of it?

Two reasons. The first was that I felt robbed, in a strange way. I would have to part with it. And if it was not Grannie's work, I'd lost that too, the proper pride of family worth. The painting had been a visual indication that there had been, if only in the past, some small artistic ability lurking in my blood. Don't laugh. I was a photographer. What's artistic in that? you say. I'll think about it and let you know.

The second reason for my lack of enthusiasm was that I was uncertain of my reception when I got home. With Evelyn, you could never be sure.

My wife is a solicitor. She had just qualified when I first met her, and I admired her for the intellectual accomplishment which had brought it about. She was certainly not a beauty, but I saw something attractive in her puckered, mobile features, her huge blue eyes, and the flaming, hectic red hair she insisted was auburn. She laughed a lot in those days. Her face at such times achieved the most adorable shapes. I thought she had a sense of humour, but it was apparently only a reflection. I made a joke; she laughed. After a while I discovered she had no sense of humour at all. Or she deliberately acquired no sense of humour. After all, a solicitor is expected to be reasonably solemn. If a client said she wanted a divorce because her husband wore his jeans in bed, it would not be politic to burst into roars of laughter.

So now Evelyn finds nothing to laugh at. She has also become a little pedantic. The law doesn't allow much freedom of deviation from specific meanings. Or tries not to. Evelyn began by allowing me no use of an incorrect word. Syntax was her god. After a while the area covered by the lack of freedom extended upwards and sideways, so that she came to expect no deviation from anything. Life was a pattern. A perfect and precise pattern. I was an extending stain that obliterated its complex line.

Naturally, she earned good money, the sort that had an overflow allowing it to grow and mature. I earned very little. A professional photographer these days has to specialize. With the modern automatic cameras, anybody can run off a spool of perfect wedding photos. So I have to look for something with less facility involved, and for the past two years I've had to look deeper and further.

This disparity in earning capacity, and thus in the provider stakes, has never been mentioned. But it has hung like a cloud around the house. I try to ignore it, laugh it away. But, as I've explained, my laughing is done alone.

When I got home, Aleric's motorcycle—her present to him on his last birthday—was propped in the drive. Its engine was bigger than the one in my Mini. I parked behind it. The house had no distinction: a detached residence in which we resided, with three bedrooms, living-room, dining-room, kitchen, and Evelyn's study. She worked evenings. Loved it. Aleric had the front door open before I reached the porch. He gave a mock little bow to the man bearing a fortune, and a lop-sided smile that was ruined by the tail-end of a sneer. I marched on through. She was in the living-room, as I guessed she would be. I stood in the doorway.

What impressed me was that she had nothing on her lap or in her hands. Always, she was reading something. Now I had her full attention. On the wall behind her there was a lighter patch on the Regency striped wallpaper where The Painting had lived. This was now under my arm.

"Darling," she said, smiling her crumpled, encouraging smile, "you own a Frederick Ashe! How splendid for you."

I stood there. Aleric edged past me and went to stand by his mother's chair. He was all attention.

"It's not a Frederick Ashe," I said. "It's an Angelina Foote. There's just a wild coincidence in the initials."

"Nonsense," she said briskly, reminding me of Margaret Dennis for one second, before I clamped down on the memory. "You've always been stupidly romantic. Your grandmother . . . didn't you tell me she came from a wealthy family? She was probably in Paris, you know the way they used to tour the Continent. Around 1912. She'd be about nineteen. I'll bet she bought it somewhere along the Left Bank, for a hundred francs or so, precisely because of the initials. You have to be logical in these things, Tony."

"You seem to know all the details." I was playing for time.

"Of course I do. Aleric's told me every detail. Clever boy."

Did I say she has no sense of humour? It's just that she doesn't recognize a joke when she makes one.

"We'll put it up for auction," she decided. "Sotheby's, I think." She had never taken any interest in it, but it had become "we" when it was a question of parting with it. "Twenty thousand, possibly. You can get yourself a new car, and we'll have the room re-papered. Some decent clothes for you. How you can hope to impress . . ."

I didn't really take in the rest. My mind, prompted by that blank patch on the wall, was roaming the house. Now that there *was* a blank patch, it drew my attention to all the other things of mine that weren't within those walls. The answer came back: pretty well everything wasn't. Apart from a few clothes in the wash and a paperback or two, all I personally owned was either at my photo-lab in town or in the Mini. I'd been away for a few days at a factory in Maidstone, getting colour shots for a set of twenty-by-sixteens in the boardroom, to remind the board members that work was performed beyond those four walls. So the floppy bag containing a few spare items of clothing, and my camera equipment, were still in the car. Nothing of note was in that house. The house itself was Evelyn's, in her name, bought with her own money. Considering the sneer on Aleric's face and that weird nose, I began to wonder whether in fact he was mine. Why else had Evelyn married me? And why in such a hurry? Perhaps that was what she'd found worth laughing at in those days.

Then suddenly my ambivalent thoughts about the painting flowed together and became one warm glow. It was mine. It was under my arm. It didn't matter who had painted it, nor whether it was worth a lot of money. I derived pleasure from looking at it. That pleasure would not be enhanced by the thought that it was valuable, nor reduced if Grannie had painted it. Rather the reverse. So I wanted no discussion about what was to be done with it. I would keep it. But not there, on that barren wall, where unfeeling eyes would rob it of its worth to me and unspoken thoughts blame me for not realizing its possible worth in spending-money.

It was mine.

I didn't know whether she had finished her exposition on how the sale would be handled, and probably on the legal aspects of ownership. Perhaps I cut in without consideration. Certainly, I recall very clearly her startled expression and how very ugly it made her seem.

"Well," I said. "I'll be off, then."

And I walked out of there.

2

It said a lot for our marriage that Evelyn didn't run after me and ask what the hell I thought I was doing. She knew very well, and she was not prepared to do anything about it. For too long we had been separate people, living under the same roof.

I was aware that she stood at the dining-room window to watch me drive out of her life. Probably she would be wondering whether I might claim alimony from her and what legal gambits she could toss beneath my flying feet. But that was where my artistic heritage came into play. I told you I'd think of something. My exit had a certain balanced pattern to it: it stated the truth in simple lines, it had design, it had composition. Until I reached the Mini, it also had dignity. Then once more the car let me down.

Nothing. Not a whimper from the starter motor. I saw her pale, expressionless face at the window. Even at that moment she failed to smile. Then something happened that added the final touch to the picture, produced the colour and the tone, the chiaroscuro. A Volvo Estate drew up at the drive entrance, Dr. Margaret Dennis got out, and she called, "Want any help?"

I think she must have guessed exactly what had happened. The Mini's door was open and the painting (now it was outside Evelyn's house it did not need the support of capitals) was clearly visible. I had brought it home; I was taking it away again.

"Want a lift?" she asked.

Clearly I could not sink to the indignity of crawling under the Mini with my magic spanner. I had only one choice.

"I'd be much obliged, if you'd give me time to unload."

She not only gave it to me, she filled it in by helping. To Evelyn, the picture she was staring at must have changed. It crackled now, and sparkled with naked colour. I'd returned home to 5 Laurel Grove with the express intention of leaving again—and with a woman. At the window she made no move. She would be preparing the legal tangle with which she would bind me.

We stripped the Mini of all my possessions and loaded them into the back of the Volvo, where they assumed a shameful insignificance. We went round and climbed in the front.

"Where to?" she asked.

"I've got a little place in town." Did my voice sound right? "A display window and my working lab. I thought I'd rig up a bed of sorts . . ."

"Sounds terrible."

"I can't afford a hotel."

"Of course not."

Her conversation was colourless. She was allowing me to take the lead. I was the custodian of a Frederick Ashe, and she had to keep an eye on me. Commission loomed. It was necessary to remain in touch. And yet . . . there was something in her attitude that hadn't been there at the Road Show, something more than the casting off of an official cloak. She was relaxed with me. There was a light intimacy in her voice.

"I can do better than that," she said. "There's a place . . . it belongs to my firm. It's used for entertaining wealthy clients. A cottage. You'd like it. You'll be safe there."

Safe? There it was again, the implication of danger.

"I can't let you go to any trouble."

"I'm not allowing you out of my sight. I've got a proprietorial interest in you, my friend." Then she laughed, a free and unforced liquid sound. "There's the smell of money around. It always makes me slightly hysterical."

"And practical."

"I'm extremely practical. The appreciation and assessment of art isn't an art in itself. It's a science. Very down-to-earth, I can assure you. We use scientific methods. It's very depressing. Contrast the artist's attitude to his work with ours! They'd weep if they knew. Sometimes I long to do wild things—forge a masterpiece, something like that. Wild, impulsive things."

I'd just done a wild and impulsive thing myself, and at that moment I couldn't find anything in its favour. There was an emptiness, a choking feeling of irrevocable error. I couldn't see any distance into the future, not with optimism.

"Such as driving to Laurel Grove . . ."

"That! Exactly! It was an impulse. I wanted to see where the Frederick Ashe had hung."

"Whether the house justified the honour?"

"Now you're being sarcastic."

"This isn't the way into town."

"Isn't it? Where does your grandmother live?"

I glanced at her, only then aware that she'd found time to change and was now in jeans and a denim jacket. "Wiltshire."

"Excellent. It's on the way."

"What is?"

"The cottage I mentioned. Where we're going. You said you intended to take the painting to your grandmother and ask her about it. Now you haven't even got transport. So I'll have to take you. The cottage is in Worcestershire. As I said, on the way."

"Got it all worked out, haven't you?"

"I told you, I'm practical. I can even put it all down as business expenses."

"Hmm!"

I was beginning to realize that leaving the Mini behind had been a mistake. Cranky and difficult though it was, it had given me independence. Now I was trapped. Talk about frying pans and fires! I'd become lumbered with another female of my wife's species: dogmatic, efficient, autocratic. Professional women! It would have been better if I'd asked her to stop the car, got out, and started walking into the night.

She was moving too fast for that to be a possibility. Her driving was a reflection of her personality, practical in that she pressed the correct things and turned the right ones, but there was an over-confidence in her expectations. Other vehicles were expected to do exactly what suited her. It seemed to work though. We sliced the night apart, in the general direction of Worcestershire.

"Keep your eyes open for a sign saying Kidderminster," she called out, racing through a crossroads.

"If you slowed a bit, I might have time."

"So much to do. You can't imagine."

Which was true; I had no idea of her intentions. All I wanted to do was settle somewhere, get something to eat, get some sleep, and think of some way I could find myself another car. I wasn't wildly happy about visiting Grannie with Margaret Dennis in tow. The odds were she'd have *me* in tow by the time we got there.

We took a corner too fast. She said, "You missed it. This is the way. Only a couple more miles." I sighed.

I had expected something remote and desolate. Hadn't she called it a cottage? Isolated it certainly was, but we drew up in front of a modern, semi-bungalow that later proved to be on two levels. When she'd parked, and we'd entered the building through a side door, we were on a wide balcony with an open stairway down to a large room that occupied the full width. She must have operated a switch inside the garage, because all the lights were on. A whole bank of curtains ran across the far wall, and I had to guess they covered a row of full-length windows.

She led the way down. "Unload your stuff later," she said. "I'll get some coffee going, then we'll see what's in the deep-freeze."

I was on edge, my nerves jumpy. For the whole of that evening I'd been in no position to control my own life. Even now there was uncertainty. I roamed the room. Paintings covered all available space on the three walls downstairs and along the head of the stairs. Genuine oils and watercolours, I could see that, and even I was able to detect they were copies. The original Constables, Turners, and Monets, etc., were in national art galleries.

Above the clattering in the kitchen, I called through the open door, "The paintings? Fakes, are they?"

"Copies. All of them."

"Who did them?"

"Me."

"The lot?"

She came in smiling, carrying a tray. "I've put something in the oven. It'll keep us going. Yes, they're all mine."

I sat on a padded stool, facing the low table. "White, please," I said. "It's not a company house, is it? It's yours."

"True." Her eyes were dark with amusement. "There isn't any company. I work on my own."

"You lied to me." I don't know why I'd assumed I could trust her, but the remark emerged with a tone of disappointment.

"Sorry about that." She glanced away. "I had to get you here."

"The painting, not me."

"You."

"They come together," I told her. "One package."

"I wanted both."

We sipped her coffee. I produced my pipe and gestured around. "From what you said . . . I suppose you'd rather I didn't . . ." I indicated the paintings.

"Oh, those! Smoke by all means. They're rubbish. It's all I was ever capable of when I was at art school. Copying. Any fool can copy."

To me, that seemed to be a somewhat sweeping statement. I'd had enough time to realize the copies were excellent work. But I'm no expert and felt I had no right to offer praise. I shrugged, which seemed to annoy her.

"Not fakes," she said intensely, "not forgeries. Copies."

"It matters?"

She banged down her empty cup and got to her feet. "Of course it damn well matters, Mr. Tony Hine. You're not *that* blasted ignorant, I hope."

But I was. Beyond her, where she stood with her feet straddled, her jet hair untidy and her high cheeks flushed, there was a copy of Monet's *Cart in the Snow,* which I recognized. I would have loved to own it, and it wouldn't have mattered to me that the brush had not been held in Monet's fingers. It would simply have been a constant pleasure to look at.

"I am, you know. Dead ignorant." Then I lit my pipe. There's a time when you know you've touched flame to a fuse, and I sat and waited for the explosion. I needed information, you must have realized. There was a question of whether my painting was a Frederick Ashe or an Angelina Foote. I needed to understand why it ought to matter to me and why its value could fluctuate from around £20,000 to nil on the answer.

She began quietly enough, after a long stare at me to decide whether I was serious.

"Tony," she said at last, "I'm calling you Tony because this is going to be personal. I've never told anybody this before, because in the art world I've never met anyone so ignorant. But of course, you're a photographer." She jutted her lower lip. It was a challenge.

"Take me to the original with my camera . . ." I was pointing at the Monet.

"It's in the Jeu de Paume in Paris."

". . . and I'll produce a colour print, same size, that's as good as that one on the wall."

"Yes?" she demanded. "Yes? Then listen to me, friend Tony. I've been involved with painting for thirty years. Yes, since I was eight. My father . . . well, never mind that. I started with copying. Every student does, and of course I went to art school. Three art schools: London, Paris, and Prague. We copied. Until of course we progressed to our own work in our own styles. All except me. I went on copying. Don't think I haven't thought about this, over and over. Maybe I started copying too young. But the basic fact was that I couldn't paint for myself. There wasn't anything I didn't know about colours, techniques, composition . . . but I couldn't *do* it. No artistic ability, you see. No flair and no imagination. I'd copied for too long. I had to look at a fixed picture, not at a scene or a model or a still life. As an artist I was a failure. Every art school rejected me."

I got up and walked round the room, just in order not to look into her eyes. She continued as though I was still sitting there. I doubt she could see.

"There'd never been anything but art in my life, Tony. It was as though the world had cast me out. My father fetched me from Munich, where I'd drifted to, took me home, and treated me like a baby. He got me to understand in the end, hammered it into me, that it didn't have to be a door that'd slammed in my face; it could be a door that had opened. He persuaded me to study art as an academic subject—the history, the techniques. And that was what I did."

There she stopped. I didn't believe she had finished, only that she'd paused for some intimation that she had my interest. Standing in front of a Renoir, I said, "You certainly succeeded in that; you got a doctorate."

"Yes. You could say I succeeded. Because I had to, or there was nothing. For my doctorate, I specialized in forgeries and in the detection and exposure of forgeries. I became an expert on the composition of pigments used for the past few centuries, on techniques, brush strokes even, and the mediums used. And at that stage I realized something else. Can you guess what that was, Tony?"

I had drawn back a curtain and was looking out into the darkness. It was after midnight, but a few lights still sparkled in the distance, below my level. I was staring over an invisible valley. She was a career woman. There'd been no time for emotional interruptions. Sexual incidents perhaps, but nothing that might have diverted her from her purpose. She was now going to tell me about accomplishment and involvement, about fulfilment. I swept the curtain shut and turned, not knowing what I could say. I smiled.

"I wouldn't care to guess."

"I realized I was in an ideal situation and had all the abilities and knowledge to paint real forgeries, undetectable ones. Not quite copies of known works. Slight changes. A tree moved, or a colour change in a hat. That sort of thing. And d'you know what?"

"Tell me."

"I couldn't do that either. Just couldn't. Not because I wasn't capable of doing it. I knew I was. But because I knew I'd be degrading myself and the original artist. Now wasn't that ridiculous, Tony? I'd at last found something I could do . . ."

"You'd already done—"

". . . and I couldn't put a brush to the canvas. The laugh was . . ." Her voice faltered, but she hadn't tripped over laughter. "The joke was on me. All my learning and studying and . . . and understanding, I suppose, stopped me. I knew how that artist had striven to develop his technique, how he'd starved to provide himself with materials, how he'd perfected his choice of colours . . . and there I was, prepared to pick up his whole life of endeavour and make some tawdry use of what had been his basic reason for living. And for what? Not for money." She waved an arm blindly. "I had what I needed. Not for fame or to fool the establishment. I was part of the establishment. So can you see why I couldn't do it? Can you, Tony?"

And there I was, caught, expected to produce a few words that in some way indicated an empathy with her point of view. She'd said she hadn't told this before. Did it matter to her that a virtual stranger, a philistine in her art world, should express an opinion? Perhaps it was because I was a stranger and yet enough of a friend for it to matter.

"I can see that it had to be *his* hand holding the brush," I ventured. "Renoir's, Degas', Constable's. His. The first stroke of the brush and your hand would wither."

"Superstition?" She pouted her disappointment.

"Not superstition. Sympathy and understanding."

I waited. She stared at me with moist eyes, swallowing. I watched the smooth line of her throat moving.

"Didn't you put something in the oven?" I asked, and went to check.

I was alone, peering into her oven. She had put in a lasagne, and it was ready. Crisply ready. I looked round for oven gloves and somewhere to put it down, and she was at my shoulder.

"Let me."

She put it on a plate, and we stared at it. Then she laughed.

"I'm starving," she said. "Let's try it."

We sat facing each other across the kitchen table. She had put a bottle of hock in the fridge. The lasagne was too hot, the wine too cold. We ate, and between bites and swallows we chatted. Nothing important. My life and my gradually escalating failure to achieve; hers and her growing prominence in the art world. "World" was the correct word. She travelled world-wide as an expert on forgeries. Her fees had bought this house and a small flat in London. She was already in sight of the culmination of a dream.

She was not a tidy person. She dumped the crockery and glassware in the sink for future attention, and said, "Let's get our stuff out of the car, and I'll show you where you can sleep."

This we did. As we returned from the garage and moved along the landing, she flung open a door. "This is my room." Flung open the next door. "You can sleep here. Or in the other room, as you wish."

I made no comment, simply walked into the second room, dumped my floppy bag and the camera holdall, and looked round. It was luxurious. She stood just inside the door. "Bathroom over there. You can take a shower if you like, while I get to work on your canvas."

It was under my left arm. I turned and looked at her. She raised her eyebrows delicately.

"Get to work?" I asked.

"You don't think I could sleep until I've at least cleaned it and taken some colour readings? Come on, Tony, I know what I'm doing. I'm not going to do it any harm."

I handed it over. "Where shall I find you?"

"Through the kitchen, the far door. Come down when you're ready."

I had my shower and felt much fresher, but my brain refused to respond. I couldn't take in the events of the day, analyse them, and produce a clear decision about my attitude. If it turned out that I was a fairly wealthy man, I still wouldn't be able to bear the thought of parting with my painting. So I'd gained nothing, except perhaps a cleaner canvas. Certainly, I thought, as I dug out a nearly clean shirt and a clean pair of Y-fronts and covered them with my disreputable working clothes, it would be pleasant to buy a couple of new outfits, in order not to soil the seats of a new car. What I couldn't balance in my mind was the loss of the painting against a transient gain in affluence.

Her workroom was a brightly illuminated and windowless laboratory, all shadow-free light, as near white as I've ever seen produced artificially. She had microscopes and magnifiers, a chemical bench, spectroscopes and viewers. On the side bench lay my painting. It was clean. I couldn't remember it like that. It glowed. Colours I had never realized as being there were now revealed in their naked glory, and new detail set my eyes roving across it.

She straightened. "What d'you think?"

"I'd intended to do it up with a toothbrush and washing-up liquid."

She flinched. "I was certain before. Now I'm dead certain. It's a Frederick Ashe, painted before he left this country. It could even be a painting of his own cottage. He was late to be using this style, you know. The French Impressionist movement lasted until the end of the century, but there he was, using the same fragmented colour techniques, the pure colours, the use of light, just as they'd done. He sold only six in his life. He must have painted many more, and this is one of them. It'll cause great excitement . . ."

She stopped, probably aware of my reaction. Her implication had been that I would let it out of my hands to be gloated over by the pundits.

"I've never seen it looking so wonderful," I compromised.

"I've analysed the yellow—"

"If what you say is true," I cut in, "that the Impressionists over there had had their day, then there must have been no end of painters over in Britain too who were picking up on the style. Hundreds. So apart from the initials, which I still say could be A.F. for my gran, there's nothing to tie it down to Frederick Ashe."

This thought, more or less, had been tracking through my mind for some time, and I was determined to get it out. It seemed I'd insulted her.

"Nothing!" she cried. "There's a dozen points. His impasto—that's the thickness and build-up of the paint. I've *seen* it, Tony, on his other known works. His use of the palette knife. Here and there, his use of a finger. The choice of colour. The yellow—I've had time to analyse that, not chemically but with the spectroscope. It's cobalt yellow. Hardly known in England in 1910, but the French were using it. He was known to have corresponded with Monet, who could have sent him pigment. When he went to Paris, Maurice Bellarmé was a close friend. *He* could have sent him pigment. And there's viridian green. Another pointer—"

Clearly, she was going to take some stopping. "All right," I said. "Pax. You know your job. Other works, you said. Six, you've mentioned. Where're those?"

She stared blankly at me for a moment, then suddenly grinned. "The great disbeliever! No, you can't very well go and see them, to compare. Two are in a private collection in this country. I haven't seen those. I *have* seen, and examined, the other four. In detail. It's my job, Tony. One in the Musée des Beaux-Arts in Rouen, one in the Lecomte Collection in Paris, one in the Staatsgalerie in Munich, one in the Metropolitan in New York. Quite a round trip that would be."

I grimaced. "Look," I said, "I can understand your enthusiasm, but I've never been one for speculation. Tomorrow, if you're still prepared to do it, we can go and ask my grandmother. She'll know. She'd have been about seventeen when this was painted. She'll certainly know where it came from."

"I can't wait to meet her."

"So . . . if you don't mind . . . I'm very tired and I'd like to get some sleep."

"If that's what you want," she said solemnly.

I nodded, a lock of hair flopping forward. "Sorry—it is."

"No need to apologize."

"There might well have been."

She turned away. "I'll be here for some time. Might as well do a chemical analysis on that yellow."

"And the green," I suggested. "Good night."

But she was already absorbed with the painting.

3

In the back of my mind there was the vague recollection of a scandal involving my grandmother. My father told me about it, but at that time I was very young and probably didn't understand. There had been, now I came to probe my memory, never any mention of my grandfather, though I had the impression his father was the reason Dad had left home. Why else had my own family been living in the Midlands, when my father's original home had been in Wiltshire?

These memories were returning to me whilst we were on the journey there. Margaret was not the sort of driver who encouraged conversation when she was behind the wheel of a car, and I'd decided she needed all her concentration to keep us on the road. Perhaps she had her own thoughts. She seemed tense and expectant, eager to get there. Certainly, she wasn't wasting any time.

"The ring road's coming up," she said suddenly. "Do we take it, or straight on into town?"

It had been twenty years. There hadn't been a ring road last time. I had been hoping that my memory would pilot me to the house, but it was doing nothing. Too much had changed.

"Surely you know an address," she said irritably, pulling into a lay-by. "The name of a street even."

"It wasn't a street. Nothing towny like that. My impression is of isolation. Countrified. A large house. She was living with a companion. Grace or Gloria."

"But the name was Hine?"

"Of course."

"Of some importance?"

"They were grocers." Not "we" were. The "they" had been automatic. "My father's grandfather was the mayor."

"Oh . . . lovely. Let's find a post office."

She drove into town, parked with difficulty, found a post office, and we consulted a phone book. There it was: Hine A., Mandalay, Forster Grove.

"Mandalay?"

"Great-grandfather was an officer in the Indian Army."

"What an artistic background you do have, Tony." Impatience was peeking the corners of her mouth.

"Let's go and find Forster Grove," I said with dignity.

I recognized the Grove at once. The trees were thicker and taller than I recalled, and the roadway more narrow. The drive entrance columns seemed closer together, and surely they had possessed gates. The drive was short, and the overhanging beeches dripped from morning rain, which we hadn't encountered on the journey.

"Looks a bit gloomy," she commented.

"My memory's of dark rooms and depression. Silence. The companion looming like a ghost in the background. It wasn't a place I yearned to return to."

"You're completely out of touch. Admit it. Your grandmother might have died, and you wouldn't know."

So what did I say when the companion opened the door? "Is my grandmother still alive?"

We were standing in the porch, staring at the stained-glass panel in the heavy front door. I had pressed the button in the frame, but we'd heard no sound. I pressed it again, and silently the door opened.

I recognized her at once, and with the recognition there came the certainty of her name.

"Hello, Grace," I said, trying to smile. "It's me. Tony."

"No need to keep on ringing. I'm not deaf, you know."

My smile was difficult to hold, she'd changed so much. She had always been large and bulky, but now she was simply ungainly, distorting the shape of clothes that she'd probably possessed when I was last there. Her puckered face was coursed with lines, her cheeks sagging in wobbling dewlaps, her eyes sunken deeply into hollowed, dark sockets. All that was left was her resilience. She could be . . . how old? She had been their maid—a young and pretty girl—when my grandfather, Arthur Hine, had died. Heavens, that had been all of fifty years ago. It would make Grace at least seventy-five. How the time marched on! But for her it would have crawled leadenly. For all those years she'd had no life except as a companion, and later almost a nurse, for my grandmother. Every bitter, lost year had carved its passing in her face.

I risked a social disaster. "I wanted to see Grandmother."

She sniffed. Her red nose indicated it was habitual. "You'd better come in. A lot of good it'll do you though. If she'll see you, she probably won't recognize you, and they've pretty well stripped the house."

This last I didn't understand. We moved into the hall, with its patterned quarry tiles and its ancient hallstand. No, no hallstand, and the black old chest wasn't there either. The hall was wide and chilly, and smelt slightly damp. The staircase to the left was uncarpeted, though I couldn't remember whether it had been before. There had been changes. Surely Grannie Angelina hadn't had to resort to selling her antiques! The stair carpet had probably been priceless. I had always understood that Grandfather Arthur had died a wealthy man.

"I'll go and tell her," said Grace, flinging open a door into what I recalled as a drawing-room. "You'd better wait."

Then she closed the door on us, and we were left alone to stare at each other.

"Stripped the place?" asked Margaret. "She couldn't mean the bailiffs, surely?"

I shook my head. Certainly not. But this room, too, was more bare than I recalled it. I would have described it then as oppressively over-furnished, but now you could have played basketball in it.

"It wasn't so empty," I admitted. "And the ivy should have been cut back from the windows, that's why it's so dark. Grannie Angelina used to say it was better not to have direct sunlight on the furniture."

"No sunlight, and not much furniture now."

"True."

We waited. Eventually the door opened. Grace, still a heavy woman, moved with silence. She now radiated disapproval. "She will see you."

"What did you mean, Grace?" I asked. "You said stripped."

"And you another of them!" She tucked in her loose lips and nodded. Her hair was iron-grey and thin. "Don't tell me you haven't come to pick up a choice bit you'd like."

"I've brought something. I'm not intending to take."

"Well, that's a turn—up for the book, I must say. The relatives have been coming here in droves. Vultures over a carcass, but she keeps on living. I hope you realize she's ninety-five now. Don't expect too much of her. But at her age, everybody's expecting her to go at any time. So it's a good idea to get in while you can. 'Dear Angelina, I've always fancied that little table in the parlour.' " She mimicked the avaricious hypocrisy perfectly, and Angelina's weak and inoffensive response. " 'Then do take it, Flora—or Mary or Rose or whatever. It's no use to me now.' No good to Angelina, no. But what about me?"

With no one she could tell it to, she had bottled up this grievance for too long. It erupted like the bursting forth of a too-long-kept champagne, the pressure of fermentation having built up as the wine grew more bitter and sour. Perhaps Grandmother's will left everything to Grace. "All of which I die possessed." Very soon she would die possessed of nothing.

My smile was mechanical. "I told you, Grace, I've *brought* something." I produced the canvas, now without its frame, from under my arm. She hadn't noticed it. I'd expected relief, but instead of relaxing, she stiffened. Wrinkles smoothed along her jaw at the tension.

"It's one of those," she grumbled.

"Yes."

"You mustn't . . . no, not show her that . . . please."

I was completely confused. Why should I not show it to Angelina? "She'll be pleased to see it again, Grace. Come on now."

"You'll remind her."

I glanced at Margaret for assistance. She was as tense as Grace, but it was an anticipatory tension, her eyes bright and high patches of colour on her cheeks.

"Remind her of what?" Margaret asked, her voice empty, strained dry.

But Grace had recovered. "It's up the stairs and to the right. The room at the end. She likes a bright room." She nodded a distant disapproval. Brightness was too revealing.

She watched us out of the room with suspicion. I followed Margaret up the stairs. Ahead there was a short corridor lit only by a small window at the far end. Before we reached it there was a cross-corridor, where we turned right. I tapped on the door at the end, eased it open because my grandmother was expecting us, and we went in.

It was a corner room, adapted over the years as a bed-sitter. Angelina was in a wheelchair, which for some reason shocked me. But what had I expected? She'd not moved from her chair the last time I'd visited, when she'd been a mere seventy-five. She was sitting half-turned away, watching something through the window, and without the aid of spectacles. The chair appeared too big for her; she was bolstered with cushions on both sides and in the small of her back. Perhaps it was this that made her seem so small. She had shrunk into her clothes. Her hands, gnarled and claw-like, were resting on the arms of the chair. Her face, in profile, seemed barely to have changed. A thousand wrinkles had taken up the sag, so that it was easy to see she must have been very beautiful when young. A soft-focus lens, and I could have made her that again. She had the long, straight nose I'd inherited, the small chin, the long neck.

She had seemed not to be aware of us. "There's that magpie again," she said, her head nodding, nodding, as though on a spring. "Why is there only one, I wonder. Perhaps the poor thing's lost its mate."

I spoke quietly. "It's me, Gran. Tony."

There was nothing wrong with her hearing. Her head snapped round. The chair swung to face us at a touch of her left hand. Her eyes were deeply set now, the blurred grey of age, but she saw me clearly, I could tell—the way they swept me from head to toe, the way she switched her attention to Margaret, critically, hungrily. She saw so few strangers.

"Charlie's boy? Then it's about time. That's not your wife. Why haven't you been to see me? Come closer, where I can see you. My eyes aren't what they were."

But she'd been able to see the magpie in the garden—what had been the orchard, I realized from a quick glance, but which was now a jungle. Her faculties seemed to be in order, though she had the trick of the very old of jolting from one thought to the other abruptly. They have to express their thoughts as they present themselves, in case they become forgotten and lost.

I moved forward into a position where she could consider me in detail, nodding and humming to herself.

"Yes, you're Tony. Not changed a bit. You nearly left it too late, my lad." She gave a little splutter of laughter and dabbed her lips with a lace handkerchief that could well have been as old as herself.

"I could hardly come before, Gran," I said gently. "Not without a certain amount of disloyalty. Do you remember what you said about my wife?"

Her eyes danced, her lips quivered. "I remember very well. And I'll bet I hit the mark. Oh yes. Another woman knows. But I see you've found a better one. Come along, dear, don't stand over there. What's your name? Speak up. Don't be shy."

"Margaret. Margaret Dennis."

"Not married then?" She meant to me.

"It's Ms."

"Now don't you use that modern slang to me, my girl. If you're his mistress, stand up and say it. Pride. You girls, these days! No pride. I shouted it out with pride, let me tell you. And why not?"

"She's not my mistress, Gran. She's a business associate, an expert on paintings."

Gran was enjoying herself though. There was no stopping her. "So now we have experts. In my day we were artists or non-artists. We didn't speak to non-artists. Are you a non-artist, young lady?"

When I glanced at her, I was surprised to see that Margaret was smiling. "You could put it like that. I study other people's paintings. We can't all reach the heights, you know."

That seemed to satisfy Angelina, who nodded and looked down at her lap for a moment. Then she raised her eyes again. "Well, sit down, why don't you. Old people don't care to look up. Of course, I was always small. You could say I've always looked up to my men. Freddie was tall, like you, Tony. Oh, so like you! And Arthur was huge. But I looked up to Freddie in a different way. I suppose you know he was a genius. Oh yes. Now, get a chair for the lady, Tony. Where've your manners gone? You never used to let me stand without rushing for a seat. Don't you remember, that fight in the café . . . the café . . ." She faltered to a halt. For one moment she had confused me with Freddie.

I went to find a chair. They were all rush-seated and uncomfortable. I heard Margaret say behind me, "Freddie?" She said it very casually, as though not to disturb an already insecure intellect. "You can't mean . . . Frederick Ashe!"

Grandmother's voice was suddenly alive with delight. "You know him? You've met him?" She stopped so suddenly that in the silence the scrape of the chair was harsh. "But he's dead, of course. So long . . . you weren't even born."

"I wasn't born," said Margaret softly, on an indrawn breath.

I had placed the painting on the surface of a chest of drawers, which was above the level of Grannie's eyes. She hadn't noticed it. Now, before I could reach her to intervene, Margaret snatched it up and offered it to Angelina.

"This is his," Margaret stated with confidence.

I put the chair behind her knees and slowly edged it forward. She sat, without a glance at me. I stood at her shoulder. Angelina had not reached up to take the painting, but allowed it to rest on her knees, her hands still gripping the arms of her chair. Her head was bent. There was silence for so long I thought she might have nodded off. At her age, that was possible. Nodding, she was, but it was not from sleep. Nodding, nodding, with tiny whimpers, and I watched the fingers of her left hand tighten on the chair arm until the blood flowed from them.

There was a gentle rustling sound, and I realized she was whispering to herself.

"The cottage. Oh, it's the cottage. That first day . . . You were sitting there. Under that window. Painting. Of course, painting. When were you not, Freddie? I was wearing my blue gown. Do you remember that? It caught on the briars. There they are, on the right. Oh Freddie, Freddie . . . so long ago . . ." She raised her head and looked at me. No—her face turned to me. She didn't see me, could not, with those swimming eyes. "So long since I saw this. Where did you find it? I gave it to Charlie."

"My father—" I began, but Margaret was briskly practical.

"Is it his? You're talking about Frederick Ashe, aren't you? Is it his, Angelina?"

The eyes focused. She dabbed at the corners.

"Of course. Stupid girl. You ought to know that."

I reached past and lifted the painting from Angelina's lap and caught a glimpse of Margaret's profile. It was stiff with concentration, her lips pale. I heard her sigh.

"You knew him, did you, Gran?" I asked in a chatty voice. "He gave you this painting, I suppose, and you gave it to my father . . ."

"Now, now!" She was skittish, lively. "You know very well how it was. Everybody knew, but they didn't say anything. Not to my face. Oh, this takes me back. Yesterday . . . it could be yesterday."

She smiled into the distance. Yesterday was any day in the past, but the painting had been cleaned and was as fresh as when it had been painted. Yesterday was the day it had been painted, or the day before that.

"Tell us," said Margaret in a small voice. But I touched her shoulder. Angelina needed no prompting. The memories—so crystal clear from so far in the past—came pouring out. Her voice had more life, was younger. Her head came up with something like pride, perhaps a personal pride in her youth and beauty.

"Father had a large estate. I was seventeen. Yes, all of seventeen. On holiday from Saint . . . oh, something. Learning to be a young lady. I walked the estate, and it was so boring. You cannot believe how boring. Daddy had told me a young painter had rented the cottage in the lower meadow, so I went to look, for something to do. And there he was, painting. He was very ugly. The beauty was inside. That little turned-up nose! The big ears! Of course, I was taught to paint at school, but young ladies had to use watercolours—so much more genteel. This painter was working in oils. He wasn't very tidy, and I felt I had to be the lady of the manor, so I told him it wasn't too bad, but he must try harder. That was what they said to me at school. "Angelina, you must try harder." Miss Trench. You know Miss Trench, of course. No? Perhaps she's retired. I never liked Miss Trench—she never laughed. I didn't see Miss Trench again. Well, fancy that, I'd never realized. But she would not have approved. Oil painting was not for the young ladies of Saint Edith's. There, you see, I've remembered."

Her lips quivered in a smile at the memory of her school. Her eyes closed. Surely she couldn't nod off to sleep now! But her head lifted, and she went on.

"Frederick said he'd bet I couldn't do any better, and young ladies at private schools didn't learn anything useful. He was Frederick then. I called him Freddie in Paris though. And I said I could if I tried, and he bet me I couldn't. So I said how much, a shilling? But he didn't have a shilling, and he said a kiss, so I knew I was going to be kissed anyway, win or lose!" The voice changed to a crisp reprimand. "And don't smile at that, young lady. It was very daring, and he *did* let me try, sitting down and doing a tiny corner of his painting for him, and he said it was very good and gave me my kiss, and said if I came the next day, he'd lend me an easel and brushes and a canvas and I could paint my own picture. So I did—and we did, all through that wonderful summer. We painted together."

She looked round vaguely for the painting and seemed confused that it was no longer on her lap.

"That was one of them," she said, moving her left hand vaguely.

"You painted it together?" asked Margaret disbelievingly.

"No, no. Silly child. Didn't I say! We sat side by side, two canvases, his palette on a table between us, and shared his colours. What he did, I did. I copied his brush strokes as well as I could. Or he copied mine. Later, it didn't seem to matter which. We found we went together. Naturally. It was destiny, and there were pointers. And that's how it was until the end."

She put a hand over her face and bent her head. Margaret seemed about to say something, but I squeezed her shoulder and we waited. At last Angelina went on, "He insisted. It wasn't his war, I told him. Wars don't belong to artists. But he joined the French army and I never . . . never saw him again."

"But—" began Margaret.

I cut in quickly. "You must have loved him very much, Gran."

"Like a child, like a woman. You couldn't possibly understand. He was my life. I never painted again."

"So there were two sets . . ."

She didn't answer directly. "Mamma disapproved. Consorting with a vagabond, she called it. My father understood, I think. Yes, Father was a wonderful man. We painted all that summer. Eight paintings."

"Eight pairs?" I asked.

"Yes. Of course. I've said that. But Mamma had her way in the end. She made my father give Frederick notice to quit. And he'd got nowhere else he could go, and hardly any money. To me, it was the end of the world. Where would he go? I asked him. He said Paris. He said he had painter friends in Paris—if he could only get there. Claude Monet and Maurice Bellarmé. So I went to see my father and told him, and he gave me money for Frederick to get to Paris, much more than was needed, because he understood what I was thinking, you see; I could tell that in his sad eyes. But he wanted only my happiness. Two days later I took my wicker-work basket of clothes to the cottage, and we went to Paris."

"We went to Paris"—such simple words, but in 1910 it would have been an act of great courage to a young woman brought up as Gran had been. She had had to be with her man. It was as simple as that, and Gran expressed it simply.

"We nearly starved," she went on, "but Freddie got work at a bistro, and I tried to sell the paintings. I sold six. Six out of all that work! For about ten francs each. But Father sent me money from time to time. Mamma never wrote. She didn't even come to my wedding, and never spoke to me again. And the war came . . ." She drew breath sharply, her lips quivering. She was silent. Her time sequence had become confused.

"The initials," I prompted after a moment. "The signatures on the canvases."

She flashed me an abrupt smile, direct from her beloved Paris. "But that was our thing, you see. Tony, you should know all this. Our initials were the same, only backwards, which Freddie said was destiny. So we each signed our canvases the same, an A and an F on top of each other. We always worked side by side. He said I inspired him. He said he couldn't do it alone. Dear man. But really we did them together. His brush strokes were mine, and mine his. Sometimes, for a laugh, we would try switching them over, halfway through. But that didn't seem to work. Isn't that strange? I've never understood that."

"You painted a great number?" I asked gently, feeling Margaret straining to get in with her questions.

"Oh yes. About eighty finished pairs. More. I destroyed the sketches before I came home."

Margaret moaned softly.

"That was in 1917?" I asked.

"Well, yes. Freddie died. I told you that. I had to come home. A single young lady in Paris couldn't have a child, could she?"

"Of course she couldn't," I agreed calmly, although my heart was pounding.

"So I wrote to Father, and he sent me the money to come home, and said he would find me a husband, who I knew would have to be absolutely dreadful, to take on a young woman carrying someone else's child. And that would be for money and status, but I didn't care about anything any more, and Father arranged everything. He was in the importing and exporting business, and he sent some of his men to pack the canvases, which was about all I had left, and I came home, to this house, and became Mrs. Angelina Hine—Mrs. *Arthur* Hine. Fortunately, he didn't live long, though long enough to father one son on me—that would be your uncle Henry, Tony. Yes. Henry." She sniffed and shook her head.

The shaking gradually subsided and her head fell forward. Her breathing changed. She was asleep.

"For heaven's sake, Tony!" said Margaret. "The paintings! We can't leave, not knowing."

Grandmother Angelina murmured something. I said, "What was that, Gran?"

"We had a bonfire," she told me distinctly, lifting her head.

"The paintings?" asked Margaret in a weak voice.

"They were in tea chests. Eight tea chests. Father imported tea. His men came and packed them for me. I marked one set of four as Freddie's with a cross so that I would know. But my husband hated Freddie. As he would, I suppose. As he hated Freddie's son when he arrived. Your father, Tony. It was like acid to him, knowing the paintings were up there in the loft. All that I had left of Freddie, except the child. But he couldn't destroy the child. It had to be Freddie's paintings. In the end he was near insane about it and said I'd got to burn them. Myself. With my own two hands. That was because he'd been unable to give me a child himself. He said I must be doing something to stop it. Ridiculous. But do you know . . . that very night . . . I'm sure it was that night, he was so fierce and triumphant with me . . . that was when I got pregnant again, the night I burned the paintings."

She puckered her lips, pondering fate.

"The canvases!" Margaret whispered.

"He asked me—demanded—what crates Freddie's were in. I'd marked four of them. A cross. Did I tell you that? But I couldn't bear the thought of destroying Freddie's work. So I told a lie. I said *mine* were in the tea chests with a cross. I could bear to lose mine. I remember that night. It was dark in the garden. Down there, in the orchard, that was where we did it. He was up in the loft. I stood on the landing and wept. I heard the chests being smashed open. He was roaring something, fury I suppose. He threw the paintings down at my feet. Grace and I took them down to the orchard. We made a pile. Eighty canvases make a big pile. He came and poured paraffin on it, but he wouldn't strike the match himself. He said I had to. He watched from up here. This very window. I lit them . . ."

Her eyes were sightless. She stared into the past, her jaw set, the wrinkles in her skin now more deeply etched. Her left hand gestured towards the painting I'd brought.

"That was the one I saved. I kicked it behind a tree, and in the morning, when he'd gone to one of his shops, I went out and wrapped it in newspaper and hid it in the garden shed. I was weeping so much I couldn't see what I was doing. Then, years later, when your father was sixteen and decided to leave home, I told him to take it with him." She sighed, breathed deeply for a moment, then was asleep again.

Margaret hissed, "For God's sake, she can't go to sleep now!"

Angelina murmured and raised her head. "And then I had nothing left of Freddie, with Charlie gone. He'd destroyed everything."

This didn't seem to make sense, because she had just told us how she had managed to save Freddie's paintings. She would have had those. But I didn't have time to question this.

Angelina put her head back and rested it against her small pillow, and stared sightlessly at the wall, until I realized she was sleeping with her eyes open. Slowly, as I watched, the lids descended.

We stood and watched her. I said, "We've tired her out."

"She can't leave it there. Wake her up, why don't you!"

"Let her sleep."

"You fool," she said, whispering intensely. "Can't you understand? He was no idiot, her husband. He probably double-guessed her, knowing she'd tell a lie about which paintings were in which chests."

"Does it matter?"

She flung her hands towards the ceiling. "They're probably still in the loft—the other set. We've got to know the truth, which they are. I'm going to wake her."

I grabbed her arm. "It doesn't matter," I snapped, "who painted what! You're obsessed."

She allowed me to draw her towards the door, but she was furious. From behind us there was a bubbling sound from Grannie. We turned. Her eyes were open, and she was smiling.

"Such a clever girl," she murmured. "That's exactly what he did."

4

Now we were drawn back by Angelina's alertness. So far as she was concerned there had been no gap in the conversation. She even raised her arm in a gesture of companionship. We were her friends.

"Did you know this, Gran? On that night, when you burned the paintings, did you know you'd destroyed Freddie's?"

She shook her head. "Not then. Not until years later."

"You didn't go into the loft to check?"

"At that time, it was a comfort I didn't wish to disturb. And I was afraid. Of him."

"Then when did you get to know?"

"Later. Much later. After Charlie left home, after Mr. Hine died." He had become Mr. Hine, I noted. "I went up then. Tried to, but I fell. It's very steep. That's why I'm in this chair."

Then how had she found out? But before I could ask, I realized that Grace must have gone up for her. "Was it, Grace?"

"Yes. She told me the marked crates had been broken open. So he'd won after all."

Margaret moaned feebly. But Grace might have made an error. "The others are still there?" Margaret asked quickly, desperately clinging to any remote possibility.

Smiling now, sleep far away, Angelina nodded. "Which is why I'm so glad Tony has come. I told myself, if Tony comes he shall have the paintings. Who else should they belong to but the grandson of the person who painted them?"

"I can't let you—" I began, but Margaret was still in there fighting.

"You're giving them to Tony, Mrs. Hine?"

"That was what I said."

Margaret turned away, and I heard her rustling in her shoulder bag. I said, "It's very good of you, Gran, and if it's in your will . . ."

"I'm not going to trouble changing it now. Don't be a silly boy. Take them with you."

"I . . . can't!" Not past Grace, not after what she'd said about vultures.

Margaret tugged at my shoulder and thrust something into my hand. It was a sheet torn from a notepad.

"What's this?"

"It's a formal deed of gift. I've scribbled it out, and it might not be legal wording—"

"To hell with your formalities."

"It's a matter of provenance, proof of ownership."

"You heard what she said. They're not works by Frederick Ashe. Not from his magic brush. So you don't have to worry."

She was agitated, her eyes wild. "I don't know. I need time. Get her to sign it, Tony, damn you."

"What is it?" demanded Gran. "Let me see. Get me my glasses; they're over there somewhere . . ." Her fingers reached for the paper.

Before she could take it, I crumpled it and thrust it in my pocket. The idea of getting my grandmother to formalize a gift was repulsive. I was family, her own grandson. I took her reaching hand in mine.

"Thank you," I said. "Thank you, Gran. I'll treasure your paintings."

She smiled, and her hand fell limply from mine. She had smiled herself to sleep.

"Let's go," I said.

"You must be insane!"

"There's no money in it, no glory in the find. They're only paintings by Angelina Foote." I picked my own from the top of the chest of drawers. "So you were right about this being a Frederick Ashe. Too bad, as it turns out."

Talking steadily, I got her out of the room and closed the door quietly.

"You'll regret this."

"What I regret is that I ever went to that Antiques Road Show in the first place." I shuffled her down the stairs.

"Your paintings . . ." she tried.

"When she dies, I'll collect them. Nobody will want them, not eighty Angelina Footes. Ah, Grace, we're off now. She's sleeping. We can see ourselves out."

Grace watched us out of the door. In spite of what I'd said, she refused to deny herself the pleasure of closing it with firm finality.

Margaret stalked to the car, lips tight, small patches of white at their corners. She slammed the door furiously.

As I slid in beside her, she rounded on me fiercely. "You damned fool, Tony. You complete and utter idiot. You should have got her to sign it."

"She gave me the paintings. Isn't that enough?"

"It is not! That Grace, she'll probably get the lot in her will. Everything that's left in the house, and those are, that's for sure."

"She'll hardly want a load of old paintings. And Gran gave them to me."

"You can't prove that in a court of law. And how d'you know Grace wouldn't want them? You know nothing. It's all contradictory. Can't you see . . . we've proved nothing. Oh, to hell with it. Let's go and get something to eat."

Being Margaret, she naturally headed for the most expensive restaurant in town, which stretched my pocket somewhat as, of course, I had to pay my share. But we got a corner table and we were allowed to eat without undue interruption.

"We know nothing," she said again. "Your grandmother's memory could have been faulty, and I think she was confused anyway."

"She sounded lucid enough to me. For her age." The soup was cold. Margaret said it was supposed to be.

"For her age," she agreed. "But as soon as she saw the painting she said, 'It's his.' "

"So? Apparently it is. Frederick Ashe's."

"She later said she needed her glasses to read the bit of paper you so cleverly stopped her from signing. So she may not have seen the painting clearly. She saw the magpie, so she's probably long-sighted."

I wasn't sure I liked the soup, and left half of it. "She also later said she was convinced she'd burned Frederick Ashe's paintings, but mine was the one she saved from the fire. So she would know it's one of his without seeing it very clearly."

"She saw it was the cottage. No question of that. She mentioned the briars. When she said it's his, she could have meant the cottage and not the painting. As it was. He was renting it."

We sat back and waited for the roast lamb. I said, "Now you're trying to persuade me that my painting isn't a Frederick Ashe and that she burned her own stuff after all. You're contradicting yourself. Surely an expert such as you can't be mistaken!"

"Oh, you can laugh. But you heard what she said. She copied every brush stroke. She used the same paints. We don't know how much alike the two sets of paintings are."

"But *she'd* be able to tell, surely."

"Of course she would," she agreed, tossing an absent smile at the waitress bringing our lamb.

"Well then," I said after she'd left, "my gran said she wrapped up my painting the morning after the bonfire and hid it in the shed. At that time she believed she'd destroyed her own. If in fact she had destroyed Frederick Ashe's, she'd have realized when she was wrapping it. Her sight was probably good at that time."

She smiled as she chewed, waited until she had swallowed, then pointed her knife at me. "Yes, but she told us she was in tears. So she might not have been able to see."

"Why was she in tears?"

"What?"

"If she thought, at that time, she'd fooled her husband, why the tears?"

"You're very unimaginative, Tony. She had been degraded. She'd been forced into destroying something precious to her, whether it was a set of her own paintings or a set of Ashe's. And don't forget, she did say he'd treated her violently the previous night. Really, Tony!"

She was, at least, in a less abrasive mood now. I allowed myself a smile very close to a grin. "You're trying desperately to convince yourself you've not made a mistake, and yet you're now saying my painting might not be a Frederick Ashe."

"I have not made a mistake. I have personally studied the four available genuine Ashes in the art galleries. However well she copied his brush strokes, they could not be so exactly alike in style. There are dozens of considerations—confidence in line, the strength of the approach, the impasto . . . I could *not* be mistaken. Yours is by the same hand as those other four."

I thought about that and decided I didn't want a pudding but was dying for a smoke. I couldn't see what she was getting at. She couldn't have it both ways.

"Haven't you missed one very important point?" I asked.

"I don't think so."

"It's this. Gran said she never managed to get up into the loft, to confirm for herself which were destroyed. So what we're discussing depends entirely on Grace. She might have made a mistake about the tea chests. She might even have lied to Gran, though heaven knows why. But there's only her word, from a quick look in the loft, which is probably very dark anyway, to say that it was the Frederick Ashe paintings that were burned. Suppose she was wrong. Then Gran *did* destroy her own, and mine, having been saved from the fire, is therefore one of hers."

"I've told you. I'm certain yours is a Frederick Ashe."

"But only because you're comparing it with known Frederick Ashe paintings in the galleries."

"Only?" Her eyes were very big. Her voice held a hint of danger. "And what d'you mean by that?"

I admit I hadn't much faith in what I was about to say, but I couldn't resist the impulse to take a dig at her precious art expert establishment. I kept the smile out of my voice.

"What if the art gallery paintings are Gran's, and not Ashe's? Then where would you be? After all, Gran said *she* sold six. Isn't it likely she would sell six of her own if her Freddie's were so precious to her?"

"Not unlikely at all," she agreed complacently, surprising me.

"I'll have to stop calling him Ashe. He was my grandfather."

"That much seems true."

"So where's my artistic heritage now—both grandparents artists!"

"Good for you."

"No need to sulk."

"I was pleased for you. For both of us. Pleased that you've at last come round to the point I wanted to make."

I eyed her with suspicion. "What point?"

"That it's absolutely imperative for us to get a good look at what's in that loft."

"Oh now . . . hold on."

"She gave them to you. They're yours."

"All the same . . ."

"We don't know how close your grandmother's work was to Frederick Ashe's. Hers could be terrible imitations. One look, and I'd know. But they're yours, in any event, so we ought to go and collect them."

I took a deep breath. "If you think I'm going to stand in front of Grace and say I've come to empty the loft . . ."

"I wasn't suggesting that."

"Then what?"

"She has to leave the house some time."

"Good Lord!"

"I'll tell you this, Tony. I feel I'm on the verge of a great art discovery. One way or the other. If necessary, I'll break in at midnight and sneak up there on my own, but for you to do it you could at least claim you were collecting your own property."

"At midnight?"

"It need not be so late."

"Why can't we just go and see Grace and say we simply want to do no more than look in the loft? Not take anything away. You did say—you'd only need one look."

"I was talking figuratively."

"Figuratively in what way?"

"I'd want to get them back to my place, clean them up, examine them in detail. Check them against yours."

"You're hopeless."

"With you or without you, I'll get into that loft."

"Without me, you could only look and leave them there," I pointed out.

"There you are then."

There I was. Stuck. I have to admit that I too wanted to be certain. I owned a loftful of canvases which could be wildly valuable or worthless apart from their sentimental value. Whatever happened, I was the grandchild of a famous painter, but it would be less unsettling to know which grandparent had become famous. Only the fear of Grace prevented me from marching up to the house and demanding my rights, and the fear of the law. How could I prove Gran had given them to me?

"So how do we do it?" I asked when we were sitting in the car.

"We watch the house and wait till Grace goes out."

"It could take days."

It occurred to me that if I'd been Grace, I would have listened at that bedroom door, suspicious that Angelina might be giving away more of the precious inheritance. It also occurred to me that Grace might be well aware that she had a loftful of Frederick Ashe paintings, that she was equally aware of their value, that eighty times twenty thousand could cushion her declining years, and that she could well spend all of them cruising the world on it. First-class.

But I didn't say anything on this aspect of it, only decided, as we had planned, that indeed our actions had to be kept secret from Grace.

It was only because of this I spent the afternoon and most of the evening skulking in the shrubbery just inside the drive of Mandalay. Margaret was parked, bored to the eyebrows I hoped, in the drive of an empty house just down Forster Grove. My thoughts reflected my condition: damp, cold, and depressed. I was considering that if I'd been Arthur Hine, intent on banishing all evidence of Frederick Ashe from my house, I would have burned the lot—both sets. It was unlikely that my gran, distressed at the time, would have counted them, especially as she was being helped by Grace. A pile of a hundred and sixty might well look like what one would expect of a pile of eighty.

Strangely, as I examined this idea more deeply, I found it a little comforting. If this were to prove correct, all decisions would be lifted from me, and I'd be back with my single canvas. Frankly, I didn't care who'd painted it.

The front door opened. The time was something after nine, and it was now dark. Heavy clouds had been massing, intensifying the gloom, but before she turned off the hall light I saw that Grace was dressed for outdoors, in a bonnet and a long, ancient topcoat. She slammed the door, and her shadow moved towards the dilapidated garage at one side of the house.

I edged my way back towards the entrance, then turned and ran.

"She's going out," I panted, yanking open the car door.

"Don't panic." She was smoking a cigarette, the first time I'd seen her doing that. "Come in and sit down, and don't slam the door too hard. She'll probably be driving past here; it's a dead end farther up."

We sat with the engine purring softly. Grace drove past in a very old Morris Minor, the model with the split windscreen. Margaret pulled out into the road, and we followed. It wasn't difficult. Grace's maximum speed was twenty-five.

We were reaching the outskirts of the town, with a few shops making their appearance, when Grace swung right and parked in the space beside The Dun Cow.

"Right," said Margaret, looking for somewhere to back and turn. "That's Grace out of the way for a while. I bet she does this every evening, after she's tucked Angelina into bed. Down here for her two halves of Guinness and a natter."

And who could blame her?

To my surprise, Margaret drove into the drive at Mandalay. If Grace returned early, we would be trapped. But clearly, Margaret anticipated that we should load the Volvo directly from the front door. She also anticipated finding an open window round the back, which she did, almost as though she was an expert at this kind of thing. Doctor of Crookery.

"You climb in and come through to open the front door for me," she instructed.

I nodded. As of now, she was in charge. My nerve was failing; I'd have made a rotten burglar. In practice, it was easier than I'd anticipated. Some latent memory guided me through the hall. The front door had a cylinder lock, so we would be able to close it behind us with no sign that we'd ever been there.

At the head of the stairs there was a small light left on. It guided us up the creaking treads and along the short, facing passage. The cross-corridor was dark. I groped for a light switch, and suddenly Margaret snapped on a torch she'd brought from the car, searching out switches.

"I'll go and look in on Gran," I said softly.

"Why on earth . . . ?"

Because, if she was awake, I wanted to say something like "I've come for the paintings, Gran, so if you hear any noises . . ." so as not to frighten her. "You look for the loft," I said, not prepared to argue about it.

She made a clicking sound with her tongue and went in the other direction. I opened Gran's door very quietly. The room was not completely dark, as there was a light on the small table beside her bed. She lay on her back, only her face showing. I went forward, making no sound, and stood over her.

The bedclothes were neatly tucked in, and she made hardly any disturbance in their smooth symmetry. Her tiny head seemed buried in the soft pillow. I bent down and carefully lifted away a lock of thin hair that had fallen over her eyes.

There was hardly any indication that she was breathing. Abruptly concerned, I bent my ear close to her lips and was just able to detect a shallow inhale and exhale. Very old people barely disturb their environment with their presence.

I turned away and left the room. The door-latch made a faint click.

Margaret was waiting for me, impatient and now nervous.

"It's at the end of the corridor," she said.

"She's asleep."

"There's a ladder."

It was not so much a ladder as open stairs, as there were treads instead of rungs. The climb was almost vertical, and once again it was my turn to lead.

"Hurry," she said.

"I'll need the torch."

There was no handrail to grip, just open steps. With one hand reaching upwards and forwards, I mounted to a trapdoor. It opened easily. I had to be careful to lower it gently as I hoisted it beyond the vertical. A waft of stale dust enveloped me.

My first stab with the torch discovered a light switch on one of the upright rafter supports. The wiring was naked. I touched the switch, rather surprised when two bare bulbs went on. It was a poor light for such a large area, but it was more useful than the torch. The complete floor area was boarded, so that we were able to move around without difficulty.

I had expected to find four tea chests standing proud in a vast emptiness. But a hundred years of family discards were scattered around, and we had to search. They were together. Four tea chests. Sealed. There were no crosses on them that I could detect.

Quite close, lying where they'd been thrown, I found the shattered and discarded remnants of what could have been four other tea chests. The metal corner bracings identified them. On these remains I could see no crosses either.

But Gran hadn't said what she'd used to mark the crosses. If it had been chalk, the dust and decay of seventy years could have eliminated all traces.

"We forgot to bring something to open them with," said Margaret, her breathing heavy and fast.

"There must be something we can use."

There was. It might have been the same crowbar Arthur Hine had used to break open the other chests.

The tops came off with creaks and groans and bangs. All four were filled with canvases. Margaret's hand was shaking when she reached inside and drew one free.

It had dust on it, and there seemed to be some darkening of age. Or it could have been the poor lighting. I clicked on the torch and held it close to the canvas. She swept her palm over it. The signature was the same overlapped A and F as on mine, the date three years later:

A 1913

"Well?" I asked.

She didn't reply at once. Perhaps I was expecting too much of her. At last, "I don't know!" she said, pain in her voice.

I left her to it and got the tops off the other three. They weren't packed tight, and old dresses that had been Gran's had been used to restrict movement. One of them was blue. I drew out another canvas at random.

"Try this one."

She shook her head and merely glanced at it. "It can't be!" she said in despair, staring at the one in her hands. "It's the same. The same style as yours. And yet it can't *be.* Yours was rescued from the fire. This is the other lot. Tony, it's impossible."

"We'll have to unpack 'em and take them down in bundles."

"Do it how you damn well please," she said in sudden anger. But the anger was at herself and her inability to make a decision. "Sorry. But, Tony, can you get them down yourself?"

"I'll need help. A full chest is too heavy. Why can't you lend a hand?"

But I knew why. When her head turned so that she could glance at me—and away—the torch caught her eyes. It was all in there, her growing panic and despair. With all her years of study behind her, the precious expertise she'd nursed was letting her down. She could not make a firm and confident decision. "You can't do that," I said quietly, guessing her intention.

"There's only one person who really knows."

"Even she—"

"She would know. At a glance." She shook my arm. "A minute. Is that too much to ask! Old people sleep and wake and sleep again. I'll be gentle."

I turned away. "We're wasting time."

She took it as agreement, and taking the canvas with her, dangling from her fingers, she backed away down the steps.

I did what I could, piling them in heaps of ten beside the opening, backing down, reaching them through, and doing it with no hands for support. There were fifty standing beside the steps when she returned.

"Well?" I said, my back to her. She didn't answer. I turned.

Even in the poor light I could detect that she was pale. Her eyes seemed sightless, her mind not with me.

"You woke her?" I prompted.

"Yes. Oh yes. They wake easily, old people."

"And what did she say?"

"I don't know. I don't *understand.*"

"Relax, Margaret. Did she get a good look at the painting?"

"She seemed to."

"And?"

She shook her head, her lips puckering.

"With her glasses on?" I prompted.

"They were on the side. Yes, I gave them to her. She took one good look at it and started shouting out . . ."

"Perhaps she took a good look at you, too, and couldn't remember who you are. I should've gone with you."

"Shouting for Grace."

"Just that?"

She nodded, her lower lip between her teeth.

"Perhaps you frightened her. Did she use your name?"

She shook her head. "Only Grace's. Shouting."

"For help, I suppose."

"She was angry."

I grinned at her, trying to shake her from the mood. "All right, so you didn't get anywhere . . . so what! I hope you didn't leave her upset."

"I soothed her."

"Right. Then we'll have to rely on you. Now, why don't you take some of these down to the car. I'm getting the hang of it now."

She spoke not one word during the rest of the transfer. There were eighty-one. I counted them as we loaded the Volvo, then went back to the landing to check that there was no visible evidence that we'd been there, put my head inside the door of Gran's room—she was again peaceful and quiet—then put out the lights we'd used, closed the front door behind me, and joined Margaret in the car.

She was smoking again. I said, "No doubt your scientific methods will reveal the truth."

I meant it as encouragement; she took it as sarcasm. She gave a small, bitter bark of angry laughter and backed the car out of the drive.

The Morris Minor was just taking the bend farther along the Grove. It was a matter of seconds. From later events, it became obvious that Grace had spotted the Volvo's headlights swinging out of the drive, but at the time she did nothing to obstruct us. We drove past each other as though neither car existed.

It was nearly midnight when we drove up to Margaret's cottage. We hadn't said much during the journey. I was busy fighting my conscience. My moral performance so far had not been commendable. I helped her into the workroom with the complete set, plus my original canvas, and we placed them in piles on her benches.

"Phew!" she said. "Some job here. I'll be at it all night."

"I take it I can't be much help?" I said it hopefully, the hope being that she would say no.

"You can make coffee, hold things, encourage."

I flung the lock of hair out of my eyes with one hand. "I'd rather hoped to get some sleep."

"Sleep!" She stared at me with wonder. "Don't you care?"

"In any event, I'm the grandson of two marvellous painters."

"And that's all? Oh, Tony, how can you be so unfeeling! It matters. They're all yours. Either you've got one Frederick Ashe and eighty-one Angelina Footes, or the other way round. And it's Frederick Ashe who's become famous. Don't you understand? Some of the great artists had pupils, who naturally learned to paint like their master. Sometimes they're almost indistinguishable. But the pupils are all called 'the school of so-and-so.' So your grandmother is going to be 'school of Frederick Ashe.' However good she was."

"She was, wasn't she? Good, I mean. In any event."

She made an impatient gesture. "Oh, you're hopeless. Put it like this. That one painting of yours, if it's a Frederick Ashe, would be a find. I bet you'd get fifty thousand pounds for it in auction. In that case, the whole eighty-one Angelina Footes wouldn't be worth more. But if the eighty-one are Ashes, then what sort of a find would that be? It'd rock the art world. You'd be—what?—worth a million and a half. Maybe more. And you say it wouldn't matter!"

"Of course it'd matter," I said gently. "I assure you I'm all agog. Couldn't be gogger. But I'm still a professional photographer, with a contract to fulfil. I thought I would hire a car—"

"You can't just turn your back on all this."

"I shall return." Why had I become caught in this facetious mood? Because I couldn't take her seriously? That was it, surely.

"You don't need to hire a car. I'll drive you where you want to go."

But I needed my independence. I wanted to be free of her forceful influence. Above all, I had to get away on my own and consider from the outside a world for which I felt no sympathy or understanding. The pragmatism was stifling me. I'd always believed the art world to be bound by love of beauty and perfection, but apparently, like everything else, it was wrapped around with money.

"You'll be busy. I'll need at least a full day at my photo lab, and you'll need a night . . . and a day?"

Then she stood back and looked at me fondly, shaking her head.

"Oh, Tony, Tony, you're quite incredible. Go away and play with your photographs. But come back with expectations. Because, whatever happens, it's more important than your crabby little photographic business."

With these parting words ringing in my head, I went to my room.

5

In fact, I did hire a car, thus straining the muscle of my credit card. There was no question of Margaret driving me. By the morning she was grey with exhaustion, having cleaned most of the paintings, and I nearly had to carry her to bed. All I got out of her was the fact that she still had no proof, either way, as to the identity of the artist who'd painted the eighty-one.

I walked into town, no more than a mile, hired a red Ford Fiesta, and headed for my own territory.

My place has a small window on two sides of the corner where Beech Street meets Albert's Fold. There's a door beside it opening into a reception area with a narrow counter dividing it in half. On the counter is a notice: IF RED LIGHT SHOWS, PLEASE PRESS BUTTON AND WAIT. The red light is above the door the other side of the counter and indicates that I'm working beyond it. In no event must light be allowed to enter at the wrong time. There was, that day, plenty of time during which the red light was glowing, because I had six spools of film to develop and around two hundred colour prints, six by four, to produce. The buzzer was silent until late in the afternoon.

I was well into the swing of it, having stopped only for a sandwich and coffee at a place just down Albert's Fold, when the buzzer went. I shouted, "A minute." Then, with the print out of the fixer and into the wash, I could open the door.

He was in his thirties, I'd guess, a large and solid man with too much colour in his face and flashing a pessimistic smile that came out all twisted. He was wearing a dirty anorak and a tweed hat.

"Mr. Hine?" he asked. "Anthony Hine?"

I nodded. Customers did not usually need to confirm my Christian name.

He flashed a leather-bound plastic card out of his inside pocket and said, "Detective Sergeant Dolan." And flashed it back before I could get a good look at it.

"Excuse me." I reached out and waited. He grinned and produced it again. I checked the photograph. It could well have been him. "Thank you," I said. "I hired the car, you know, not pinched it."

"I'm sure you did. Are you the grandson of Mrs. Angelina Hine?"

Tingles ran down my spine. My palms rested on the twelve inches of counter between us, but I couldn't prevent my fingers from curling.

"Yes," I said stiffly.

"Then I'm sorry to have to tell you that your grandmother died last night."

His eyes didn't leave mine, and he probably noticed they'd gone out of focus. I was thinking that Gran had possibly been dying when I bent over her, dying when Margaret allowed her to return to her last sleep. And we'd not known. Could we have done anything . . . ?

"Sir?"

I cleared my throat. "I'm sorry. I saw her only yesterday."

"So I understand."

"You've come from there?" My eyes focused. His head was tilted, the hat slid sideways, he poked it back. "It's quite a distance—how did you trace me?"

"An address book. And this place is in the Yellow Pages . . . you weren't at home, you see."

"No."

"Your wife said you'd left her. In fact, walked out."

"That's correct." Had she said I'd gone off with another woman?

"You left with a painting, I understand."

So . . . not with a woman, with a painting. "It's mine. My father handed it on." He smiled encouragingly, so I continued—couldn't stop myself. "Which was why I went to see my grandmother."

"The painting?"

"To check who'd painted it."

"That . . . and the others?" he prompted.

My reception area is so small that there's no room for chairs, just the twelve inches of counter and its button. I was backed up against my darkroom door, but our faces were still only a yard apart. There was no retreat. He smiled. It seemed to peel the skin from my bones. I couldn't say, "What others?" He clearly knew.

"We discussed the ones in the loft," I admitted. Admitted? It felt like an admission.

"In what way?" He waited, but it was all too complex for me to go into. "To what end?" he suggested helpfully.

"She said I could have them. A gift."

His eyes at last slid aside. Some of my best work graces the walls, twenty by sixteens. He eyed them with approval. "But a photographer," he said, "especially an expert, wouldn't give wall space to a bunch of mouldy old paintings."

"This one would."

"But you didn't take them with you when you left."

"It would've seemed too . . . well, eager."

"They're not there now. In the loft. I looked."

"You were told to look?" I guessed.

"Certainly. By the companion. Grace Fielding. She saw you leaving the second time. Late. After ten. Did you realize she saw you leaving?"

I shrugged. "I thought so at the time. Does it matter? I mean, they were mine. I went back and collected them. I didn't fracture any laws."

"Breaking and entering. Burglary."

"I didn't break anything, and surely I could enter my own grandmother's house."

He pursed his lips. "Try theft," he suggested.

"But they're mine."

He lifted both palms, smiled, and said, "And there we have it. Are they yours? That is exactly the point."

It had been hot in the darkroom, but was cool out there, and I was down to my shirtsleeves. Nevertheless, the shirt was sticking to my back, and he was watching with interest the drop of sweat trickling down my nose. I'd been trying to keep Margaret out of it, but now I needed her and had to mention her.

"They are mine. She said she wanted me to have them. I've got a witness."

It seemed not to impress him. "Miss Fielding told me you went there with a woman. I don't think there can be any dispute that your grandmother wanted you to have them. But she's dead. The legal processes take over. There's a will. Grace Fielding tells me that she gets all of which your grandmother died possessed. That's the phrase. In this case, she died possessed of the house, and everything in it at the *time* of her death. In the house, Mr. Hine. Do you see what I'm getting at? If she died before you took those paintings out of the front door, then what you were doing was theft. You were stealing from Grace Fielding."

I was taking slow, deep breaths. For him, the speech had been long, and I'd had a chance to recover my wits.

"She was alive when we left."

"You're certain of that?"

"We looked in on her twice—three times, but I didn't go near the bed the last time. She was breathing very shallowly, but she was alive."

"Hmm!" he said. "Yet Miss Fielding arrived just after you'd left, that second time, went straight up to Mrs. Hine, and found she was dead. Now don't say she couldn't tell. She's experienced. She can take a pulse. Your grandmother was dead."

"I see."

I saw very clearly. There had been only minutes in it. Grace could make a legal fight of it. She surely would if she believed the loft paintings were by Frederick Ashe, who was becoming collectable. Grace, in fact, might well have spent some time that afternoon persuading Angelina to retract the gift. She would certainly have been furious when she spotted the Volvo leaving and then discovered, as she must have done, that the loft had been emptied of paintings.

"I see," I repeated. "So you've come here to charge me with theft?"

"Oh no. No, no," he said emphatically. "It's not as simple as that. I've spent a long while with Miss Fielding. She told me that after you left the first time, she guessed what you'd come for, so she spoke to your grandmother about it. In the end, your grandmother agreed to write to you and tell you she'd changed her mind about giving you the paintings. Miss Fielding was upset about the number of valuable items that'd been given away already. Are you following this, Mr. Hine?"

So Grace had listened at the door. "Closely," I assured him.

"The old lady, you see, might well have been breathing shallowly, as you said. It wouldn't have taken any great effort to prevent her from breathing at all. A hand over her mouth and nose, that's all it'd take. There would probably be no struggle. What I'm trying to say to you is that the ME has said there're signs that she was suffocated. The post-mortem will clarify it. We thought you ought to know. For now, we're treating it as a murder enquiry."

He was saying this in the same unemotional and casual way he'd been using before. Perhaps, to him, the death of a woman of ninety-five was a very minor occurrence; she'd been so close to it. But to me it was the opposite. She had had so little left. Every passing day made the trespassing minutes more precious. And she'd been robbed of the diminishing time left to her.

"Mr. Hine?"

I shook my head, clearing my eyes. "I'm listening."

"You can see the point, I'm sure. The possibility is that you went there the second time and she woke and told you what she intended to do. Which was to cancel her gift. But you wanted those paintings. How did you put it? You would give wall space to them. You *wanted* them. So you would not want her to retract her gift in writing." He cocked his head and waited. It was quite clear what he meant.

"Are you making a charge?" I managed to say.

It was then that the basic unreality of the scene swept over me. I was standing aside, mouthing words that had been scripted for me, and I could discover no emotional background to lend them force. For the past forty-eight hours I had been moving in an insecure world, prompted by impulses and reactions rather than reason. I'd been carried along by it, finally retreating into my darkroom to be embraced by my firm and structured life. But I'd opened the door on to the world again. My routine life should have been there too, to be lived or confronted or opposed. But real. Now there was no home and no family, only a fantasy involving paintings and a throw-back to my ancestry. And I was now being virtually accused of murder. Did I laugh in this man's face, did I demolish his reasoning with well-structured but dignified rhetoric? No. I merely said in an empty voice, "Are you making a charge?"

The way he shook his head was not denial; it was disbelief. He'd seen everything, but I was a new discovery.

"You'll naturally be shocked, Mr. Hine. You'll need time to think. All I'm asking is that you keep yourself in touch. I may need to find you again."

At last I laughed, but it was the natural humour of a man who can find amusement in his own dilemma. I *was* amused. "I've only got one place where I can lay my head, and I can't give you the address. I've been driven there, and I've walked away from it. I can find it again. It's near Kidderminster, I know that much. And there's here. Follow me home . . ." I stopped and gestured helplessly. "Follow me to Dr. Dennis's place, and that'll be it. For now."

"This Dr. Dennis?" he asked. "This is the witness you spoke about, at your grandmother's?"

I nodded. We were now talking naturally, me trying to be helpful, as would a normal law-abiding citizen, he probing gently without pushing it.

"It's Dr. Margaret Dennis. She's an art expert."

"Well known?"

"Internationally," I said, with reflected pride.

"Then we'll be able to trace her. And trace you. This association with her—can I ask?—is recent?"

"Very. Her interest is professional."

"Your private life—"

"Is none of your business. I merely mentioned it in case my wife—"

"She told me there was a woman."

"The same."

We stared at each other. I could read his thoughts. I smiled, allowing them to mature. He pushed his hat on more firmly.

"If you get any more news," I said, "you know—the post-mortem, I'd like to know."

"I'll see you're kept fully informed, Mr. Hine. Closely." He nodded, opened the outer door, and left.

I returned to my darkroom, where I had a high stool in front of my bench. My legs felt weak. I wanted a smoke and filled my pipe. It's rarely that I smoke in there, because of the poor ventilation. This time I did, unable to get back to my work, and attempting to clear the situation in my head. I was trying not to think about Grannie Angelina's death.

I had declared that I was not really concerned about the provenance of the eighty-one canvases. In either event, they had been painted by one of my grandparents. But this didn't mean that I wasn't concerned about owning them. In fact, there was a deep and hard core of possessiveness growing inside me. They were mine. Gran had wanted me to have them. Yet now there was a hint of dispute over their ownership.

Grace could well put up a legal battle about them, monetary value or not. They'd been the last straw in a series of gifts extorted from Gran, trading on her generosity. There was going to be trouble from Grace, and hell, I'd got all the distracting trouble I could handle.

Determined to be professional and refusing to brood uselessly, I forced myself to return to the prints and, as always, became completely absorbed within a couple of minutes.

The cottage—I had to continue to think of it as that—was dark when I arrived there, but Margaret came at a touch of the bell-push in the porch. I heard her rapid footsteps up the staircase. She opened the door, snapping on the light at the same time.

"Where have you been? For God's sake . . . Tony, I needed you."

She might well have been my wife. I smiled, smoothing the mood. "It's a big job. Ten hours solid. I'm whacked."

She was jumpy, her eyes jerking around, her hands moving in small gestures. Her make-up was minimal, her hair mussed, her clothes stained. One hand held a cigarette between two fingers. Her lips plunged for it, and she drew smoke in greedily. She turned away. It was almost a command to follow. We nearly trotted through the kitchen, and I had only a moment to notice the scattering of quick snacks and empty cups and the saucers lined with cigarette stubs.

Inside her workroom there was a flat glare of white, pitiless light. She closed the door, the gesture being allied with the closing of my dark-room door. Inside here was her life, but whereas for me there had been another life, for her this had long been the nucleus of her basic existence.

She had completed the cleaning, the whole eighty-one, and had them ranked all round the walls, perched on her benches. They glowed, they danced. Sunlight shone from them, mocking her artificial tubes. Here was Paris in the spring and summer and on into six or seven autumns, but it was a Paris where the sun always shone. Frederick Ashe—or Angelina Foote—had loved sunlight, had tried to recreate it, and had succeeded. I stood, caught in awe.

"You've had a busy day," I said at last.

"I have." Her voice was harsh. "I've had five under the spectroscope, I've analysed the pigments . . ."

"But we know they shared the same palette."

She moved a hand in quick rejection. "There was a chance, damn it."

"But . . . nothing?"

"Not one clue. Hers or his! I've agonized over brush strokes and techniques, the force of the impasto, the . . . the vision. They could be his. His, Tony!" Her voice was unsteady. She had worked too hard and too long. "But look round them. Go on. Take your time. Tell me what you see."

I glanced at her. There was a bitter harshness to her voice that I didn't like. Then I walked round slowly. These were mine. All this beauty really belonged to me. Did I say they mirrored Paris? Well, yes, but there were a few that held a tang of England. There was one that held more than a tang. I turned with it in my hand.

"You put my original one amongst them," I accused her.

She flicked me an empty smile, bent, and picked up a canvas from behind a chair. "No. This is your original one."

One in each hand, I turned them over. She was correct. The one she'd just handed me was mine. I knew this because there was a small scorch mark on one of the wooden stretchers which I'd never been able to understand but now did.

"Look at them," she said fiercely. "Go on. Tell me if you can see a difference between the two."

Of course there were differences. No two brush strokes can be identical, no loading of the brush, even from the same palette, equally full. Nevertheless, they could well have been painted by the same person. Yet there was one difference, one that was immediately apparent to a photographer. Perspective.

"They were painted from slightly different viewpoints," I said, not because that proved anything, just as something to reassure her. Certainly, from the wildness in her eyes, she needed reassurance.

"I saw that. D'you think I'm a complete fool!" Her voice was too loud. She modified it. "There's more of the side of the cottage in the one than the other. One tree is farther over to the left than in the other. It fits, Tony, for heaven's sake. They sat side by side—say three feet apart—so of course they would see the view from slightly different angles."

She had reasoned this out. At the end, she was managing to speak reasonably. Then she spoilt it by waving wildly round the room and crying out, "But I ought to know which is which! It's driving me mad. I'm an expert. People pay me to fly round the world. I say yes, this is genuine, that is a fake, and they take my word. I ought to know, blast it, and I don't." Then I saw that it was fear in her eyes. "I ought to know, Tony," she said with a catch in her voice, "I *have* to know."

"Perhaps one of them was left-handed," I suggested, introducing a light touch.

"What?"

"Sitting side by side, using the same palette, one of them would have to lean over awkwardly to reach it. But if one was left-handed, it'd solve it for them. Perhaps that was why they always shared a palette, placed between them."

"Don't be a fool, Tony. Please."

"Just an idea."

"You don't realize what we've got here, do you! It's a great art find, the find of the century. We can't keep it a secret and hide them all away. Some time I've got to produce them and say yes, that's Frederick Ashe, and that one's Angelina Foote. Me. The expert. And I'll need to point out why I say that, and be confident. Confident! And I'm lost. I can't get hold of anything positive I can latch on to. Don't you see, Tony? I don't know which of those two in your hand is Ashe's. And I should be able to!" she wailed, whipping her hands up and sending her hair flying.

"If one of them was left-handed . . ."

"Oh for God's sake."

". . . and we knew which . . ."

"Will you please—"

". . . we'd at least know—or be fairly certain—which of these two was done by who."

She paced a while. My suggestion seemed to have sailed right past her. She stopped, pointing a finger at me. Maybe it was the light that made her seem so pale, but after all she was conceding a defeat.

"There's only one thing for it. We'll have to go back to your grandmother and ask her—show her both—and ask her which is which."

She was asking me to do this, and her reluctance was in no way linked with her belief that I might be hesitant to comply. She was hating herself for admitting the necessity.

"I'm afraid we can't do that," I said gently. "She died last night."

She sucked in her breath so sharply that it fluttered her lower lip. "Then she was . . . dying when we saw her?"

I wasn't going to go into the ramifications. "I don't think we could have helped her."

"Oh hell! The poor old thing. I upset her. You don't think that could . . . oh no. No! I don't know . . . I can't see . . . there's nothing I can think of. Oh . . . Tony!"

She stood before me, arms now limp at her sides. Her eyes were brimming with tears, though whether at my grandmother's death or at her feeling of helpless defeat I couldn't tell.

"You'll think of something."

"I've thought and thought." Her hands came up in small fists in front of her. "I've racked my brains, nearly driven myself mad . . ." Then she moved to stand facing me, raised her fists, and thumped my chest. I allowed the two canvases to slip from my fingers, slide down my legs, and flop gently to the floor. I took her elbows, then slid my hands up to her shoulders.

"It's going to be all right, Margaret."

She searched my face for confidence she could cling to. "But it's not!" she moaned. "Everything's . . ." Her voice sank to a whisper. "Everything's going to nothing."

Tears welled on to her cheeks. This was the young Margaret, home from art school as a failure. I was her father. She needed comfort and understanding. And who better than me to understand, who'd made my photography a retreat from unpromising reality? But her case was worse than mine. Hers was not simply her obsession, it was her life and her only reality. She had worked for it, fought for it, hacked herself a notch in the hierarchy of art knowledge, and always she had to be aware that the higher she climbed, the farther her fall if she made one incorrect identification. She was exposed and vulnerable, and however successfully she had trained herself into a practicality and severity fitting her status, beneath it there was a woman refusing to admit her basic frustration.

So I kissed her on the forehead as a comforting father, kissed her on the eyelids with gentle understanding, and on her lips as no father would kiss her. There were aeons of desperate longing in her lips, and her hands tightened around my neck in a frantic desire for security and self-confidence.

I lifted my face from hers. Her eyes were huge.

"In the morning," I pronounced, as one who knows, "it will seem different. You'll see." My voice betrayed none of my own lack of self-confidence.

She didn't answer. She clung to me again, and the morning was a long way away.

6

We stared at each other across the breakfast table. She was relaxed, her face naked of make-up, her hair in a tangle that I found delightful.

"You said it would look different," she said. "And it doesn't." But it was delivered with a smile.

Whatever I'd said to her in the night, I had not mentioned the possibility that Gran's death might not have been natural.

"I've been thinking about it."

"Oh? When?"

I grinned at her. "Between times."

"I'm not sure that's a compliment."

"But I was thinking for you."

"Hmm!" She nodded, sipped coffee. "Such as?"

"Two things. This left-handed business . . . no, don't laugh. It's valid. Listen. If both were right-handed—or both left-handed, of course—they could well have switched positions from time to time, to share the strain of reaching over. If so, we're in trouble. But if one of them *was* left-handed, and the other not, the odds are that they always painted together in the same positional relationship. You're with me?"

"Oh certainly. With you, but not convinced."

"Then consider this. We don't know whether my original one is Ashe's or Grannie's. But if we did, you'd have a clue. Am I right there?"

"If we knew that, you idiot, we'd have the truth here and now."

"But there are six others around. Presumably those have all been assessed by other experts, your peers, whose judgement you'd respect. Yes?"

A spark of interest had entered her eyes. It died when she realized it would mean deferring to other opinions. "I see what you mean. But how does it help?"

I had to work it out as I spoke, clarifying the situation in my own mind.

"Let's look at what we've got. Things we know. We know two sets were painted, and from what you say, they're almost indistinguishable from each other."

She nodded glumly. "You're right there."

"We also know that my original canvas is not from the same set as the eighty-one. We know this because it's matched with one from the loft set, apart from the fact that it was painted from a slightly different viewpoint."

"I can't argue with that."

"But what we don't know is whether the other, already-known, Ashes are part of the loft set, which would make the original complete set eighty-seven—"

"Angelina said more than eighty." She nodded her permission for me to continue.

"Or from the other set, the same set as mine, and not destroyed because they were sold in Paris, long before the bonfire."

"If we knew, what would it prove?"

"Accepting . . . accept it for the moment . . . that the other six can be attributed to Frederick Ashe, then we'd know whether to attribute the whole loft set to him or only my original one."

"How would we know?"

"By whether the six match with six in the loft set and by the question of the viewpoint of the painter."

To my surprise and disappointment, she looked down miserably at her cup and moved it around with one finger at the handle. She looked up.

"I'm afraid I've already thought of that. Something like it, though not the left-handed business. I was frantic for ideas. Do you know what it's like . . . ? No, of course not. I thought I was going insane. So I phoned all four of the art galleries. And there's a snag."

"You'd have to go there?"

"Not that. They haven't got the paintings now."

"Sold? They'll know who—"

"Not sold. Stolen. In the past two years. All four. Clever, slick, and efficient robberies, aiming for those specific canvases. The Frederick Ashes."

I thought about that. It took only a second. "A collector. Somebody interested in Frederick Ashe."

"Naturally."

"But there's still the other two. In a private collection, you said."

She made a dismissive sound, pursing her lips. "There's a man. He's known in the trade. He sends a representative to bid for him when there's something he wants, with simple instructions—no limit. He can afford to. His wealth is legendary, but where he got it from is doubtful. There've been rumours, ranging from drug-smuggling to stock exchange irregularities. Rumours only. But he has a house, almost a fortress, and rumour, again, has it that he owns a huge collection of paintings. The snag is, nobody's ever been allowed to see them. But of course, whatever his wealth, he can buy only what's offered for sale. It's he who owns the two other Frederick Ashes, and legitimately. The odds are that he's got the whole six now. So what can we do there? I ask you."

I looked at her across the table. Elbows on the surface, her hands cradling a coffee mug, she was staring wide-eyed at me and making a tiny moue of embarrassed surrender. And that was exactly what she was doing: she was *asking* me. Some time in the night, she had come to terms with herself. She could not wholly admit that she was beaten, not to the extent of calling in fellow experts. They might shame her by displaying greater knowledge and a more firmly established scholarship. But she could dare to display her weaknesses to a friend—an intimate friend—who wouldn't be ashamed to use unartistic methods of proof. So she was asking me, but meekly, in a way suggesting surrender to a stronger character than herself—a man. It was this part of it that was false, but I didn't let her see I realized it. In practice, I was becoming personally involved with the puzzle, and didn't mind playing the game, if that was what she wanted.

"I don't fancy tangling with a man like that," I said, "but we don't have to discard it out of hand. Call it number-three option."

"Number three?"

"I can see two other ways of going at it. One of them is the left-handedness. It might be possible to show that one of them *was* left-handed. If so, we apply it to the pair of near duplicates we've got, and it'd tell us who painted which."

"Small chance there." She nodded. "What else?"

"My gran said Grace had told her it'd been the Ashe paintings that went in the fire. It was from that set that mine was rescued. Right? We thought Grace could have made a mistake, or even have been lying. So she's obviously the first one to tackle. Ask her, and see what comes from it."

Interest sparked in her eyes. She thrust back her chair. "I'll take a shower. We'll use my car."

"No. I intended to do it alone." I smiled at her, taking the edge off it. But all the same it was a challenge. Was she going to take charge again, now that I'd made my suggestions? Or try to.

"I'd like to hear what she says." Then she made a gesture of dismissal. "All right. If that's how you want it."

"I've got an excuse—a reason. It will be natural to call and offer my condolences. They were together for more than sixty years."

"Of course. I'm being thoughtless. You must go alone. But it'll be awkward for you."

"Perhaps."

More than awkward, embarrassing. She had fed the police with information that had virtually led to a murder charge against me. She was certainly going to make trouble over the paintings. No, "awkward" was a pallid word for it.

When I was ready to leave, I put my head inside Margaret's laboratory, where she'd once more plunged into her work. I'd suggested that things would look better in the morning, but this was artificial daylight and everything looked the same. Had I realized it, the solution was already there for the taking, but at that time we hadn't run out of options, and neither of us looked closely enough.

I drove away to see Grace.

The day was sunny, and I'd hoped it would make the place look less devastatingly gloomy. But it did not. The trees had grown wildly with their freedom, and no sun penetrated. Pessimistic, then, as to my welcome, I was not surprised when Grace tried to slam the door in my face.

I put my foot inside and used my shoulder as a buffer. "We've got to talk, Grace."

"Thief!" she shouted.

"We ought to discuss the paintings."

"There's nothing to talk about. You stole them. Go away."

"We *are* talking about them. Now wouldn't it be more sensible to do it sitting down? Like civilized human beings."

She would not like it to be suggested that she was uncivilized. She had been the companion to a lady. Didn't that make her a lady too? The pressure eased at my shoulder, an eye appeared at the gap.

"You're a thieving swine," she said temperately, "but I suppose you'd better come in. Never let it be said I wasn't polite."

I entered. The emptiness of the house was overpowering, with an atmosphere of aching loneliness that was Grace's own. Could she bear to live with it here alone? Would she wish to? The house would certainly be hers. She could sell it. She would not be derelict. Or so I told myself.

She led me into the drawing-room where we had first waited. It was full of whispering stillness and of chill rejection. Grace seemed unaware of any inhibition. She took one of the four remaining Regency dining chairs and sat primly on it, leaving me to do the same or to stand. I chose to stand, to give myself room to move around. At least I could disturb the air, my clothes making rustling sounds to which the room listened hungrily. Grace waited. She'd made her opinion known. She sat still. There was no indication of mourning. The curtains were as wide as they'd been before. The room itself mourned, though it hadn't seen Angelina for . . . how many years?

I went straight to the attack, though gently. She was not a fragile woman, as my grandmother had been, but she was not young.

"I've been told," I said, "that you're making a claim to the paintings.

"They're mine. Everything that was in this house when she died. Mine. You can't get round that."

"Then surely it all rests on exactly when she did die," I suggested.

Her head snapped up and her eyes gleamed. "I saw you leaving. The car pulled out of the drive. I recognized it. I drove up to the front door. A minute, perhaps. I went straight up to her. Ran. I didn't trust you. Another minute. And she was dead then. She died before you got them out of the house. So there."

She was in no way senile. She knew how things stood. I smiled at her. "It's almost as though you're saying I killed her, Grace."

"I wouldn't put it past you."

"Come now. That's a serious accusation. Why should I? What would I gain?"

"The paintings from the loft, that's obvious. They're mine. You bring them back here, or I'll have the law on you."

"But she said she wanted me to have—"

"Said," she jerked out, her face quivering with the triumph. "Only said. She'd said to me she'd take it all back. In writing."

"I see." The pen being mightier than the word. "But how could I have known she'd promised you that, Grace? If I didn't know, I'd have no reason. Surely you can see that."

"You woke her up. Got it out of her."

I paced a little, trying to make my feet disturb the silence beyond our voices, but the carpet was heavy.

"You've worked all this out," I conceded.

She nodded, jowls quivering. "You're not getting one over on me."

"I'm not trying to."

"It sounds like you are to me. But you can be sure of one thing—I'm having them back. Or I'll want to know the reason why."

"The reason why," I said, though the remark had been rhetorical, "is that I'm satisfied I've got a legal and moral right to them."

Her feet stamped so hard on the carpet that she nearly shot herself out of the chair. "We'll see about that. Just you wait."

"What can they mean to you, Grace? A bunch of old paintings, that's all they are. It's not as though they're valuable."

She leaned back, crossing her arms as though she'd said the lot. "It's the principle of the thing."

"Unless you believe they *are* valuable, Grace." She glanced away. "Is that it?"

She sniffed, and her lips sucked in, then prodded out again.

"Do you believe they could be valuable?" I persisted.

"How would I know?"

"Well now. That's the point. There was a bonfire. Do you remember the bonfire, Grace? But of course you do. Mr. Hine threw a batch of paintings down from the loft, and they were burned. He thought he was throwing down the set painted by Frederick Ashe. You know who he was, I suppose?"

I waited. Her eyes were fixed on a patch of mould in the far corner of the room. They flickered back to me and away again. "Her lover." It was delivered with contempt.

"But Angelina thought she'd fooled him—fooled her husband—and believed she'd burned her own paintings. Though perhaps he was too smart for her and threw down the canvases painted by Grannie's lover."

"He wasn't stupid, Arthur wasn't. She called him a shopkeeper. To her, that was an insult. But he was a clever man. Owned six shops. A clever man."

"I'm sure he was."

"And don't tell me he married her for money," she said violently, once more facing me fully, her hands free and gesturing. "He never made any secret of it. I heard him tell her that. Arthur always called a spade a spade. He said she was like spoiled goods, that they had to pay him to take her off their hands." She smirked. She'd memorized the exact phrase.

"So," I said, after a small interval during which this endearment was allowed to settle, "so, he was possibly clever enough to double-guess her, and he threw down the Frederick Ashe paintings he knew she treasured."

"Yes," she said, pride in the inclination of her head.

"Do you *know* he did that?"

"Not know." She was cautious. "Not really know."

"And yet—and my grandmother told me this, Grace—and yet she said that you went up into the loft for her because she couldn't manage it herself and you came down and said the Frederick Ashe ones had gone."

"How would I know that?"

"Because she'd told you that his had a cross on the tea chests."

She pouted sullenly. "As like as not."

"Did you tell her those were the ones that'd gone?"

"I seem to remember I did."

"Come now, Grace. It's something you wouldn't forget. Did you go into the loft and check if the chests still there had a cross on them? Or not?"

"I went into the loft, yes."

"And did they—at that time—have a cross on them?" It was now becoming difficult to moderate my voice.

She lifted her chin. The wattles fell back. "I didn't trouble to look."

I took that in, letting my mind juggle with it a little, but it came out again unblemished.

"And yet you told Angelina that it was the batch of Frederick Ashe paintings that she'd burned." I made that a statement.

She answered with impatient definition. "Yes."

"But you didn't *know* that?"

"No."

"Then why did you say it?"

I had the feeling that it was not I who'd led her gently to that point, but she who had teased me along to the question. She smiled. I'd got to it at last. But there was such secret malice in the smile that I nearly recoiled.

"Because I knew it would hurt her," she replied, nodding in emphasis. "And I knew she'd never be able to get up there and check for herself."

"But why in heaven's name should you want to hurt her?"

"Because I loved Arthur, and he loved me, and Angelina killed him."

"Figuratively speaking, of . . ." I stopped and stared at her. The hard buttons of her eyes challenged me. "You did say killed?"

"If pushing him down a staircase is killing, that's what she did. I saw her do it. She killed him."

I had to turn away. She had led me into an uncharted realm of conjecture, and I was afraid to go ahead. It was something I didn't want to know.

"You don't want to believe it, do you?" she jeered at my back. "Your precious grannie, the angel. Just because of her name. Angelina!" she cried in disgust. "She was no angel, I'll have you know."

I turned back to her. Her name was Grace, but there was no grace here. She leaned forward, tightly embracing the venom. Spittle decorated the corners of her lips.

"Tell me," I said quietly, facing it full on.

"Why d'you think there's no carpet on the stairs?"

"What?"

"His blood. It wouldn't wash out. She had it taken away."

"His blood."

"He was carrying a drinks tray—glasses, bottles, everything. She was just behind him at the top of the stairs, at his shoulder. He'd never let her walk in front of him. A lady always goes first, he used to say. You follow, my angel. He called her his angel. That was a laugh, but Arthur always had a sense of humour, you can say that for him. There've been times—"

"Grace!" I cut in, and for the first time I was unable to control my voice. "For God's sake keep to the point."

"There's no need for blasphemy." Then she gave a bitter laugh. "I want you to understand."

"Oh, I do." Arthur had hated his angel all their married life. Or loved her, in spite of himself. If he'd not, why the corroding jealousy for a man long dead? I decided not to probe that matter with Grace. "The stairs," I said more quietly. "Arthur and his tray."

She nodded, her lower lip loose. "He'd got no spare hand for the banister. He was a big man, heavy. I was behind, along the corridor. I saw her take his elbow. He glanced round. She twisted him and put all her weight into his back, and he was gone. She shouted at him all the way down." She stopped abruptly, then whispered, "Shouted *at* him. Hatred. Yes."

"He broke his neck?"

"What?" She tore herself from the memory. "No. It was the glass. The jugular. You know the jugular?"

"Not exactly, Grace, but I'm sure you do."

"I might have saved him," she said in a dead voice, "but Angelina was having hysterics and grabbed hold of me, and wouldn't let me go. Hysterics! Not here! It was on purpose. Hard as nails, she was. I couldn't get to him, she hung on so, and his life ran away down the carpet."

"You mentioned the carpet," I put in quickly. "When was this, Grace? Roughly."

"On the sixth of May 1934."

"Your memory is very clear, I must say."

"It was the day after your father's sixteenth birthday. The day after he went away."

"I see." I caught at the tide of it, hoping to get as much as possible before the ebb of the tears. "So the batch of paintings, the ones remaining after the bonfire, had been in the loft for how many years . . . fifteen? Sixteen?"

"All of that."

"The bonfire was soon after my father's birth, I understand."

Again I had the impression she was encouraging me, leading me on. She was leaning forward like a crumpled gnome, her face bright with intentness.

"That would be the time," she agreed.

"And in all those years my grandmother, who must have been uncertain which paintings she'd destroyed, didn't go up and check?"

"How could she?" She raised both palms and slapped her cheeks in an ecstasy of revelation. "Arthur had a padlock put on the trapdoor—right after the fire, that was."

"Yes. He would. That sounds like his line of thinking. So that after his death, when Grandmother had the key . . . that was when she tried to get up there?"

"So stupid. She couldn't wait."

"And she fell?"

"Yes. She fell. It seemed like a judgement on her."

"Very true. You saw that one too?"

"I was right behind her."

"Right behind? On the steps, d'you mean? And she didn't take you down with her?"

Her face was so solemn it must have hurt. "She was reaching up with both hands to the padlock. I could see—her feet were six inches from my nose, so don't say I couldn't see—her left foot was slipping off the tread. I shouted, but I was too late, and she went. I sort of, you know, flattened myself against the steps and hung on. She went right over me." She waited, challenging me to criticize her own role in this, to mention how close her own hands must have been to my grandmother's ankles. I said nothing. She sighed. "It was her spine. She was paralysed all down one side."

Thus making her completely dependent on Grace. Why had she not dismissed her and taken on a more amenable and amicable companion? Fear? Fear of what Grace had seen when her husband died? And Grace—she had stayed because of the power she could wield, the taunts, subtle and outspoken, she could throw around, the misery she could inflict by telling my grandmother that she had, with her own hand, destroyed her lover's life-work in a bonfire. And Grace had not even bothered to check the truth of this!

No wonder the house held an atmosphere of doom. The two women had lived with this between them, holding them in its grip for over fifty years. Hatred is a stronger emotion than love. Hatred feeds on itself; love needs replenishing.

And yet . . .

"You told me you loved him," I said, trying to discover something in this house that hadn't gone sour. "And he you. Were you lovers?"

"Sometimes he visited her. They slept in separate rooms."

"And when he was not with her . . ."

"He was with me."

"A passionate man—"

"Don't throw your fancy words at me, young man," she cut in fiercely. "We were young, and we were in love. Sex, that's what all you young people look for and think about. We could not have gone on in this house together if we'd not had each other. Oh, I know, you got your dear Angelina's story, her grand passion, like a story book. And *that* you approve. Don't deny it. I can see it in your face. Why should it have been any different for us? We loved each other. I think . . . if it hadn't been for me . . . he'd have gone insane in this house. We laughed and we cried together, and we whispered our secrets to each other. And I watched him die on that staircase."

For the first time there was life in her face. Suddenly I could see that she would have been pretty, with that mobile, chunky face, pretty in a joyful, outgoing way, generous in her giving and in her enjoyment of life. It was a fleeting glimpse, the most painful moment of my visit, then it was gone. I took out my pipe and stared at it, not daring even to consider lighting it.

"And when you were whispering together, Grace, laughing together, didn't he tell you how he'd tricked Angelina and thrown down from the loft the ones she *didn't* want to burn?"

Her mouth fell open and she gobbled, positively gobbled in an attempt to control her tongue. "No!" she managed to get out at last. "That's not true."

"But that's the sort of thing he would talk to you about, Grace. It's the exact type of intimate joke you'd exchange."

Then she was on her feet, both arms raised, her scarred and arthritic hands clenched, and she flew at me. Not in the way Margaret had flown at me. This was furious outrage. She had trusted me with her intimate thoughts, and I'd seized on them and used them against her. But I had to know. The damned thing was becoming an obsession. I wanted to help Margaret. Yes. But there was something more important than that now. The paintings, in one way or another, had been the cause of one death and a crippling accident—even a second possible murder. All these thoughts flitted through my head in the couple of seconds it took me to capture her flying wrists, to find myself inches from her distorted face, feeling the spittle from her fury spattering me, and then to try to shout her down.

"Be quiet, Grace! You'll do yourself an injury. Take it easy, for God's sake!"

Then her face, made for it, crumpled into tears, and I almost had to catch her as I helped her back to her chair. She found a handkerchief from inside her garments and pressed it to her face, sobbing and sobbing to a point where I realized it had become false. She didn't want to look up at me.

"But it's true," I said softly. "You've got to admit it, Grace. He would have told you."

I waited, and eventually she shuddered and raised her face, dabbing at it futilely. "He never did."

"I can't believe that."

"You can just please your damned self," she said distinctly, separating each word for emphasis. "Now, will you please go."

I did so, after a last, doubtful glance at her, but I waited in the hall, knowing she would have to watch me out of the door. She came after me, briskly now, her head up again.

"Oh . . . one thing, Grace," I said.

"What now?"

"She was paralysed down her right side. I noticed that. So at the end she'd learned to use her left hand. What was she before her fall, right- or left-handed?"

"What're you up to?"

"I just wondered."

"She was right-handed, if that does you any good."

I smiled at her. I didn't expect to see her again unless she took me to court over the ownership of the paintings.

When I turned from her, a large, dark car was parking behind mine in the drive. The first person out of the rear door was Detective Sergeant Dolan.

7

For a moment I was uncertain what to do. Did I nod, walk over to my car, and drive away? But that would signify an abandonment of Grace. I advanced on to the drive and waited.

A tall, thin, and sour man got out of the other side of the car. He stared at me across the roof, said something quietly to Dolan, and on his reply gave instructions. Then he and the driver, who was a woman in a plain costume, not a uniform, advanced on Grace. I heard the thin man ask whether she was Grace Fielding. At her murmured response, they disappeared into the house.

"So here you are," said Dolan, as though they'd been scouring the countryside for me.

"As it happens, yes."

"Just off?"

"That was my intention."

"Spare a minute? Come and sit in the car."

We sat side by side in the back of the police Granada. He was treating me as an old and valued friend.

"A social visit, was it?"

He was offering me an escape route. "Not really." I tried to get my pipe going, my system shouting out for nicotine. "I came to discuss the paintings."

He gave a soft chuckle. We weren't staring at each other, so a smile would have gone to waste. "Not a friendly discussion, I'd guess. The Super's going to be mad, you smoking in his car."

"Let him. I don't mind getting out and driving away."

He touched my elbow. "He'd like to hear that I'm keeping you fully in touch."

"There're developments, then?" I wound down the window and blew smoke at the open air.

"The post-mortem report's in. A verbal one anyway."

I glanced at him. "And?"

"She was suffocated. A hand over her mouth and nose. There was no struggle."

"I don't suppose there would be," I said, feeling sick at his casual tone.

He seemed to be marshalling his thoughts, as there was a pause. Then he slapped my knee. "Have you tried the beer in The Dun Cow?"

"No," I said cautiously. "Haven't had the time."

"The draught bitter's good, and they've got a pin-ball machine."

"Exciting. That'd tax your mind."

"She goes there every night. Two halves, and she plays the machine. Thumps the side, as they do. It's supposed to achieve something."

"Yes. This is Grace Fielding you're talking about?" Watching his nod, I struggled for a mental picture of her, half a pint in one hand and thumping the other palm against the machine. "Are you telling me something?"

"The machine's painted brown. The paint's flaking. All that thumping, I suppose. And it's not often dusted." He cleared his throat. "There were traces of dust and tiny flecks of brown paint in your grandmother's lungs. We've taken samples from the machine for checking."

He must have been a wow in court, with his precise and exact explanations. There was only one question I needed to ask.

"You're taking her in?"

He shook his head. I'd turned to face him. He said, "I shouldn't think so. If that'd been the intention, the Super would've sent me. No—he's playing it softly. He's a sneaky devil. If he gets a straight admission, that would change things. But I doubt he will. She struck me as a hard woman."

"She doesn't admit much. But she was upset—"

"You upset her?"

"Not purposely. One thing led to the other. I doubt she can stand much more, but I don't think you'll get an admission."

"So he'll go gently. Just questions. He knows we've got no case as it stands. Nothing the court wouldn't throw out. At this stage anyway."

"Why're you telling me this?"

"You're an interested party."

"Don't kid me, Sergeant. The police don't show their hands unless they want something. What d'you want from me?"

He grinned and, to his credit, came out with it. "The paintings. Information on them. Why is she making such an issue about them?"

So we were back to the paintings. There was no getting away from the subject. "My grandmother had been giving away bits of furniture and ornaments and things, all of which cut down Grace's possible inheritance. The paintings—me taking them away—was perhaps a camel's back situation. She spotted us driving away. She couldn't stand the thought. The way Grace put it, it was the principle of the thing."

"Hmm!" he said. I hadn't supplied him with the fact that these gifts had been Angelina's only way to hit back at Grace's malice. But perhaps he guessed. "Are they valuable?" he asked.

"I don't know. Perhaps. It's a question of who painted them."

"Perhaps she knows they're valuable. Grace Fielding, I mean."

"That's what upset her, me trying to find out. But she wouldn't admit to knowing a thing about them."

"We might be able to persuade her."

"Beat it out of her?"

He raised his eyebrows. "If necessary," he said solemnly. "You on her side or something?"

I laughed. "You're tricky, Sergeant. I said it as a joke."

"I'll try it in the canteen and let you know how many laughs I get."

I sighed. "She'd looked after Angelina for most of her natural life. She'd hardly kill her now . . ."

"Unless she knows they're valuable. From fury. A last straw, as you said."

I was silent. I could hardly tell him that Grace wouldn't destroy the person on whom she could vent her hatred. He would think I was mad. At last I ventured, "I don't think she knows what they are, valuable or not."

"You *are* on her side." He spoke accusingly, wonderingly.

The house had witnessed too much distress already. I shook my head.

"She was your grandmother, for Pete's sake!"

"I'm aware of that."

"You're a bit slow on the uptake, that's your trouble. Haven't you realized . . . if we take her in, charge her, and get an admission that she killed Mrs. Hine—or if we eventually get a conviction—then it'll show that your grandmother died after you'd left the house, and then there'd be no denying your legal right to the paintings."

"I hadn't thought of it like that."

"Then think about it."

I stared at him, not sure any more that he was the friendly and understanding man I'd thought him. Understanding, yes, but in a sly, furtive way. He was trying to use my emotional responses to force me into revealing every fact that Grace had told me. One of them might clinch the case. I had no reason to feel any sympathy for Grace, but I couldn't find it in me to hate her.

"All right. I'll think about it," I promised, and opened the car door. From outside, I leaned into the open window. "And if they turn out to be valuable, I'll let you know."

I left him a waft of smoke, walked to the Fiesta and got inside, and only then realized that I was blocked in by the Granada. So I had to sit and wait, with nothing to do but think.

I realized, thus thinking, that the provenance of the paintings had now become imperative. It was no longer a question of value, nor a matter of assisting Margaret in her ego problems, but a matter of laying a ghost. Those canvases had sparked too much tragedy. I had to know to what extent it was justified.

At last the superintendent and his driver emerged. They did not have Grace with them, but she stood there at the door, still open six inches, and peered out at them. When the Granada backed out, she shut the door firmly. It indicated that she considered me a very minor menace, in comparison.

I reversed out and set off back to Margaret's place, stopping only to post off the proofs for the factory at Maidstone.

It occurred to me that opening the front door was the first time that day she'd taken a breath of fresh air. Her stance was dejected and weary, her face blotched, her make-up nil, her eyes red with strain.

"You're late," she said. "I've got something cooking. I only hope it isn't spoilt."

"It can't be that bad; I'm starving."

She stood back from me. I could tell she was poised to demand how it had gone, but she restrained her impatience until we were halfway through the meal. At last, "Well? Did you discover anything useful?"

"By useful, would you consider an accusation by Grace that my grandmother killed her husband?"

Her fork was poised, waved, then she said, "Is the old fool completely insane?"

"I think not. There was a hint, too, that it was Grace who caused Angelina's accident."

"A hint?"

"She almost boasted about it."

"Dear Lord, what a house!"

"I don't think I want to see it again, ever."

I then went on to tell her what had happened during my visit there, to the best of my recollection. Her dinner grew cold on her plate. Not mine; I ate between bursts of speech.

"And did she know what crates Arthur Hine took the paintings from?" she demanded before I could get into that bit.

I considered how to put it. "She said she didn't . . ."

"Of course she knew!" Margaret burst out.

I looked down at my plate. "She wouldn't need to know. Her purpose was to *say* to Angelina that the Frederick Ashe paintings had been destroyed. She wouldn't need to know the truth."

"Then why is she so possessive about them?" she demanded. "She must know they're valuable, that's all I can say."

"How could she, Margaret? You people, living in your tight little art world, you seem to believe the great British public can't wait for the latest news about art. It's not so. The odds are that Grace doesn't know how well known Frederick Ashe has become."

"Oh, you're a fool! Don't you want to know the truth?"

"Very much so." What I didn't want to do was watch her face, so I went to get the coffee. "But not by conjecture. Proof positive."

"Which we're never going to get. That woman knows the truth, and you let her get away with evasions."

"She told me one thing," I claimed equably, putting a mug under her nose. "Angelina was right-handed." She looked down. "It's not much, but it's something. Unless she was lying, of course."

I sat down opposite to her again, uneasy at her hair-trigger temper.

When she still hadn't spoken after two minutes, I asked, "And your day—how did it go?"

She looked up smiling, but with an obvious effort. "Something, possibly, achieved. Very little, but I got something. I drove up to London. There were catalogues to be consulted, and the records of art gallery collections. I wanted to find reproductions of the four Ashe paintings that were stolen."

"And you did?"

She pouted. "Black-and-white in three cases, and only a description in the fourth. But it did seem, working from memory of course, that they could have near duplicates in the loft set." At my eagerness, she shook her head. "It means nothing. Most artists paint more than one canvas of their favourite scenes. It doesn't have to mean . . ." She stared past me, her eyes vacant, and licked her spoon absently. "It occurred to me to search for biographies. They're sometimes very useful. The authors use reproductions of little-known works, because the pictures are important to the reading matter, not because they're fine works." It was clearly a practice of which she didn't approve.

"I can see you found something. Let's have it. Whose biography was it?"

She smiled like a temptress, her eyes narrow, her tongue flicking her lips. "Maurice Bellarmé. Your grandmother mentioned him. He was apparently a close friend. There was a reproduction of one of Bellarmé's paintings that he simply called *Angel, 1914.* She was very beautiful, Tony. And there was another. *Frederick Ashe, 1914.* It was this one that caught my attention. It was a picture of Ashe working on a canvas. They often did this, the artists in those days, using each other as models. And Tony, Ashe was painting left-handed."

She produced this nugget of interest as though it didn't glitter with the perfection of a pure and definite clue. I opened my mouth, and she put a finger to my lips.

"I don't want to make too much of this, Tony. After all, if they'd both been right-handed, he'd probably have sat to her right when they painted together. Then he would be the one to reach across for the palette, out of politeness."

"Politeness to their womenfolk wasn't rejected in those days."

She didn't rise to it. "But with him being left-handed, it's almost certain he would sit to her right. Almost."

"If he sat to her left, they'd both have had to reach across," I agreed.

"Exactly. So we could surely take it as proof."

"Almost certainly."

She raised her eyebrows. We were both being very cautious, because we were aware that we were taking Grace's word for it that Angelina had been right-handed.

But I had a ghost to lay. Ghosts demand truth, because they can see through deceptions and evasions, see through each other.

"Let's take a look at the matched pair we've got," I suggested, and she was up off her chair so fast it nearly went flying.

It was me she'd wanted to persuade. Or rather, she had wanted me to persuade myself. Already she had made her decision, but her attitude had changed since we'd first met. Then it had been a matter of plain and uncontestable statement: this is, and this is not. Her confidence had carried her forward, and she would not have expected to be forced into persuading. Now she was confident, but it was qualified. I was the one who now had to be persuaded. It was, perhaps, flattering. But it was out of character.

We put the two paintings of Frederick Ashe's cottage side by side, in the way they had been painted, which was apparent from the slightly different points of view. We separated them by a distance of three feet from each other, the approximate amount apart they would have been on their easels when they were painted. In these positions, the difference in perspective gave them a fresh reality.

My own canvas—I checked the scorch mark on the back—was the one on the right.

Margaret sighed and seemed to sag. Frederick Ashe, left-handed and sitting to the right of Angelina, must have been the one to paint my canvas.

"So that's it," she said. "That's the answer. Ashe painted yours, and it was rescued from the fire. So the rest of his, apart from the six we know about, were destroyed. You've got eighty-one Angelina Footes."

"Haven't I!" I said with pride.

"Don't you care, damn it?" she shouted.

"Not much."

"The whole damned batch wouldn't fetch as much as your one Frederick Ashe."

"Probably not. School of Frederick Ashe. You said that."

"Oh . . . you're impossible."

"What d'you expect me to say?"

"At least . . . at least show some sort of disappointment. What's the matter with you? You nearly had a fortune in your hands, and now you've got . . . what?" She made a wide, sweeping gesture, almost swinging herself off her feet. "A load of tat, not worth getting rid of."

"I didn't intend to. However it turns out, I'll have a houseful of paintings by both my grandparents." But no house to display them in, I recalled. Fleetingly, I wondered what Evelyn would say if I took home eighty-two paintings. How many canvases per wall would that be, counting the bathroom? I must have smiled.

"And it's nothing to smirk about," she snapped.

"You're taking it too seriously."

"Of *course* it's serious."

"Ah! Perhaps you're thinking of the time you've wasted. Time lost and no fee. Tell you what, take any half dozen. Go on—"

She slapped my face.

Startled, I could do no more than stand there rubbing my cheek. She had her lower lip in her teeth.

"Sorry," I said. "But you're so . . . so intense. I was trying to lighten . . ."

"It matters," she whispered, half turning away.

She had poised herself on the springboard of her career. One leap into the heights of a major art discovery, and she need never descend again. She'd be in orbit. But the springboard had collapsed, and her enthusiasm was drowned. To me, too, it mattered, I recalled. My ghosts demanded their absolute proof.

I said gently, "This doesn't have to be positive. Let's look at it logically."

"You and your damned logic." But now she was more calm, even with a hopeful undertone in her voice.

"Grace could have been lying. We know she lied to Angelina, one way or the other. It's in her blood—lying. If she knew Angelina was left-handed, it would be almost instinct for her to say she was right-handed."

"Weak," she decided emphatically.

"All right. Weak. Try this, then. That reproduction you found in the biography of Maurice Bellarmé—it was of Frederick Ashe. But that could've been printed backwards. It happens, you know. I had it happen with one of my pictures in a photo magazine."

She pouted. "That's unlikely. You're trying to encourage me, aren't you, Tony! Oh, I know you. Getting to, anyway. You don't like to hurt people. You're too soft. And I know you're as disappointed as I am. But you pretend. You *are* disappointed, and it's me you're disappointed in. Well, I'll tell you something, and if you interrupt I'll kill you, Tony. You're not as disappointed in me as I am. This is my job, and I'm supposed to be an expert. Expert! I've failed. All right, it's taken me a day or two, but now I can face it. I'm finished, and that's it. There's nothing else I can do with these paintings of yours, or decide to do. So . . . as far as I'm concerned, that's the end of it. We assume the loft batch is Angelina's and . . . I don't know . . . I'll sell them for you, if you like. I don't know!"

The thought crossed my mind that if she was so certain she had "failed," how could she be equally certain that the loft batch were Angelina's? But I didn't say so. Her brilliant mind was coldly analytical, and there wasn't much room for warm logic. What I did say was "It's not the end, you know. There's still that man you mentioned, who has those two—and perhaps all six—of the accredited Frederick Ashes. We go to him—"

"You must be mad."

"I don't see why we shouldn't."

"You don't go to a man like that and expect to be welcomed and shown round his collection. The Queen couldn't get in there without the SAS behind her."

After contemplating this image for a moment, I said, "I'd thought of something more subtle. All we want to know is whether his two (or his six) have got near duplicates in the loft set. As my original one has. If so, then it indicates that the loft set must be Grannie's, because we have to accept the six are Frederick Ashes."

"Indicates! Indicates!" she said impatiently. "And how could you tell just by looking at them that they've got near duplicates?"

"We ask him."

"We take all that batch of canvases to him . . ." She stopped, realizing that this was not what I'd implied.

"No. I'm a photographer. Remember? I'll take shots of all eighty-one, full frame, and do prints. They'll be good, I can promise you that.

And we take him the prints. We say nothing. We let him do the talking."

"I don't like it . . ."

"What harm could there be in trying?"

"I'd just as soon abandon the whole thing."

I grinned at her. "Rightee-oh. So we load 'em all in my car, and I'll do it round at my lab. It'll be inconvenient, but I'll manage somehow. Then I'll go and see him myself."

"No," she said.

"No?"

"I'll . . . I'll come with you. I'll have to. What if he lets us see the canvases! You wouldn't know what to look for."

"Of course. I'd forgotten that. But I'm such an ignorant pig . . ."

She thumped my arm. "Where's your camera, you big fool?"

One thing about her, the volatility of her temperament maintained the interest. Nursing my arm, I went to fetch my Pentax. I was still having to carry all my possessions around with me in the car.

8

She expected me simply to walk round her workroom, shooting away and capturing perfection. It's not like that. Strictly speaking, it should have been done with the camera mounted on my enlarger stand, each canvas face up on the base and with a spotlight each side. But I was equipped for no such niceties. I used a 50mm lens on the Pentax and loaded in a slow film for finest grain and maximum definition. This meant that I would have to handle fairly slow exposures, as the diaphragm had to be stopped down for a decent depth of field, to allow for any lack of squareness to the subject. I couldn't use a flash on the hotshoe, because it would throw back reflection, and I didn't want to use an extension flash, because of the fall-off of light intensity across the canvases.

Margaret couldn't understand my laboured precision, so I explained. She still didn't understand. I did one at a time, perching them on a chair, leaning them against the back, and relying on her flat and white artificial light. It worked out at one-tenth of a second of f11, which was too slow for hand-held shots, so I used the tripod.

Eighty-one frames. It seemed to take an eternity. Three spools.

"I'll get straight on to this in the morning," I told her. "Another all-day stint."

"Right. You do that. I'll try to find out who owns those two Maurice Bellarmé canvases."

"Why trouble?"

"You said . . . the picture of Frederick Ashe in the biography could've been printed backwards."

I grinned at her. She wasn't missing a trick.

We went to bed. Together. It seemed natural and inevitable. Mostly, we slept. Our second night together, and we were both so exhausted that we slept! Yet, come to think of it, we had become so attuned to each other's moods and characters that there was a hint of strain between us that inhibited relaxation. At least, so I felt. For once, I did not feel she had been completely honest with me, and it was in attempting to decide in what way that I fell asleep.

My automatic alarm woke me early. I was a self-employed man, used to fixed hours as a regular routine, and I had work awaiting me in my darkroom. I took a shower, got a quick breakfast inside me, and took her up a cup of tea at eight. She groaned and rolled over when I kissed the back of her neck. Her eyes were smeared, her cheeks puffy. The jet-black hair, I noticed, showed lighter traces at the roots.

"What time . . ." Her eyes cleared. "You're dressed!"

"Early birds. It's eight o'clock."

"Can't you ever rest?"

"No." This was true. How could I rest when I was competing with Evelyn in the rivalry for income? The fact that I was no longer doing so hadn't yet seeped into my system. I still could not relax. Damn Evelyn. "I'll be off," I said. "It's another big day in the dark."

"No wonder you're so pale. Hurry back."

"You know I will."

I kissed her on her naked lips, savouring the perfume of her, and turned away quickly. Why ruin my applaudable efforts for an early start?

It was a fifty-minute drive. When I pushed open my photolab door, there was a bulky brown envelope dragging against the floor. Not delivered through the post. No name on it.

On my narrow counter I slit it open. There was a note with the contents, from Evelyn:

> Tony,
>
> For God's sake, make arrangements for your post. If you want a complete break, then do it. From next Monday I shall return all your mail as gone away. Which you have. I want to organize my life on that assumption.
>
> Evelyn

It had been a mistake even to have started using my home address for business purposes, simply because Evelyn maintained an office there. Now I would have to arrange with the post office for my stuff to be forwarded to my tight little workplace. One good intake of mail, and I wouldn't be able to get the door open.

There were two new commissions, one of them a lucrative and technically difficult assignment for a glossy magazine, to cover a pop group's tour. Just try working in that psychedelic lighting! Forcing myself not to think of this or of Evelyn, I got down to work in the darkroom.

They were good, better than I'd expected. I did a complete set at six by four and glossed them, put them in an envelope, and left. It had taken me nine hours. I was drained, and pains kept running up my back and across my shoulders. I went in for a coffee before tackling the run back to Margaret's. These long stints in the darkroom did terrible things to my eyes.

"Get a darkroom assistant," Evelyn had said. "You're the photographer, not the stinks-room mechanic."

But part of the job was the quality of the prints. It was something of which I was proud.

"Good?" Margaret asked as she let me in. "Are they good?"

I simply handed her the envelope, and followed her down the stairs.

She poured us drinks, and while I sat quietly and tried to make myself unwind, she went through them. She looked up with a smile.

"I didn't expect this. The colour's marvellous."

I shrugged. "It's done with chemically linked dyes. They can't be perfect, but you have to try to get the best there is from the materials."

"I could put a lot of work in your way—"

"Not that sort of thing, thanks. It's mechanical. I like variety. It keeps the interest going."

"But these—"

"I could bang those up to twenty by sixteen and print on specially grained paper, and most people would just as soon have them as the original painting. But I suppose that offends your sensibilities?"

"Somewhat. But if it gave pleasure—"

"Condescending, that's what you are. The poor, non-aesthetic horde, who don't appreciate your art!"

She flushed. "What's got into you, Tony? You'll hardly let me finish a sentence, and when I praise you—and genuinely, I assure you—you throw criticisms at me." The patches of colour were high, and her eyes seemed out of focus.

I looked at her above my glass. If I hadn't known better, I'd have said she was on drugs. It was some sort of emotional high that possessed her. Had there been a breakthrough in her endeavours?

"Sorry," I said. "It's been a heavy day." A bad one. I couldn't get Evelyn's message out of my mind, and I hadn't found time to get to the post office. But most of all, with my brain tired, I was unable to find sympathy for Margaret's art-establishment-oriented ideas. I was clinging desperately to my ghosts. The blooms of high colour on her cheeks were still there. "I see *you've* had a good day," I added as a palliative.

She looked away. "If it's any satisfaction, I haven't. I've been tracking around, trying to locate the whereabouts of those two Bellarmé portraits. All I can come up with is that they're in a private collection. Somewhere. So there's no joy there." She grimaced at me. "You're hungry?"

"Yes. Very."

"It's all ready. You see, I'm still considering your welfare."

We ate in silence, which gave me time to realize how expertly I was able to ruin relationships with my moods. The trouble was, I could put forward no good explanation for them. I could well have kept my mouth shut. But no. Perhaps I'd been too pleased to see Margaret again and had relaxed, allowing built-up tension to take control. I'd known for some time that I'd been trying to do too much on my own—the photography, the processing, the paperwork and accounts. But I'd been reluctant to seek assistance. I treasured the complete pattern of expertise. Proud, that was it. Big-headed, even. It doesn't do to face yourself over an Irish stew.

I gave myself excuses. My whole life was being set aside to cater for this provenance business. Did I resent this? No, to hell with that. The paintings were mine. I had to know the truth.

After a lemon meringue pie—she was quite a cook; it was perfect—I tried a suggestion.

"I suppose it's too much to ask you to call in another expert? A second opinion."

Her eyes were dark under her eyebrows when she glanced up. "Yes, too much. You shouldn't need to ask that, Tony."

Over the coffee she told me what she knew of the big man we would now have to approach. His name was Renfrew Coombe. He lived in a large house on the edge of Exmoor in Somerset, and so far as Margaret knew, the police had no active interest in him at that time. Several art historians had attempted to gain access to his gallery but had been shown the inside of the door, even if they'd got beyond the outside. He was no longer an active villain, but it was said that his old team—as it was politely called—was still with him. He was protected, though there was no longer any suggestion of violence. He never answered his own phone. His secretary was illiterate, inasmuch as no replies were ever received, not if they concerned the collection.

"Then we go and knock on his door," I suggested, "and we see what happens."

"Tomorrow?"

"Only because it's too late tonight. I've got a business to maintain."

She said idly, "And if the eighty-one turn out to be true Frederick Ashes, would it tempt you to retire?"

I grinned at her. "I'd turn amateur, but I'd still be a photographer."

"And I," she said, "would still be a consultant on art."

"Even more so."

"Yes."

We parted on the landing. There were no words said on this arrangement; it just happened.

"An early start?" I asked.

She nodded. "We've got to find the damned place."

We used her Volvo, because Margaret thought we needed to make an impression. On such a man as Renfrew Coombe, nothing less than a gold-plated Rolls would have made an impression, but really, she wanted to do the driving.

It wasn't as difficult to find as I'd expected. We stopped in town so that I could fix the forwarding address business with the post office, and I popped into a stationer's to get an Ordnance Survey map covering Exmoor. One inch to the mile. It covered every tiny hamlet, and I noticed that a number of them had Coombe in their title. I studied it as Margaret drove, and discovered something about the sort of man we were going to visit. He had decided to retire from crookery. It befitted his self-esteem to retire to somewhere bearing his own name. This he had managed to bring about.

It is a simple thing to change the name of a country. They do it every month in Africa. It is also possible to change the name of a county if a boundary adjustment also adjusts the political balance. It even happens that towns change, by being squeezed out—Wellington in Shropshire is now no more than an appendage to Telford. But just try changing the name of a village. Then you have the villagers to deal with, and they won't even let you change the name of their local pub.

So Renfrew Coombes had searched around and discovered that there was a village called Renfrew Coombe. It was simple to drop his final *s* by deed poll. I learned later that he'd bought the freehold of the whole village just so that his address would be Renfrew Coombe, Somerset, England.

It was such a man whom we hoped to impress and persuade.

We discovered the village as we popped over a stone-built humpbacked bridge. A wriggle in the road, and there it was, a row of cottages, one public house, and a tiny village store. We slowed, wondering whether to ask directions to the big house, but I sensed the atmosphere and whispered for her to drive on.

A fair number of the original residents were still hanging on. You could tell which they were, those people on the street who looked like furtive extras in a film set, equally nervous in spite of a lack of cameras, but uneasy with their new neighbours. Coombe had managed to empty a few of the cottages and fill them with his own men. These, too, were obvious. They were the ones with newly colour-washed walls, the brightly painted front doors, and the professionally landscaped diminutive gardens with roses sweeping up the walls. The occupants of these cottages lounged in doorways, from time to time flicking cigarette ends at their fuschias, then disappearing inside to their phones to report a sight of a stranger. Strangers were suspect. The publican, too, lounged in his doorway. The pub was now part of the film set, might even have been no more than a false front. Beer might still have been obtainable inside, if the regular citizens weren't too dispirited to find out. Or maybe the cellar contained an armoury.

Shaking myself from these fanciful thoughts, I looked ahead. "There," I said. "Just beyond that rise."

What I'd seen might have been the ruins of a castle, but it was the only sizeable building in that hilly, tangled landscape. It was possibly half a mile away. The road became increasingly unappealing, perhaps as a discouragement. The map showed it to continue onwards, but the surveyors had allocated it no more than a dotted line.

One or two buildings speckled the rises each side and could have been farmhouses, though their bright and recent paintwork made them suspect. I was aware of being observed with suspicion.

It had once been a castle, guarding a ford and offering a grim front to the north. It had been built on from time to time, with scant attention to previous styles, and perhaps had more recently been improved by an intake from Renfrew Coombe's millions. It was depressing and unwelcoming. A mist would have improved the prospect.

We drove through an opening in the surrounding high wall, directly into a large courtyard. I would have expected a gate across that opening, with a guard. But against what would Coombe need to protect himself? Certainly not burglars; they would appreciate the risk. The law? There was nothing specific to level against him. Ordinary visitors such as ourselves? There was a very large, solid and iron-studded door to serve that purpose. It could be closed firmly on an unwelcome face.

Which was what happened.

Margaret had performed a wide, smooth swing round the courtyard, which was entirely stone-flagged and liberally mossed but which once must have rung to the hooves of armoured cavalry. We stopped opposite the door and got out. Nothing moved. I could hear no bird-song, no bleating of sheep or barking of dogs. The door towered above us under an inadequate porch. There was no bell-pull or button, only a large knocker in the form of a lion's head. I lifted it and banged firmly. Twice. The echoes sang away inside the house.

After a minute or two we heard the approaching clack of steel-tipped heels. The door opened without a creak. The man staring at us was tall, thin, in his fifties, bald, and wearing a black butler's jacket with too much spare material around the chest. He said nothing. We failed to impress.

"We would like to see Mr. Coombe," I told him.

"He doesn't see visitors."

"There's something I'd like to show him."

Bushy eyebrows were raised. He watched my hand reaching towards the bulky shape in the side pocket of my anorak, and his eyes changed. The door slammed shut. We heard his heels retreating, steadily, unhurriedly.

I banged again. The heels retreated. Once more. Still the heels. Again. The heels stopped. Finally, I gave it a regular tattoo. The heels began to approach.

By this time I'd decided what had worried him. Renfrew Coombe had enemies, undoubtedly. The package in my pocket was suspect. This time I was prepared, and had one of my six-by-fours ready in my hand. The door opened. His right hand was behind it. I held up the print.

"Show him this and he'll see us."

"Bugger off."

"If you don't, I'll send it by post, and he'll be looking for another flunkey."

He eyed me with venom; then, as it seemed innocuous, he reached out a tentative hand. I released the print. The door closed. The heels retreated.

We walked round the courtyard, stretching our legs after the long journey. The moss was slimy and the flags uneven.

"You think he'll see us?" she asked.

"Daren't refuse." But I wasn't as confident as I sounded.

"But will he let us leave again?"

"We've got the paintings."

She wrapped her arms round herself and shuddered. "I can't see we'll gain anything."

"Maybe not. It's worth a try, though."

We were over by the courtyard entrance when the door opened again. He stood there and crooked a finger. I put a hand to Margaret's arm. Walk slowly, make him wait, show confidence.

The inside was a surprise. I hadn't expected the grand hall still to be rush-strewn, and perhaps the suits of armour would have been retired. But the full transformation was staggering. Only the walls and the windows were the originals. The echoing heels had been slamming hard on to black-and-white checkered marble. The walls had been treated to a pine coating, and the wide, black oak staircase, as it must have been at one time, was now decorated with chromium supports to a black leather-faced pair of hand rails. The full-width stair carpet was purple nylon. The scattered furniture was chrome and plastic. I wouldn't have been surprised if each leaded diamond pane hadn't been double-glazed. Large, white-painted radiators stood where the armour had mounted guard.

It seemed inconceivable that a man with such anarchic taste could own a unique collection of art treasures that he coveted. But of course, he didn't covet them. They were not there to be looked at and admired; they were there because other people would have liked to have them, and Coombe had them. That was their purpose.

The steel heels led us past the staircase and through a door at the side. He waited until we were inside, received a signal from his boss, then the door closed behind him.

This was Coombe's personal office. It had received professional attention from a colour-blind interior decorator. Rugs too precious to be walked on hung against the naked stone of the wall, the spaces between them occupied by tall white columns, each bearing a goldfish bowl with a single exotic fish in it. The splendid proportions of the large and tall windows were ruined by low valances and net curtains dyed red. There were a lot of windows; it was a long, high-ceilinged room. At one end was a round fountain, into which the little boy tinkled endlessly away. He'd been lacquered pink. The wall-to-wall carpeting was one huge flow of white, like a snowfall. The desk, too, was white, though it had started its life in the study of one of the Louis. Chairs, cane and rush, stood around in negligent disorder. Only two chairs were comfortable, these being deep leather easy chairs with studded backs. In one sat a young, pale man with polished hair and a bored expression. In the other, not behind the desk, sat the man who must be Renfrew Coombe.

By this time I had become resigned to failure. A man who could live in these surroundings could not be expected to have any appreciation of art or understanding of it. He wouldn't know a Toulouse-Lautrec from an Aubrey Beardsley. It was on his personal knowledge that I was relying. My confidence sagged. He seemed to confirm my assessment by holding up the print and saying, "What's this?"

I walked forward. I was no longer aware of Margaret's presence; perhaps she was stunned by the room. Standing in front of him, I answered, "It's a print, a photograph of a painting I own."

It was then that I became aware that his was an orthopaedic chair. His feet rested on its extension, his back was moulded to its adjustable contours, as far as such a back could be manipulated. He was a gross man, whose fat had absorbed his outline to the point of inhibiting his movements. The hand holding the print almost engulfed it, the thumb obscuring most of the surface. His face was a pear, with the jowls resting on his shoulders. Whatever neck there had been was absorbed. No shirtmaker could have produced a collar that wouldn't be ridiculous. He was wearing a white, polo-necked jumper.

Angrily, he stared past the thumb at what was revealed. "So what?" he barked, his voice deep and throaty.

"It's a Frederick Ashe. As the owner of the only ones in a private collection, you might be interested . . . I thought."

"Tcha!" he said in contempt, then he tore it across, across again, and tossed the pieces over his shoulder.

The youngish man—I now realized he could have been forty—moved uneasily, then subsided again. In the corner of my eye I saw Margaret studying the manikin. She was keeping her options open.

"Feel free," I said. "I have the negative as well as the canvas."

"When I buy, it's at auction. Now get out of here."

Reaching over the chair arm, the young man had rescued the portions of my print. He hooked a low table towards him and jigsawed the pieces together, then he glanced up at me. His eyes, ice-blue, contained interest, and I knew that all was not lost.

"There's another eighty of them," I said, keeping my voice casual.

"Eighty-one canvases in all. I've got photos of all of them. Want to see?"

I drew out my packet slowly so as not to trigger any violent reaction. I held it up. Coombe stared at me, then waved his hand. "Paul."

His assistant reached towards me, forcing me to go to him. Smiling, I slipped the set out of its envelope and handed them over.

With the expertise of a card-sharp, he put them down on the table and fanned them out. Then, delicately with spatulate fingers, he edged each one sideways so that he had a full view, and moved along. Six of them he slid fractionally downwards. I barely noticed the action. Then he swept them together again, rose to his feet with athletic grace, and went over to his employer.

There was whispering and grunts in response; then Coombe said something and Paul walked with silent stealth from the room.

We waited.

Coombe was not an entertaining host. He interlocked his hands and placed them on his stomach, where they rested like a coil of hosepipe, and closed his eyes. I moved over to Margaret's side. She glanced at me. Her eyes were dark, her cheeks pale.

"A waste of time," she whispered.

"I think not. He hires the brains, and Paul's his curator."

She looked away, shuddered when her eyes fell on the fountain, and murmured, "I'll scream if I don't get out of here soon."

But it was a long wait, and she didn't scream. Paul at last returned. He held the batch of prints in one neat block, and went directly to his employer. There was more whispering. I edged closer.

At last Coombe raised his eyes. They were flat and empty. Paul, with a smirk, handed me the pack of prints. I slid them into my pocket.

"Right," said Coombe, rumbling aggressively. "So you've got eighty-one forgeries. Why should I be interested?"

"They're not forgeries."

He went on as though I hadn't spoken. "I'll take them off your hands. Eight thousand the lot. Take it or leave it."

"Why should you want them if you think they're forgeries?"

That was a mistake. The hands uncurled and the fingers flexed, like dying snakes. His face was suffused with blood. Paul took my arm quickly.

"Out!" he said.

We left. Margaret led the way. Paul stood in the hall and watched us on our trip to the door. A roar of fury sounded behind him, and he retreated, the door closing quietly.

Steel-tips was waiting to see us out. He bowed mockingly. We left. I knew why Coombe wanted to relieve us of the canvases, forgeries or not. He could not risk them coming on the open market and thus throwing doubt on the authenticity of his own. Even, perhaps, of demands coming from high places that his own should be inspected.

I said, "Drive away slowly and keep going. Stop when we get the other side of the village."

This she did. By that time I'd confirmed what I suspected.

I had, as was my normal practice, banged on the back of each print my rubber stamp, which includes all the details required to trace a negative in future. Such as the number in the batch. In this instance, I'd done a print from each negative, so that the prints were numbered simply 1 to 81. I now possessed 2 to 81, number 1 being in four pieces on the formica top of that low table.

But they were no longer in exact order. Paul had paid special attention to the six he'd noticed. These six were now together at the bottom of the pile.

"Got him!" I said in triumph. "We now know he's got all six of the Frederick Ashes. And we know which ones from the loft set are paired with his."

Margaret didn't seem as pleased as I'd expected. "But we don't know whether his are painted from right- or left-biased viewpoints of your six."

"But surely they must be the same as my original canvas, a right-hand viewpoint."

"Hmm!" she said doubtfully. "But sometimes artists do more than one painting of something they like. Those six could've been picked out by that evil-looking young man just because they're similar to the six Coombe has."

"You do take some convincing."

"And you, Tony? Are you convinced? Don't forget, you're as good as agreeing with me that the loft set are all Angelina Footes. I hadn't noticed you agreeing with me lately."

I grimaced at her, changed it to a grin. "So we need to have another go at it. Is that what you're saying?"

"Another go at Coombe? Heaven forbid!"

"But don't you see, we've now got something on him. We know he's got those four stolen paintings."

"So?" she asked, with no warmth.

"We phone him. We put it to him that on this evidence the police could apply for a search warrant. In exchange for our silence, we demand that he should let us . . . or me, if you like, and I'll take photos . . . let me, then, have access to his collection, and—"

She jerked the car into violent movement. I shouted, "What the hell!" But she was glancing at the rearview mirror.

"There's a car just come over the bridge," she said. "I'll have to lose him."

"You're crazy."

"Don't you realize what you've stirred up! And you talk about threatening such a man! He wants those canvases."

"Over my dead—"

"If necessary," she said. "If necessary."

She set out to lose the other car. It was faster than the Volvo, and more powerful. But they didn't stand a chance. Thugs have a fine regard for their own lives, but Margaret had none for ours.

9

In order to reach the village of Renfrew Coombe we had had to take the Porlock-to-Lynton coast road and strike off south into Exmoor. After that, there had been only one route. This road, out on the moors, is about twelve feet wide, and you either follow it or bump along through the scrub. Closer to the coast the road is no wider, and tall hedgerows encroach very intimately. So when I say that Margaret set out to lose the car on our return journey, she could not do so until we were nearing

Porlock, because they could afford to hang back, knowing she had no alternatives.

But Porlock is approached by way of Porlock Hill, from this direction being downwards. The hill is steep, and it winds. Cyclists are advised to get off and walk, and the few escape roads—steep ramps of sand to slow you down—are signposted. They occur where the fall becomes one in four, and always on a corner so tight that you can catch a glimpse of your own rear wheels as you take them. Most people tackle the whole thing at around twenty, up or down. But Margaret had no patience for this sort of thing.

She took it in second gear with the revs flying high, driving on brakes and throttle, so that the whole three quarters of a mile was done in one screaming, wriggling dance round the bends. I didn't think a Volvo Estate would do this sort of thing, but it did. Approaching the top of the hill, the car behind had closed up. Where he thought we might disappear to, except through Porlock and on to the Minehead road, I couldn't imagine. He made the mistake of trying to match the Volvo, and we lost him at one of the escape roads, which he took, or nearly. It made an expensive noise behind us as we slowed through the village of Porlock.

"Was that really necessary?" I asked.

"We daren't let Coombe know where the paintings are."

"Oh!" I said in dismay. She had prodded free a thought.

She slowed even more, glancing sideways. "Oh what?"

"My rubber stamp, the one I bang on the back of my proofs—it's got my home address on it, and both my phone numbers."

She nodded. It was just what she might have expected. "Then you'll have to keep away from your home."

"Didn't intend going there."

"Perhaps not. But every time you come to my place you'll have to make sure you're not followed."

Life was becoming increasingly complicated. "Every time I come?" I asked. "I thought you'd pretty well drained every drop of knowledge from the canvases."

She drove a mile before she replied. "We'll see. We've got to discuss this."

Which we did when we reached her place. Now that we knew which photos had attracted Paul's attention, she could concentrate on those.

She had never seen the two Ashes he owned legitimately, and the catalogues contained no more than a description. But she had certainly seen the other four in the galleries from which they'd been stolen. As far as she could tell from memory, those four were now in the hands of Renfrew Coombe. If they were not, why had Paul shown such interest in pictures of canvases almost matching them?

We had got back in time for a quick lunch and were now sitting out in the sun on Margaret's patio, which overhung the valley. I was feeling lazy, which made me uneasy. Lounging around in the middle of a working day felt strange. My disorientation increased. I could see this business hanging around for ever.

"There's only one thing for it," I said at last. "We'll go to see him again . . ."

"We will not."

". . . or I'll go to see him again, and say we—or I—believe that his Frederick Ashe paintings might not be genuine. The odd lie never does much harm. I'll tell him that if I can see them, there's a method of making sure. I wouldn't tell him anything about the left- and right-viewpoint theory, but with a bit of luck he'll be worried enough to let me take a peep—"

"I forbid it."

"Forbid?"

"It's too dangerous for you."

I noticed that she'd now excluded herself. "I don't see that."

"He wouldn't dare to let you see inside his gallery."

"Paul could bring them out. Just his two legitimate ones would be enough for what I want. I'd simply compare them with the photos and confirm that they're right-viewpoint versions of the ones in the loft set. That'd make 'em the same as my original one."

Her lower lip tucked between her teeth, she turned and stared at me. "Promise me you wouldn't go inside the gallery." Her eyes were very dark.

"If you wish. I don't see that it matters."

"Oh, you are slow! What does he know about you? You could be an undercover man from the Arts Section of Scotland Yard. You might see something that'd make you a dangerous liability."

"If he thought I was a policeman, he wouldn't dare to touch me."

"All the same . . ."

She was flushed, her eyes moist and bright. I couldn't understand her attitude. Was it concern for me? To be sure, we had a natural empathy for each other; we could bear to be in each other's company without strain. Looking back, I realized that this was partly what had stood between Evelyn and myself. We had both had to work hard for a continuing domestic peace. Not so with Margaret. Our intimacy had grown rapidly, but I didn't think it had developed to a position where she could be concerned deeply for my safety.

At last she said simply, "I don't want you to go."

"Because you now know enough about the paintings to stake your reputation that the eighty-one from the loft are not Frederick Ashes?"

She looked away from me over her valley, then reached sideways to her cigarettes on the metal table between us. She spoke with her eyes still averted, so softly that at first I wasn't sure I'd heard her correctly.

"I know enough about that loft set to be certain of one thing—nobody would ever dare to say they're *not* by Frederick Ashe."

"Pardon . . ."

"Don't be a fool, Tony," she said sharply, snapping her head round, dragging the cigarette, still unlit, from her lips. "You know what I mean."

I stared at her dumbly.

"You do!" she cried. "We could put them on the market as Frederick Ashe canvases, and not one art expert anywhere would dare to dispute it."

Then she spent quite a while getting the cigarette going, giving me time to absorb this new concept.

Where, now, was all her high-flown professional morality? At no time had there been any reason to question it, and in fact her probity had ruled every action she had taken. Now, all of this was to be jettisoned, was it? And why? In order to make a quick fortune for me and a fair commission for her, but mostly to secure her treasured acclaim for this remarkable artistic find! How could that be? I just couldn't imagine her smiling at a gathering of her enthusiastic peers when inside she would be squirming. Oh, the bitterness of the thought that she was betraying her trust as an international expert, she whose word was pristine truth!

"Less," I said, "the six that're duplicated in Coombe's collection and my single one."

"What?"

"To prevent any backlash from Coombe, any protests, any awkward questions . . . to play safe, there would have to be no duplicates."

I'd confused her. "Yes . . . of course," she said.

I shrugged. "Suits me, then. It'd save all the trouble of seeing him again."

"There's that too." She smiled. Though she tried to conceal the fact, there was relief in it. But there was not enough behind her eyes, no affection, no hint of passion, to make me accept that her relief was for me.

"I really must catch up on my work anyway," I went on casually. "I'll spend another day at my photo-lab." I laughed. "Oh, don't worry, I'll make sure I'm not followed. You can work out how you're going to unload seventy-four of the canvases on to an innocent world."

She grimaced. In spite of what she'd said, it was not a task she would enjoy. But during the rest of the day, she did much to reinforce the impression that her concern was for me personally. She became more affectionate and attentive. She probed me about the details of my profession, and seemed fascinated. From her bedroom door she looked at me in a way not usually lavished on me, and throughout the night she protected me with her strong arms. I had no fears. It was no longer necessary to have future contact with Renfrew Coombe, and I was going to become a millionaire. Wasn't I?

I regretted only that my recent incursions into the art world were turning me into a cynical bastard.

In the morning I covered what I was beginning to feel was my regular commuting run, and as usually happens when you're overwhelmed by work, more commissions had arrived in the post. One of them was a lulu, the pictures for a brochure covering holidays in Norway, all expenses paid, plus a generous fee. The satisfaction this produced was slightly dimmed by the recollection that I was shortly to become a millionaire. I would be able to buy the travel firm! It was also undermined by the fact that it arrived by way of Evelyn, who had included another charming note:

Tony,

I need a settled address to which I can direct the serving of divorce proceedings. Of course, to claim desertion would be futile after so short a time, so I have had a man follow you, and evidence of adultery is available. Please let me know whether service of the writ may be made at your business address or at the home of Dr. Margaret Dennis.

Your immediate reply will be appreciated.

P.S. Please do not claim that my address is still yours, as I have had the locks changed.

P.P.S. Aleric sends his regards.

E.

I threw it to the floor and stamped on it. The disaster it spelled out was not my divorce, but the fact that Margaret's address was now known to a third party. It was dangerous. I went quickly into the darkroom, where I had my phone on the end of the bench, intending to call Margaret to warn her. It rang beneath my fingers and I snatched it up. If it was Evelyn . . .

"Mr. Hine?" A man's voice, like dark brown velvet. Another commission? I unearthed my best voice.

"Tony Hine speaking."

"Ah! Fine! This is Paul Mace. You'll remember me perhaps. At Renfrew Coombe."

"I remember you." I was cautious, no longer being particularly interested in what Coombe might have to offer.

"Mr. Coombe has been thinking about your proposition."

"I don't remember making a proposition; I simply told him what I have."

"And which he would like to acquire."

I took a deep breath. "Mr. Mace, I own eighty-one Frederick Ashe canvases. These I intend to offer at auction, and your employer will no doubt put in a bid—"

"You don't understand."

"It's you who doesn't. Tell him I don't intend to include the duplicates of the Ashes he now has—or believes he has. I don't want to embarrass so important—"

"Will you listen!"

I stopped. It had been difficult to maintain the formal style anyway. Then I said, "I'm listening, but any offer under—"

"He's making no offer."

"No?"

"I've been told to instruct you to bring all your canvases here and leave them for our examination and possible destruction."

"Instruct me! Now listen here, you slimy little—"

"We have your wife."

"Just listen . . . you what?"

"We are holding your wife here as a—how shall I put it?—as guarantee of your sensible behaviour."

I laughed. His timing had been perfect. I laughed, and he made clicking noises of disapproval with his tongue.

"We shall hold her until—" he began.

"You can hold her for ever, as far as I'm concerned. Hasn't she told you—Obviously not. I've left her. She's suing me for divorce. I don't *want* her back, you loon."

"Come now, Mr. Hine."

"Then go and damn well ask her."

"We have your son too."

"And you can keep him as well." This I said with equal force, but I was recalling that Aleric had Frederick Ashe's nose and his ears, so it did seem that he was my son after all. But he had a different view of life from my grandfather's, I told myself. "He'll love it there," I said. "You'll be able to train him as one of your heavies or hit-men or whatever."

"Really, this is absurd," he bleated, no longer brown velvet but brushed nylon.

"Isn't it!" I agreed.

"You'd better speak to her."

"Who? Evelyn? No thanks."

"Here she is now."

And there she was. Evelyn had always been addicted to smooth, legal invective, each word cutting quietly to the bone. All this polish had disappeared. She was a very angry woman.

"Tony, I'm going to kill you for this!" she shouted. "You and your blasted paintings. Give the man what he wants, and let me go home. You hear me?"

"I hear you, Evelyn. Tell me what happened."

"Be damned to what happened. Just do as I say."

"Tell me what happened."

"How can I talk—"

"What happened, for heaven's sake?"

She turned her face from the phone, but didn't cover it. I heard her shout, "Get out of this room, you nasty little creep. Out!" A pause. I heard the distant slam of a door, so unlike Paul. Then she was back to me.

"I'll tell you what happened, if it amuses you. Two men came to the door. They told me to put my coat on. *Told* me! I protested. They used force. Force on me, Tony. I shall never forgive you. They entered my house against my will. Aleric was there. They used physical violence on him, then they took us out to the car."

"He's hurt? Aleric—is he hurt?"

She snorted. "Nothing hurts him. He was unconscious when they took us out, but he'd broken some fingers. Not his own. Do not interrupt, Tony. Let me say it. They brought us here, wherever here is, and they tell me we'll be driven home when you surrender some paintings you seem to have. Paintings. Plural. I don't know what it means or what it's about. You've only got one damned painting, which I'm glad to see the back of—"

"Evelyn!"

"So just you do what he wants, or by God I'll sue you for damages due to negligence—"

"Evelyn!" I shouted. She was silent. I waited, and could hear her breathing.

At last, "Well? Make it good, Tony."

"It *is* good. What if I tell you I now own eighty-one paintings, all valuable? Possible total value around a million and a half. That's pounds sterling, not lire or pesetas. Pounds. Do you seriously imagine I'm about to give them away?"

In saying this, I was assuming that Paul Mace would be listening on an extension line. It did no harm to set him worrying. All the same, it was a mistake. Evelyn hissed gently between her teeth.

"Are you telling me the truth?"

"Though I haven't been able to prove they're valuable," I added quickly.

But the damage was done. "No wonder he wants them." I could almost hear her mind ticking over.

"It's not quite like that."

"So what can we do?" she asked, my ally now in our combined distress.

"I take it you've already told him the legal aspects of what he's done, and explained how you'll have the police on him when you get out of there?"

"What are you talking about? It's what *you're* going to do that matters. What *are* you going to do?"

She was thinking in terms of ransom: How many paintings was she worth, and how many would we have left, and what sum of money would they get us? Her mind was already running in terms of a resumption of cohabitation.

"I don't intend to do anything about it. I've explained that to your friend Mace."

"You're not—You'd leave me—Well, let me tell you—"

"It's quite simple," I explained patiently. "When he realizes he can't use you to force my hand, he'll let you go. Simple."

I felt her shudder, felt it right through the phone system. She did that when she was forcibly taking control of herself. Then she spoke quietly, in her most biting tone.

"No! No, Tony. I see through you now. You're intending to share it all with your marvellous Dr. Dennis. Doctor of what, may I ask? You'll have to tell me some time. But not now. Now you're going to listen. Do what I say, or you'll have nothing, you and your fancy woman. You're forgetting something, Tony. I know her address. If you do not bring the canvases, or whatever they are, and bring them now . . . *now,* Tony . . . I'll tell him. And his men will fetch them. I'm quite certain that's where they'll be. Do I make myself clear?"

The situation was very clear to me, but not exactly as Evelyn assumed. I had wanted a good excuse for going there again, and now, with a bit of luck, I had been able to implant in Mace's mind my confidence that I held eighty-one Frederick Ashe canvases. My bargaining power with these was stronger than Coombe's with Evelyn. This, too, I had firmly implanted.

"I will come, Evelyn," I said.

"With those—"

"As quickly as possible. That'll be at least four hours from here."

"Four hours!"

"You don't know where you are, but I do. Four hours, at the very least."

Then I hung up before she could extend the delay, and immediately dialled Margaret's number. Quickly and succintly I explained what had happened. I told her to make arrangements to take the canvases somewhere else. Somewhere safe.

"I know just the place." She sounded a little breathless.

"Oh? Where?"

"Sotheby's."

"But you can't . . ."

"They know me. They'll take 'em in."

But that hadn't been the reason for my protest. Such a distinguished firm of auctioneers, with more than adequate security, could quite well protect the canvases. The trouble was, she was rushing me. I still wanted my proof, even if she didn't, and I wasn't keen on the way she was confining the options. Before I knew it, they'd be putting them under the hammer. She seemed to sense my reason for hesitation, and laughed.

"Oh, don't worry. They won't even look at them. It'll just be a batch of canvases, miscellaneous."

"If you say so. But if I've got to go there and see this Coombe character again, I might be able to get some more information."

"I don't like you going at all."

"But you'll agree I've got no option."

I could almost hear her grimace. "I suppose not, though what you hope to achieve I can't imagine."

To tell you the truth, I wasn't sure myself. But somewhere in the back of my mind was a feeling of outrage that he should have abducted my wife and used her to apply pressure on me. To be sure, my opinion of her was not at its highest, but she was still my wife. And Aleric? I wasn't sure about him, my long-implanted opinion of him controlling my thinking even now. But the outrage still applied. Certainly, I couldn't turn up with the canvases, as demanded; I'd now virtually put them out of reach. All I could hope was that I could talk my way through and out of it. One thing was certain though—I had to go.

"I'll play it by ear," I said, adopting a false confidence.

On this inconclusive note, we hung up. I spent a little time printing another copy of the photo that'd been torn up, and left. I managed to close and lock the front door before Detective Sergeant Dolan tapped me on the shoulder.

"Lucky I caught you," he said amiably.

I couldn't agree to that, so I grunted. "I'm in a hurry."

"I'll walk you to your car."

But what he had to say took longer than that, and we finished it sitting inside my hired red Fiesta.

"There's news?" I asked.

"You're not going to like it."

"Say it, damn you."

"Touchy, aren't we! All right. Grace Fielding has committed suicide. She left no note, so we don't know why. But we can guess."

"It all got on top of her," I decided emptily.

I knew why, didn't even have to think about it. My taking of the paintings had indeed been a last straw. All those years of wasted life, and the reward for them had been pared away, culminating in my grand effort in clearing the loft. Perhaps she had realized they were of value, and I had them, and it was all going to be too much strain to wrest them from me. Despair had overcome her, and she'd taken her own life.

"How?" I demanded.

We had reached the car, and I had to lean on the roof.

"Apparently she'd climbed into the loft for something or other . . ."

Looking for crosses on the crates perhaps, I thought, but I said nothing.

". . . and she seems to have found a length of rope up there and tied it to one of the beams—damn it, Hine, d'you want me to describe it? She jumped through the trapdoor hole. Her feet were tapping against the loft ladder."

I got into the car, hoping I wouldn't be sick inside it. I'd badgered her to that end. Don't tell me otherwise.

"What took you to the house?"

"The forensic evidence. The dust and the specks of brown paint."

"You mentioned them."

He slid on to the seat beside me, having been talking through the open door. "Funny thing, the paint didn't match up, the stuff from the pin-ball machine against the flecks in your grandmother's—"

"I know what you mean." I was fumbling with my pipe, but the tobacco wouldn't find the bowl.

"And what she expected to find in the loft I can't imagine. Certainly not canvases."

He had his chatty mood going again, smooth and gentle, but with the persistence of a road drill.

"I couldn't say," I mumbled.

"A pity she didn't wait for my news," he observed.

"For God's sake!" The pipe wouldn't draw. I stared at it in disgust and groped for my brain. "What did you mean by 'apparently'? Apparently she climbed into the loft, you said. Seems to have found some rope. You sounded doubtful."

I felt him shrug. "Just that it's strange. At her age, it'd be an effort even getting up there. And she had sleeping tablets available."

"She normally took them?"

"Your grandmother did."

"Simpler," I agreed. "It would've been."

"More pleasant, perhaps," he decided. "Less unpleasant, say." He touched my arm. "You get my point?"

"I get it."

Nevertheless he insisted on enlarging on it. "I can see you're blaming yourself. Oh yes you are. You got those paintings out of the house pretty smartly, because you knew she would object. You knew it would upset her. You knew there was going to be a protest, probably legal, as to the ownership . . . and, incidentally, where are they? And what're you doing with them? I hope it's nothing to do with disposing of them, because that'd make it look as though you knew she was going to commit suicide. Which would be ridiculous, of course. The sad thing about it—and I'm sure you'll appreciate this—is that she was in a fairly strong position regarding the ownership. It was beginning to look as though your grandmother was dead before Grace Fielding arrived back home, so that the paintings would be considered as part of the inheritance. I wonder whether she'd have taken her own life if she'd realized that. And she would have realized it, if I'd got there in time with the forensic evidence."

He said all that in a steady, ruminative voice, as though he was merely musing to himself out loud. I might not have been there. But he knew very well that every carefully considered word was like a hammer blow at my conscience. There was nothing I could say.

He slid out of the car, swung the door, but caught it before the latch got it, drawing it open again.

"For your information, she seems to have died intestate, so I doubt there'll be any dispute about your ownership of the canvases. Unless further evidence comes to light." He nodded. "Of course."

"I . . ." But he'd slammed the door.

Cocking his hat on the side of his head, he strolled away, rolling slightly. I sat there. It was a long while before I found I could start the car and drive away with any confidence.

Heading towards the M5 and Somerset, I had to try to convince myself I had an adequate reason for going there.

10

It was nearly three in the afternoon when I came within hitting distance of my objective. For several miles I'd been fighting those tight curves and the steep rises and falls, and it was quite abruptly that I came out on to the moors above Renfrew Coombe, with the turn-off to the village a mile ahead.

The hedges had disappeared as though trimmed by giant shears. Each side now was a low bank or gorse, and there was no difficulty in turning off on to the green-brown carpet and stopping to consult my map. I wanted to be absolutely certain of my location and my possible escape roads. There was a likelihood that I'd need them, as I hadn't Margaret's driving ability to rely on if I found myself in trouble. I got out of the car to pin-point the village.

It was somewhere below me in a cleft between the round-topped hills, which marched away in all directions. This high above sea level, they were all capped brown with gorse, not yet green, and since it was early June, they were possibly not going to be able to achieve it. In the valleys, as though they'd tumbled from the peaks, were folds of green trees, too far below for me to identify them, but a solid, bright green, so probably deciduous. They fell down the lower slopes like a tossed green duvet in a ditch, and it seemed that no habitation could exist beneath their tight mass. Yet my map confirmed it. Renfrew Coombe was below me—or, rather, below a point half a mile farther on.

I drove that half-mile, and there found a bare, red-earth, pull-in space, into which I nosed the car gently because the fall in front of me was steep. I got out and had another look. The brown slope fell below me at an angle of thirty degrees, directly into the cleft of the valley. Now I could see slate roofs and sun-caught thatches beyond the belt of trees. The map indicated a distance of less than a mile. As the crow flies, the saying goes, but from there he'd be falling.

I backed out and drove on, downhill now, steep and winding, and again abruptly between high hedges and then between trees, massed each side and meeting above me, the sun pattern on the tarmac dazzling. Then there was the bridge and the village. I hadn't before noticed how constricted the cottages were, with the hill slopes so tight behind them and the rock-strewn brook facing them across their meagre street.

My approach was noted and relayed. When I rounded the final bend and turned into Renfrew Coombe's courtyard, the front door was already open, and the goon stood waiting.

"Mr. Mace is expecting you," he said, almost bowing. It was an honour, he implied, for me to be invited beyond the door.

Paul Mace was standing at the rear of the echoing hall, but this time the other side of the stairway. There was no friendliness in his eyes as he gestured towards me in a peremptory manner. Then he reached back to open the door.

It was a sun room, in that the roof above it had been removed and glass substituted. Everywhere was glass, and the room looked even larger than it was because some of the glass was mirrored. Green tangles of growth had been encouraged to climb the walls and to hang from the glass ceiling. Potted exotic plants crowded from all sides. The humidity was high, and the temperature controlled at about a hundred degrees. From the branches of a tree that might eventually bear bananas, two marmoset monkeys gibbered at me, peering suspiciously at a stranger.

"They're outside," said Mace, his voice tense with distaste. "Outside" was a place of which he did not approve.

There was a tall door consisting of a single sheet of plate glass, and beyond it a wide spread of terrace. It was slabbed with imported granite and sported a balustrade and half a dozen Greek statues, which could well have been stolen there and shipped clandestinely. Beyond it, down a wide sweep of ten shallow steps, was a lawn.

To achieve a flat, smooth lawn it must have been necessary to chop into the hillside. On this lawn they were playing croquet, my wife and Renfrew Coombe.

Surely I hadn't been mistaken when I'd thought his chair to be orthopaedic. Certainly, from his bulk, I'd assumed he was incapable of standing on his own two feet. Yet here he was, massive even against a backfall of huge oaks, planting those great feet firmly and smacking a ball vigorously, though inaccurately. Evelyn was laughing. She must have been winning, because losing was never, for her, a source of joy. But Coombe was enjoying it. He could, after all, afford to lose a game here and there when nothing rested on victory. My impression was that he was being gallant and deferring to her lack of experience. Evelyn was as close to simpering at his jovial attentiveness as I've ever seen her.

He need not have deferred. Evelyn could take on anything and succeed. All she would need was a sight of the rules, and as long as there was a sufficient number of "provided thats" and "notwithstandings," she'd have them tamed at once. Her cold and analytical mind would then compute the angles and impacts required, and before you'd know it, she'd have you retrieving your ball from the shrubbery.

In this instance there was no shrubbery, just a steep drop into a million or so trees, so that when Coombe watched his ball disappearing over the edge, he raised his meaty shoulders, jutted his flabby lower lip, and growled heartily, "You win. You're too good for me."

"Who could be good enough for you, Renfrew?" she asked, taking his arm, hanging on it like a poor, weak feminine person and allowing him to pilot her up the steps.

Ye gods! I thought. They fancy each other! I'm on a winner here. Though, of course, she was probably only undermining him with her charm. But why didn't I ever encounter that charm? She was flushed with it, short of breath from it. It was years since she'd been short of breath with me.

"Mr. Hine is here, sir," said Mace, his voice cold.

"D'you think I hadn't noticed! Clear off, Paul, there's talking to be done."

"I think I should be here to advise—"

Talking down to his employer from the terrace was one thing, but now Coombe had reached the top step. He loomed over his slim and effete curator. "You'll do as I say," Coombe told him, and after one glare at me Mace turned and walked away round the corner of the house.

As my eyes followed him, I noticed that one of the statues was attended by my son, Aleric, leaning against it. This all seemed strange to me, that he and his mother should, supposedly, be under restraint, when Aleric could simply have disappeared into the trees. Though perhaps there were invisible guards, or Aleric had been told there were and didn't care to risk it. He flipped a hand in my direction.

"Hi, Pa! How's it going?"

"Fair, son, fair."

"We will sit," Coombe announced, "and talk in a civilized manner." He led the way to one of the round, white-painted metal tables and drew back a chair for Evelyn. She smiled up at him as he slid it behind her. Then he sat himself, and the chair sighed. I sat opposite to them. It was a triangle of three people, yet my impression was that I was opposite them. Strange.

Coombe pressed a bell-push. "We'll have tea. I import my own Darjeeling. You'll like it."

Evelyn smiled. She liked it all, it seemed. "My short stay is coming to an end." There was sadness in her voice.

Aleric realized that he was not invited to join us, but he strolled across and found a closer statue to embrace.

Coombe said, "You'll stay to tea, then your husband can drive you home, with a standing invitation—"

"I've got a feeling she won't be going home," I cut in.

"What!" Evelyn slapped her palm on the table surface.

"Though it seems to me you won't be displeased," I assured her.

"What the hell d'you mean?"

I looked away from her furious eyes. "I haven't brought the canvases."

I expected Coombe to be choleric in his anger, but all he did was rumble a little in his chest, then smile in a most unpleasant manner.

"That was very stupid of you," he said gravely.

"They're no longer available."

"You're lying, of course."

I shrugged. Something that Detective Sergeant Dolan had said came to my assistance. "They're kind of involved in a bequest. The Chancery Court, or something like that, is holding them until there's an inquest—"

"For God's sake, Tony!" Evelyn cried. "Don't talk legal gibberish to me. You're just trying to be clever. I can't *afford* to get stuck here . . ."

"Now, now, Evelyn," said Coombe heavily. " 'Afford' is an irrelevant word. You stay as my guest. Until I say otherwise," he added smoothly to me. But his eyes were twin buttons of black ice.

"I can't stay here!" Aleric suddenly put in agitatedly. "My bike! What about my bike?"

We ignored him.

"There's something you ought to understand," I said quietly.

"Understand!" Evelyn reached across and snapped her fingers beneath my nose. I'd never seen that done before. "All I understand is that you're being deliberately awkward."

"I was talking to Mr. Coombe. He's the one who needs to understand."

"Let him speak, my dear." Coombe clasped her other hand in his, where it disappeared. "But first, here's something for *you* to understand, Mr. Tony Hine. Your wife has told me she's shortly to be free of you and will have more spare time. I'm in need of legal advice, and she's agreed to represent me in all legal matters. Various departments and institutions are trying to tie me down with their complications, and she will help me. So when you speak to me, you're also speaking to her. Have I put that correctly, Evelyn?"

This was a different man from the one I'd met before, who'd seemed to rely on Paul Mace too readily and whose only weapon had been a hectoring voice. He was smooth and he was patient. He was deadly. I couldn't decide who was fooling whom, as clearly a man such as Coombe would already be surrounded by a barrier of legal finagling, and a woman as astute as Evelyn must have realized that.

"The point is, Tony," she said, "that when I divorce you, I shall claim the paintings as part of my settlement. I've explained this to

Renfrew, and you—from the way you're speaking—must realize your legal hold on them isn't very strong."

Did I tell you how clever she is? This wasn't a warning to me, it was a stall she was presenting to Coombe. He had only to be patient, and all would fall into his ample lap. Heavens, I thought, she had realized I was in danger from him, and she'd thought this up as a protection—for me! I looked down at the table, not wishing her to read the expression in my eyes.

"The snag is," I explained, looking up, "that the paintings I've got *could* be worthless, in which case we're sitting here arguing about nothing."

At this point a manservant appeared along the terrace with a large tray, which he placed in front of Coombe, who glanced at him.

"You took your time," he snapped.

"I'm sorry, sir. The cream had gone off."

"Well, watch it, sport." He turned, smiling at Evelyn. "Will you be mother?"

It was revolting.

"Could well be worthless," I persisted. "There were two sets painted at the same time, by two different people, one of them Frederick Ashe. It's almost impossible to tell one from the other. All I've had to go on is the one painting I've always owned, which is duplicated in the new set of eighty-one. Is anybody listening to me?"

Evelyn was concentrating on the teapot, Coombe on the strawberries and cream and on her.

"Listening," Coombe growled.

"It's impossible to say," I went on, raising my voice a little, "at this stage, with any certainty, if my own painting is a Frederick Ashe, and its mate in the other batch what you might call a copy. And this'd apply to the rest of the eighty-one, of course. The odds are that this new lot are copies and worthless."

Coombe flicked his eyes at me from beneath the thick bushes of hair that he called his eyebrows. "You would naturally say that. I'd prefer my own opinion."

"Which is just why I came. To help you form it."

"But you haven't brought the paintings, so how would you do that? Milk second for me, my dear."

I took out my envelope of prints and slapped it down on the table.

"With those. There's one photo of each of the eighty-one, as you know. One of them is duplicated by my own, and I've got reason to believe your six are too."

"My *what?*"

At last I had his attention, full frontal, all that unlovely face in one concentrated scowl. It had not been intentional. I knew I'd made a mistake before the words were out, and possibly a fatal one.

"What did you say?" he asked heavily.

"He said 'your six,' " Evelyn offered, smiling at me sweetly.

He glanced at her warningly, then said to me, "Why do you say that?"

Honesty, I decided, would deflect his fury from me. "On my previous visit here, when I got this batch of prints back, six of them were out of order, all together at the bottom."

His face was now red. He mouthed something and jabbed at his button. "Paul!" he snarled.

"And as," I went on, trying to keep the momentum going, "the only four you hadn't got have been stolen from their rightful owners and as you're the sort of man who can arrange such things, I naturally assumed you were simply putting together a full set of Frederick Ashe."

Paul appeared in the doorway of the sun room.

"Though, of course," I qualified, "it now seems they might not be Frederick Ashe paintings at all. If," I explained placidly, "the new set of eighty-one are."

Coombe crooked a finger, then pointed it at the terrace surface in front of himself. Paul advanced and stood there. His face was pale and pinched, so he must have sensed the atmosphere.

"You," said Coombe, "are a bloody fool."

"Sir?"

"You gave him back his photographs with six of them—yes, I said six—in one set at the bottom."

"Oh." Paul stared into the distant trees, where a corpse might lie hidden for years.

"So now," growled Coombe, "while you're still around, you'd better arrange for another room for another guest, because we daren't let him go. And get a team out to collect those canvases."

"No point," I said quickly.

"What?" His head swivelled at me with the ponderous weight of a swing bridge.

"They're no longer at that address. Gone to Christie's, I think. Or was it Sotheby's?"

Coombe bounced to his feet, the metal chair clattering away, and vented his fury on Paul. "By God, I'll break you for this! Every soddin' bone. They'll put 'em up for auction, and I'll have to bid for every bleeding one, you ape, you stupid, worthless moron."

Paul's immaculate suit seemed to become a size too big for him. Perspiration dripped down his nose. "I'll . . . I'll . . ."

"You'll what? Raid Sotheby's?"

"Or Christie's," I suggested helpfully. "Or both."

Paul made a whimpering sound.

"There's an easy solution to it," I offered. The head again swung towards me, shoulders following. "You pay me their estimated value, a million and a half, and I give you a deed of assignment. Evelyn can draft it—"

"Damn you, I'll see you dead first."

Evelyn put in, "Aren't we becoming too agitated over this? Simply because Tony *believes* you have all six of the Frederick Ashe paintings, it isn't necessarily a danger to you."

Coombe stared at her blankly. "He can go to the police. D'you think I can risk them coming here—with a search warrant! Talk sense, Evelyn, or keep your mouth shut."

She flushed. I could've told him he'd made a mistake. But she persisted. "What can he take to the police? A story of photos in a certain order? A theory he's worked out from that? They'd laugh him right out into the street."

Slowly, as though hypnotized by her calmly confident court voice, Coombe relaxed. Recognizing this, Paul Mace scuttled for the fallen chair and brought it back for his boss's superior backside, and after a moment Coombe sat. But his face was still dark with anger.

"After all," she added, patting his hand, "he hasn't actually seen them."

Once again, I realized, she had come to my assistance. All sorts of unpleasantness had been lining up for me, and one thing I could not afford at that time was to be restrained forcibly. But in assisting me, she had, though she couldn't have understood the importance to me, successfully put a stopper on my plans to get a sight of the actual paintings in Coombe's gallery.

In fact, this was really why I'd gone there. It would have been possible to make my position clear on the phone, but I'd had the hope that I'd be able to con my way into his gallery and check his paintings against my prints, in this way confirming—or otherwise—that his were painted from the same relative viewpoint as my own original one. This, Evelyn had effectively blocked. All the same, there's no harm in trying.

"I don't know what all the fuss is about," I complained. "What if I did see your Frederick Ashe collection? There'd be nothing to gain, me dashing off to tell the police. All I'm interested in is finding out whether my eighty-one are Frederich Ashes or not."

All that did for me was to provoke one of Coombe's better glares. "You must be soft in your head. How'd you come to marry such a gormless idiot, Evelyn?"

"I can't remember. Certainly I can't imagine, now, any good reason."

"Well . . ." I said. "I'll be off then, seeing that nobody loves me around here. All I'll say is that I'm not parting with any of my canvases until I know the truth about them."

If Coombe was a gambler, that might get him, I thought. The risk of allowing me to see his six, against the possibility of making a profitable deal. It didn't work. He backed only certs.

"You'll stay where you are until I've decided what to do with you."

He snapped his fingers, having seen Evelyn use it so effectively, and he and Paul Mace moved to one side. I stared at Evelyn, and she at me.

"It's all gone to your head, hasn't it!" she said sadly. "A week ago, and you were the same old plodding Tony I've always known; now you've got this obsession—"

"The truth, that's all I want."

"The truth is that you've got me in this mess, and you don't seem to care if I stay in it."

I tried to work out how much I cared. "Mess? You seem to be enjoying yourself."

She smiled thinly. "I might get some well-paid work out of it."

"Don't be a fool!" I rapped back sharply, annoyed that she, so perceptive normally, could be so easily taken in.

"Don't you call me—"

"He's leading you on. The easiest way to hold you here, that's what it is."

She was shaking her head. "Oh no, Tony. If you think we're not watched every minute, you're mistaken. And overhead. What we're saying now, somebody, somewhere, is listening to."

It was a warning. I shrugged and got to my feet, ostensibly with impatience but in reality to check her statement. Nobody was in earshot, nobody was watching us. I thought she was mistaken, but Aleric caught my eye and inclined his head fractionally.

I had been paying too little attention to our son, taking him for granted. But he'd heard what we'd been discussing, and knew what was going on. He heaved his weight from the statue and strolled over to me.

"You sure are in trouble," he said, making it sound admirable.

"So it seems."

"Then give him the paintings. It's no skin—"

"You heard. They could be very valuable."

"Oh . . . sure . . ." He shrugged lazily and looked sly.

"And incidentally, I now know that both your great grandparents were artists."

"You don't say! What do I do, roll about in ecstasy?"

I should have become used to his casual dismissal of everything not in his restricted sphere of experience, such as discos and fringe drugs and motorbikes.

I grimaced at him. "Please yourself. I thought you might be encouraged to think you could one day amount to something."

"A painter? Garn!"

"Have you seen my grandfather's paintings in the gallery here? Or possibly my grandmother's, of course."

"Haven't troubled."

"They wouldn't let you near them anyway."

He winked. Nodded. What he said contradicted the visual evidence. "Never get in there."

I began to wonder whether he had something to say, to tell me, and had been laying a smokescreen. I spoke resignedly. "I suppose you're right."

"When y' get outa here, Pa, can you go and see about the bike?" he asked.

"Bike? Yours?" It seemed totally irrelevant in its context.

"I left it in the drive. It'll get nicked."

"Yes. Well certainly, I'll do that. But will they let me go?"

"Sure to. With you here, they're gettin' nowhere. Put it in the garage for me, Pop, will ya?"

"It'll be locked. Your mother always locks it."

"The key's on the hook in the kitchen."

"But she's changed the house locks. How do I get in?"

His gaze slid sideways, as though he was considering this obstacle. "You know the big glass door that faces the trees. At the back."

That was what his eyes had rested on, the plate-glass door. We had no such door at home, and no trees at the back. "I know what you mean." I knew now why he'd introduced his motorbike into the conversation.

"It'll be open," he said with confidence. "You'll see. Just try it."

I thought about that. What was he suggesting? I tested him out. "The neighbours'll think I'm a burglar."

"Not if you come through the trees."

"After dark? I'd get lost."

"You gotta torch, ain't ya?"

"It'd be seen."

"Odd flashes. You could do it. Three flashes—who'd see them?"

"If somebody did . . ."

"Not in the trees. Nobody'd be there, would they?"

"And all this for a blasted motorbike!"

"It's important, ain't it?"

"Depends on the point of view," I told him.

He grinned. This was the first time he'd treated me to a genuine grin of pleasure instead of a leer. "Yeah, an' I reckon it's time you thought of mine, if I can think of yours."

He'd certainly given some thought to mine. I gave him a considering look. For too long he'd been an unpleasant object in the background of my existence, best ignored. I hadn't tried to probe his depths, because his creed demanded a shallow outlook on life. It appeared I might have been negligent. He had known exactly what was going on, had weighed up the pros and cons, and had made a decision. He was on my side, even though there were facets of my character he could not know about. He hadn't wasted his time here. He had learned the details of the set-up and worked out how the security might be probed. Not bad for a nineteen-year-old layabout.

"You'll be getting bored here," I suggested.

"Yeah. You got to do somethin' though, ain't ya!"

I agreed and would have pursued our growing intimacy if Coombe's voice hadn't summoned me. "Hey you!"

I turned. A decision had been reached. I went over to him. "You called?" Evelyn turned, frowning, on her chair.

"We're going to let you go," Coombe said, "because there's only you can get those paintings back from Christie's or wherever. Which you will do. Understand me? You will bring them here and let Paul have a look. He says he can tell if they're Frederick Ashe paintings or not."

"He's seen the photographs. They ought to tell him."

Paul Mace stood, his lips thin, his eyes brooding. "Not good enough. I need to touch the paint. Feel the texture. It's an instinct. Not many of us have got it."

But the strain showed around his jaw and in the tic at the corner of one eye. He was laying everything—possibly even his life—on his ability to make a decision. Or perhaps he was counting on the fact that there was nobody around there who could dispute it.

I tossed in a challenge. "And what if I don't come back?" What could Coombe threaten now? Evelyn's life? Aleric's? I wondered whether he was sufficiently certain of my reactions if he did.

Coombe didn't fall into the trap. "Then we come after you. You can't hide away for ever. I might be able to save Evelyn the trouble of divorcing you, and she'd get them as an inheritance."

Nicely put, I thought admiringly. Nothing messy, such as breaking a few limbs. I would simply die. I turned to Evelyn. "I'd like my painting to go to Aleric, Evelyn, please."

She stared at me, her lips moving but no sound emerging. I was aware that my remark had been based on something close to hysteria, and Aleric understood.

"Say, Pop, that's great!" he burst out.

Then, to my surprise, Evelyn picked it up. She had never before ventured into light farce. "I always told you that you ought to make a will," she said.

"Oh, get him out of here!" Coombe growled angrily, and this Paul Mace did with obvious relief.

The goon stood at the open front door, watching me drive away. Aleric stood behind him, his thumb up.

11

I drove to Lynmouth to get something to eat and to buy a torch. It was early in the holiday season, and not crowded. Time needed wasting, so I spent it watching the river flowing out of the gorge, and strolling round the harbour. But when the sun was low on the horizon my nerves pressed me into action. There was no point in trying to reach Coombe's residence until late, when all but a minority of the guards would be asleep, but I had no idea how long it would take me to navigate that valley from the road above. I was relying on one basic fact: all I had to do was keep heading downhill until I reached the trees that Aleric had mentioned.

I realize now that I must have been in a state of euphoria, brought about by the sheer magnitude of Coombe's villainy. To a person like me, he was so far from anyone I had ever before met I was quite unable to contemplate him as a serious obstacle. I was nervous, but strangely confident. I was over-simplifying.

It was dark on the Coombe valley, with only a glow on the horizon beyond the hills facing me, when I edged the nose of the Fiesta into the parking place I'd used before. This in itself was tricky, as I dared not use lights, and yet it had to be far enough in from the roadway not to attract attention from any night travellers. I did it by moving a few inches, getting out to check, moving another foot, until I had the front wheels right against the fall-off. I checked that I had with me all I needed.

The bulk of my photographic equipment I'd left locked away at my photo-lab, and I'd brought along only my little Ricoh. A photographer would feel naked without at least one camera. This Ricoh is useful in that it slips away into my anorak pocket with scarcely a bulge, is light, and yet is a true 35mm job with a good lens, though with rather a wide angle. I'd also pocketed my smallest flashgun, with an extension lead. As I've explained, for what I had in mind—and I'd had it in mind all the while—a flashgun used on the hot-shoe of the camera is unsuitable. I was fully equipped, my torch in my other pocket.

All I needed was the resolution to start. Standing there, watching the valley becoming more and more black, I suddenly doubted my ability to carry it through. I was wearing jeans and my cleated walking shoes, so was well equipped in that way, but I was not a hill climber, and it was damned frighteningly dark. There was only one thing to do, which was to get going. So I did.

What became evident at once was that the gorse—I assumed it to be gorse—which formed a solid carpet six inches thick, not only dragged at my feet but was slippy. I found also that it was difficult not to break into a run, the slope being so steep. The fact that I could no longer see the ground meant that each foot went down blind, and they never seemed to reach a firm surface when I expected them to. The jarring began to shake my spine. It was more effort to steady my progress than if I'd been climbing.

I was only a hundred yards down from the road when a new difficulty arose. During daylight I had looked down, and the impression had been of a smooth surface all the way to the trees. I discovered that this was not so when my right foot, descending in its turn, met nothing. I pitched face forward, and it was only reflex action that enabled me to twist and land on my left shoulder. The drop had been only a foot, but the shock was great. I tried to prevent myself from rolling, scrambling with my feet and digging my fingers in, and finished up spread-eagled, glued to the slope with my face in the gorse.

Gingerly I rolled over until I was sitting. It seemed I was stuck there. How could I continue if the surface was ridged and pitted, with rock breaking through the ground and the soil washed away beneath it? I had no way of being certain that all the sudden drops were of no more than a foot. The only thing I could think to do was to use my torch.

But this slope, I recalled, had risen almost from Renfrew Coombe's terrace, though slightly to one side. A light could not possibly go unobserved. I looked back. The peak was outlined dimly above me against the lighter sky. I could just detect the nose of the car. The temptation was to begin the climb back to it; this was something very much removed from my normal experience.

I decided to give it a little more time. There was a possibility of being able to back down, feeling with my feet and with my hands trailing in the gorse. This I managed for perhaps a hundred feet, by which time my face was becoming scratched and my hands sore. I tried it seated, edging down in tentative jerks. Nobody's behind can stand this for long.

Wearily and desperately I got to my feet, realizing I'd have to take it blind and risk the falls. Or go back. No, to hell with that! Aleric would laugh me out of existence.

I put one foot in front of the other, repeated it, and was moving again, and discovered I could reach down with each foot with more confidence if I progressed with bent knees, in a semi-crouch. My knees began to ache. Pain shot up behind my thighs. But I progressed.

Twice more I fell, the second time over a drop of three feet, which flung me in a tangle of pain on to a bed of small rocks. Something moved beside me. More skilful feet than mine clattered away. Hill sheep. I groaned and rolled over, staggering to my feet before blissful inertia could capture me.

Now, I realized, I was in sight of the house. I could see lights at windows too extensive to belong to any of the cottages. I had time, all the time I needed, I told myself. I stepped forward.

Some minutes passed without incident, and I realized I was now walking on a different surface. Lower down, grass took over from the gorse. Hence the sheep, I suppose. Also, when I could raise my head from the concentration of stepping forward, I noticed I could no longer see the lights of the house. For a moment this baffled me. Then I realized I had reached the tree line.

Now that my eyes had become accustomed to the darkness, I could see the dimly separated shapes of the trees. In assistance, the moon was rising. Not a full moon, but better than nothing. I wondered whether, once inside the tree cover, I might dare to use my torch.

I had covered no more than ten feet when I discovered I would have to.

My confident assumption that I needed only to move downhill now became a bad joke. Bruised and scratched and aching, I wanted only to sit down, lean back against the bole of a tree, and wait for daylight. But this I dared not do.

I moved onwards, but the trees, their roots massed, had tossed up the ground unevenly. There was no down or up. It was all up and down combined. Besides which, I realized, I did not require to move down-hill, because there I'd find the village. The big house should now be somewhere on my right. And possibly higher, I supposed.

Two hours later, still stumbling over root boles, I was using my torch unsparingly, in despair and frustration. In this way, having fumbled up a rise, I suddenly noticed I was walking on smooth and level grass. It could be nothing else but the croquet lawn, the only level surface for miles. I cut the torch, promptly hooked my foot in a croquet hoop, and fell flat on my face.

When I lifted my head, I saw first a reflection of the moon in glass, then, below it, three winks of light. A torch. I groped for mine and flicked back. Three times. Aleric was there.

I clambered to my feet. Clear now of trees, I discovered that the moonlight revealed the lawn and its hoops. I loped across, up on to the terrace, and directly to the plate-glass window. It opened. Aleric, a monkey on his shoulder, was standing there. I could have thrown my arms around him, but the monkey might well have objected.

The reason I could see him was because a faint green light filtered through the shrubbery around us. An all-night light, apparently. It showed me a chair. I collapsed into it.

"Never again," I said, keeping my head down. "Never."

"I thought you'd got lost."

"I did."

"We'll have to move. He might come round soon."

"He? Round?"

He prodded a shape on the floor with his foot. "The guard. They leave one sitting in here all night. He's doped."

I had forgotten guards, burglar alarms, all the protection Coombe would have laid on. "The alarms!"

"Difficult to rig a glass door without the wires showing," Aleric said briskly. "I found 'em in two minutes."

I was in no mood to move, but my breathing was steadying. "The guards? Doped, you say?"

"Pa, I ain't been lounging around doing nothin'. Been making myself useful. Made out I was hopin' to be taken on the strength. They let me take round the coffee. I put barbiturates in, for tonight's guards."

"Where the devil—"

"I carry 'em. Bennies and barbies."

"You're on drugs?" I was appalled.

"Nar! But you gotta carry 'em. Uppers and downers at least. Or you're out, Pop, way outa the stream."

"Ye gods."

"We gotta move. You all right? You're not as young . . ."

"I'm fine. Lead on."

He took me up a rear staircase and confidently along corridors. We dared show no lights, but the moon through the high windows helped. Aleric had certainly looked around. He knew every step of the way.

We rounded a corner. I stopped. At the end of a short corridor a light shone. There was a door and beside it a chair, on which a man was seated.

"It's fine," Aleric told me in a confident voice. "He's asleep."

As he was. A mug stood beside him on the floor, and his chin was down on his chest. Beside him was a tall container of sand, used as an ashtray. The door showed a steel surface, with a single round keyhole, beneath it a knob not intended to turn.

"That does it," I said. "It's a high-security lock."

"Dad, now ask yourself. You've got this door with a special key. Are you going to carry it around with you? No . . . you'd be scared of losing it. Maybe there's a duplicate, but you'd be afraid of losing that one too. So where do you keep it, handy for the door but concealed? Think, Pop."

I thought, but nothing came. He was running his fingers through the sand in the ashtray bin. They came up holding a peculiar cylindrical key with tiny protrusions around it. He had to turn it in the lock three times, then there was a faint click, and the door swung open.

It was an impenetrable black inside. Aleric eased the door shut, pocketing the key, and pressed a switch. He raised his voice to normal.

"Reckon we're all right in here, Pa. Nobody'll hear. But make it quick, huh?"

Now that we were no longer whispering, I could confirm what I thought I'd already detected. Gone was the slurred and lazy clipping of words, the vernacular of whatever was in at that time. Inside this bulky slouch, who was my son, there was a normal human being. A competent one too, judging by the calm and matter-of-fact way he'd managed this.

"Two minutes," I promised. "Once I've found what I want."

I said that because the gallery was confusing. What I'd expected was a large room with paintings hung on the walls, but that would have been too conventional for Renfrew Coombe. What he had was alcoves and corners and bits tucked away. He also had mirrors. For such a physically unattractive man, he had a strange addiction to mirrors, though perhaps he considered himself an example of *homo perfectus.* Whatever the reason, mirrors he had, and the impression was that he owned twice as many paintings as in fact he did.

"Cor strike!" said Aleric, wandering around.

It was no use asking for his help, because it was I who knew what the Frederick Ashe paintings looked like. Fervently I hoped Coombe had them hung in one batch. I walked through quickly, my eyes darting around. There was a sense of urgency.

The collection appeared to be all Impressionist and later. Some I wouldn't have given hanging space to. The mirrors confused me. Walking round what I took to be a corner, I banged straight into one.

Aleric said, "Did they get paid for this? I could do better myself."

"They usually starved," I told him absently. "The people who make the money are the investors. I'm looking for . . . ah, there they are!"

They were, as I'd hoped, all in one line, six of them with the familiar overlapped A and F, and conveniently at my eye level. There were some more paintings farther along and also in an alcove behind my shoulder, but I hadn't time for browsing. Behind me was a wall of mirrors, in which the six were reflected reversed, and there were more mirrors each side of them.

"Come and give me a hand," I said. "I'll want you to hold the flashgun. Point it at each painting from a spot just above my left shoulder. Get it?"

"Gotcha."

I plugged in the lead, switched on the flashgun, and told him to watch for the little red light after each flash and tell me when it came on. "That's when it's charged."

I got a near-full frame at a metre, and they were all the same size: twenty by sixteen. It meant I'd have to use f16 and guess distance, as there was no rangefinder or focusing screen on the little Ricoh. But I'm used to guessing distance. I steadied the picture in the viewfinder and the flash operated.

"Little red light," he said. I took the next.

The charging time was around ten seconds. We had all six on film in three minutes, so I did them again for luck. Or rather, I started to do them again, but at the second one Aleric suddenly said, "Psst!" just as I was taking the shot.

My nerves were so stretched that I jerked the camera as the flash operated. "What the hell!"

"I thought I heard something. Just a sec." He ran softly back to the door.

Ten seconds later he was back. "He's stirring. Making groaning noises."

"I'll finish this."

"Then hurry it, Pop, for Chrissake."

I completed the second run, dismantled the flash, and slid it all into my anorak pocket. "Let's go."

We stood at the door and extinguished the lights, then opened it and peered out. The guard was grumbling to himself and trying to lift his head. We slipped out and stood beside him as Aleric quietly closed the door, giving the key its three turns, then buried it in the sand again.

We ran, our feet silent because they barely had time to brush the floor. Aleric's memory was immaculate. We burst into the sun room and stopped. This guard was groaning too, but the light was too dim for us to see him.

"Quick!" said Aleric.

"You're coming—"

"No, Pa. No. The guards'll keep quiet, even if they guess they were doped, and nobody'll spot the alarm wire's cut. Unless somebody breaks in, I'm in the clear."

"I don't like it."

"Y' know I've gotta stay with Ma, now don'tcher! Get going, Dad, please."

He had the plate-glass door open. Behind him, a shadow stirred in the dimness. A voice said, "You're going nowhere."

The green light was ghastly, but as he stepped forward, I could see enough to recognize Paul Mace. There was also sufficient light to catch a glint of green from something he held in his hand. Surely, I thought in panic, that couldn't be a pistol!

Aleric took a step towards him. Somewhere beyond Mace, from the direction of the great hall, I heard shouts.

"Go, Dad, go!" Aleric shouted.

I hesitated. The pistol moved, and one of the monkeys jumped down on to Mace's shoulders. Aleric seemed to skip, his foot shot out and upwards, and Mace cried out. The pistol cracked sharply, but more weakly than I would have expected, and a pane of glass shattered in the roof, shards tinkling down.

"Get going!" howled Aleric as the door burst open behind Mace and white light thrust in blindingly. He seized the doubled Mace and hurled him at the group pushing their way in. "I'll hold 'em!"

I turned and ran across the terrace and the croquet lawn, my torch on because of the hoops, and plunged over the end, rolling down the slope and into the trees.

I stood, caught a glimpse of the moon just before I entered the trees, and placed it in my mind. Upwards, I had to move upwards, but I would find the slope only if I could hold a line. There was now no chance of using the torch. I prodded it into my pocket and stumbled forward, hands outstretched and with every nerve standing out, reaching for clues as to my surroundings.

There were shouts behind me. I heard a booming voice call, "Spread out. Don't let him get away." Distantly somebody was screaming. I had to assume it was Evelyn.

They could use torches. I saw them flickering through the trees behind and to the sides. Only the boles of the trees hid me from their sight, but my guardian angel, the moon, was hidden behind the massed young growth of the leaves above.

From time to time I stopped, panting, my legs shaking. By moving my head sideways I could catch an occasional glimpse of the moon. It indicated that I could not simply run away from the torches. They were trying to head me off and must have realized where I wanted to go. But I had to be true to the moon. A clear night—was it a clear night? I wondered—and I might survive. If it clouded over, I was done. They would be carrying not only torches but weapons.

The flickering torches now arced widely to my right. My intention was to head left, but in that direction they were closer together. I forced myself to trust the moon, caught one more weak gleam from it, and staggered in the indicated direction. Surely, I prayed, I would feel the slope under my feet soon. But the torches were closer. They were even closing in on me from both sides.

Branches lashed my face and I tasted blood on my lips. I tripped constantly, recovering from reaction, my reasoning now becoming confused. There were no more shouts. The torches seemed to be one blurred mass. For a moment I paused, my shoulders against the bole of what must have been an oak, my head back, gulping in great lungfuls of air. A man walked through a brake of shrubs thirty feet from me. I backed round the tree, my heart leaping about wildly.

In the split-second I'd seen him, his torch searching, I had noticed we were on opposite sides of a clearing. He entered it, and stood, his head turning, cocked, listening. Somebody shouted, "Over here." He moved to his left, which was towards me. I flattened myself against the tree. He walked past me, his torch and his attention focused ahead. Then he broke into a trot and crashed his way towards the shout.

I walked out into the clearing, because there was a chance that here the trees didn't meet overhead. It was a correct guess. I got a good look at the moon just before the clouds rolled in front of it, and forced myself to stand and calculate. Keep it over my right shoulder, I told myself, and go straight ahead. The difficulty was that most of the torchlight was in that direction. But it was, I realized, slightly at a higher level.

They had reached the slope.

Resolutely I marched towards the higher area. Then I had an idea. I drew out my torch, switched it on, and left it on. I yelled, "Over on the right!"

And then I ran. I had become one of the hunters. They thinned. What had seemed a solid mass of torches, closer to was scattered. I came to within a hundred yards of the nearest, then I put off my torch and found I could steer my way between the individual lights. But it was slower going. I tripped more often, now more from exhaustion than obstructions. Yet I detected a rise, and in the direction I wanted to go. As the searchers progressed farther, they had of necessity to spread out. I slipped and scrambled between two of them, and the trees were thinning ahead of me, the slope was becoming more pronounced, and abruptly, before I could calculate the danger, I was standing on the steepening grass slope.

But now I was in the open, and it needed only the swept beam of a torch to locate me. On that slope, I would be an open target. Yet the moon, my saviour, had now hidden itself away behind a heavy bank of cloud; otherwise I would have been as visible as a fly crawling up a wall.

I moved stealthily, my eyes turning over each shoulder in turn to see whether torches were coming my way. Occasionally light shone through the upper bank of trees, but nobody shone in my direction. Perhaps they thought they'd cut me off. I moved stealthily because I could barely move at all. I ached all over and my chest seemed to be congested. All I knew was that I was progressing slowly upwards, my arms and hands doing most of the work now. Eventually I would come out on the upper road, hopefully in sight of the car.

But hopefully would not do, I realized. If I could not see my car and didn't dare to use the torch, I would not know in which direction to walk. In one of the clefts the sheep had been using, I sat and thought about it. Far below me in the valley there was now no visible activity. The possibility was that I'd been spotted, and they were advancing silently, no longer needing their torches. Definitely, I would need to head directly to the Fiesta. I stood and stared upwards. The moon, behind cloud that was now breaking up, supplied a slightly lighter backdrop for the brow of the hill. It seemed smooth, apart from one indefinite shape, far over to one side. I had to risk it, and struck out on a diagonal line, rising and to my right.

Almost at once I was in gorse again. At least it meant I was progressing. But the drag on my ankles, which had been only a nuisance on my way down, now became close to disabling. I moved slower and slower. The shape on the horizon grew in size and took on form. It was the protruding nose of the car. I was now below it, with only two hundred yards to go. Straight up. My brain, robbed of oxygen, was swimming. I wanted to lie down. With my eyes firmly on the objective, the Fiesta, I felt it was growing larger than my progress justified. I stopped, waiting for my eyes to clear.

I discovered that although I was now still, the nose and bonnet were still growing larger. It was moving towards the edge, towards me. Then the front wheels were over the edge, and the acceleration became definite. The nose tilted, and it was charging down the hillside towards me.

There was nowhere I could go. I was directly in its path. For one moment I forced myself to my feet, and stood swaying, and watched it coming, rustling the undergrowth, bucking and bouncing. Then I threw myself face down in the gorse. Yet still I could not cover my face with my arms. It fascinated me, robbed me of all conscious thought. There was nothing but terror. The bouncing increased. The nose dug in. Its tail came up, and the whole car left the surface, plunged down again, nose in, pitched right over, and the terrible crashing sound preceded it as the hammered metal protested. It bounced on its roof. A door flew clear. It leapt again, and it was on me. I wrapped my arms round my head. I think I was screaming, but I could not have been heard.

The bonnet pitched in only ten feet from me. The din flattened me. It arced over my back, and as it landed behind me, a wheel flew off, and the tailgate hung by one hinge.

I twisted and watched it down into the darkness of the trees, the noise decreasing as its bulk grew less and as it distanced itself from me, until eventually it was taken by the trees and cushioned by them into silence.

There was no fire, because the ignition wasn't switched on.

I lay, panting and gasping, lay for a full five minutes before I could force myself to my feet again. It didn't matter any more at what point I reached the road. All that I could think about was that I'd have quite a difficulty with my report to the hire firm. I couldn't get my mind from that, but when I did, I realized that, inside the car, there had been my set of prints of the eighty-one loft pictures.

I crawled up to the road and began to plod along it.

12

I reached the coast road about equidistant between Lynmouth and Porlock just as dawn was breaking. On the bank of tight moor grass at the verge I sat and tried to recover. There were decisions to be made and plans to be drafted, but my brain would not operate. There was a light emptiness to me. I saw clearly, but could not associate image with fact.

When I'd recovered my breathing, I lit my pipe. Usually it helps. This time it made my head swim. Which way should I go? That was the first decision to be made. Porlock was nearer home, if there was a home to go to, but in Lynmouth or Lynton I'd be more likely to find a car-hire firm. But would my credit card now carry any financial weight? Unlikely. Worry about that later. Worry right now about the fact that Coombe's men might come looking for me, and there was nowhere I could hide.

On this open road, high above the Bristol Channel, there was very little cover. The naked moors spread in both directions, steeply downhill inland. I could only sit and wait, and pray that they were still searching for my body on the slope. They would assume I had reached the Fiesta and stupidly engaged forward gear instead of reverse. Or would they? Perhaps not. The car hadn't pushed itself over the edge. No, they would probably know I had not reached the car. In any event, they would need to locate what was left of me.

Pleased now that my brain was working again, I tested out my other senses. Sight and hearing. Out there in the open, engine and tyre sounds give prior warning. I heard a vehicle coming from the Porlock direction and prepared to scramble over the meagre bank behind me. But the multiple curves revealed it long before the driver could have seen me. It was a white van.

I stood in the roadway, too weary to raise a thumb. He stopped. It was a newspaper delivery van. The driver got out.

"You all right?" he asked. "You look terrible."

"Car accident," I told him. "Can you get me into Lynton? I'm about done."

"Sure. Hop in. Hey, you look awful!"

Hopping in was out of the question. He helped me up. It was seven o'clock. He asked no questions, but I thought he deserved answers.

"The inland roads are tricky at night. I missed a turn."

"Nasty. You ought to see a doctor."

"It's only," I lied, "superficial."

He took me into Lynmouth, where I sat in the cab as he dumped his parcels of papers. Emptily, I watched him. He drove me up to Lynton, told me where I might hire a car, and dropped me outside an early-opening café. It was just after eight. I thanked him.

"I can't tell you how much—"

"Do the same for me some day," he said cheerfully. "Drive the next one more careful like."

I used the men's room while they prepared me a pot of tea and bacon and eggs and chips. Truly, I did look terrible, my face black and my hair tangled, bits of gorse stuck in it and all over me, my clothes torn and slimy with green, the left knee out of my jeans. I was bang in fashion. I tidied up as best I could, but it would be a fool who'd let me step inside a hire car.

I ate voraciously and downed two pots of tea. The pipe tasted better, and my head remained where it was. I was ready for the next step.

The car-hire firm was dubious, but computers never lie, and this one confirmed that I had a balance sufficient to pay for a week's hire plus insurance, in advance. Perhaps, this early in the morning, the computer was half asleep. I drove away in a blue Metro with a fault in its silencer.

Three and a half hours later it was making a loud noise in my home town. I had decided on a sequence of procedure. First, park, walk round to my photo-lab, and observe it to check whether it was under surveillance. I saw nothing suspicious. Second, nip inside quickly and dial Margaret's number. This I did. It rang and rang, but there was no reply. That meant two things: one, that I had nowhere to go, which in turn probably meant I'd have to sleep rough at the lab—dangerous because Coombe probably knew by then where it was located—and two, that I had comparison shots of Coombe's six paintings, and nothing to compare them with, my set of eighty-one prints having been in the crashed Fiesta. So . . . I would have to run off another set of the whole eighty-one, or at least go through them until I found six that would match.

But before that, I wanted to try out a slim chance. Aleric had been very subtle in suggesting how I could enter the Coombe residence, so there was a possibility he'd been doubly subtle. Wanting to try this out, I deferred the photographic work and was just pulling shut the outside door when I heard the phone ring.

I dashed back inside and grabbed it up. It was Margaret.

"Tony! Where have you *been?*"

"You know damn well. Coombe's place."

She didn't ask if I'd had any luck. "Listen, I've got some news. Not good, I'm afraid." Her voice was brisk and businesslike.

"I'm getting used to that. Say on."

"I didn't take them to Sotheby's—"

"Didn't?"

"I took them to a friend of mine, who's got a gallery just off Bond Street."

"I thought we agreed—"

"And he's a bit of an expert on the Impressionists."

"I thought you were the expert."

A slight tang entered her voice. "There are others."

"You said you didn't want a second opinion," I insisted, a little needled that I'd expended so much effort in obtaining evidence, and all it had needed, for Margaret, was a consultation with a friend. Also a little needled, to tell you the truth, that there was a friend she could run to.

"I can change my mind, can't I?" she demanded.

"If you wish."

"And he says—"

"An opinion."

"He says he's certain the eighty-one are not Frederick Ashe works."

I allowed a pause to build up, trying to recover my equanimity.

"Tony?"

"Margaret, I've got what we were after. Six photographs of Coombe's set of Frederick Ashe. We can check the business of the right or left viewpoints and at least—"

"You got *in* there? Inside the gallery?"

"Yes. How else would I do it?"

"And that's all you've got to say?"

I didn't understand what she meant. "What else is there? Oh yes, I've got those six, but I've lost the set of photos of the eighty-one. So . . . to save reprinting the lot, wouldn't it be better to check against the original canvases?"

There was a slight pause, then, "Do you think that would be a good idea, Tony?"

"It's the best one."

"Correct me if I'm wrong, but you'll surely have had difficulty getting into Coombe's gallery."

"You could say that."

"And he's not pleased about it?"

"Not noticeably."

"Then he'll certainly have you followed, and it wouldn't be sensible to lead him straight to the canvases."

"I can't see that it matters if you're so certain they're not by Frederick Ashe."

There was a snap to her voice. "Don't be foolish. They're worth *something . . .*"

"I was forgetting—school of Frederick Ashe. But what happened to the idea of selling them as genuine?"

"Now I ask you! One expert, that's all I've needed to go to, and he said, without a doubt, they're not by Frederick Ashe."

"Quick on it, wasn't he? It took you days . . ."

She didn't like that, but I wasn't in any mood to be considerate of her sensibilities. "Never mind that. It was only a suggestion."

"Yes," I said. "I see," I said. Which I did. It had been a suggestion that made it unnecessary for me to visit Coombe. But I'd done that, and I was safe. Nothing much had happened. "Coombe would still be in the market for them," I suggested.

"He wouldn't expect to pay, he'd just take them," she said acidly. "By force, or whatever was necessary."

"Not if we can prove to him they're not Frederick Ashes."

"Why are you being so difficult, Tony?" she asked, her voice wearily conversational. "Everything I say is sensible, yet you do nothing but quibble."

"Shall we say I'm tired."

"Then do get some rest."

I was about to ask where, but she didn't give me the chance. "I'll be in touch. Goodbye for now."

And she'd gone before I had time to ask for her number, her new address, anything. It was highly unsatisfactory, and it seemed clear to me that her interest had died the moment she decided the loft set were not by Frederick Ashe. Her interest in the paintings and in me.

So now I was committed to another stint in the darkroom, to produce prints of the six Coombe shots and of the six they matched from the loft set. If I could locate them.

But first . . . I locked up and went to the meter where I'd left the Metro. Then I drove home. By home, I mean Evelyn's house. I drove a roundabout route, using every device I'd ever read about to avoid being followed. Only when I was certain I was not did I head for Evelyn's.

I was playing a hunch on the way Aleric had said it. His meaning could have been taken at face value, that the house might be entered from the rear. This I had to test. I needed somewhere to lay my head.

The motorbike was in the drive, as Aleric had said. I went round the back and tried the French window into the living-room. She might well have changed the lock on this too—though I had never carried a key to this door—but as Aleric had claimed, it opened. The relief was immense.

I had brought along all my photographic equipment, the workplace being too vulnerable in my opinion. With this unloaded from the car I felt better. After that, the first thing was to get a bath and a change of clothing . . . and decide the next move.

The advantage of this place as a refuge from Coombe was that Evelyn would have told him she'd changed the locks, so it was the last place he would look for me. I would have to be careful not to show a light after dark though.

Evelyn's departure had been so abrupt that she'd left the immersion heater switched on, controlled by its thermostat. So I enjoyed a glorious, blissful soak and felt much better for it. And, unfortunately, sleepier. I'd lost a night's sleep, and the reaction was setting in. I went down and raided the deep-freeze and cooked a decent meal, by which time the thought of bed was so overwhelming that I went out into the garden hoping that fresh air would revive me. It had begun to rain. That helped. I turned my face up to it.

It was three o'clock in the afternoon. I decided I had wasted too much time; Coombe's men could be closing in from all directions. I went up to Aleric's room and searched the drawers in which he kept items I cared not to linger over, and found the spare keys to his bike. I discovered his leathers inside his wardrobe, and his boots and his crash-hat. A disguise. The bike would also be difficult to catch, if I needed to use evasion. And if I could handle it.

I unloaded the film cassette from the Ricoh and put it in my pocket, shut the French window, and clumped round to the front.

It had been nigh on twenty years since I'd ridden a motorcycle, and that had been a 250cc BSA. They had changed. This thing was a 1000cc V-twin, with a self-starter, and shaft-drive instead of a chain, and a whole set of control buttons on the handlebar console that I had to sort out. It was heavy, but Aleric and I are about the same size, so the seat height seemed correct and, straddling it, my feet were firmly on the ground, and the weight disappeared.

I did what I thought to be the right things, and the engine thrummed into life with a strangely off-beat pulse. I engaged gear. We were moving.

It felt like a dream and at once became part of me. All the old joy of being on a bike flowed back. The acceleration took my breath away.

One advantage of a motorcycle is that you can park it almost anywhere. I left it in the yard behind a nearby pub and walked to my photo-lab, looking, I hoped, very unlike Tony Hine. I went in as though I were a customer, though having to use the key spoiled the image a little. Once inside the darkroom, I shut the door and wasted no time. Off with the leathers and into the tank with the film, and while that was proceeding, in the intervals between solution changes, I got out the loft canvas negatives and tried to discover, from memory, which ones might duplicate the six from the Coombe gallery. I was working in white light at this stage, but the task was near impossible.

I now had the negatives cut into lengths of six frames, but for colour it's not just the black and white that're reversed but also the colours. This makes identification difficult. I put aside the strips that had possibles on them, completed development of the film, and hung it in the drier. You can't rush these things. I needed prints of the Coombe gallery six before I could proceed further.

In practice there were twelve Coombe gallery prints, as I'd run through them twice, thirteen if you counted the spoiled one. This one I printed too, before I realized what I was doing, which is an indication of how tired I was. My concentration was failing. What with having to work now in near darkness and the lack of ventilation, my head was throbbing and my eyes were going out of focus. Aware that I was rushing it, not taking my usual care on colour control and density, I knew it was probably a botched job.

While they dried and glazed, I opened the door for a breath of air, but I didn't dare to go as far as the street.

With the six best Coombe shots to go on, I managed to find the matching six from my original photos of the loft set. That there were six that matched was an advance in my knowledge of the situation. It confirmed there had been two sets of eighty-one canvases, and that out of one of the sets, only seven now existed.

I slapped the six loft-set prints into the glazer, switched everything off, and lit my pipe. Home—Evelyn's—and bed, that was the next thing on the programme. Comparison of the prints could wait until later.

At first I thought it was my pipe burning rank. It couldn't have been the enlarger overheating, because I'd turned it off. It was burning I could smell. Of necessity, a darkroom door has to have a good seal, but, now in white light again, I saw that smoke was seeping from under and round the edges of the door.

Without thinking—I was long past considered thought—I opened the door . . . and slammed it again. Outside there, where my tiny reception office had been, there was an inferno.

Coughing already from the smoke, sweat streaking my face, I switched off the glazer, peeled off the prints, and crammed the day's production into my pocket. I scrambled, falling twice as I raised one leg from the floor, into Aleric's leathers, put on his crash hat and his driving gloves, and slammed down the visor.

Then I opened the door again. Even through the helmet I could hear the roar, through the visor I could feel the heat striking my face, and already there was the smell of scorching riding kit, before it became overwhelmed by the choking smoke. There was no other way but through it. I tried to avoid the counter, not simply because it was beneath it that the fire seemed to be centred. Coughing and choking, and rapidly losing my sense of direction, I fumbled towards where the door should have been. There was no light from the windows, which were blocked by my show prints. I came up against something solid. Flames ran up it, so that the chance was that it was a wooden door. Heat pounded at my back, and I thought the overtrousers were alight. I grabbed for the latch and turned it, and pulled. The door would not move. The heat—or something else—had wedged it.

Inside the helmet there were whimpering noises. I could see nothing, as the smoke was in there with me. Forcing myself to the effort, and against the pain of retreating towards the centre of the heat, I took a pace backwards and kicked out with my foot, flat on. Futile, of course. The door opened inwards. Then, with fury and panic, and a reserve of energy I didn't realize I possessed, I attacked the door, kick after kick. Pain racked me. My breath caught, and I drew in fumes and smoke. I kicked, and a panel gave way. Air rushed in. I fell to my knees, reaching for it.

It was what the fire had craved. Air. It sucked it in, and what had been a roar became an explosion, and with my face to the gap, aware that through it was coming not just air but the wail of sirens, I lost consciousness as a rush of water flung me on to my back.

13

It is a good way to catch up on your sleep, but not one I would necessarily recommend. I regained consciousness in a hospital bed, remained awake long enough to discover I was suffering from an intake of smoke and fumes, and minor burns, then apparently slept for twelve hours under an oxygen tent. With a little help from a needle, no doubt.

A policewoman was waiting for me. She smiled. The nurse smiled. My face was stiff and sore, so I didn't. A doctor came and checked various things and said I was doing fine, and that the policewoman had a few things to ask, if I was up to it. I had things to ask, myself, but kept them for later.

It appeared that the fire had not been accidental. How could it have been, with nothing to start it in the reception area? Did I know anything that would help the police? Had I enemies? Had I offended anyone recently?

Oh yes, and yes, and yes, but I wasn't going to say so. Would they send a local bobby to arrest Renfrew Coombe? I could just see it. I shook my head only once, a painful process, and afterwards said, "No, sorry," to every question.

The young policewoman, who had started off all smiles, finished with annoyance on her face and a shake of the head that indicated sadness for me. Enemies who projected such fear in their victims were just the ones the police wanted to interview.

I was alone. Carefully I assessed the damage. The visor had not given full protection. The lower half of my face was stiff and burned even now. My calves were bound and padded. I touched one, and even through the padding it hurt. My hands were fine. My chest ached when I breathed in too heavily.

That was me, physically.

But the damage in other directions would not mend. My darkroom, its equipment, my records, and my filed negatives had all been destroyed. That meant a large hole in my career. It meant I no longer had the negatives for the eighty-one loft paintings. Nor—until I became active—could I reach the paintings themselves. Not even then, come to think about it, because I could not reach Margaret, and the only phone number she had for me was now extinct.

All I did have, and these had been placed on the bedside cabinet for me, was the set of photos from the Coombe gallery and the matching six from the loft set. As there was nothing else to do, I sorted them out.

I chose the best six of the Coombe shots and laid them beside the other six. It was easy to tell which were which, because Coombe's paintings had been framed, and this was just visible round the edges of the prints.

The position was at once clear. The Coombe paintings, as in the case of my own original one, were in all cases right-biased viewpoints. It told me that mine and his had been painted by the same hand. No, I'll qualify that. The odds were that they had been painted by the same hand. And if Margaret's search of the archives had to be considered valid, Maurice Bellarmé's painting of Frederick Ashe indicated that he was left-handed. Therefore, he had most likely sat to the right of grandma Angelina.

So I'd progressed not one iota. It simply confirmed what Margaret had said, that the eighty-one loft paintings had been done by my grandmother, and the other seven by Ashe.

I put them aside and lay a long while trying to recapture my enthusiasm for the truth. Proof positive. That was what it had been. A kind of crusade. But even the crusaders must have felt a similar lack of enthusiasm when they'd had the stuffing knocked out of them.

It was true that the paintings had already brought about too many deaths. Arthur Hine, Angelina, Grace Fielding. But all I was doing was keeping the legend alive by trying to add my own to the list.

Then I thought of Coombe, the acquisitive Renfrew Coombe, who had obtained most of his paintings by theft and was prepared to maintain their inviolability by murder. He could not afford even the suggestion that his might not be genuine Frederick Ashes, and needed to destroy anything that might be used as a questionable comparison.

I thought of Coombe, and a spark of anger grew. He was unassailable. His arrogant assumption of this was infuriating. He assumed now that I would surrender the paintings gladly. Gladly? I'd see him in hell first. Angelina Footes or Frederick Ashes—to me that no longer seemed relevant. Their possible value was an issue not even under consideration. They were mine, to do with as I pleased, and if what I did in some way annoyed him, then I would do it twice, and twice as vigorously.

Thus musing, I fell asleep, and awoke to find Detective Sergeant Dolan at my bedside.

"They're going to let you out tomorrow," he said, shaking my hand as though I was an old friend long lost. "We'll probably be taking you in."

"Protective custody?"

He didn't think that was amusing. "That'd be a good idea. It'd save a lot of argument."

"Who's arguing?"

He drew up a chair, and took the question seriously. "The Super and the Chief Inspector. The CI's all for charging you on what we've got." He stared at my flaming chin. "You feeling all right?"

"I was. Keep to the subject. Charging me with what?"

"Murder. Your grandmother and Grace Fielding."

He made the whole issue sound a bore. If there was something better he could be doing, he would be elsewhere.

"And you?" I asked. "What do you think, Sergeant?"

"Me?" He shrugged. "Who cares what I think?"

"I care."

"Well, if you must know—and if it matters—I think you're a prize idiot, but not a murderer."

"And nobody cares what you think?"

"Not at the office, where it counts."

I wondered where that left me and wondered why he'd come. He seemed to read my mind. "But that isn't why I'm here," he admitted.

I waited, but he wasn't ready, seemed *distrait* and wouldn't meet my eyes.

"Why am I a prize idiot?" I asked quietly.

In answer, he reached over to the bedside cabinet and picked up the pack of photographs I'd been looking at. He flipped through them as though they were holiday snaps.

"The car in your drive," he said, "was hired in Lynton. That's a hundred and eighty miles from here. A long way to go in order to hire a car, especially when you already had one on hire."

"I lost it."

It seemed not to register. "But Lynton is only a few miles from the home of Renfrew Coombe, art collector and well-known anonymous philanthropist, one of our richest and dirtiest crooks, and the owner of two Frederick Ashe paintings." He jutted his lower lip and tilted his head, examining the quality of my photography. "At least two," he amended.

"I've heard about him."

He flapped the pack of prints against his other palm. "And it's Frederick Ashe paintings you're interested in, Mr. Hine, if I'm not mistaken, so the coincidence gets a bit too much to take."

"That's an opinion, Sergeant."

"Mine." He nodded. "Not the Super's, nor the DI's. Just an idea of mine." He switched topics again. "Had a word with the doc on the way in. He says there're contusions and bruises and scratches not involved with any fire. This is your body we're talking about."

"It sounded like me."

"So I've got this feeling you've been tangling with our friend Coombe. Just a feeling. And that's not healthy, Mr. Hine. We want him. Want him badly. Got anything to say to that?"

He tossed the prints on my lap, or rather, on to the bedcover beneath which my lap was hidden. It was a challenge or an offer or a veiled suggestion of alliance.

"You've looked at these?" I took them up and shuffled them, then put together the six from the Coombe gallery, the ones showing the canvases as being framed.

"Before I woke you up."

"Right. Then I'll tell you something. Not officially, Sergeant. Just you and me."

He inclined his head. Maybe it was agreement.

I went on, "The paintings from the loft, which my grandmother gave me, may or may not be Frederick Ashe works. Equally, the ones Coombe has may or may not be what he thinks they are—Frederick Ashes. Both can't be right. So I took photographs of the ones Coombe has. These six here, the ones showing the frames. Six, you'll notice, when he's only supposed to have two. The other four have been stolen from national galleries in the past two years. Are you interested?"

He looked up at me, directly in the eyes, probably for the first time since he'd entered my tiny personal ward. "Possibly." But his eyes were bright.

"So . . . in his gallery are four paintings that can be shown to have been stolen. Right?"

He picked up the theme. "So I take those photographs to the Super, and we get a search warrant. For years we've been looking for evidence that'll get us inside there."

I shoved them under my pillow, just before his questing hand reached them. "No you don't. I've lost the negatives in that fire, so these are all I've got."

"I'll have them officially copied for you."

"I'm not letting 'em out of my hands."

"I'll legally impound them as evidence if I have to."

I grinned at him. "Evidence of what? That they're photographs, and that means nothing. You'd need an affidavit from me, to provide the proof that I took six specific photos of paintings on the wall of his gallery. No, let me say it, Sergeant. You see, whereas you could subpoena me to a trial and get me on oath, there's nothing you can do to force me into swearing an affidavit. My wife's a lawyer, Sergeant. Details rub off over the years."

His brows had lowered. He wasn't certain what to say. "Why're you telling me this, if it isn't going to do me any good?"

"I owe him, Sergeant. He tried to kill me, or have me killed. I owe him a lot. But I need you to give me time. It's a *quid,* as my wife would say, *pro quo.* Give me time, and you'll have your evidence. But there's another point. I now think that I can prove to him that the paintings he has are not by Frederick Ashe." I tried to sound convincing about this, though all the evidence was to the contrary.

"I don't like the sound of this. You're thinking in terms of revenge."

"Partly. But you see the snag? No? Well, if I succeed and convince him that he owns copies, what good would it do you to get a search warrant? He'd claim they weren't stolen, because they're only copies. And it'd be Coombe, and not the prosecution, who would subpoena me as a witness, to prove in court that they're copies. You get my point?"

He levered himself to his feet. His face was flushed and his voice was a growl. "Oh, I get it, don't you worry. You offer with one hand and take away with the other! You're too bloody clever by half, strikes me."

"I need time." I was fighting for it.

"You might get all you need in gaol."

"Now don't be niggly."

He took a deep breath. "You're talking about going to see him again?"

I nodded solemnly.

"Then it'll be protective custody for you."

"If I'm around when you come next time."

He leered. "You'd better be." He paused with his hand on the door. "And now, you see, you've put it right out of my mind. Why I came. Your son—Aleric is it?—he's been found in a ditch in Wiltshire."

"Wh-wh-*what?"*

"Oh, he's alive. A broken bone here and there, cuts and bruises, but he'll live. They've got him in Salisbury General, if that's any use to you." He shook his head. "I shouldn't be telling you this," he admitted sadly. "It'll only make you more stubborn."

He had the door open and again paused. "Oh . . . something else. There's a lady to see you."

At last he got through it.

They had propped me against a couple of pillows, an awkward position, neither sitting nor recumbent. I tried to lever myself upright, wished I could have been shaved—though my chin was too sore—worried about my hair. Evelyn? Evelyn! How could it be?

Margaret put her head round the door tentatively, eased the rest of herself inside, then stood with her palms to her face. She seemed nervous of what she would find.

"Tonee-ee-ee! What have you been doing to yourself?"

"I was done to. Come in and sit down. It's good to see you, but how—"

"Are you all right? Let me look at you."

Grinning, I discovered, hurt. I was not pleased to be stared at like a barbecued burger. She sat. I thought she was about to burst into tears.

Of course, I had to remember that her life was spent in the company of painters usually long dead and thus out of harm's way.

"How did you manage to trace me here?"

"I kept getting the unobtainable signal when I phoned your photo place, so in the end I drove down . . . and found the place gutted. Oh, Tony! I stood and looked at it, and my mind . . . I just couldn't make it work." Her face puckered. I had never seen her so attractive. "Then in the end I went round to the police, and they told me you were here."

She drew in her lower lip, nodding, seeming nervous about my possible response.

"Out tomorrow," I assured her. "It's not as bad as it looks."

"You *say* that . . ."

"Because it's so."

"I *told* you not to go there again. That man's powerful and vicious . . . and . . . you *did* go there?"

"I've told you this. I didn't just visit, I managed to get into his gallery."

"I didn't believe you. You actually got in?"

"I did. But not with his permission."

"Oh, you idiot. You've annoyed him."

"Hopefully. And worried him too, with a bit of luck."

"You got a look round? You'd be the first one—"

"There wasn't time for that. It was a matter of a quick in and out."

"Oh."

She looked past me, her eyes vague. I couldn't decide whether she was disappointed or not. Possibly, and because she hadn't been with me. There was a pause. We had been batting question and answer at each other and seemed to have run out of both.

At last, "But it's not serious?" she tried again, eyeing me discouragingly.

"As long as you don't kiss me."

Her little laugh was awkward. She got to her feet and leaned over me and kissed me gently on the lips. It was like an electric shock.

"There," she said, nodding as though she'd given me an injection, and she sat down again. "Now tell me all about it."

I told her the whole thing. Not for one moment did her eyes leave my face. She searched it. There was agony in her eyes. It took a long while, and when it was over, she produced a tiny handkerchief and wiped the palms of her hands.

"You're lucky to be alive," she said huskily.

"Yes."

"And you didn't— No, I can see you wouldn't have had time to look round his gallery." It was the third time she'd asked that.

"Why should I trouble? I headed straight for the six so-called Frederick Ashes."

"But there must be some wonderful things . . . I'd give anything . . ."

"I'm sure you would."

"But you got your photos?"

"I've got 'em and they're printed. It's about all I've rescued from the fire, those and the six new prints they match from the loft set." I gestured. "There they are," I said negligently.

If she'd noticed them before, there had been no sign. Now her hand pounced on them. I gave her a couple of minutes.

"The ones showing frames—"

"I realized," she said sharply.

"You'll notice his are painted from the right-biased viewpoint. The same as my original one."

"I'd noticed that."

"Which seems to show—"

"What's this one?" she demanded.

She was waving the spoiled shot, me having jumped when Aleric said, "Psst!"

"I jumped just as the shutter went off. Better throw it away."

She looked at me doubtfully, glanced at the waste-basket, and asked me, "Have you *looked* at it?"

I took it from her. There wasn't much to see. It was just a shot involving two paintings, angled in the frame of the photo and painfully out of focus.

"I'd got the focus at a metre or so," I explained. "These paintings were farther away, so they're blurred. The flash has got a bounce response, so the exposure's all right . . . ah, I see what you mean. You told me the two by Maurice Bellarmé were in a private collection. His private collection. Well, well!"

"Those are Bellarmé's paintings, the ones he called *Frederick Ashe* and *Angel.* I recognized them."

I peered closer. "You can see that Frederick Ashe is painting. And look at this—you can just detect that he's got the brush in his left hand."

She sighed. "So it's most likely he'd sit to the right of her when they worked together. So yours and Coombe's, painted from the right-viewpoint position, must almost certainly be Ashe's, and the loft set are therefore your grandmother's."

"Angel," I said softly.

"As Bellarmé called her."

I handed it back to her. "So you were right first time. One look at mine, and you said Frederick Ashe. And you must be right about the loft set." I looked directly at her and tried not to grin. "With a little help from your friend."

She grimaced. "They're not exactly worthless, you know."

"Can you see what she's doing?" I asked, pointing at the print in her hand.

"You're not listening, Tony."

"I can't make it out. She's not painting, is she?"

"Something domestic," she said impatiently. "In those days, women were expected to be motherly and domestic. Will you listen to what I'm saying!"

"Say on."

"The loft set. I can lay on an exhibition—"

"Not yet," I cut in.

"I don't understand."

"I owe Coombe a favour, and I intend to get something out of him. I can't kill him, though I'd like to. But I can squeeze *something* out of him. Money. I'm going to sell him the six canvases that match the six he's already got."

She jerked to her feet. "You're crazy."

"I think not."

"You're not to go near him."

"Not alone, I agree. I'm not going alone. I'll need you with me, Margaret."

"Me?" Her eyes were wild.

"The art expert. To back me up. To help me persuade him that he has to have those six."

"I will do no such thing."

"Then I'll do it alone."

Furiously, she moved to the door, flung herself back, stood over the bed, and almost stamped her foot. "You'd never get out alive!"

"Yes I would. I'd persuade him that he has to have them, but I wouldn't be able to tell him where they are. No—don't tell me. 'The need to know,' they call it in the trade. The secret service trade. What you don't know they can't extract from you with their nail-pullers and things. No, come to think of it, you'd better not be there, because you *do* know. Forget what I said. I'll phone you when I get back—you'd better give me a number to call . . ."

"Damn you, what're you trying to do?"

"Get back at Coombe."

She was almost in tears. "How can I let you go alone?"

"I said forget that bit."

"Forget it! Forget! I'd have it on my conscience."

"I forbid you—"

"Forbid! Who the hell're you to forbid? I go where I like."

"But this you wouldn't like."

"If you insist on going, then I'm going with you. But what you hope to get out of it . . ." She shook her head miserably. "You frighten me, Tony. I don't . . . can't understand you."

To tell you the truth, neither could I, and I was frightening myself. But then, I've always been easy to frighten. Offer me violence, and I would go to pieces. Always have. It's something to do with imagination, I think. I never had any difficulty in imagining the pain about to be inflicted on me. So I would back off. But now— Oh yes, frightened I was, though for some reason I wasn't feeling like backing off. You take so much, experience enough pain, and there comes a time when anger overrides the fear. The anger I was feeling wasn't a transient thing. With every minute it was gaining strength. Mind you, I wasn't any happier about the anger than I was about the fear, but there was an outlet for the anger. The same outlet, hopefully, would also blanket the fear.

"I didn't mean to frighten you," I said gently. "You can walk out of here—I'd never know where to find you—and I wouldn't blame you—"

"I'm staying at the Metropole in town here."

"A bit of a dump, that."

"And I'll be there. When you're ready, Tony."

"You're leaving? We haven't really talked . . ." I meant in any way personal.

"There'll be time. Other times."

"The Metropole," I said. "I'll be in touch."

She kissed her palm and blew me a kiss. I watched the door close behind her and wondered why she'd registered at a hotel when she'd driven from London for no more than an exploratory visit.

Then I realized she had not yet registered. She had noticed the hotel as she drove past and had now deliberately severed her one escape route by deciding to stay there. The thought warmed me.

I gave it ten minutes, then I pressed the buzzer for my nurse and, when she came, asked how I could make a phone call. She went and fetched a trolley complete with pay phone and plugged it in. I called my friend Terry Bascombe, the only other pro photographer in town, by which I mean the only one who did his own processing.

"Tony!" he said. "I heard. Jesus, I'm sorry mate. What can I do for you?"

Good old Terry. "Can I borrow your darkroom for a couple of hours?"

"Any time, old son. What for?"

"I'll need a copying stand—six prints, that's all I want to copy. Six by four—"

"Where are you?"

"In hospital, you idiot."

"Then how can you— Have you got 'em with you?"

"Well, yes."

"I'll come straight there. Get 'em done, and back with you tonight. That do?"

I was silent.

"You know I can do a good job, Tony," he said.

"It's not that. How are you at picture framing?"

"Lousy. I thought you said six prints."

"It's a masking job. Tricky."

"Ah!" he said. "Sounds interesting. I'll be right round."

He hung up. I lay back, relaxed. It would leave me a clear day I hadn't counted on, and could use.

The idea was beginning to clarify.

14

At ten the next morning I limped out of the hospital in shirt and jeans and Aleric's boots, but carrying his leathers in two plastic bags. My legs were painful, my face felt stiff, and I became short of breath very easily. But as long as I didn't break into a run, I was fine.

There was no reason to run, no sign of Dolan's protective custody, no lurking shapes behind the hospital trees. I strolled to the bus stop, collected Aleric's motorbike from behind the pub in town, and rode to Salisbury.

This was quite a long trip, though it gave me plenty of miles in which to become used to the bike. By the time I reached the other hospital, I was pulling and kicking the correct things by instinct. Nothing else on the road had a chance to keep in touch with me.

I took off the leathers again, intending to look respectable on this visit, and not wanting Aleric to see how I'd mistreated his riding kit. They weren't leathers; they were a wax-treated black fabric, which was why they'd burned through around my legs. The holes had provided a cooling draught of air to my burns, and the limp was now much smoother.

He was not in intensive care, but looked as though he ought to be. There were fractures not apparent, but a tent inside the foot of the bed indicated trouble with his legs. He did not at once see me there, so I had time to study the damage to his face. What I could see of it. He was extensively bandaged, but minor damaged such as the purple and black bruises had been left showing. His right eye was almost closed, the left brow swollen. In his right hand, which had a stiff-fingered cast on it, he was gripping a pad of paper, in his left a black felt-tipped pen. Aleric is ambidextrous.

I cleared my throat. He looked up. For a moment his eyes went blank, then he said, "Hi, Pa! They told me you'd had it." Not one to display emotion, my son.

"Not so far wrong, at that."

"Get yerself a chair. Hey, this is great."

I reached a chair over and sat down. He wasn't moving his jaw much. "When did they tell you that—me being dead?"

"Just before they dumped me in the ditch."

I gestured. "What happened?"

"Oh . . . this? Yeh. Well . . . a couple of 'em held me and that ponce Mace worked me over with his gun."

"I see."

We stared at each other. Conversation was difficult. I cleared my throat.

"I suppose you're lucky, on the whole. They tell me there's nothing serious."

"More'n they told me. Feels serious from where I am."

"I bet. What've you got there?"

"What? This?" He turned it round. He'd been sketching on his pad of paper. He seemed ashamed of it. "Gotta do something. The nurse over there got me this. It's her. See the likeness?"

And I did. I grinned at him. A mistake. I winced.

"You ain't too good yourself, Pop," he observed, cocking his head to favour his better eye.

"My continuing existence is not wanted. A bit of a fire, that's all."

"All?"

"I got out of it."

"Sure you did."

"I'll have to buy you a new riding kit. I was wearing it at the time. I've borrowed your bike as well. Hope you don't mind."

"Help yourself. Hey, I'd like to see this. You'll kill yourself."

I raised my fist to give him a friendly punch, then thought better of it. "I was riding motorbikes before you were born."

"A tip, then. Don't accelerate on right-hand bends. It pulls. Something to do with the shaft-drive transmission."

"I'll remember that."

There was another pause. Awkward. Apart from the motorbike, we had little in common.

"I'm gonna do the sister next," he told me at last, gesturing with the pen.

"I don't think they use that word now. It's sexist."

"The boss-lady, then. Don't see her much though. Got nice eyes."

"I hadn't noticed. Look, I'll see you again, Al. I've got to get away now. Things to be prepared, sort of." I put back the chair. "When I see him—any message?"

"See who?"

"Paul Mace."

"You ain't goin' back there!"

"It isn't finished."

"When?"

"Tomorrow."

"Can't you put it off? Give me a couple of days—"

"No, Al. Thanks, but no. I've got to get your mother out of there. I'll give him your best wishes. That do?"

He looked at me without expression, then away. "I can't wait to try colours," he said. "Look out for yourself, Pop."

"I'll do that." I turned abruptly and went out.

As I'd told Aleric, I'd ridden motorcycles before he was born. But that had been more than twenty years earlier, and three hundred and twenty miles in a day was now more than I could take. By the time I reached home, I was hanging on to the bike rather than controlling it, and my head was swimming from concentration. It was an effort to lift my leg over it and lower it on to its stand, and for a moment I had to steady myself before stumbling round to the back to get into the house. It was only when I had coffee filtering and was cutting a cheese sandwich that I remembered I hadn't checked for miles about being followed.

It was eight o'clock by the time I was feeling as though I would live. The skin over my shins felt tight and hot. My pipe tasted fine again and didn't affect my breathing, so I went to the phone in the hall, taking a chair with me. Directory enquiries gave me the number. It rang a long while before it was snatched up. I sensed the snatch from the tone of voice.

"Yes?"

"Paul Mace, please."

"Speaking. Who the hell—"

"It's Tony Hine."

A pause. I heard him take a deep breath. Then, "Where are you?"

"Let's not be funny, eh?"

"We thought you were . . ." He stopped.

"Dead? Yes, I'm sure you did. But I'm not."

"You'll wish you were. Don't waste my time, Hine. We were eating."

"Too bad."

"D'you know where your damned car finished?"

"Tell me."

"On top of the pub."

"Oh dear. Then you'll have found the photos in the glove compartment?"

"I've got 'em. Now get off the bloody line."

I gave it five seconds, but he didn't hang up. I had him. Curiosity, and perhaps fear, held him.

"I was hoping you had those pictures," I told him. In fact, everything depended on it. "You'll realized, of course, that they're photos of the eighty-one I hold."

"Copies!" he snarled.

"So what I want you to do—"

"You *want!*"

"What Coombe wants you to do, though he doesn't know it, is sort out the six that match with the ones in the gallery. You'll remember which those are, I'm sure."

"Will you get on with it!" His voice was cracking with tension. He had sensed my confidence.

"Plenty of time. Don't panic." I paused again. Let him panic. "Now what you're going to do is take those six to the gallery and compare them with the six on the wall."

"Don't you give me orders," he snapped.

"You'll be glad I am. Listen. Are you listening?"

He was breathing hard. He said nothing.

"Are you listening?"

"Yes." It came through like a whiplash.

"Right. I know you believe my lot are only copies of the ones your boss has. So you'll take those six and compare them with the others, then you'll come back and tell me what you've seen."

"I'll see you in hell—"

"No. You'll come back and sit by the phone, and I'll call you back in fifteen minutes. Oh—one thing. I take it that Coombe has relied on you completely when it comes to authenticity? Yes? Then you'll sit by that phone, friend, because you're in for a shock."

I hung up. I was trembling. I felt great.

Then I went and poured another mug of coffee, took my time over it, and exactly seventeen minutes after I'd hung up I dialled the number again.

He gave it one ring, then I heard him breathing. "Well?" I asked.

"I see what you mean."

This was a different Paul Mace, chastened and scared.

"They're painted from different viewpoints—correct?"

"So . . . it seems."

"Two people, sitting side by side, sharing a palette between them on a table. Eighty-one were done like that. Eighty-one pairs, Mace. Seven left of one set. Guess which set your boss's come from!"

"You can't pull that one." He was trying to sound more forceful. "I know a Frederick Ashe when I see one. Ours are his."

"Ha!" I said. "I know another expert who thinks the same. But you're both wrong, and I can prove it. Prove, Mace. Not persuade or argue. Prove. And to back it up, I'm coming there tomorrow, about three, say, to do the proving."

"You're out of my mind."

"No. You'll see. You'll tell Coombe what I've said, and to save any waste of time, you'll tell him to have a certified bank cheque ready, made payable to me to the sum of three hundred thousand pounds—"

"What!"

"Which he'll be willing to part with by the time I've finished, pleased to. For *my* six. Get it?"

More heavy breathing. Then he laughed thinly. "By all means come. Welcome! I wouldn't miss this for the world. Somebody trying to con Renfrew Coombe out of three hundred thousand . . ."

"I'll see you, then."

"You'll see me."

"Good. I didn't want to miss you. Until tomorrow . . ."

I hung up. Though it hurt, I laughed.

Then I went to bed early, resting up for the big day tomorrow, though I didn't sleep well. Mace had been correct. I couldn't actually prove anything. It was, after all, going to be a con trick, and by the very nature of it, I was unable to rehearse the participants. But I had a good idea of their reactions. On these I had to rely.

In the morning, after a large breakfast and a bath, a tentative one because I wasn't sure about the legs, I rang the Metropole. I asked for Margaret Dennis, and they paged her. Knowing the Metropole, I guessed it would be a shout from the desk. In a couple of minutes she came on.

"You were quite correct, Tony," she said.

"About what?"

"It is a crummy place."

"Yes. We'll have to meet up for lunch."

"Not here, I hope."

"No. There's a service station just this side of junction 19 on the motorway . . . the M5."

"Aren't we travelling together?" she cut in.

"I didn't think it'd be a good idea. Assuming you still want to be in on it."

"You know I do. But I've got the Volvo here—"

"I've got a hired Metro, but—"

"And we could talk about it on the way down."

There was a pause. We'd been interrupting each other so briskly that we were both out of breath. In the end, it was I who broke the silence.

"I thought we'd discuss it at the service station. Eat there, then tail each other to Renfrew Coombe's place."

"Well yes, but—"

"No buts. I'm likely to be followed, and I don't want you involved if there's trouble. I'll start early and go by minor roads to shake anybody off. Then we meet at this service place . . ."

"I hate eating on motorways."

"Yes. It's a pity. It ought really to be a good meal if it turns out to be our last."

"You're trying to put me off," she said sharply, not at all amused.

"Exactly. I can manage on my own."

"No you can't, and you know it. You need an expert. You said that."

"All right. Shall we say one-thirty at the service station? There'll still be time to back out."

"I have not the slightest intention of backing out," she said with chill dignity. "Yes, I'll see you there. Goodbye for now."

"Be seeing you. And drive carefully." But I didn't think she heard the last words, the line had gone dead.

I was inside Evelyn's private little office when the doorbell rang. It set my nerves jangling. Nobody was supposed to know I was there. But that was optimistic, based on the theory of being where I was least likely to be. I peeped round Evelyn's curtains, from where I could see the front door. It was Detective Sergeant Dolan. Of course he knew, because of the hired Metro in the drive.

Sighing, I went to open the door.

"It's just the wrong time for protective custody," I said.

He was dangling from his fingers a set of car keys. "You left these in the Metro."

"I lost a set of keys once, and it caused me a hell of a lot of trouble. Now, when I've only got one set, I leave 'em in the car."

"Dangerous."

"Toss 'em on the seat as you leave."

"You're using it?"

"Not today. Keep 'em yourself if you like, then you'll know where I am."

He laughed. "You're a tricky bugger, Hine." I noticed he kept them in his hand. "I came to see you about that affidavit you mentioned."

I didn't turn away, because I didn't want him in the house. "I bet you've promised something to your Super."

He shook his head, the hat wobbling, and tossed the keys in his palm. "Haven't mentioned it. This is just you and me . . . you said."

"So I did. Well, don't worry, you'll get it."

"When?"

"Heavens, Sergeant, don't push. Tomorrow, if I'm still around."

He grinned. "You'd better be. They're getting a warrant, and tomorrow's when we're taking you in."

I stared into his eyes. They didn't flicker. He turned away and walked off cockily, tossing the keys through the Metro's open side window as he passed. It was a gesture that indicated he didn't care where I went, because he would know.

Having watched him drive away, I went back to Evelyn's room. I couldn't find what I wanted in her desk drawers, so had to try her briefcase, which had combination locks on the latches. Before going to the length of breaking it open, I tried an idea. It was a three-digit lock and her birthday was 17 March. I tried that—173—and it worked. It didn't for the other latch, so I tried mine, 23 May—235. It worked. I found this strangely moving.

I was wearing slacks and my old tweed jacket, because it had large inside pockets. From the briefcase I took a sheet of her law stationery, folded it in four, and put it in my left-hand inside pocket. I banged her little rubber stamp on its little inked pad and slipped that into an outside pocket to pick up fluff. In my outside breast pocket I clipped her Sheaffer fountain pen, and I was ready.

I had the photographs waiting on the kitchen table. There were two sets, six in each, one of the photos of Coombe's paintings and one of the matching ones from the loft collection. These I put behind my wallet in the right-hand inside pocket.

The set of six copies which Terry Bascombe had printed for me I carefully placed in my left-hand inside pocket, next to the blank sheet of law stationery.

It was vitally important that I didn't get them mixed up.

I was ready. It was an early start, as I intended to take a meandering cross-country route by way of Bridgnorth and Ludlow, then across to pick up the M50 the other side of Hereford, and thus to the M5 at junction 8.

There was no intention of using the Metro, never had been. I climbed into the motorcycling suit and went out to Aleric's Yamaha.

The road to Bridgnorth is fast. Along it, I saw no sign of being followed, though the rearview mirrors on the handlebars had a tendency to vibrate and shatter the reflection. Once I'd taken the new bypass around Bridgnorth and was on the Ludlow road, the hills and the winding turns gave me little time to watch my tail. I poured the bike into the corners, having mastered the trick of using power to lean me into left-handers, and easing off for right. I was riding as I'd always done, rolling the twistgrip with my right thumb, my fingers resting on the front brake lever.

Ten miles short of Ludlow, I became aware that a car was on my tail. There'd been little traffic, and I wasn't pushing it, merely trying to hold a steady fifty. There had been opportunity to pass me, but it hadn't been taken. I raised the speed. Fifty-five, then sixty. I could still hear it behind me, but the bends were so close together that I had no chance to turn my head. The road surface was poor. The mirror images were jumping all over the place.

As I said, I had heard it, and the implication of this took some time to sink in. Inside a crash-hat, and on a 1000cc twin, you don't expect to hear anything. I heard it because its muffler was blown. I saw it as it edged up at my right elbow, along one of the rare straight stretches. It was my hired Metro. The cheek of it; they were using my own car with the intention of pushing me off the road.

Then it was not an intention but a fact. The car eased across my nose. There is a technique in this. The nearside tail of the car has to touch the bike's front wheel. No more than the tail at sixty, or the car might itself be ditched. It was during the two seconds when the calculation was being made that I had time for evasion. Fingers already on the front brake, ease it on. Not too hard, it would raise the weight off the rear wheel enough for it to break away if I stood on the brake pedal. I felt the speed drop, rolled the throttle off, and the tail of the car skimmed my front wheel by two inches.

It accelerated away, its broken exhaust blatting back in defiance. I could have chased it, but I didn't know who was driving it—hadn't had time for a glance—and pistols might be brought into play. The Metro was doing about seventy when it disappeared around the corner ahead.

I stopped, a little shaken. The ditch that side of the road was deep. I propped the bike up and got off and had a smoke, waiting for my nerves to settle. Clearly, it was optimistic to expect that I'd seen the last of the Metro, unless I could once more get ahead of it. I would have to keep an eye open for side roads, in which it might be lurking.

Getting going again, I settled into a steady fifty, but, as these things usually do, the speed crept up to sixty as I gradually relaxed, seeing nothing of the car. There was always a chance I'd already got in front of it. With this thought in mind I began to put on the pressure, forcing the bike round the bends.

I had expected it to wait down a side, minor road. In practice, the driver had chosen an open farm gate on the right-hand side of the road, catching me by surprise. It was a nice bit of straight. The speedo was on seventy, and suddenly it was pulling out, right across my nose.

The driver was taking a big risk, because over three hundred and fifty pounds of metal moving at my speed would make a nasty hole in the side of a Metro. I was fifty yards short when my reactions snapped in. They were as sharp as they'd ever been. I rolled off the throttle and eased on the front brake, feeling it in, judging by the bite and the dip of the nose. Short, sharp dabs of the footbrake; I didn't dare to allow either tyre to break away. The over-run on the shaft drive applied its torque, and it wanted to turn right. I let it. The Metro had gone a yard too far, assuming I would try to squeeze through under his nose. I aimed for the tail. It moved forward another six inches. I leaned into the right turn until I was opposite the gap, then I rolled back the throttle and gave it the lot, felt the tail kick, and the torque helped me throw the nose round the Metro's tail.

I was right over, my left shoulder dipping. I felt the wind-fluttered sleeve of the suit brush a corner of the tailgate, then I hauled the bike upright, stuck my head down, and fed in the power until I was up to eighty and too near the next corner, scrambled round that, and settled down to put miles under the wheels in as short a time as possible.

I didn't relax until Hereford forced me to, but by that time I was satisfied I'd lost the Metro. I picked up the M50 and drove east, picked up the M5, and settled into the middle lane, heading south.

Because of all this, and in spite of the fact that I'd taken a roundabout route, I was much too early for Margaret. It was barely one o'clock when I rode into the service area. I stripped off the suit and locked it in the panniers, locked Aleric's crash-hat to the bracket, locked the steering—so many damned keys on his ring—then went to have a coffee. Afterwards, I strolled, placidly smoking, around the car park until Margaret's Volvo turned in. By that time I was relaxed and, indeed, more than a little pleased with my performance on the bike.

I opened the door for her. "Had a good journey?"

She stood beside me. "Very easy. And you?"

"No difficulties."

We stood and looked at each other. I grinned, and she threw herself into my arms, her lips at first firm and cool, but then melting. Not, this time, an electric shock but a warm bath of intimacy.

For a moment she held herself away from me, her eyes moist and her hair wild; then she put her head on my shoulder and clutched me close.

"Oh, Tony! Tony! Why did you have to do it like this? Every minute I've been worried."

"And all for nothing," I said softly. "Come and eat. I've seen the menu. You'll love it."

There comes a time when a tone of levity needs to be introduced.

15

Worried or not, ten minutes in the Ladies restored her to normal, and in practice she had been a few minutes late arriving, the worry not bringing about any panic speeding, so that we didn't have much time to spend on eating. I had said three o'clock to Paul Mace, and I'm the sort of person who likes to be prompt. I didn't want them worrying too.

Over the meal I explained roughly what I had in mind. As I'd expected, there were objections.

"If you expect me to lie for you Tony . . ."

Her professional integrity was creeping back. "Only to back me up."

"But if *you're* lying—"

"With a bit of luck, I shan't have to."

I followed the Volvo down the motorway to Bridgwater. From there we were on ordinary roads. Margaret showed no inclination to linger. I managed to keep her in sight. Put it like that.

One behind the other we rolled smoothly into the courtyard of Coombe's stately home. The front door opened before I'd got all my riding equipment off. I let him wait. Margaret lit one of her rare cigarettes. I realized she would probably be meeting Evelyn, which could well be as unnerving as meeting Coombe.

The gaunt retainer led us through the hall, through the sun room, and out on to the terrace. There, a tableau was being played out. It held all the gruesome viciousness of a medieval ritual, and for several moments I had difficulty in reminding myself it was real.

Evelyn was standing to one side. When I had last seen her, there'd been evidence of joyful self-indulgence, even if hysteria hadn't been far away. But now, I saw, she was quiet and withdrawn, her face pale and her clothing untidy. She had had no chance to change for several days. Her face had encountered soap, but with no make-up her complexion was sallow. Her hair, usually so flamingly flamboyant, now seemed lustreless.

She saw me and took a pace forward, then, seeing Margaret, she stopped. Her mouth formed the word "Aleric?"

I nodded, smiled. "He'll be fine." But it was said absent-mindedly, my attention being captured by the scene on the terrace.

Previously, apart from the episode in the woods, I hadn't seen much evidence of Coombe's armed back-up. Now they were all there, lined up with their backs to the balustrade. They, I thought, hadn't even noticed my arrival, their attention being concentrated on the tableau, as though they might have been witnessing a keel-hauling with Captain Bligh in charge.

I reminded myself that I had been expected at three o'clock. It was three minutes past, so the whole thing could have been staged to impress. Or perhaps not.

Coombe was standing, in a dark blue tracksuit he'd have had to get tailored, with his fists on his hips. Paul Mace, shrunken and grey, was swaying in front of him, legs apart to prevent himself from falling over, holding in his right hand a three-inch paintbrush and in his left, by its handle, a half-gallon can of white emulsion paint, its lid off. He seemed unable to move.

Coombe made a pretence of having just seen me. He waved, all friendly and jovial.

"Come on over. You can help him."

Not sure I wanted to, I nevertheless strolled over. "Anything to oblige. What's going on?"

"It's a courtesy I extend to my employees when they're about to leave us. He puts a cross where he'd like to be buried. We simply lift a couple of the flagstones. Come on, Mace, we can't take all day on it."

Mace's grey lips opened, but nothing came out.

" '*Pour encourager les autres,*' " I suggested.

"Eh?" said Coombe.

"Bonaparte," I told him. "When he—"

Evelyn cut in. "Voltaire." She always likes things to be correct.

"What?"

"Voltaire wrote it. A sly dig at the British when they shot Admiral Bing. 'To encourage the others,' he said."

I stared at her. Everybody stared at her. She fidgeted with her fingers and blushed. I turned and grinned at the line of men against the balustrade. Stiff, vicious faces stared back.

"Funny!" said Coombe, aiming it at me. "Perhaps you'd like a go. Give him the paint, Paul. And the brush."

Paul Mace sagged. In his eyes, tears appeared. His employer had called him Paul. Limply he offered me the brush, but he had difficulty lifting the paint can enough to offer that.

I took them. The brush was in my left hand. I put down the can in order to change over, and straightened.

"Well?" I demanded.

"A cross. Where you'd like to lie in peace."

I considered him with fascination. It was impossible, with this man, to decide where a joke finished and serious conversation began.

"I get a choice?"

He waved an arm. "Feel free. Where you'd like to lie."

I lifted the can and dipped in the brush, giving myself time. When I had it well loaded, I lifted it out and painted a cross on his chest.

"On top of you, Coombe."

He was late reacting. Suddenly his face suffused with blood and his fingers tightened into huge fists. I think he would have lashed out, in spite of a disinclination towards doing his own dirty work, but somebody giggled. He turned ponderously; he couldn't whirl. The row of faces went stiff, and Evelyn belatedly screamed.

I had been right about the scream, the night I raided the gallery. I recognized it now. Never before had I heard her do that. Somehow, one never expects screams from a solicitor.

I turned to her and laughed. Not at her, not at Coombe's discomfiture, but at the fact that in painting that cross I had seen where my absolute proof lay. Relief and elation prompted that laugh, and when I turned back to Coombe, I found that he, too, was laughing. Or at least had recovered his good humour enough to smile and make a whickering noise.

It was then I realized that Coombe had astonishing reserves of character. How else could he have risen to the position he now held, a multi-millionaire in command of a group who feared his very glance? He had a great control over his emotions. When he needed calm and considered thought, he achieved it. Now, he needed every iota of his subtlety, because he had recognized my laugh for what it was.

"I hope," I said, "that you've got that cheque prepared."

His eyes narrowed. "A piece of paper can be torn to shreds."

So he had been sufficiently influenced by my continuing persistence to feel uncertain about his own position. Which meant he was already tentative about the authenticity of his six paintings, which in turn would explain the predicament in which Mace had found himself. And this in spite of the fact that four of them had been stolen from accredited sources, national art collections.

It wouldn't be the first time that experts have been wrong, including Mace and Margaret.

"Let me see it," I said.

For one moment the anger returned. Then he snapped, "Paul!" and at the same time gestured behind his back. Released at last, his consort of hooligans dispersed rapidly for cover.

Paul Mace, recovering rapidly now that the attention had drifted from him, reached into his inside pocket and produced a wallet. From it, he took a cheque. He held it up before my eyes, not letting me reach it. It was a certified cheque.

I put down the paint can, carefully placed the brush across it, then smiled at Coombe. "A hundred thousand?"

"At the most, they're fetching twenty thousand each."

"They?"

"Frederick Ashes."

"Good. So, if you're agreeing that mine *are* Frederick Ashe—"

"I'm agreeing nothing." Coombe's face was dark again.

"Then I propose to prove that they are, and yours are not, and when I've finished doing that, I think you'll be pleased to produce the second cheque you've got ready, for the other two hundred thousand."

"Tony!" moaned Evelyn feebly. She now knew enough about Coombe to know he was not to be taunted.

"Pff!" said Coombe in disgust. "All this talk about proof, and you're arguing with two art experts." He nodded, his lower lip vibrating. "That's right, I've checked on our Dr. Dennis. Her reputation is world-wide. Mace was quite jealous. Weren't you?" he jerked out, not looking at Mace.

Mace, disconcerted at becoming Mace again, mumbled something.

"Weren't you?" Coombe snapped.

"In comparison, my experience is limited," Mace admitted.

"So let's hear from the lady." Coombe beamed at her, like a malevolent laser. "What do you think of my set of Frederick Ashe?"

Margaret was caught unprepared. "Well, I don't . . . I haven't seen them, of course."

"The photographs," I prompted.

"Well yes, I've seen those, but the actual canvases are a different proposition. Ask me again when I've seen them."

"Ah!" said Coombe. "That, I'm afraid, is impossible."

Margaret shrugged. She managed to get into it an element of contempt for Coombe's cageyness. "I'd hoped to be shown round. Your collection's legendary."

Coombe lifted his head. "We're wasting time. Hine, you'd better get on with it. Let's hear about this proof of yours."

I tried to repeat Margaret's shrug, but it hadn't her impact. "I'll need to go with you into the gallery, and I'll need Mace with me, and Dr. Dennis to confirm a few points. Otherwise, there is no proof."

Coombe stood before me like a rock. He made a movement as though to cross his arms, then realized the paint on his chest was still wet. His face darkened at the thought. "Paul," he said, "you might as well tear up that cheque."

I smiled at him. "Then we'll be off, though I did hope for a cup of your Darjeeling before we leave."

Evelyn took a step forward. I glanced at her. She became motionless. I added, "Over the tea, we can discuss the basis of my proof."

Coombe considered it for a few moments, then a couple of teeth appeared, one at each corner of his mouth. He was smiling. It was terrifying.

"Paul," he snapped. "A minute."

Then he turned away, and he and Mace walked away along the terrace, conferring animatedly. I was left with Evelyn and Margaret, my predicament no less fraught.

"Evelyn," I said, "you ought to meet Margaret Dennis. My wife, Margaret."

Margaret had moved no farther than a yard from the plate-glass door. She made no move now. Evelyn inclined her head coldly and with reserve. She was not at her best in dirty jeans and a crumpled shirt and was facing a woman who could always look smart and poised whatever the circumstances. Nevertheless, Evelyn managed to convey a contained dignity. She turned to me.

"You haven't told me about Aleric, Tony," she said. The voice had a beckoning quality. It was a quiet request. I moved towards her, to face her so that I could watch Coombe and Mace beyond.

"He's a bit knocked about. They've got him in Salisbury General. Nothing that won't repair. He's more disturbed, I think, at finding that two of his great-grandparents were artists."

"What? You're being clever again."

"My grandmother, and Frederick Ashe."

She absorbed that in a flash. "I didn't like her," she said definitely.

"Never mind that now," I told her firmly, and to my surprise she didn't snap straight back at me. "We haven't got much time. You heard what I said to Coombe. I need you in that gallery. So play along with it, please."

Her eyes searched my face. "You're different, Tony. You've changed. What are you up to? And what's all this talk about three hundred thousand pounds? That's nonsense, of course. Isn't it?"

I shook my head. "I've seen Aleric. Coombe's going to pay for that. Call it compensation, if you like."

She bit her lip. "I can't make you out. Tangling with a man like *that.*" Her head jerked towards him. "There's a basic precept in law: Don't take on a case until you know the strength of the opposition."

"This isn't law. There's nothing legal about it. He's going to pay."

"But you're such a simpleton!"

"They're coming back. Will you help me?"

"For Aleric, yes."

"Not for me?"

Her lips flickered. "You'd be lost on your own."

Coombe was coming back, but not Mace, who had disappeared inside the house.

"We'll have tea," Coombe grumbled. "You can talk. Then we'll decide."

"Has Mace gone to get the strawberries and cream?"

He sneered at my humour. "He's making preparations. In case."

He didn't say in case of what, but I guessed that Mace was heading for the gallery. A man appeared, sent no doubt by Mace. He arranged four chairs around one of the tables. We sat, Coombe and I facing each other, the two women disconcertingly facing each other. Coombe lifted his head. The tea-tray appeared. No delay this time; Coombe's rumbling mood of near explosion had upset everyone.

As the man leaned over the table, I caught a glimpse of the butt of a gun under his left armpit. I watched him leave and had the impression he went no farther than just inside the door.

"Now," said Coombe, "talk."

"There's a story behind it," I said, and watched his fist clench on the table surface. "Frederick Ashe met my grandmother, who was Angelina Foote at the time, and she was just about seventeen. Quite apart from a natural affinity for each other, they had other things that linked them, such as the fact that one of them was left-handed and they had the same initials, only reversed. And the fact that they were both painters. She learned to work in his style and went away with him to Paris in 1910. They used to paint side by side, with their palette on a table between them, and they invented the same signature for their paintings, an A and an F, overlapped. All this I got from my grandmother very recently. Margaret was there. She can confirm it."

I glanced at her. She was sitting with her fingers interlocked on the table in front of her, her eyes on them, saying nothing. Evelyn sat the same. I nodded to Coombe.

"Looks like you'll have to be mother."

His bushy eyebrows lifted. He frowned. He reached for the pot.

"So," I went on, "there were two sets of paintings completed, each of eighty-one canvases. Out of one set, six were sold in Paris, and these are the ones now in your gallery, Coombe, and one went to my father and on to me. The other complete set I now have. The whole point is, which set was painted by who?"

"Sugar?" said Coombe, looking at Margaret.

"Pardon? Oh, I'll help myself, thank you."

Having attracted her attention he asked, "Is he making this up?"

"Not one word. It's all true."

"And it doesn't get us anywhere," he decided.

"Oh, but it does." I reached inside my right inside jacket pocket and produced the two sets of six prints each. "One of these sets is of your own six, Coombe, and the other set is of the six matching ones out of the complete batch of eighty-one." I spread them out in front of him. "Check 'em. Go on. Tell me what you see."

Coombe had a reluctance even to look down at them. For too long now he had paid people to do things for him. He wouldn't, for instance, do his own killing. Paul Mace was the person he paid to look at photographs for him and probably to arrange the theft of paintings that Mace had decided Coombe should own. It was now beneath Coombe's dignity to do anything for himself. He probably had someone whose sole duty it was to go to the toilet for him.

Crooking his finger like a fractured banana, he sipped his tea, then growled, "Mace has told me."

"Told you what?"

"That they're painted from slightly different viewpoints. If it matters."

"Oh it does. It does. Two people sitting side by side and separated by a table on which they have their palette—and one of them is left-handed. Now ask yourself, wouldn't it be more convenient if the left-handed painter sat at the right of the table? It would save either of them reaching across with the brush. You agree?"

He grunted. Evelyn had not touched her tea, but her eyes were fixed on me. There was a light in them I hadn't seen for years. Encouraged, and because Coombe hadn't answered, I demanded, "Don't you agree?"

Margaret stirred uneasily.

"Margaret?" I asked.

"You know I agree. We've already discussed this." For one moment she glanced at me. There was bewilderment in her expression. She believed that this presentation would get me nowhere, in fact would play right into Coombe's hands. Perhaps Coombe recognized this. Mace would have briefed him fully, in so far as Mace himself understood the implications. But Coombe's face had set into an expressionless front. His poker face this was, though no doubt he had someone to play poker for him.

"Do *you* agree?" I insisted to him, determined to provoke a response.

"You're pushing it, Hine," he said, his voice grumbling at my presumption. "Don't press your luck."

"I'm only asking you to agree that it would've been more convenient for them to paint in that relative position, the left-handed one to the right of the table. Not that it proves anything."

Margaret made a sound in her throat. Evelyn's cup clattered in her saucer. Nobody had looked at the strawberries and cream.

Coombe said nothing.

"How in God's name does anybody do business with you!" I cried.

"Nobody does business with me. I do business with them."

"Then *do* something."

He poured himself another cup of tea. I had disturbed him, or he'd have poured three others too.

"Or I take my eighty-one to Christie's, and they sell them as Frederick Ashes, whether they are or not, and your six'll be worth nothing. Damn it all, Coombe, are you stupid or something? I'm offering you a business proposition, not robbing you of something."

"Three hundred thousand," he barked. "That's robbery."

"I'll prove to you it's not. If you'll just agree. The left-handed painter would most likely sit to the right. Yes?"

"Much more of this . . . I agree. Yes. Paul explained that. So what?"

"So look at the photographs," I shouted. A man appeared at the end of the terrace, another in the open doorway. I grabbed up one print from each batch and waggled them in front of Coombe's face. "That's one of yours. This is one out of the eighty-one set. Which one is painted from a right-hand point of view? Look, damn it. They're not going to bite."

He stared at me through the space between them. I registered the fact that I was destined to place my cross on the flagstones.

"Look, or I'm leaving."

A corner of his lips twitched into a sneer. His eyes re-focused. He actually looked at the photographs.

"Mine," he growled, "is painted from the right-hand side, yours from the left."

"Fine. Good. That's something." I put them down on the table surface, then collected them all up, patted them into neatness, and slid them back inside my jacket. "For your information, my original painting, the one that came to me from my father, is the same as yours. It's painted by the left-handed artist."

He lost his temper. It had to come some time. His huge fist slammed down on the metal surface of the table and a dent appeared. The tray danced.

"I've had enough of this!" He put back his head and raised his voice, and in the woodland the rooks rose in droves. "Mace! Where are you? Carter! Phillips! Green!"

The two men I'd noted came running, and a third appeared from behind me. Mace walked from inside the sun room so appositely that he must have been lurking there.

"You wanted me, sir?"

Coombe was on his feet. "What the hell's the idea of letting this madman come here? It was your idea. Yours, Mace . . ."

"With respect, sir—"

"I want no blood on the terrace," Coombe cried. "It soaks in. But I want him silent."

It was not the remark of someone out of control. His fury had been measured. Evelyn didn't realize this and flew at him, hammering as far up his chest as she could reach. Coombe picked her off and handed her to one of his men, who steered her back to her chair. Margaret seized on the diversion to whisper to me, "What are you *doing,* Tony?"

"Getting somewhere," I murmured. Aloud I said, "Let's get along to the gallery and confirm it, shall we!"

"I think it would be best, sir," Mace suggested.

"It's ready?" said Coombe.

"As you said."

"Then we'll go there, and let this idiot dig his own grave."

I realized then that this had been his intention all along. Mace had expressed an uncertainty Coombe couldn't live with. I was the only one who could return his continuing existence to its former complacency.

"Come along, Evelyn," I said. "You mustn't miss this."

"I'd prefer to."

I took her arm. "I need you desperately."

"You won't need me, Tony," said Margaret in a distant voice.

"Oh but I do."

"You know it all."

"This is your reputation we're talking about. Your expertise. Your integrity. You're surely not going to allow me to say what I like?"

She managed a smile, but still hesitated.

"Besides," I went on, "you said you'd give anything to get inside that gallery."

"Not my life. As it'd be if I saw too much."

"Then don't look."

Coombe raised his voice. "Aren't you coming?"

"Be with you."

With one woman on each arm, I followed Coombe and Mace through the sun room.

16

We used a different route from the one by which Aleric had initiated me to the gallery, up the main staircase, with one of the gunmen leading, then Coombe, tailed closely by Mace, myself following with a lady each side, and two more gunmen behind us. The pace was steady and measured, like mounting a tumbril.

Margaret hissed in my ear, "I don't need you to hold my arm."

"I got the impression you were about to turn and run."

"I don't see why you need me."

"You will."

We marched on.

Evelyn hissed in my other ear, "Let go my arm. I think you're out of your mind."

"I can't do it without you."

"Well, that's an admission."

The gunman turned to the right at the top. It was like a conducted tour, though Coombe blocked most of the view. We turned a corner, and we were in a corridor I recognized, if only because it needed artificial light in the daytime. At the end sat the guard alert and prepared, watching our approach nervously.

Mace already had the key. He held it up for all to see, like an illusionist. The guard stood to one side. The door swung open, and Mace reached through a hand and put on the lights. We entered. Mace closed the door behind him, locked it, and dropped the key in his side pocket. It clinked against something else metallic. He set his shoulders against the door, plunged his hand into the same pocket, and smiled thinly.

I could barely detect the smile, because when I said "lights," the plural was hardly applicable. There was a small one above the door, trapped in a wire cage, and, farther into the darkness of the gallery, six strip-lights above six paintings.

Mace had performed well. He had switched off all but the appropriate lights, and as they were hooded, the illumination extended for no more than a yard in any direction. Quite efficiently, the other secrets of the gallery were kept.

The one guard ahead and the two guards behind were still in their relative positions, but the one in front had disappeared into the darkness and the ones behind had slipped into deep shadows. Nevertheless, I was aware of them.

We stood facing the paintings. Coombe turned massively.

"There they are. Tell me what you can see that isn't in your damned photographs."

"Not me," I said. "But Dr. Dennis hasn't seen the actual paintings before. Perhaps she can tell us something."

Smiling, I turned to her. The light, angled deliberately on the canvases, offered a very poor reflected glow at face level. Margaret seemed to be confused. Her shrug and her gesture of resignation told me more than her expression. Her voice was empty of emotion. "What d'you expect me to say?"

"Well," I said encouragingly, "we know these are by the same hand as my original one because all seven are duplicated in the eighty-one set. Mine, you were sure, is a Frederick Ashe."

"Mmm, mmm," she said when I paused.

"And you seem to be sure that the eighty-one are all by my grandmother. So look at these. Go on, Margaret, touch 'em and smell 'em, whatever the technique involves. Would you say they are genuine Frederick Ashe works?"

Still she hesitated—I was introducing nothing new—then she went to them, and we waited. I took out my pipe. "No smoking in here,"

Coombe grated. I shrugged. Something to play with, that's all it was, something to occupy my shaking fingers.

She did all I'd suggested, plus a few other things, making it look good. She produced from her shoulder bag a contrivance I hadn't seen before, a magnifier with an open-work wire frame, for placing over the surface. She used it mainly to study the signatures. Whatever the canvases told her, they took a long time to yield their secrets.

At last she turned. Back-lit, her face was cut into hollows. I could see her lips move, but she was whispering.

"I'm sorry," I said. "I didn't hear that."

She spoke too loudly. "My opinion hasn't changed. These are by Frederick Ashe. I'm sorry, Tony."

"Just what I said," Mace called out from the door. He sounded jubilant and relieved.

"So that's the end of that," Coombe decided. "Let's go."

"Wait." I still held Evelyn's arm and I could feel it shaking. "Margaret, do you agree that these were painted from a right viewpoint, so probably by a left-handed painter? Would you like to see the photos again?"

She frowned. I was becoming pedantic, flogging the same point over and over. She said, "I don't need to, thank you. These are right-hand viewpoints, compared with the six that match them."

"Good," I said.

"Good?" Evelyn jerked my arm. "What's good about it?"

"It was what I expected. They're by the same hand as my own original one, from the house."

She groaned. "So all right. So you own a genuine Frederick Ashe. That was what this lady expert told you in the first place. Nothing's changed. Why can't you let it lie, Tony? Why can't you?"

"You're wasting my time," Coombe said harshly. "I've had about enough of you—"

"But you agreed."

"I agreed what, damn it?"

"That the person who painted your six and my own, which are painted from a right viewpoint, must have been left-handed."

"No!" he roared. That sound in the labyrinth of his gallery bounced around and back, returning in a mirror image, but still as no. "Most likely! Most likely!"

"Very well."

"So let's get out of here."

"In a minute. There's more."

"More what?"

"Evidence. Dr. Dennis found a reproduction of a painting in a biography. It showed Frederick Ashe to be painting left-handed."

"Well that *proves* it!" Coombe bellowed. "You stupid or something?"

"Sometimes pictures get printed backwards in books."

"And sometimes people get carried out backwards and feet first."

Mace permitted himself a soft snigger, and Coombe beamed at him in approval.

"There's another photograph I want to show you."

Coombe clamped his hand on my shoulder, nearly bearing me to the floor. "No more pictures. I've had enough."

"Then I'll describe it." The grip on my shoulder increased, but I managed to speak through the pain. "When I was here—as you know I was in here—there was one shot I spoiled. I jerked. When I printed it, it showed two blurred pictures of paintings, one of them actually *of* Frederick Ashe. The same painting as was reproduced in the biography. You've got the painting here, Coombe. The biography was of another painter, Maurice Bellarmé."

The fist was removed. I straightened. He made a hissing noise through his teeth.

"The camera swung to the right," I said. "There must be an alcove or something just there."

Coombe made no move. Evelyn whispered, "He's hurt you!" I touched her fingers. Margaret turned away in disgust at my foolishness.

Coombe said carefully, "There is no alcove there."

"My photograph showed Ashe, as far as I can tell, painting left-handed," I said softly, offering it, praying he would react. "What is there, Coombe, if not an alcove?"

"A mirror."

I laughed. "It's as I guessed. I got mirror images. So the Bellarmé paintings . . ."

I turned, my eyes searching the shadows behind me.

"Stay where you are!" Coombe rasped.

There was movement along the aisle. Two pairs of feet appeared inside the edge of the illumination. I was very still.

"What're you afraid of?" I asked quietly.

Coombe grumbled deep in his chest, then he moved past me, his hand swooped down, and a switch snapped on. I stared into the alcove that had been behind my right shoulder, as the two tubes flickered, then steadied.

Coombe could not have owned what he thought to be a complete collection of Frederick Ashe and not also have owned a portrait of the artist. The two portraits went together, Ashe and his angel. My grandmother. Still they were not separated. There they were, side by side.

Bellarmé had been their friend. He had painted Frederick Ashe as though he was working on a portrait of his angel, who, as Margaret had said, was performing a domestic chore in her painting. She was darning one of his socks. Ashe would not, of course, have been actually painting. Hadn't they always painted side by side? But Angelina Foote seemed actually to be darning. The concentration was there, and her beauty, the transparency of her complexion, and in her expression her devotion to such a minor item relating to her Freddie—his sock. Bellarmé must have had a sense of humour because his picture of Ashe seated on a hard-backed chair at his easel showed him to have one foot bare.

"It's her!" cried out Evelyn involuntarily. "Your grandmother, Tony!"

She had last seen Angelina twenty years before, when she was younger than my most recent memory. I felt choked, unable to speak. I wanted to meet these people, as they were then, and meet Bellarmé. And shake his hand in congratulation. The two works were superb.

Frederick Ashe was holding the brush in his right hand, Angelina Foote had the sock on her right hand, and the needle was poised in her left.

I cleared my throat. "You didn't tell me this, Margaret."

She was behind my left shoulder. I turned. She was shaking her head, in bewilderment or in rejection. I couldn't be certain.

"Or perhaps they were both printed in the biography backwards," I offered.

"I don't . . . remember."

"Never mind. It doesn't matter now. The point is, we've got our proof at last. My painting and the six in here being painted from a right viewpoint, were done by my left-handed grandmother, Angelina Foote. *Now* what d'you say, Margaret?"

She gestured. She turned and stared at the six on the other wall. "I don't know. I don't *know,* damn it!"

"Anybody can make a mistake," I said comfortingly.

"But not me!" she cried out.

"You're insisting you didn't?"

"No. Yes. I don't know. Leave me alone. Please."

She looked round frantically, as though seeking a chair for her shaking legs.

"We need chairs, Coombe," I said briskly. "Three chairs and a table."

"Will somebody please tell me what the hell's going on!" he appealed, and the two guards moved closer.

"What is going on," I told him, "is exactly what I promised. I said I'd prove that you own six paintings which are not by Ashe. I've just done that. With Ashe shown to be right-handed and Angelina Foote left-handed, it's inconceivable that they would paint in any other arrangement than he on the left and she on the right."

"Then what d'you want with a table, goddamn it!"

"Because we now have to complete our financial arrangement."

"I'm not sitting in here to discuss—"

"I'm not asking you to either sit or discuss. The sitting part is for my wife and myself, and there's nothing to discuss. I'm going to legalize the situation. My wife's a solicitor. Doesn't that make sense?"

"In here?"

"I thought you'd prefer that," I said innocently. "Then, if you don't agree with what I'm going to do, there'll be no chance of me getting away before you can tear things up. Get it?"

He stared at me broodingly, then he wobbled the upper stack of his chins and barked, "Mace!"

Paul Mace came running. He was revitalized. "Sir?"

"You been listening to this?"

"Every word."

"Well?"

"My assessment of the paintings was perhaps a little—"

"Never mind that. What's he up to? That's the point."

"What I'm up to," I put in, "is the tying up of the loose ends. What you'll see and hear is going to be enough to justify fifty thousand pounds for each of my six genuine Frederick Ashes, to replace yours. So we need a table. And chairs."

"Mace!" snapped Coombe. "A table and chairs. This I've got to hear." He put back his head and laughed. "Fifty thousand!"

Mace turned to the two guards. "Get 'em."

They went into the back of the gallery to search, each carrying a torch. There would be places to sit, and tables on which to place ash-trays that dared not to be used. We waited. Coombe stood in massive menace, Mace moved restlessly, and Margaret went to stand looking at the six paintings, perhaps not even seeing them. Evelyn leaned against my shoulder, her lips close to my ear.

"What've you got in mind, Tony?"

"An affidavit. A water-tight, uncontestable affidavit. I'll pay your fee later."

"You can have my advice free."

"I know what it would be: Give him what he wants—six paintings. Give him, Evelyn? Never. I'm going to hand him a rattlesnake with fangs at both ends."

"You're an idiot!"

Then why did she squeeze my arm supportingly?

They came back with the chairs and the table. Margaret seemed to have recovered, and waved hers away impatiently. The table was placed in the centre of the aisle, where it received only a spill of the light from each side. I put the chairs facing each other across it and held one for Evelyn. Normally she would have frowned at my impertinence. This time she threw me a quick smile and sat. I walked round and took the seat opposite.

"Can we get on with it?" Coombe demanded.

I smiled up at him. "Can you see all right?" I asked Evelyn.

"Yes, thank you."

"Right." I plunged my hand into my left-hand inside jacket pocket and produced the folded sheet of law stationery, opened it up, folded it back the other way, and put it in front of her reasonably flat. I plunged again and brought out six photographs.

Mace, who'd been watching me very closely and with suspicion, pounced in, and whipped them from my fingers. "Wait a minute," he said. "What's this?"

They were the wrong set, the prints of the six from the loft set.

"Whoops!" I said. "My mistake." I grinned at him and produced another set. Held them up. "All right? You can tell these are the ones . . ." I gestured towards the wall. "The frames. They show."

He frowned at my prints, then nodded, stepping back. I reached inside my side pocket and found Evelyn's rubber stamp.

"Breathe on it and it'll work," I told her. "Is that all you need?"

She flicked me a look under her eyebrows. She has never plucked them. They caught the light redly. "I'd prefer the atmosphere of my office, otherwise . . . yes, I can manage. What is it you want me to say?" She looked round. "If I'd got something to write with."

"Forgot." I produced her Sheaffer.

She laughed. "Tell me."

"I want to swear something to the effect that the six photographs herewith referred to—I suppose we'll have to mark them in some way . . ."

"I'll put something on the back of each one. I hope the stamp'll hold out."

"Yes. Herewith referred to . . . are of canvases to be seen on the premises of Renfrew Coombe, at Renfrew Coombe, Somerset . . ."

"So that's where we are!"

"Where they are hanging—"

Coombe's hand slapped down on the law stationery, confirming his contempt for anything relating to the law. "What the hell *is* this?"

"An affidavit."

"Paul!" he shouted.

Mace, at his shoulder, stepped forward.

"What's he playing at?"

"I don't know, sir."

Evelyn looked up at Coombe. "I'm notarizing an affidavit."

"And what," he rasped at me, "do you intend to do with it?"

"Take it to the police. I promised Detective Sergeant Dolan—"

"He's insane!" bellowed Coombe.

"If you'll just listen . . ."

"Perhaps, sir—" Mace began.

I cut in. "I'm just about to tell you why my six paintings are worth fifty thousand pounds each. If you'll only listen."

I stared into Coombe's face. Slowly his hand lifted. "Say it."

"I will take this affidavit and the photographs of the six paintings to the police. They will go to a magistrate—"

"A Justice of the Peace," corrected Evelyn.

"Thank you. A JP then. And they will get a search warrant."

Coombe was rumbling, close to an eruption. I held up my hand.

"I happen to know they've been trying for years to get something, anything, that they can use to get into here. They'll pounce on this. And I can guess you've been expecting something or other from the police. But you'll notice that the affidavit will read premises. Not gallery. By the time the police arrive, you'll be expecting them. These six paintings here will then be displayed in your hall or your study, or whatever you call it, and if you've got any sense, the two Bellarmés will be there too. Because you'll be able to show that the six paintings covered by the affidavit are *not* by Frederick Ashe, but are copies, so that none of them could have been stolen from the galleries who've unfortunately lost them. And because that covers the information in my affidavit, they can't look any further. You can even let them take them away, because by that time you'll have the six genuine versions of the same paintings, which I shall bring to you, displayed here in the gallery. And you can laugh them out of the house, knowing that they'll never be able to try a search warrant again." I took a deep breath. "There. Isn't that worth fifty thousand each to you?"

Coombe was wheezing, his huge chest shaking, and the cross on it vibrating. I realized what was happening. He was laughing. Then he raised his mauler, and I thought for one appalling moment he was going to slap me on the back. But it descended on Mace's shoulder.

"What d'you think, Paul?"

"I like it, sir. I like it."

"Then do it," he boomed at me.

So we did it. All through my exposition, Evelyn had been drafting the affidavit and annotating the backs of the six photographs. All I had to do was sign, watch her bang on her rubber stamp (with seven breaths it just managed to work seven times) and add her signature. I picked it all up, folded the affidavit round the certified photos, and slipped the package inside my jacket. I got to my feet.

"No!" said Margaret.

Nobody had been taking any notice of her. She had been silent in the background. Thinking, no doubt.

"No?" I asked.

"It isn't valid," she plunged in, almost breathless with it, her hair flying about with the emphasis. "It won't work."

"And why not?"

"Because it is *not* valid. Not enough to support legal action, or anything else based on authenticity. Tony, I'm sorry. But I can't let you walk out of here and have the whole thing crumble away . . ."

She stopped, biting her lip. I'll swear she was close to tears. Because of this, I spoke quite gently.

"Tell us why it isn't valid."

"Because you can't—positively—argue that two people, right- and left-handed, would sit the way you've described. It isn't *proof.* They might not have done that. They might have both leaned across to use the palette. It's possible, Tony, and you know it. Just possible."

I sighed. "Oh, Margaret! I did hope you wouldn't say that. You see, there's another proof. I was keeping it in reserve." I smiled at her. "Just in case you did say it."

She gave me a long, considered look, then pressed thumb and fingers to her forehead, and said dismissively, "Let's hope it's better than your last load of proof." Her tone sharpened. She was unable to control her tension. "It wasn't proof, and you know it. Ask her—ask your wife. She's the solicitor. Everything's black and white with that lot."

I turned to Evelyn. She gave me a crumpled smile. "Evelyn?"

She shook her head. "It wasn't proof, Tony. Not what you could take to court." She said it sadly.

"Then we'll have to give this other thing a try."

"A try! Do you mean to tell me it's something you haven't tested? Tony . . ." She could think of nothing to add.

I ran my fingers through my hair and tried to grin. "It was only half an hour ago that I got the idea."

"Can we get on!" shouted Coombe.

"Right." I stood face on to him, my eyes level with the cross. "The idea came to me when I did that cross. One of the strokes has to come after the other, and crosses it. You can see. Even though it's dry, you can see which came second."

He tried to peer down at his chest, but one of his chins got in the way, so he went and stood in front of the nearest mirror.

"He's right, Paul. Come and have a look at this."

Paul Mace did. He prodded the chest. "Yes. But I don't see . . ."

"It's like this." I looked round for something to draw on, but there was only the affidavit. I took it out of my pocket and used the back, borrowing Evelyn's pen.

"These two people," I said, "Frederick Ashe and Angelina Foote, were so intrigued by the fact that they had the same initials, only reversed, that they both used the same combined form of initials. They used the F and the A overlapping, to sign their paintings. So they look the same. But they wouldn't be the same, would they? Ashe would naturally do the F first, then add a down stroke to complete the A. And Angelina would do the A first, and add a cross stroke at the top to make the F. Like this."

I did it quickly, and found it quite difficult, but managed a reasonable representation.

"Frederick Ashe," I said. "F.A." And I drew:

"But this would be Angelina Foote. A.F.":

"You can see the difference is mainly in the top left-hand corner. It all depends on which stroke does the overlapping."

I looked round. Margaret, distancing herself from my antics, had withdrawn into the shadows.

"Margaret, may I borrow your magnifier?"

She came forward, plunging into her shoulder bag. "If you must. But I've got no faith in this."

"We'll see."

Mace and Coombe were almost in my back pocket as I bent to the paintings on the wall. The magnifier was a superb instrument, bringing the image up very clearly. There was absolute silence behind me. I moved slowly along the line of six, stopping from time to time to wipe the lens, as sweat was dripping from my forehead. It was not easy. The texture of the paint beneath the initials obscured the result, and the clarity of the overlap depended on the fluidity of the paint that'd been used to inscribe it.

I straightened. Margaret was now pacing. Evelyn watching me with strain in her eyes.

"Give me side-lighting and a camera with a macro lens and I could blow the initials up to ten by eight, and there'd be no doubt. I'm certain of two, not so certain of the other four. Mace, you want to take a look? It's the top left-hand corner, remember."

He took the magnifier. I stood and watched, playing with my pipe to stop myself from screaming. He straightened and nodded to Coombe.

"Numbers 1 and 4?" I asked.

"Yes. Those for certain."

"And what did they indicate?"

"The cross bar at the top of the F came last."

"Which is a definite and unarguable proof that they were painted by Angelina Foote?"

Mace stuck out his lower lip. It cost him a lot to say it, but he managed to get the words out. "They're Angelina Footes."

My legs went weak. I leaned a cheek on the table. "Right then. Fine." I picked up the affidavit and waved it. "So what I've got here's not just evidence that'll bring the police rushing round, but on the back there's absolute proof that what they've come to see are only copies, not genuine Frederick Ashe paintings."

I could tell that Coombe was delighted at the outcome. He was shortly to acquire the genuine Ashes and the evidence to make complete fools of the police. He would perhaps invite the TV newsmen to bring their cameras along. His delight was expressed in the fact that he unzipped the top six inches of his tracksuit and a quarter of an inch of a smile.

"My cheques then, please," I said.

"When you bring your six."

"Oh, come on, Coombe. If I brought six paintings, I'd leave with no cheques and no paintings. If I take the cheques and don't bring the paintings, d'you think I'd expect to live long enough to spend any?"

He contemplated this. Then he said, "Paul." Mace produced two cheques. The total was three hundred thousand pounds. I folded them, my fingers uncertain, and tucked them in with the affidavit.

"Your wife stays," said Mace flatly.

"Oh . . . Tony!" she wailed.

"It's all right, love," I assured her. "It's only another day. Back tomorrow with Coombe's paintings—"

"And how d'you intend to do that, Tony?" Margaret demanded from the shadows. "You don't know where they are."

"Oh my God," said Coombe. "The clown doesn't know where to put his hands on them."

17

She advanced into the light. The starkness of the tubes drained her face of colour, its shadows hid her eyes. There was a tense authority about her. She had made a decision.

"But Margaret," I said quietly, "you know where they are."

"And why should I tell you? I've listened to all this, to you calmly proving that you own eighty-one genuine Frederick Ashe works—his complete collection—then you happily promise to let this ape here have six of them!"

"For good money, Margaret. Your commission—"

"To hell with my commission. What do I care for that! It was a find! The complete set and a way to authenticate them. And you'd rob me of that!" Her voice was brittle. It crackled round the gallery. Nobody said a word. "You'd break up the collection just so that this thieving swine, who hasn't got one atom of feeling for any of his collection . . . so that he can get one over on the police and go on with his rotten, underhanded pirating of art treasures . . ."

"Be quiet, woman," put in Mace.

"Quiet! Oh, you can easily silence me. And don't think I would care.

Tony, I just don't understand you. You prove you own all that beauty and perfection, and before I can begin to take it in, you start to split it up!" Her voice was breaking with the emotion of it.

I took a pace towards her. "But, Margaret, you've known all along that the loft set are the genuine Frederick Ashes."

"What?"

"You used your magnifier just now. D'you think I didn't notice? I did, because I'd only just thought of the idea. And the first thing you examined was the initials. Now be sensible, Margaret. You're an expert. You know all about signatures. It's one thing you'd think about, that overlapping business of the initials."

"I don't know what—"

"But you do. Your first sight of my painting . . . and you said Frederick Ashe. But at that time you knew nothing about the story of the two sets. When you *did* know, you couldn't wait to get your hands on the loft set. And in that loft you had no magnifier, and not enough light. You had to know! Had to. So you said you would wake my grandmother and ask her. Then you came back and told me she'd shouted for Grace. As I suppose she would, because she'd found herself looking at a genuine Frederick Ashe when Grace had told her they'd been destroyed. Of *course* she would shout for Grace, and of course you would want to know why. And my grandmother would have told you why. There was no reason for her to keep it from you."

"Conjecture." But Margaret barely parted her teeth.

"Perhaps. But it sounds right, and when you consider what followed . . . You knew, in that second, that this was a wonderful discovery, and it was *your* find, *your* glory, *your* rung right to the top. As long as it *was* your find and they didn't belong to that fool, Tony Hine. So . . . I must not be allowed to know what I had. Who knew what I'd do with them? Give them away or some damn fool thing like that. But my grandmother would have told me, if you gave her the chance. So you covered her mouth and nose with your hand, Margaret . . . No, don't talk about what you intended. Don't say you only wanted to stop her from shouting out for Grace. Because I wouldn't believe you."

"Who cares what you believe? Anybody can say anything. It's all lies. You're making it up!" She spoke in frantic appeal, as though I might be persuaded to stop doing it.

"I'm afraid I've got into the habit of trying to prove things. What I've just said can be proved. The dust on your hand also had bits of brown paint in it. They—the forensic people—can analyse the paint specks that were found in my grandmother's lungs and analyse the brown that Ashe used—"

"You could have done it."

I shook my head. "Dusty I was, but it was from the crates. It was you who wiped a hand over the surface of one of the canvases."

"I'm getting out of here. Tell your stupid ideas to the police."

"The door's locked.

Her chin lifted. I caught a glint in her eyes. "Then tell it to somebody else." Then she turned her back on me and tucked her hands beneath her arms against a chill that wasn't there.

It wasn't difficult to understand her. In the formative years there had been her frustration that she could not become an artist. Then the cold, ruthless determination to master something which she herself had called a science and not an art. She would have had no emotional feeling for it, so that she'd succeeded in something to which she had had to drive herself. And somewhere in the intervening years all emotion had died, until she was no more than an unfeeling machine, one that wouldn't balk when the ultimate opportunity presented itself.

"I could forgive you almost anything, Margaret," I said quietly, "except the cold-blooded murder of an old lady in her bed. I could even forgive you the three attempts on my life . . ."

"Tony?" Evelyn whispered.

I reached back and touched her hand, and went on, "I know I was supposed to accept that they were the work of Coombe's men . . ."

"Now hold it right there!" Coombe snapped.

I didn't glance round. "But how could they have been? The first one, on the hill above here—Coombe couldn't have known I'd come from up there. His men didn't even chase me up the hill. So I must have been followed, and you knew, Margaret, that I was coming here. The second: you were the one who knew I'd be working in my darkroom. The third: you knew my hired Metro was in the drive at my home. So you see, by that time I knew it was you who was trying to kill me."

She whirled round and stared at me with challenge. "Knew! Knew!" she snapped in contempt.

I continued as though she hadn't spoken. I had to get it all out, before it choked me.

"I didn't understand why you wanted me dead. I thought your idea was to pass off a lot of Angelina Foote paintings as Ashes, and that I might object. But it was better than that, because you knew by that time exactly what you had. And only I knew you had them, and Grace Fielding, she knew. But she died. Suicide, they thought, though there are doubts. I haven't got any doubt at all. Grace not only knew about the paintings, she was also threatening legal action, because she knew that my grandmother was dead before we left that house."

"Ye gods," said Coombe. "What have we got here!" He spoke in a voice of awe.

"You've got to admit she's got plenty of nerve," Mace commented.

"More than you can know," I told him. "She had to get Grace Fielding into a loft—probably on the pretence of looking for crosses on the old crates—and strangle her there, then put a noose round her neck, and push her through the trapdoor opening."

Evelyn made a high, shrill sound of disgusted protest.

"Exactly," I agreed. "And she would have had to climb down the ladder past her dangling body."

Coombe whistled absently.

Margaret, apparently annoyed that the catalogue of her activities should have drawn admiration from such an uncouth oaf as Coombe, turned to face us again. She advanced on me with a determination that was quite admirable under the circumstances.

"This is pure imagination," she said briskly. "It wouldn't stand up for one moment."

Evelyn tugged at my sleeve. "She's right, you know. In law, you haven't produced anything that would convince a magistrate, let alone a jury."

Encouraged by this apparent support from such a quarter, Margaret went on, her voice professionally crisp. "One: Grace probably killed your grandmother and committed suicide from remorse. Two: your accidents were the work of Coombe's men, though the police would never be able to prove that. Nor that I had a hand in them. And three," she produced in triumph, "I didn't know the loft set was all Frederick Ashe until you proved it just now."

"No?"

"If I'd known, I wouldn't have come here."

"It was because you knew that you couldn't afford not to. But you did know, and this is one thing I can prove. And with it, your motive."

"You can prove nothing," she said in disgust.

"The biography of Maurice Bellarmé," I reminded her. "It's most unlikely that the reproductions were printed backwards. Not in a work like that. I think that book will show them printed as they were painted, and from seeing them you would have your proof, if you still needed any, that Frederick Ashe painted the loft set. You were vague about that biography. You didn't want me to come here, because you knew those two paintings were in the Renfrew Coombe collection. Probably it told you so in the biography." I turned to Coombe. "Ones you actually bought legally?" I asked him.

"Of course," he said gravely.

I returned my attention to Margaret. "And I'll make a bet that the biography you said you hunted out in London is in fact in your own library, at what you modestly call your cottage." I held out my hand. "May I have the key, please."

"You may not."

"It'll save me breaking in to collect the six for Mr. Coombe."

"They're not there. I told you—"

"Of course they're there. You told me you'd moved them, and I was able to tell Mr. Coombe, quite convincingly, that they were safe in London." I turned to him again. "Were you convinced?"

He lifted his eyebrows. "Completely."

"So . . . your cottage is the one place they'd be, Margaret." I waggled my fingers. "The key, please."

"You're not having it."

I sighed. "I can ask Mace to pull on all the lights. I can ask Coombe to get two of his men to carry you, if necessary, round the gallery, so that you can't help seeing every painting he's got. And then, Margaret, he wouldn't *dare* to let you stay alive."

Furiously she reached her hand into her bag, fumbled, and produced a set of keys.

"Thank you." I looked at them. "I'll use the Volvo." It was a statement. "And all I'll ask Mr. Coombe to do is hold you here in the house until the police arrive. It's them you'll have to convince."

Panic caught her. "But you can't—"

"I know, Margaret. You've heard so much about the little trick he's going to play on the police that he might decide it's safer to remove you, anyway. I'm sorry. A little worry won't hurt you." I grinned at Coombe. "Perhaps you'll be careful to keep her healthy, if only to offer some little morsel of comfort to them by handing her over."

He clapped his palms together. A hundred or more paintings shuddered. But he was only expressing pleasure. "I can't wait for them."

"Fine," I said. "So we're all agreed? Then you can open the door, Mace."

We trooped out in much the same order as when we'd arrived. I had a little difficulty walking straight, but Evelyn took my arm. Margaret did not take the other, though she walked beside me, her head up, a small defiant smile on her lips. She was still fighting.

I said to Coombe, "Tomorrow afternoon I'll be back with the six paintings. You'd better make room for them in the gallery and start hanging the others somewhere near the front door."

He nodded. Mace was frowning. He was not happy with the arrangement, though he didn't know why. Evelyn came with me to the car. "Is that Aleric's?" she asked, noticing the bike.

"I've been using it."

"You're too old for that sort of thing."

"I'll bet I've got more experience than him."

We stared at each other. She smiled. "You should have been a solicitor, Tony." It was her ultimate in compliments. She capped it by leaning forward and kissing me briefly on the corner of the mouth.

"Tomorrow," I said.

"Yes."

I drove away in the Volvo. The trip was uneventful, apart from the fact that I had to stop at three service stations to use their toilets. It's free, now, you know.

When I got home I managed to contact Detective Sergeant Dolan. When I told him I had his affidavit ready, he said he'd be over in the morning.

And so he was. He was waiting for me when I got back from the bank.

I had been their first customer. I had cherished an expectation that the size of the cheques would at least raise an eyebrow. I had imagined that the deputy manager would have me in, to discuss investment.

Even, perhaps, the manager. But . . . nothing. Not even the bat of an eyelid from the cashier.

That sort of money safely in his account gives a man confidence. I felt solidly comfortable when I dealt with the sergeant. We were in the kitchen, disposing of a pot of tea. He made no comment on the fact that we'd had to go round the back to get in.

I explained the situation to him in detail, showed him the proof sketches on the back of the affidavit, and gave him the relative photos with the affirmations on their backs. Inside, I was laughing.

"Make it tomorrow," I said.

"The day after. We'll need to rake in an art expert and so on."

"Right. Now we'll go and pick up the paintings."

"We?"

"I want you as a witness."

What Dolan was a witness to was the fact that the complete set of eighty-one loft canvases, plus my original one, were there. But more important, to the fact that the Maurice Bellarmé biography was in Margaret's library. As it was. The paintings were printed, side by side, exactly as they had been in the gallery.

"So you'll need another warrant," I told him.

"So it seems. But we already had our suspicions."

"Of me," I reminded him.

"That too."

I collected together the relative six paintings and packed them carefully. Margaret had all the correct materials for packing paintings. Dolan took along the biography of Maurice Bellarmé. It was in French, but it was the pictures that mattered.

"You'll need a magnifier," I said. "For the initials."

"Have to buy one."

"I thought all detectives carried a large magnifying glass."

"Ha!" he commented.

After lunch, I drove to pick up my wife.

This time I was not even allowed to enter the house. Coombe stood in the open doorway, watching whilst Paul Mace came out and opened up the package in the back of the Volvo. Each canvas received a searching examination. He used Margaret's magnifier. In the end, he raised his head and nodded. They were genuine Frederick Ashe paintings.

Coombe gave a bleak smile.

"Is it all right if I take my wife now?" I called.

"She's here."

Evelyn came from the front door. She stood there a moment as though this was a special brand of fresh air, then she smiled and walked towards me.

I had another package, especially for her, inside the Volvo.

"What's this?"

"I popped round to see Aleric's latest girlfriend. She's about your size. I've borrowed her riding kit for you."

"I'm expected to—"

"Yes. You'll love it. I can't take the Volvo, now can I! It'd be theft." I handed Mace the bunch of keys. "Tell Dr. Dennis that I'm keeping the key to her cottage until I've taken away the rest of my paintings. It'll be under the flower pot by the front door."

He said he would do that. Everything was calm and civilized.

"When?" he asked.

"The police? Oh, I couldn't say. They don't confide in me. Tomorrow, perhaps, or the day after. You'll be prepared?"

"We're ready now."

While we'd been talking, Evelyn had been climbing into the overtrousers and trying to master the snaps on the jacket.

"I feel an absolute fool," she said.

I caught a glimpse of Margaret at one of the windows upstairs. If she found it amusing, there was nothing in her expression to confirm it. I was reminded of Evelyn at her window. There was the same complete lack of emotion.

"All you've got to remember," I told Evelyn, "is that you lean with me. Don't try to lean against the bike."

I supported the bike as she climbed on. Then we were away.

One advantage a bike has over a car is that it limits conversation. From time to time she shouted something, but inside the helmet I could make nothing of it. I made one unbroken run of it. My technique was now as good as it had ever been. No incorrect decisions, no hesitations —straight through.

She climbed stiffly to the ground, removed the helmet, and said calmly, "I really enjoyed that."

I laughed.

Two days later, Dolan visited us and told us what had happened. The police had arrived at Renfrew Coombe in a large contingent, headed by a superintendent. The police were not armed, though there was a wagon full of men in camouflaged battle jackets and berets, but with no weapons visible. They were not called into action.

The Superintendent told Mace he had a warrant to search the premises for six paintings, four of which were believed to be stolen. The leading group was politely invited inside. The main group of police dispersed themselves in a surrounding movement.

Coombe's six paintings had been displayed in the hall. The Superintendent stood and stared at them. The art expert examined them. In his hand he had six photographs with my signature on the back of each.

"These," he said at last, "are not the relevant paintings. They do not correspond with the photographs attested to by a Mr. . . . er . . ." He turned them over. "A Mr. Anthony Hine."

At this point there was a certain amount of aggressive movement, some of it violent. Coombe's men had been out at the front to consider the implications of the camouflaged jackets and surrendered their weapons without argument.

Coombe, restrained by four large policemen, shouted, "These are the paintings. I watched him sign the damned photographs."

But the photographs I had attested to, and quite correctly because the paintings were now on Coombe's premises, were the six Terry Bascombe had copied for me, from the loft set. He'd done a grand job. What it entails, this masking, is exposing your six prints under the enlarger with part of the printing paper masked off, so that it only exposes the bit you want. Then you reverse the masking, covering the portion you've just exposed, and print the other part you want. For the first run he had printed six picture frames from the set of pictures in Coombe's gallery, and for the second part of the job he had printed my six matching canvases, from the loft set. So he'd framed them, and they looked, at a superficial glance, as though they were prints of Coombe's own paintings. Which they weren't.

Remember the name. Terry Bascombe. Any time you need a special job doing.

The Superintendent was able to point out that as the paintings reproduced in the six photographs were not on show anywhere he could see, it would be necessary to search deeper. This, of course, now included the gallery, and quite legally. It was part of the premises mentioned in the affidavit.

It was in the gallery that the art expert really came into his own. With a free run of the display, he trotted in ecstasy from one canvas to the other, discovering, quite apart from the ones they had come for, twenty-seven major works that had been given up as lost, having been stolen over a period of twenty years.

Charges were made, arrests were made. Coombe quivered in dissolution in his special chair.

There was an unexpected bonus. I had told Dolan about the episode of the white cross, and he'd passed it on to his superiors. On an inspiration, prompted by a complete lack of any sense of humour, the Superintendent had tried an experiment. He ordered the slabs on the terrace to be lifted.

For two days his men worked at it and uncovered three skeletons and one decomposing corpse. The corpse still contained the bullet that had brought about its death, and the forensic experts later matched it to Mace's gun.

The trials are expected to last several months. The Superintendent has made much of his triumph on television, but I have seen no mention of Detective Sergeant Dolan.

That was six months ago. Aleric is now at home. He is working at this time in acrylics. I tell him I can now afford to send him to any art school of his choice, but at the moment he seems to want to remain at home. I never could understand him.

Evelyn intends to continue with her practice. This I expected. I intend to continue as a professional photographer. This she didn't. I am having a proper photo-lab built, with a reception area, and already I've engaged a secretary-receptionist and a lab assistant—this as Evelyn had suggested. Both are young women. Evelyn disapproves, of the lab assistant particularly. She believes this is not a proper profession for a young lady. I don't think I'll ever understand Evelyn either.

The four paintings from the collection found in the gallery have now been returned to the art galleries from which the thefts were made. But now they have genuine Frederick Ashes in place of the Angelina Footes they originally owned. I wonder whether any of their acclaimed art experts have noticed the difference. I wonder whether Ashe should now be described as school of Angelina Foote and whether it matters.

Unfortunately, this now leaves Renfrew Coombe as the legitimate owner of two genuine Frederick Ashes. But it'll be a long while before he'll be able to gloat on the fact.

I have kept only two, my original painting of the cottage with the morning sun, which after all was painted by my grandmother, and its mate from the loft batch, painted by my grandfather. I have them displayed side by side on the sitting-room wall, in their relative positions, Grannie's on the right. After all, she was the one who was left-handed.

The remaining seventy-four I have donated to the National Gallery. After much thought. For after all, my grandmother *was* dead before we got the canvases out of the house, so that they were legally part of the legacy to Grace Fielding. So I have no right to them. So I've given them away.

No right or not, I nevertheless listened carefully to the gentleman who came from the Home Office, and I made no protest. In view of my gift, it is hinted, I shall see my name in the next honours list. A CBE, or perhaps an OBE. Who am I to argue?

And that about wraps it up.

Oh, I nearly forgot. The second warrant was not used, because Dr. Margaret Dennis was not at Coombe's house. He claimed she had given his men the slip and got away. Maybe that is so. But perhaps his nerve went, and he didn't dare to allow her to speak to the police.

Wherever she is, she will never be able to utilize the expertise and world-wide acclaim she fought so hard to acquire.

ROGER ORMEROD lives in Wolverhampton, England, and he is the author of more than twenty novels of suspense. He entered the Civil Service in 1937, serving ten years in the County Courts. He has also worked as a Social Security inspector, postman, and television playwright. In recent years, he has devoted himself to his flourishing career as a novelist and to his photography and painting. This is Mr. Ormerod's second novel for the Crime Club.